"Oh, it's nothing much," Case said, rocking back on his heels. "A little matter of a dead man in the dining room. Your waiter, Luigi, found him under your celebrated Round Table."

Benchley, as if reading Dorothy's mind, said, "You think it was something he ate, Frank?"

Case frowned at him.

"Not a chance," O'Rannigan said in all seriousness. "It was murder. He was stabbed."

"Stabbed?" Woollcott said. "In the middle of the Algonquin dining room?"

"Stabbed through the heart," the detective said.

"Just a minute," Sherwood said. "Was this someone from our circle?"

Frank Case shook his head.

"That ain't the half of it. He was stabbed," O'Rannigan grumbled emphatically, "with a fountain pen."

Benchley looked to Dorothy. "Mightier than the sword, indeed."

She replied, "He took his writing a little too close to heart."

Murder Your Darlings

An Algonquin Round Table Mystery

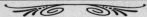

J. J. Murphy

AN OBSIDIAN MYSTERY

OBSIDIAN

Published by New American Library, a division of
Penguin Group (USA) Inc., 375 Hudson Street,
New York, New York 10014, USA

Penguin Group (Canada), 90 Eglinton Avenue East, Suite 700, Toronto,
Ontario M4P 2Y3, Canada (a division of Pearson Penguin Canada Inc.)
Penguin Books Ltd., 80 Strand, London WC2R 0RL, England
Penguin Ireland, 25 St. Stephen's Green, Dublin 2,
Ireland (a division of Penguin Books Ltd.)
Penguin Group (Australia), 250 Camberwell Road, Camberwell, Victoria 3124,
Australia (a division of Pearson Australia Group Pty. Ltd.)
Penguin Books India Pvt. Ltd., 11 Community Centre, Panchsheel Park,
New Delhi - 110 017, India
Penguin Group (NZ), 67 Apollo Drive, Rosedale, North Shore 0632,
New Zealand (a division of Pearson New Zealand Ltd.)
Penguin Books (South Africa) (Pty.) Ltd., 24 Sturdee Avenue,
Rosebank, Johannesburg 2196, South Africa

Penguin Books Ltd., Registered Offices:
80 Strand, London WC2R 0RL, England

First published by Obsidian, an imprint of New American Library,
a division of Penguin Group (USA) Inc.

First Printing, January 2011
10 9 8 7 6 5 4 3 2 1

Copyright © John Murphy, 2011
Cover art by Vince McIndoe/Lindgren & Smith, Inc.
All rights reserved

OBSIDIAN and logo are trademarks of Penguin Group (USA) Inc.

Printed in the United States of America

To my own little vicious circle—
Karin, Betsy and Mary Jane

Whenever you feel an impulse to perpetrate a piece of exceptionally fine writing, obey it—wholeheartedly—and delete it before sending your manuscript to press. Murder your darlings.

—Sir Arthur Quiller-Couch

Kill your darlings.

—attributed to William Faulkner

In all reverence I say Heaven bless the Whodunit, the soothing balm on the wound, the cooling hand on the brow, the opiate of the people.

—Dorothy Parker

AUTHOR'S NOTE

Although real people walk through the pages of this book, it is a work of fiction. I do believe that Dorothy Parker and the other members of the Algonquin Round Table would have encouraged the embellishment of fact to tell a good story—and I hope you will as well.

FOREWORD

In the 1920s, there were no Internet, no wireless phones, no satellite TV—no TV at all. Even radio wasn't commonplace until the later twenties. Instead of text messages and e-mail, people sent telegrams or employed messenger boys. For music at home, they listened to a Victrola or sang around a piano.

For entertainment, New Yorkers had dozens of theaters in which to see plays and a number of movie palaces where they could see silent films. ("Talkies" didn't arrive until the later twenties, too.)

For information, New Yorkers lacked twenty-four-hour cable news networks. But they did have a dozen daily newspapers to choose from. Presses ran day and night, printing morning editions, afternoon editions and special editions (*"Extra! Extra! Read all about it!"*).

At this time, the people who wrote the news also became the news. A new class of writers, editors and critics emerged. A loose-knit group of ten—and their assorted friends—gathered around a large table for lunch at the Algonquin Hotel. They went to the Algonquin because it welcomed artists and writers—and because it was convenient and inexpensive. Their daily lunch gatherings were known more for wisecracks and witticisms than for the food they ate. But they buoyed one another with merriment and camaraderie. They thought the fun would never end.

Chapter 1

Dorothy Parker stared at the pair of motionless legs protruding from beneath the Algonquin Round Table.

This, she thought, *is what you get for showing up early.*

She was never early for anything. Often, she was the last one to arrive. Today, despite her best intentions, someone else had arrived before her.

"Under the table before lunchtime?" she said to the pair of legs. "Even I wait until after noon to wind up there."

The legs didn't move.

Nobody else was in the darkened dining room. The room had no windows, and the lights were dimmed. It was unusually silent. She could hear only the muted clatter coming from the kitchen as the chef and his staff busily prepared lunch. But no waiters emerged through the swinging door.

Her dark, soulful eyes clouded over. Those demure eyes belied her sharp mind. They peered out from the shadows of a very pretty, but now troubled, face.

She gently nudged the toe of her little scuffed shoe against one of the legs. "You should stand up when a lady enters," she said. "Hurry up. One might come in at any moment."

Still, the legs did not stir. She knew something was dreadfully wrong, of course. But joking about it was more appealing than shrieking.

The legs belonged to a short, slender man. Even in the dimness, she could see that his black shoes were expensive, narrow and highly polished. Dove gray spats covered the tops of his shoes and his ankles. Above the spats, the man's trousers were charcoal gray and pin-striped. Above the trousers, the immaculate white tablecloth draped down like a shroud.

Dorothy prodded the legs again, harder this time. Again, no response.

She glanced once more at the door to the kitchen. Still closed. She turned to look toward the entrance to the dining room. People milled about in the lobby, just a few paces away.

She should go. She should get someone.

She didn't. Curiosity got the better of her. She leaned forward and lifted the tablecloth. She saw the man's vest. It didn't move—it didn't rise and fall with his breath. Then she saw something thin and metallic sticking out of his chest, surrounded by a dark crimson stain.

That was enough. She dropped the tablecloth. She hurried toward the kitchen door and flung it open. The kitchen was bright and busy. The waiters, the kitchen staff and the chef fell silent and turned to look at her.

Before she could say anything, Jacques, the chef, stopped her with an impatient stare. He halted his mallet in midair over a flattened fillet of veal.

"We know," he said, exasperated. "There is a dead man in the dining room. We told Mr. Case, and he called the police. Now, unless you know what killed him, don't bother us."

Dorothy quickly recovered her composure. "Perhaps it was something he ate."

She turned on her heel and let the door swing closed. Behind the door, she could hear the chef cursing at her in French. Without a glance toward the body under the

Round Table, she strolled calmly through the dark toward the threshold to the well-lit hotel lobby.

Across the lobby, she spotted her longtime friend and coworker at *Vanity Fair* magazine, Robert Benchley. He stood in the light of one of the large, sunny windows at the front of the hotel. He was busy fiddling with his pipe and spilling tobacco on his sleeve.

Seeing him, as she did every day, she felt a subtle thrill. She wasn't nervous or anxious. Just the opposite. Robert Benchley was perhaps the only person with whom she felt completely at ease. When she was alone, she often felt distracted, isolated, on edge. When she was with him, she felt like herself.

She couldn't wait to tell him about the body—in her most casual, offhanded way. He would be horror-struck, appalled and thoroughly amused. He would—

Suddenly, a hand touched her sleeve.

"Excuse me? Miss Parker?"

She turned to face a short, skinny, droopy-eyed young man in a baggy houndstooth suit. His whisper-thin mustache and scraggly beard, which barely covered a narrow chin, made the young man look like a suffering artist or a homeless vagrant—Dorothy couldn't decide which.

"It's *Mrs.* Parker," she corrected him. "May I help you?"

"I'm a writer, from Mississippi." He nervously shifted from foot to foot. "That is, I want to be."

"You want to be from Mississippi or you want to be a writer?"

He wasn't offended. In fact, he smiled. It was a tender smile, she thought.

"I want to be a writer." He clutched a handful of dog-eared pages. "I was hoping you might take a look at what I've written and give me your honest thoughts."

She looked at him squarely. Her voice, as always, was just above a whisper. "My honest thoughts would curl the wallpaper, sweetie." But she accepted the papers he handed to her. "What's your name?"

"Billy—William Faulkner."

"Billy Faulkner, you came all the way up from Mississippi to hand this to me?"

"Well, not exactly." He continued to shift from foot to foot. "You see, I've been working in New York a few weeks. I'm a great admirer of your poetry, and I read about you in the newspapers—"

She interrupted. "When in doubt, tell a lie, my boy. Save the truth for your writing."

"Well, then, yes." He smiled halfheartedly, still fidgeting. "I came up from Mississippi just to show this to you."

"That's better." She sensed instinctively that he was a kindred spirit. And she usually followed her instincts— much to her despair. "Now, why are you quaking like a snake before Saint Patrick? Are you nervous to speak to me, or do you just have to go to the lavatory?"

"Both, ma'am. I've been waiting here for quite some time—"

"The men's room is down that way. Come back and join us for lunch, won't you? The conversation is lively— though the company today quite literally pales in comparison," she said, thinking of the lifeless body under the table.

"I'd be honored. Thank you." He gently shook her hand and headed to the men's room.

She continued across the lobby to her old friend, who was now preoccupied with a pack of matches.

"Good afternoon, Mr. Benchley," she said.

Robert Benchley looked up and smiled as he lit his pipe, the corners of his merry eyes creasing.

"Mrs. Parker. How are you today?"

"Just dreadful," she said cheerfully. "And you?"

"Couldn't be worse, Mrs. Parker," he said brightly. "Ready for lunch?"

"Not quite." She'd tell him about the dead man—at just the right moment to make his jaw drop. Instead, she said, "I found another stray dog."

"Oh, Dottie, not again."

"The poor thing was lingering right by the door," she said. "He tiptoed up to me as if he knew me. I saw immediately that he needed someone to protect him, to shelter him from the storm."

"Storm?" he cried. "It's a lovely spring day. The birds are shining. The sun is chirping."

She sighed. "The forlorn in New York face a storm every day, Fred."

"Let's save the drama for the theater. And stop calling me Fred." He exhaled a puff of smoke. "Is the poor thing even housebroken? You never clean up after these wretched mongrels."

"Is he housebroken? Why, he's in the men's room right now."

Benchley tilted back his hat and scratched his head. He had an expressive oval face that usually framed a wide smile. But now his mouth and brow were knotted as tightly as his bow tie.

"Ah," she said. "Here he comes now."

Benchley turned to see not a mangy stray dog, as he had expected, but a skinny, bearded young man in a baggy suit.

"That's your stray dog?" Benchley said.

"Mr. Robert Benchley, meet Mr. Billy Faulkner. He's a writer, too."

The young man lowered his chin in modesty. But there was an eager glint in his drooping eyes.

"That's my hope." He held out a slim hand. "That's why I came to New York, to meet famous writers like yourself and Mrs. Parker. Very pleased to make your acquaintance."

"Someone misdirected you," Benchley said, shaking Faulkner's hand obligingly. "Most writers in New York don't do much writing. They spend their time talking and drinking bootleg liquor. That's what we do, at any rate."

Faulkner hesitated. "I presume you're pulling my leg."

"I never joke about such serious things as writing or—"

"Or liquor?" Faulkner said.

Benchley grimaced. "You'll find yourself in jail for stealing a man's punch line like that."

A rising clamor on the other side of the room caught their attention.

"What's the hullabaloo?" Benchley said, peering at a small throng that had now gathered at the partition dividing the dining room from the lobby. A bellhop was busy attaching a makeshift curtain—apparently a bedsheet—between the partition and the wall, closing off the view to the dining room.

"Nothing much," Dorothy said. "Just a dead man under the Round Table. Perhaps he passed out, and then he passed on."

"Passed—*what?*" Benchley was more perplexed than aghast.

"A dead man," she repeated, "under the Round Table."

"Dead? You mean dead drunk or—"

"Just dead. Stabbed, apparently."

Benchley considered this. "What a peculiar way to check out of a hotel," he said. "Did you see the body?"

She nodded.

"So whose body is it—or rather whose was it?" he asked.

She bit her lip. After seeing the dead man, she had quickly turned tail and run away. She hadn't even looked at his face.

Across the lobby, two men at the edge of the gathering noticed Dorothy and Benchley and made their way over. The two men couldn't have been more different.

Alexander Woollcott was short, plump and imperious, with a round, pale face like a snowman's. Behind owllike glasses were hard, glinting eyes like little lumps of coal. Despite his girth, Woollcott had the quick, nervous movements of a bumblebee.

The other man, Robert Sherwood, was startlingly tall—more than six and a half feet—and uncommonly thin. His straw boater sat askew on his narrow head as if it hung carelessly on a hat rack. Just above his upper lip perched a fuzzy black caterpillar of a mustache. Sherwood moved like a giraffe, with a methodical, stiff, cantilevered grace, as he crossed the lobby. The pompous, pudgy Woollcott reluctantly followed.

Benchley said into Faulkner's ear, "Do you recognize those gentlemen?"

Faulkner's nod was like a genuflection.

Benchley smiled warmly and put a hand on the young man's shoulder. "The walking telegraph pole is Robert Sherwood. He works with Mrs. Parker and me at *Vanity Fair* magazine. Why, I've known Mr. Sherwood since he was just this tall." Benchley raised his hand as high as he could reach. "The overstuffed sausage next to him is—"

"Alexander Woollcott," Faulkner mumbled. "The drama critic for the *New York Times*. I've read a ponderous amount about him."

"Ponderous indeed," Benchley said. "Then you should know he doesn't pronounce his name *wool-cot*, but *wool-coat*. He's very particular about it."

"Now, now, Mr. Benchley," Dorothy said. "Don't poison impressionable young minds."

"No, I'll leave that to you," he said.

Woollcott snorted as he greeted them. "It's not their minds that she's interested in."

"Put the daggers away," said Sherwood, towering over them. He looked amiably toward Faulkner. "Did a new cowboy mosey into town?"

Dorothy began to speak, but Woollcott snapped, "Introduce your snot-nose yokel some other time. Right now, a very serious matter is much more pressing."

"And what's so dire?" she said, casting a silencing glance at Benchley and Faulkner. "Are they not serving rice pudding today?"

"They're not serving lunch whatsoever," Woollcott said. His nasal voice was high and rising. "The dining room is closed off. The police have been summoned."

"No meal for Aleck," Benchley cried. "Muster the police! Police the mustard!"

"Apparently it is a matter for the police," Sherwood said in an even slower, graver tone than usual. "I overheard the waiters chattering. Something very bad has happened."

Woollcott dabbed a silk handkerchief at his glistening forehead. "Of course it had to happen today of all days. Today, when I invited Leland Mayflower to join us."

Dorothy had a sickening feeling all of a sudden.

"Leland Mayflower, the drama critic for the *Knicker-bocker News*?" she said, genuinely alarmed. "Why in the world would you invite him to lunch with us? He's your fiercest competitor. You two hate each other."

Woollcott's beetlelike eyes became slits. "Because he sent me word that he had some extraordinary news he wanted to share in person. Probably some little unnoteworthy achievement of his that he wants to brag about. By allowing him to lunch with us, I had hoped I could parade the shriveled old crow in front of you all and finally demonstrate what a scheming, backbiting fraud he is."

"Sounds like it would have been a jolly good time," Benchley said drily. His glance to Dorothy conveyed that he also had a suspicion. "Perhaps you can intercept him on the street."

"Excellent idea," Woollcott said, oblivious to Benchley's sarcasm. He floated off like a hot-air balloon.

Sherwood watched him go, then turned to his friends. "Truth be told, I'm no fan of Leland Mayflower either. I wouldn't mind seeing him get his comeuppance."

Dorothy put a hand on Sherwood's elbow. "You have every right to begrudge old Mayflower, of course. He didn't give your play a review. He gave it an obituary. He was a malevolent old shit."

"Was?" Sherwood said.

"Never mind Leland Mayflower," Benchley said hurriedly. "You haven't met our new friend, here."

"This is Billy Faulkner," Dorothy said, ushering him forward. "He's a hopeful young writer from the South."

"Hopeful, eh?" Sherwood said. "Don't pin your hopes on a writing career, my son. It's not too late to consider more lucrative and honorable employment, maybe as a tax collector or a gigolo."

"Those didn't really pan out," Faulkner said.

Sherwood's laugh was deep and resonant.

"I've decided to take him under my wing," Dorothy said.

"Watch out, Billy," Benchley said. "She's no mother hen. Cuckoo bird maybe."

Sherwood said, "Birds of a feather flock together."

"Go flock yourself," she said. Then she saw a knot of men arrive. "Now what fresh hell is this?"

Three policemen entered the hotel. The first man was a heavyset detective in a snug brown suit and a brown derby hat two sizes too small. Two officers in navy blue, brass-buttoned uniforms followed him. They quickly crossed the mosaic-tiled floor and were met at the front desk by the manager of the hotel, Frank Case.

The solicitous Mr. Case had sensitive, apologetic eyes and a bald head like the dome of a cathedral. Dorothy, Benchley and Sherwood knew him well. They watched him, his hands clasped, talk tactfully with the policemen. Then they watched Mr. Case lead the men through the crowd, between the curtains and into the now well-lit dining room.

A few moments later, Frank Case and the policemen reappeared. One of the white-aproned waiters, Luigi, joined them. From across the lobby, Luigi looked right at Faulkner and pointed him out to the other men. The policemen moved forward. Frank Case and Luigi followed.

Dorothy didn't like the belligerent look in the detective's dull gray eyes.

"You," the detective barked at Faulkner. "What's your name?"

Faulkner trembled. "William—"

"Dachshund," Dorothy said.

"William *Dachshund*?" the detective said, shouldering his way past Benchley and Sherwood. "A German, are you? I'm not surprised."

Dorothy said, "And you are?"

She noticed that the heavyset detective seemed to have no eyebrows. It gave the man an appearance of constant alarm. His small, almost clownlike derby hat seemed about to tumble at any moment from his big head.

He looked down at her as if just noticing her. "Detective O'Rannigan."

"Orangutan?" Benchley muttered. "A monkey, are you?"

"What was that?" he spat.

Benchley merely smiled innocently.

Sherwood addressed the hotel manager. "What's this all about, Frank?"

Now Woollcott reappeared, still agitated. "Yes, what the devil is this all about?"

It took a lot to disrupt the sangfroid of a hotelier such as Frank Case. He attempted his usual calm demeanor, but not entirely convincingly.

"Oh, it's nothing much," Case said, rocking back on his heels. "A little matter of a dead man in the dining room. Your waiter, Luigi, found him under your celebrated Round Table."

Benchley, as if reading Dorothy's mind, said, "You think it was something he ate, Frank?"

Case frowned at him.

"Not a chance," O'Rannigan said in all seriousness. "It was murder. He was stabbed."

"Stabbed?" Woollcott said. "In the middle of the Algonquin dining room?"

"Stabbed through the heart," the detective said.

"Just a minute," Sherwood said. "Was this someone from our circle?"

Frank Case shook his head.

"That ain't the half of it. He was stabbed," O'Rannigan grumbled emphatically, "with a fountain pen."

Benchley looked to Dorothy. "Mightier than the sword, indeed."

She replied, "He took his writing a little too close to heart."

"Shut up, wiseacres," the detective said. Then he jerked a thumb at Luigi. "Here's the good part. The waiter here says he saw your Mr. Dachshund loitering suspiciously in the lobby late this morning."

Luigi hunched his shoulders innocently. Dorothy patted his arm as if to say not to worry.

"You can't blame the wop for squealing," the detective said, then turned to Faulkner. "As for you, Dachshund, don't move from that spot. We need to have a little talk with you."

Chapter 2

The detective and uniformed officers moved away, with Case and the waiter following. As soon as they were out of earshot, Dorothy grabbed Faulkner's sleeve.

"Let's get him out of here," she said to Benchley.

"Okay," Benchley said. "Why?"

"We have to hide him," she said, "so he'll be safe."

"Well," Benchley said, "there's the matinee of Ziegfeld's *Hotsy-Totsy Hootenanny!*, which is playing to an empty house. You can bet no one will see him there."

She turned to Faulkner. "Come on, Billy. I live here at the Algonquin. I have a suite upstairs. You can hide out there."

"Hide?" Faulkner said. "But I haven't done anything."

"That didn't stop them from arresting Sacco and Vanzetti," she said.

"Those two are accused of being anarchists and common criminals," Woollcott said, eyeing Faulkner. "Is Mr. Dachshund an anarchist or a common criminal?"

Faulkner stepped forward with an eager smile. "I'm a writer as well as a tremendous fan of yours, Mr. Woollcoat."

Woollcott's mouth puckered. "*What* did you just call me?"

Faulkner's smile faltered. "Mr. Wool"—he glanced at Benchley—"*coat*?"

"It's Woll*cott*, you cotton-mouthed country bumpkin." His furious nasal voice made it sound almost like *wool-cut*. "Where's the constable? He should clamp you in leg irons."

Faulkner shrank back.

"It's my fault, Aleck," Benchley said, giving Faulkner an apologetic smile. "I was playing a little joke. Now, see here, Billy, this fine fellow's name may be spelled *W-o-o-l-l-c-o-t-t*, but his name's pronounced *Windsock*."

Woollcott huffed, his face turning red.

"You boys stop fooling around," Dorothy said. "Everyone knows it's not *Windsock*. It's *Windbag*."

Benchley slapped his forehead. "Oh, how right you are, Mrs. Parker. He's a Windbag, all right. One of the prominent New York family of Windbags. They're right up there on the social register with the Blowhards, the Braggarts and the Balderdashes. Now, I've met quite a few Windbags in my day, and Aleck here tops them all—"

"Enough!" Woollcott roared. His face was nearly purple.

"Oh, never mind, Aleck," Benchley said. "It's no fun teasing you if you're going to get so sore about it."

"Sure it is," Dorothy said. "That's the fun of it."

Woollcott eyed her squarely. "Crawl back into your web."

"That's the spirit," Benchley said. "Now we're old pals again, right?"

"Wrong," Woollcott said. "I shall shake the dust of this group off my feet." He turned abruptly and glided away.

Dorothy again grabbed Faulkner's sleeve. "As for us, I'm going to drag Billy here off to my web."

"I'd tag along, but I may play mortician," Benchley said.

"Mortician?" Faulkner said.

Sherwood leaned down conspiratorially to Faulkner.

"Mr. Benchley subscribes to morticianry journals. He and Mrs. Parker cut out embalming pictures and hang them above their desks at work. Just for laughs."

"For laughs?" Faulkner said. "I don't get the joke."

"Neither does the publisher," Dorothy said. "Just another reason why our days at *Vanity Fair* are numbered. Now, come on."

She grabbed Faulkner's elbow and pulled him toward the elevator.

"Excuse me, Officer," Benchley said to the uniformed policeman who stood at the entrance to the Rose Room, the Algonquin's main dining room. "Perhaps I could be of assistance."

"Buzz off," the officer said. "No nosybodies."

"I'm a licensed mortician— Ah! Detective Orangutan," Benchley said as the detective emerged from the makeshift curtains. "I was just telling your boy in blue here—"

"I heard you," the detective snapped. "What's your name?"

"Robert Benchley."

"Mine's O'Rannigan. Get it right, see?"

"Of course. Now, as I was saying, Detective Orang— O'Rannigan, I'm a licensed mortician. Perhaps I could be of help if you allowed me to look at the deceased."

"The deceased can wait for the coroner," O'Rannigan sneered. "And so can you, if you're looking for funeral business."

"Ha-ha. Nothing could be further— Now, see here, Detective Orang—Orienteering," Benchley said. "The time of death— A warm body cools at a certain rate, you understand. That is, a dead body, not a warm body. But that, you understand, is what a mortician is. No, just a minute. A mortician can determine that a warm body cools to a dead body. I mean, the time, of course—"

Frank Case appeared at Benchley's side.

"Detective O'Rannigan," Case said, "Mr. Benchley

moves more widely in literary and dramatic circles than I do. Perhaps *he* could identify the body."

"Well, why didn't you say so?" O'Rannigan said. He reached out a meaty hand, grabbed Benchley's arm and pulled him through the curtain. "Go take a look. Tell us who the stiff is."

He shoved Benchley into the wide, brightly lit dining room.

Square-paneled, dark wood wainscoting reached ten feet up the walls. Above this, the plaster was painted a dusky pink, which gave the Rose Room its name. The famous Round Table, with place settings for ten, sat squarely in the middle of the room. Had the dining room been a stage, then the great Round Table was at center stage.

Benchley moved toward it, reluctantly now. He was remembering what they say about curiosity and the cat. He stopped when he reached the Round Table. He noticed a small black notepad on the table. Then he looked down and saw the pair of motionless legs splayed on the floor, protruding from beneath the immaculate white tablecloth.

The elevator lurched to a stop. The elevator operator—a spidery elderly gentleman with greasy gray hair, a shabby uniform and an unreliable memory—feebly grabbed the inside accordion gate and methodically dragged it open. Then the man reached out a skeletal arm and clutched at the outside elevator door, which screeched as he slowly opened it.

"Thank you, Maurice," Dorothy said to him. She hurried Faulkner out of the elevator and whisked him down the silent, shadowy hallway toward her suite.

"Mrs. Parker," Faulkner stammered, "there's something I neglected to—"

But he slowed as they reached the door.

"Well, come on," she said.

"Is there—," Faulkner said, cautiously polite. "Is *Mr.* Parker at home?"

She flung open her apartment door. "Forget him. Just get inside quick."

Faulkner smelled the stale odor of cigarettes that barely masked the gamey stink of wet dog.

"So," he began again, "Mr. Parker is *not* at home?"

"Don't waste a precious thought about him," she said, shoving Faulkner inside. "I certainly don't. I stuffed him in a broom closet a few years ago and haven't seen him since. Now, just keep quiet. I'll see you later."

Faulkner, just inside the doorway of the darkened apartment, opened his mouth to protest. "There's something—"

She yanked the door closed and scurried back down the hall to the elevator.

Benchley, despite his subscriptions to morticianry journals, had never been alone in a room with a dead man before. He decided that today was not the day to change all that. Let someone else identify the body. Yes, that would be best. He turned around to leave, only to find himself face-to-face with O'Rannigan.

"Go ahead," the burly policeman said. "Take a gander."

"Actually, I agree with you. This is a case for the coroner."

"What, you afraid?"

"In a word," Benchley said, "yes."

O'Rannigan shoved him aside, squatted down and whipped back the tablecloth. Benchley flinched and looked away.

Then his curiosity got to him, even before O'Rannigan did.

"Take a gander," the detective said.

But Benchley was already looking. He stepped forward and bent down to take a better look.

The dead man's face was pale gray, and so was the man's hair. He wore gold-framed pince-nez on the bridge of his long, bony nose, and his short beard was trimmed neatly in a pointed Vandyke on his chin. He wore an old-fashioned, high, stiff collar and a silk cravat with a silver stud. A pink rosebud sprouted from his bouton-niere. Benchley could almost smell it. A nearly perfect circle—almost black—stained the man's charcoal satin waistcoat around the fountain pen, which dug deep into the man's heart.

Benchley stared at it. Then someone was shaking him. Benchley heard a man's voice, as if from a distance.

"You listening to me, buster?" O'Rannigan was say-ing. "You okay or what?"

"Yes, yes," Benchley said, as though waking from a doze.

"So you know him or not?"

"That's Leland Mayflower." Benchley stood up. "He was the drama critic for the *Knickerbocker News*."

Chapter 3

In the lobby, Alexander Woollcott stood in the midst of the other ten or so members of the Vicious Circle, as they called themselves. Dorothy had just returned.

"What an insult," he said. "How dare Mayflower invite himself to our lunch and then show up late?"

"Oh, he's late all right," Benchley said, staggering into the lobby. "But he was likely early. Now he's late."

"You look ghastly pale," Dorothy said. She gently laid a hand on Benchley's arm.

"I'm not the only one."

"What nonsense are you prattling about, Benchley?" Woollcott said.

"Leland Mayflower is late because he is now the late Leland Mayflower. To become the late Leland Mayflower, he must have arrived here early."

Robert Sherwood seemed about to topple from his great height. "You mean that Mayflower is the man who was stabbed?"

Benchley merely nodded.

Woollcott's already sallow face turned gray. "The man had one foot in the grave. Who would want to kill him?"

"That's what I aim to find out," said Detective O'Rannigan, looming up behind Dorothy. "Now, who do we have here? I want everyone's name."

"Just a second," she said, turning back to Benchley. "You said Mayflower was early, which in turn made him the late Leland Mayflower. Are you implying that if he had arrived on time, he wouldn't be dead?"

"Well," Benchley said, "if any one of us had been there, we would have either seen the murder or discouraged the murderer from carrying it out."

"Or been stabbed ourselves," she said.

"Exactly," Woollcott said, his nasal voice rising. "The only question is, why Mayflower?"

O'Rannigan said, "Maybe one of you had a grudge against old Mayflower. Maybe someone here took a fountain pen and wrote old Mayflower off. You know what I mean?"

The group reacted angrily. Sherwood was the first to respond. "You can't think any one of us had anything to do with this atrocity." He leaned over, trying to intimidate O'Rannigan with his height.

The detective responded only with a skeptical look.

"Preposterous," Woollcott huffed. "If anything, this wicked pen-wielding murderer meant to attack someone in our group. Undoubtedly, the murderer mistook Mayflower for a member and killed him instead of one of us."

"That's a nice theory," O'Rannigan said. "But wasn't this Mayflower a drama critic? And I'm guessing you're also a drama critic. And doesn't that make him your direct competition?"

"Well, I—" Woollcott became flustered, then recovered haughtily. "I have no competition."

"Not anymore you don't," O'Rannigan said, pulling a notepad from his jacket pocket. "Now, let's hear your names and any connection you might have had with the deceased. Let's start with you, chubby."

Dorothy mumbled, "That's the potbelly calling the kettledrum fat."

"My name is Alexander Woollcott," he said grandly, ignoring her remark. "I am the drama critic for the *New*

York Times. I am not a murderer. But I knew the deceased, as you call him, as a friendly rival."

"A competitor," O'Rannigan said.

"Truly, he's not my competition," Woollcott sneered. "The *Knickerbocker News* is not in the same class as the *Times*."

"But you had plans to meet Mayflower here?"

"He planned it. Mayflower left me a message to that effect. He knows I lunch here every day. The Vicious Circle is an informal yet admittedly exclusive group, and he was not a member. Mayflower indicated he had some petty triumph that he wanted to brag about. Probably wanted to make himself appear superior to me in front of my friends."

"Good thing none of them showed up," Dorothy said.

"Just wait your turn, little lady. I'll get to you," O'Rannigan said. Then he looked up at Sherwood. "How about you, beanstalk?"

Sherwood spoke slowly and told the detective his name. "I'm an editor for *Vanity Fair* magazine. I didn't know Mr. Mayflower personally—"

"But he knew you," O'Rannigan said.

Sherwood shoved his hands deep in his pockets. "I suppose so."

The detective tapped his pen to his notebook. "Let me guess. You're not only an editor. You're an aspiring playwright. Am I right so far?"

Sherwood nodded slowly.

"And Mayflower was a drama critic. You wrote a play and Mayflower panned it. Not just panned it—he crapped all over it. Still on the right track?"

Sherwood nodded again. "But that doesn't make me a killer."

"Doesn't make you an innocent schoolgirl either, does it?" O'Rannigan said. He turned to Benchley. "Now, Mr. Mortician, what's your real name and occupation?"

Benchley told him his name. "As for occupation, I'm a writer."

"Gee, what a refreshing change of pace. What do you write?"

"I just published a book last year," Benchley said proudly. "*Twenty Thousand Leagues Under the Sea.*"

O'Rannigan was astonished. "You wrote that? You're pulling my leg. I loved that book. Captain Nemo and the *Nautilus* and all. That was you?"

"Guilty as charged," Benchley said, his smile never faltering.

"Well, I'll be." Then O'Rannigan was back to business. "Now, you identified the stiff—the deceased—so that means you knew him."

"Only casually, as one knows others around town," Benchley said. "Saw him at most first nights, but I don't think I ever actually spoke with him."

"First nights? What's that?"

The group murmured in derision. The look on O'Rannigan's face revealed that he knew he'd said something stupid.

"A first night means the opening night of a play, that's all," Benchley said genially. "I'm also the managing editor for *Vanity Fair* magazine—did I mention that?"

"Jeez, everybody's a critic. So Mayflower was your rival, too?"

"I don't have an enemy in the world," Benchley said, almost embarrassed to admit it.

"We'll see about that," the detective said, turning to Dorothy. "Your turn, little lady. I guess you're a critic, too."

"Some might call me that," she said.

"Tut-tut," Benchley said. "Mrs. Parker is making quite a name for herself as a serious poet."

"Serious poet?" Woollcott sneered. "She's hardly Longfellow. She writes light verse about flappers and puppies."

Dorothy shot him a dirty look.

"Stop right there, Woollcott," said another member of the group. This man was short, with an enormous nose in a narrow face. His shrewd eyes glistened from under bushy eyebrows. He looked like a supremely intelligent anteater. "Mrs. Parker's poetry is as light as a bed of nails. Mark my words, she'll be remembered long after the rest of us are gone."

O'Rannigan interrupted. "And who are you? A poetry critic?"

The man's voice was gruff. "Franklin Pierce Adams, columnist in the *New York World*. You've heard of me."

O'Rannigan was sheepish. "Of course I've heard of you, Mr. Adams. You're the most famous newspaperman in America. Everyone in the country reads your column. First thing I do when I open up the *World* is turn to 'The Conning Tower.' Why, I used to read your articles in the *Stars and Stripes* during the war."

Woollcott snorted, "Most famous newspaperman indeed."

"Beg your pardon, sir," O'Rannigan said meekly to Adams, "but duty requires that I ask your relationship, if any, to the deceased."

"I understand," Adams said, fingering an unlit cigar. "I ran into Mayflower here and there but didn't know him well. He was one of the older generation of newspapermen. Still, he is—or was—the prize bull at the *Knickerbocker*. Can't imagine what they'll do without him. As for a motive, Detective, I once lent him fifty dollars in a poker game. He never paid me back. That was more than ten years ago. Does that make me a suspect of Mayflower's death?"

Woollcott said mildly, "It makes you a suspect in Mayflower's debt."

"What's that supposed to mean?" O'Rannigan said.

"I've never seen Mr. Adams lend anyone a dime in a poker game," Woollcott said. "He wouldn't lend an ear to Caruso singing the national anthem."

Adams scowled. "So Mayflower taught me my lesson—neither a borrower nor a lender be."

"And now you've taught him a lesson," Woollcott said haughtily.

Adams laughed derisively.

"It does sound strange," Dorothy observed. "Mr. Adams would sooner part the Red Sea than part with a red cent."

Some members of the group chuckled at this.

O'Rannigan, his face reddened, turned on her. "That's a fine way for you to talk after Mr. Adams defended your rotten old poetry—" Then a thought struck him. "Just a doggone minute. Where the hell is your Mr. Dachshund? I ordered him to stay right here!"

Dorothy bit her lip. "I suppose he ran astray."

Chapter 4

"Didn't you hear me?" O'Rannigan bellowed, inches from her face. "Tell me, where is your Mr. Dachshund?"

"No, I didn't hear you," she murmured. "You'll have to speak up if you want a person to listen to you."

"You know where he is. Take me to him. He couldn't have gotten far."

She and the burly detective locked eyes. Neither one spoke for a long moment.

Then Woollcott broke the silence. "She rents a suite upstairs. Maybe he's up there."

She glared at him. Woollcott adjusted his small round glasses on his large round face. "Oh, but don't listen to me. I'm just an old windbag."

"Come on." O'Rannigan grabbed her elbow. "Let's go upstairs."

"Without a chaperone?" she said as he tugged her across the lobby. "What will the neighbors say?"

"Let me join you," Benchley called, hurrying up behind them.

She gave Benchley a knowing look.

Benchley halted. "Then again, maybe I won't. I have to see a man about a pocket watch."

O'Rannigan shrugged. "Suit yourself." He pulled her toward the elevator door.

"Oh, no," she said. "I can't ride the elevator. I have claustrophobia. I panic in confined spaces."

"Confined spaces? What do you think of an eight-by-ten-foot prison cell?"

"Very little. Why don't we take the stairs? You're not afraid of a bit of exercise, are you?"

"I exercise every day." He puffed out his barrel chest, his heavy torso straining against his tight suit jacket.

"Every day ending with a *Z*," she muttered and turned toward the stairs.

"What'd you say?"

"I said, I live on floor eighteen."

That stopped O'Rannigan in his tracks. Dorothy entered the door to the stairway. Behind her, O'Rannigan cursed under his breath; then he followed her through the door.

As soon as Dorothy and the detective entered the stairway, Benchley darted to the elevator and pressed the call button. To his amazement, the door opened immediately. Maurice, the elderly elevator operator, shuffled out.

"Just a minute," Benchley said. "I have to go upstairs."

"And I have to go to the can. Guess who goes first."

Maurice ambled across the lobby. Benchley, helpless, watched him go.

Finally, Benchley stepped into the elevator. He looked at the controls. He was a disaster with anything mechanical and afraid to fiddle with anything electrical. The operator's panel of levers, switches and buttons seemed impossibly complex. But he had to get Billy Faulkner out of Dorothy's apartment before O'Rannigan could bully his way in. Benchley knew she was counting on him. He decided he would take control of the elevator himself.

He flipped one of the switches and the lights went out.

*   *   *

Dorothy climbed the next flight of stairs. She called over her shoulder to the detective. "Just so you know, I'm not in the habit of letting strange men into my room."

A few steps behind her, she could hear O'Rannigan already starting to breathe heavily. They had only passed the landing to the second floor.

"Huh, yeah? That Dachshund looks like a strange bird to me."

"He's a perfectly lovely southern gentleman. Are you implying that I can't land any men other than strange ones? That I have to kidnap them and hide them in my room?"

"No, but if Dachshund is in your room, you'll have bigger problems than landing a man."

"So you do think I have problems landing a man? This is what it's come to. Our public servants insulting single women. I should write to my congressman."

"I never said any such thing." He began to wheeze. "Don't write your congressman."

"Now you're telling me what to do." Her quick, bird-like movements carried her up the stairs briskly. "I can't land a man. I can't exercise my civil rights. What next? I suppose you probably want all homely women shut up in an institution somewhere so they won't bother you busy policemen. And you won't have to look at them or think about them."

He exhaled forcefully. "No, of course I don't want all homely women shut up—"

"So you think I'm homely, do you? That's what you said just now. I'm homely."

"Ah, jeez."

Benchley had turned the overhead light back on. He took another hard look at the operator's controls. But he quickly gave that up and looked at the elevator door-way, which was still open. He knew that old Maurice, as well as every other elevator operator, always shut both the outer door and the inner accordionlike gate before moving the elevator up and down. So that must be the first job to perform. Benchley found the handle for the inner gate but couldn't budge it. Then he tried the handle for the outer door, but it, too, was immovable.

How could a frail elderly man like Maurice move these leaden doors, and do so hundreds of times a day at that?

In times of trouble, Benchley always considered the logical, levelheaded approach, which he then quickly dismissed. He daydreamed instead. He now imagined he was Samson, trying to move a gigantic boulder or a massive marble column. He squared his shoulders, threw back his imagined thick lion's mane of hair, planted his feet wide, took a grip of the handle with his imagined mighty fists, inhaled a deep breath, then pulled with all his might. He suddenly flew backward and landed with a jarring thump.

He lay there and said to himself, "Haven't had one drink today and already I'm flat on the floor."

Something had tripped him, he realized. Something had caught at the heel of his foot. He lifted his head and inspected the dusty elevator floor. There, below the operator's controls, was a large black button set into the floor. It was about three inches in diameter and was raised about an inch off the floor. The button was scuffed and well worn.

Benchley stood up and tentatively pressed the button down with the ball of his shoe. He winced, but nothing happened. Holding the button down, he again tried the door handle. To his amazement, the door moved easily, and he pulled it closed with a satisfying snap. He tried the inner gate and closed it just as smoothly.

Of course, one would never see this safety button, Benchley realized. Maurice and every other elevator operator must always be standing on it.

With confidence now, Benchley took another look at the operator's controls. He flipped a switch. The lights went out again.

With the door now closed, it was completely dark

inside the elevator. He couldn't locate the light switch again. He found a lever and drew it toward him.

The elevator began to move.

It was on its way up, going fast. Benchley felt his stomach flip and felt the strange pressure of gravity pulling against his body. He looked out through the small, saucer-sized window in the outer door. The elevator was flying up the floors quickly.

He suppressed a growing anxiety. "Now, what would old Samson do in a pickle like this?"

On the third-floor landing now, Dorothy waited and watched Detective O'Rannigan slowly climb the stairs one flight below. She tapped a fingernail against the railing and considered how long it would require for the average person to ride the elevator up to her suite, fetch Faulkner, bring him back down to the lobby and whisk him out to an Automat or a coffee shop or some other safe, neutral waiting place. She guessed it would require about eight to ten minutes at the most.

Since it was Benchley, she doubled that number.

"What floor do you really live on?" O'Rannigan said.

"I told you once. First, you imply that I'm a spinster who kidnaps strange men. Then you call me homely. Now you accuse me of being a liar?"

"I know you're a liar." He stood two steps below the landing and now looked her in the eye. "There ain't no eighteenth floor. There's no more than twelve stories in this building."

"Frank Case would argue that. He says this building has a thousand stories. Sit down and talk with him and he'll be glad to tell you a few—"

"Cut the cute talk," O'Rannigan huffed. His wide, thick shoulders were hunched forward and his browless eyes seemed menacing now. "There's been a murder committed and you're doing what's called obstruction. You keep it up and two things are going to happen. One, things will get rough, even though I don't like roughing up ladies. Two, I'll haul you into the lockup overnight just to teach you a lesson. Now, start talking, and don't make it cute. Which floor do you live on?"

Dorothy's eyes went dull, defeated. "Just one from here."

"That's better." O'Rannigan brushed by her and began climbing the next flight of stairs. His dull, loud footfalls gave her the beginnings of a headache.

The elevator continued to rise rapidly and even seemed to be gaining speed, though Benchley knew that was not possible. Then he had an idea. He lifted his foot off the floor button and then braced for a sudden halt.

But the elevator did not jerk to a halt. It still soared upward.

"At least I know what they'll inscribe for my epitaph," Benchley mumbled to himself. "He rose to new heights."

Now he grabbed for the controls, flipping every switch and lever his fingers could find. Suddenly, the light went on. Looking at the control panel, he recognized the main lever and tilted it back toward its center. The elevator slowed and eventually stopped. Benchley sighed in relief.

Then a loud banging came from the outer door. Benchley pressed his shoe against the floor button and slid open the doors to discover he had reached the top floor, the penthouse suites. And in the doorway, wearing his tennis whites and carrying a racket, stood the motion picture star Douglas Fairbanks.

"Finally," Fairbanks said, stepping up into the elevator, which was off by a full foot above the level of the floor. "I've been waiting a dog's age—" He stopped short. "Benchley, is that you?"

"Certainly it's me, Douglas."

"But an elevator operator?" Fairbanks was aghast. "What kind of a job is this for a man like you?"

"Oh, well, you know what they say. It has its ups and downs."

*   *   *

O'Rannigan stomped along the fourth-floor hallway. "You're not going to tell me which room is yours, are you?"

"Sure, I will," Dorothy said.

O'Rannigan stopped. She almost bumped into him.

He said, "But the answer will be a lie, won't it?"

"Would I lie to you? A detective with the police force?"

The detective squinted. "Why are you trying to cover for this Dachshund? What's he to you?"

"He's an innocent, lost little boy, trying to find his way," Dorothy said, without thinking. "I know he didn't kill anybody."

"Then he's got nothing to be afraid of. Now, what's your room number?"

"Four twenty-six."

O'Rannigan shook his head. "I'm a detective, and I can read you like a book."

"Is it a good book?"

"It's fiction and fantasy."

"I knew it wasn't a romance. At least you didn't say it was a tragedy."

"Cough it up. What's your real room number?"

Dorothy bit her lip, thinking how to respond.

O'Rannigan said, "Like I told you, I'm a detective, so now I'm going to do a little easy detective work. Give me your room key. Now."

He stuck out a hand that was as large as a salad plate. She stared at the policeman's big hand a moment. Then she opened up her purse, fished inside and dropped her key ring into the man's open palm.

He smirked. "I just knew a bobbed-haired vamp like you would never have bothered to take the number off the key."

She didn't mind about being called a vamp. "I don't have bobbed hair," she said, insulted.

O'Rannigan looked at the key fob.

"Two thirteen?" His expression twisted in anger, and he shook a meaty fist in front of her face. "On the last floor down—the third floor—you said you lived on the next floor."

"I said I lived one floor away, *Detective*. You were the one who jumped to the conclusion that I lived on the floor above, not the floor below."

He grabbed her by the elbow and dragged her back toward the stairs.

This was cutting things too close, she thought as O'Rannigan hurried her along. Benchley probably hadn't taken Faulkner safely out of her room just yet. Or had he? She secretly crossed her fingers and hoped so, for all their sakes.

Chapter 5

Benchley knocked on the door of Dorothy's suite. "Billy, come on, now. We have to go."

Faulkner opened the door. He held a highball glass of amber liquid.

"What's that?" Benchley said.

"I think it's supposed to be bourbon. But it tastes like lighter fluid."

"Let me see that." Benchley deftly snatched the glass from Faulkner's hand, put it to his lips and swallowed it before Faulkner could say a word.

"Well?"

"Puts hair on your chest." Benchley coughed. "Then burns it off again. Let's go."

He handed the empty glass to Faulkner, turned and strode away quickly.

"Go? Where?" Faulkner shut the apartment door and hurried to catch up. He still carried the glass in his hand.

Benchley called over his shoulder, "To the elevator, of course. Douglas Fairbanks is operating it and he doesn't have all day. He's a very busy man."

"*Douglas Fairbanks* is operating the elevator?"

*   *   *

Dorothy Parker reached the second-floor landing before Detective O'Rannigan. She stopped and fished in her purse.

"Quit stalling," he puffed as he descended the last few stairs. His face was redder than before. A ribbon of perspiration stained the headband of his derby.

"Smoke break." She removed a cigarette from her bag and popped it in the corner of her mouth. "Have a light?"

He made a fist. "No, but I'll make you see stars."

"Now, that's the last straw." She flung the cigarette to his feet. "First, you call me a spinster. Then you call me homely, then a liar, then a vamp. And for the second time in mere minutes, you threaten me with violence. If this is the state of law enforcement today, then I prefer anarchy. I refuse to help you any longer!"

She flattened her back against the hallway door and crossed her arms.

"Suits me fine." He reached past her and grabbed the door handle. "You ain't been doing nothing but running me around in circles anyway. I have your key. So what do I need you for?"

He pulled open the door and pulled her along with it. Her shoes skidded along the tiled floor.

Now he was in the hallway. But she was after him.

"I know what you're doing."

"Yeah," he said over his shoulder. "I'm about to apprehend a murderer."

At the far end of the hall, far beyond the hulking silhouette of O'Rannigan, she heard the elevator door close. She hoped that was Benchley and Faulkner making their escape.

"That's not all you're up to," she said.

O'Rannigan glanced at the numbers on every door they passed. They had nearly reached her suite.

"Yeah, I'm running you in for obstruction, too." He stopped at her door, room 213. "Ah, here we are."

"That's not what I mean." She lightly laid her hand on his as he inserted the key into the lock. "You came up here to see my boudoir."

He looked at her momentarily and sneered. Then he threw the door open with a crash. "Awright, Dachshund. Come out!"

O'Rannigan pulled away from her and entered. Dorothy held her breath and remained standing at the doorway.

"Come out now, Dachshund," he yelled, stomping about. "Don't make me tear this lady's place apart to find you."

She peered through the door. Her suite was small—a small parlor, a small bedroom, a small bathroom, no kitchen. Even this tiny residence was more than she could afford. Most months, she handed Frank Case an empty envelope. Case was decorous enough never to mention that she'd failed to enclose a check. (She knew he liked having writers, actors and artists in his hotel, often to his financial loss.)

The detective raced from room to room. In the bedroom, he was startled to see a lumpy figure in the small bed. He grunted in triumph and yanked the covers away.

But it wasn't Faulkner. It was a surprised bug-eyed, bat-eared Boston terrier. The ugly dog had a mangy short-haired coat the color of vomit.

"Come here, Woodrow," Dorothy called, crouching down. The dog leaped off the bed and into her open arms.

"Woodrow?"

"Woodrow Wilson. Named after the only politician I've ever trusted. Until he sent us to war. A noble failure, like this dog."

The detective scowled and continued his search. In just a few moments, he had inspected all the possible places a man could hide—under the bed, behind the sofa, in the closet, in the bathtub and that was all. He had come up empty. He stood in the middle of the parlor, baffled.

Douglas Fairbanks was several years older and several inches shorter than Benchley, though Faulkner noted that the famous movie actor's clean, handsome, unwrinkled face looked younger. Fairbanks wore his characteristic pencil-thin moustache. He held the elevator operator's lever with one hand and a tennis racket with the other. He pulled the lever and the elevator began to descend.

Faulkner suddenly realized he still had the empty highball glass in his hand.

"What's that?" Fairbanks said.

Faulkner was as surprised as if the celluloid version of Fairbanks had spoken to him from the screen. "It—it used to be bourbon," he answered.

"Not on your life," Benchley said. "If that was bourbon, I'm a monkey's uncle. It was bootleg whiskey distilled through someone's boot. But never mind that now, Billy. We have to get you out of here." The elevator came to a halt. Benchley spoke like an elevator operator. "Here we are, ground floor. Ladies' dresses up, men's pants down. Thank you for shopping at Macy's."

Fairbanks reached to open the door.

"Just a moment, Mr. Fairbanks," Faulkner said hurriedly. "There's something I need to tell Mr. Benchley."

"Right now?" Fairbanks frowned, which failed to ruin his good looks. If anything, it brought his matinee-idol features into sharp relief. "I'm late for a tennis date."

"Have no fear, Douglas," Benchley said. "She'll wait. *You* don't need to worry about that."

"*She* is Florenz Ziegfeld."

"Florenz Ziegfeld, the Broadway producer?" Faulkner sputtered insensibly. "She's a he. I mean, he's a man."

"That's a generous description," Fairbanks said. "I

would have called him a greasy rat. In any case, get on with your discussion so I can get to my game."

Faulkner looked doubtfully from Fairbanks to Benchley.

"Oh, he's okay," Benchley said to Faulkner. "Whatever it is you have to say, Douglas won't bother to repeat it. Unless it's something flattering about him."

"All right," Faulkner said, speaking low regardless. "I was trying to tell Mrs. Parker something important before she shut me up in her apartment."

"Something important?" Benchley said. "About what?"

A loud banging came from the other side of the elevator door, followed by the muffled bawl of an old man.

"Let me in, you crooks," came the creaky voice of Maurice, the elevator operator. "You stole my elevator."

"Never mind him," Benchley said. "What was it you wanted to tell Mrs. Parker?"

Faulkner's voice dropped so low, Benchley had to strain to listen. "I saw a suspicious man in the lobby this morning. Before that drama critic was murdered."

"A suspicious man? Suspicious in what way?"

"There was something dark and dangerous about him," Faulkner said.

Maurice hammered his fist on the door again. Fairbanks sighed.

Benchley's eyes were fixed on Faulkner. "Why didn't you tell us this before? Why didn't you mention this when the police detective was questioning everyone, including you?"

"I don't know." Faulkner looked down at his hands. "I went dumb as a stump."

Benchley turned to Fairbanks. "Open the door, Douglas. Time to go."

When the doors opened, Maurice stood there, puffing and as hot as a steam engine. Benchley, Faulkner and Fairbanks ignored him and entered the lobby.

The elderly elevator operator stood fuming. He spat, "You can all go to hell."

Over his shoulder, Benchley said, "Guess who goes first, Maurice."

Now that Dorothy knew that Benchley had taken Faulkner from her room, she wanted to catch up with them quickly. That meant getting rid of O'Rannigan.

"It's just a small place," she said. "Only enough room to lay my hat—and a few friends."

The detective ignored her. He stood in the center of the parlor, his hand on his round jaw, his gaze off in the middle distance.

"You see?" She moved toward him. "We're alone. Just like you planned."

"Like I planned? I planned to find Dachshund—that's what I planned. Now where the hell do I look?"

"Look right here." She fixed her eyes on his. "Isn't this what you expected to find?"

He backed away a step. "What are you talking about?"

She approached him like a cat stalking a mouse. "You called me a liar? Maybe. You called me a spinster? Someday probably. You called me a vamp? Definitely."

She put her tiny hand on his chest. He batted it away as if it was a spider. He raced out the door, like a child running from a haunted house.

She turned and watched him go. This, she thought, was always what happened when she threw herself at a man. It made him run for the hills.

Chapter 6

Inside the Automat at Forty-sixth and Broadway, just three blocks from the Algonquin Hotel, Dorothy gazed at the mirrorlike wall before her. The wall was made up of tiny doors, each about the size of a postcard. Within each chrome door was a small window, and behind each window, a plate of food. There were macaroni and cheese, ham-and-cheese sandwiches, creamed spinach, Boston baked beans, stewed tomatoes, slices of blueberry pie.

But she wasn't looking at the food. She wasn't even looking at the windows. She looked at the thousand reflections in the glass and chrome. Sure, her reflection was there. Her brimless cloche hat was pulled low, almost covering the dark bangs on her forehead. She wore a deep blue dress that was stylish without calling attention to her shapely petite figure.

But she wasn't interested in her own reflection. Instead, she watched a thousand Robert Benchleys sitting around a table of friends. She saw a thousand of his smiles, two thousand of his merry eyes. She again felt that familiar precious heartache. All these Benchleys here for her alone, yet she couldn't keep a single one of them. She heard his mellifluous voice behind her.

"Did I ever happen to tell you about the time Mrs.

Parker and I both swore off drinking? We were at Tony Soma's speakeasy one night, holding up our end of the bar . . ."

Benchley was telling a story he'd told them all before, entertaining them in order to cheer them up. He spoke as though nothing horrible had happened, as if he had not seen Mayflower's corpse less than an hour ago.

"Tony was there, as usual, standing on his head and showing off, singing opera. Well, Mrs. Parker and I were greatly enjoying ourselves, by which I mean we were drinking hand over fist, although that's a certain way to spill your drink . . ."

Benchley had given Dorothy a handful of nickels. She popped one of these in a slot, turned the knob and opened the tiny door. She withdrew a liverwurst sandwich. Then she bought a dish of rice pudding, then a slice of pecan pie. She went over to the enormous silver coffee urn, where the steaming black liquid poured from a brass spout in the shape of a dolphin. Again, she watched the elongated reflection of Benchley in the silver urn.

"Before we knew it," he continued, "the night had turned into the wee morning hours, and we realized it was time to go before we started seeing pink elephants. It was just a week before Christmas, and a soft, silent snow was falling when we finally went outside. Then suddenly, under the Sixth Avenue Elevated, we saw a line of elephants approaching . . ."

She smiled. Benchley was getting to the good part.

In many ways, he was her opposite. Opposites attract, they say. But then again, in other ways she and Benchley were much the same. They perceived things through the same eyes. But they differed in how they reacted. Walking down the street together, they once witnessed a very minor tragedy. A little boy had trotted along, his one hand in the hand of his grandmother, his other hand holding a balloon on a string. A woman, walking in the opposite direction, had removed a cigarette from her mouth and tapped off the ash with a long, careless finger. As she did so, the hot end of the cigarette came in contact with the balloon, which burst with a sharp bang. The woman either did not notice or did not care, because she didn't stop. The boy was at first shocked, then heartbroken.

Dorothy and Benchley had witnessed the same incident, and both, without saying a word, felt in their hearts the little boy's utter despair. But their reactions were completely different. She wanted to embrace the crying child and cry with him. Misery loves company, she thought.

But Benchley always handled things in a brighter way. He bent down and said something funny—she couldn't hear what it was—and for a moment, the child forgot his sadness. Then Benchley performed the old sleight-of-hand trick, pulling a nickel from behind the child's ear. He handed the coin to the boy and told him about a shop around the corner that sold balloons that were even bigger than the one the boy just had.

Benchley continued his story, "The elephants walked in single file, trunk in tail, padding through the snow, and on the tail of the last elephant hung a red light. I turned to Mrs. Parker and said, 'That's it. No more booze. I'm on the wagon.' 'Me too,' she said. And then, to steady our nerves, we turned around, went back inside and ordered two double brandies."

She set the cup of hot coffee on a saucer, and, carrying this and the three other dishes in her arms, she walked carefully over to the improvised Round Table.

"I asked her, 'Did you see anything just then? You know, anything out of the ordinary?' 'Nope. Did you?' she said hopefully. And Tony turned to us and asked if we had seen the elephants. 'Elephants? You mean you've seen them, too?' I said. Well, he explained, the Ringling Brothers Circus was in town and the elephants were marching to the Hippodrome."

The group burst into laughter, attracting the sidelong glances of other diners.

"And that's when we decided that never again would we swear off drinking," Benchley concluded.

Faulkner rose when he saw Dorothy approaching, burdened with dishes.

"Oh, Mrs. Parker," he muttered in his southern accent. "Why didn't you call me for assistance? Chivalry is not dead."

She looked at the other men at the table, none of whom rose to help. "No, chivalry's just sitting on its fat ass."

Woollcott harrumphed. "Dottie is right. Couldn't we at least have lunched at a proper restaurant, with waiters to serve us? Here we are, the literary lights of New York, eating humble pie with the common folk at a Horn and Hardart's."

"I don't mind," she said. "Usually, all I can afford at the Algonquin is a hard-boiled egg. And I can rarely afford that."

She set the sandwich in front of Faulkner and patted his hand in a motherly way. She took a sip from the cup of hot coffee. When she looked up, she saw a man standing by their table.

"Heavens to Betsy!" said the normally laconic Robert Sherwood. "Bud Battersby, where did you suddenly come from?"

Merton "Bud" Battersby was the editor and publisher of the *Knickerbocker News*. He was middle-aged yet had an eternally boyish face. But his typically apple-cheeked countenance was now drained of color.

"I just came from the Algonquin." Battersby's voice was that of a sick cat. "Your waiter, Luigi, told me you'd all be here. He told me about Leland Mayflower, too."

Sherwood rose out of his chair and laid his long hand on Battersby's shoulder. "We couldn't believe it about Mayflower. We're so sorry, Bud."

"That's good of you, considering what Leland wrote about your debut play."

Sherwood shrugged it off.

Woollcott's nasal voice squeaked, "Yes, what *was* that nasty line Mayflower wrote in his critique of your play, Robert?"

Neither Sherwood nor Battersby answered, both embarrassed that Woollcott would bring up such a thing at a somber moment.

"I believe," Woollcott continued, "it was, 'Even the Savior himself couldn't breathe life into this deathly boring drama.'"

Marc Connelly, a Broadway playwright riding a recent tide of success, drew in a sharp breath. He sympathized with Sherwood's first professional attempt at theater. "Oh, Aleck, really!" Connelly snapped. "This is no time for your juvenile jeering."

"I disagree," Benchley said jovially, trying to revive the lighthearted mood of just a few moments before. "If we don't laugh, we'll cry. Please, Bud, join us."

"Join the Algonquin Round Table for lunch?" Battersby said, suddenly less stupefied. He quickly dragged over a chair. "How could I refuse?"

"We're the Automat Round Table today," Dorothy said. "Come one, come all."

"Verily, that is true," said Woollcott, eyeing Faulkner narrowly. "Now, Battersby, what can you tell us about Mayflower's unexpected demise?"

"What can I tell *you*?" He slumped in his chair. "I can't tell you a thing. That's why I'm here. What can you tell me?"

"Very little," Woollcott said. "They found Mayflower under our Round Table, stabbed in the chest with a fountain pen."

Battersby leaned forward. "A fountain pen? What kind of fountain pen?"

"What kind?" Woollcott said. "The kind you write with, old boy. What else? Ask Benchley; he was there."

Battersby turned anxiously to Benchley, whose merry smile faded. "You were there? You saw who did it?"

"Oh, no," Benchley said. "I went in . . . afterward."

"Well, I never," Battersby muttered. "Did you see what kind of pen it was?"

"Well, no. Is it important?"

"I don't think so. Not important, I hope. Just very odd."

"Very odd, indeed."

Battersby sat up. "What I mean is, Mayflower was the spokesman for Saber Fountain Pens. They run an ad with his picture in the *Knickerbocker*. The same ad runs in every *Playbill*."

"Good heavens," Benchley said. "I think it *was* a Saber pen."

"The bottom of the pen had that texture—"

"A herringbone kind of texture on the barrel, yes. Helps you to grip it better. What's that slogan they have in their advertisements?"

"'If it's not a Saber, it just won't cut it,'" Battersby said.

"By using a Saber pen to murder Mayflower, the one he himself endorsed, do you think someone was trying to give Mayflower a message?"

"I'd say he got it," Dorothy said. "But who? And why?"

All eyes turned to Woollcott.

"Why look at me?" he sneered. "I told you, I'd murder him in print before I'd ever lay a finger on his bony old body."

"Didn't you try to get that endorsement contract for Saber pens?" she said. "Didn't you talk to them about being their spokesman?"

Woollcott's fat cheeks puffed out. "By Jupiter, I won't sit here and be accused like that."

"So go sit somewhere else, and we'll accuse you anyway," Frank Adams said, jutting his cigar in his mouth.

Connelly said, "No one's accusing you of anything, Aleck."

Battersby intervened, addressing Benchley. "Let me ask you again about the scene of the crime. Was there anyone else in the room? Did the police question anyone? Or did you see anyone strange or sinister in the hotel this morning?"

Benchley shrugged. "There was no one else in the dining room, except for Detective Orangutan and me and, well, Mayflower. The murder had already happened before I got to the hotel. A small crowd had gathered in the lobby, but I didn't take notice of anyone out of the ordinary."

"I saw someone," Faulkner mumbled cautiously.

Everyone turned to look at the young, scruffy southerner.

"You saw someone?" Dorothy said.

Faulkner, glancing at Benchley, tried to hide a gulp. "I saw him in the lobby. Very tough-looking fellow. His eyes were dark and hard, but vacant. I was in the lobby waiting to introduce myself to Mrs. Parker and—"

Battersby interjected. "What did the man look like? Can you describe him? His height, his size, his hair color, that sort of thing?"

"I'm not good at describing physical traits," Faulkner said. "He had empty black eyes. That's what I remember most. Like a bear's eyes—black, hollow, soulless but full of mindless destruction. That, and he had a tooth on the chain of his pocket watch."

"Horsefeathers!" Woollcott cried. He threw his cloth napkin across the table at Faulkner. It landed in Dorothy's coffee cup. "There's a towel for your Dachshund, Dottie. He's wet behind the ears."

She plucked the coffee-soaked napkin from her cup. "Dry yourself, Aleck. You're all wet." She flung it back at Woollcott.

It landed with a soft splat against the silk handkerchief in his breast pocket. He swatted it away as if it was a tarantula. He stood up, aimed an angry glare at her and stormed off toward the men's room.

She looked at Faulkner. His face had turned red.

Battersby also looked at Faulkner. Then, after a moment of recovery, Battersby said, "What's eating Mr. Woollcott?"

Benchley explained to Battersby how Leland Mayflower had planned to meet with Woollcott at the Algonquin. "Now Aleck will never know what Mayflower had up his sleeve. His curiosity is probably killing him."

Then Benchley described how the body had been found and the subsequent confrontation with the police detective. He said, "Woollcott thinks that whoever murdered Mayflower was really trying to kill one of us, one of the members of the Round Table. Mayflower simply arrived at the wrong place at the wrong time, Woollcott says."

Battersby nodded slowly, taking this in. He removed a pad and pencil from his jacket pocket and scribbled some notes.

"What are you doing?" Dorothy said.

Battersby continued writing, not looking up from his notepad. "I'll have to write the story myself for an extra evening edition of the *Knickerbocker*. This is news after all."

"That's the spirit," said Adams, chomping on his cigar. "Nothing stops the news. Mayflower would want it that way. But you'd better hurry. I telephoned in my story a few minutes ago. You wouldn't want the *World* to scoop you on a story of one of the *Knickerbocker*'s own, would you?"

Battersby looked up at Adams. He spoke plainly, without a trace of guile. "Didn't you have a grudge against Mayflower? Something about a loan for a poker game?"

Adams groaned. "Oh, let's not start that again."

Chapter 7

That evening, Benchley was dressed for the theater in top hat, black tie and tails. He sat down and unfolded the extra afternoon edition of the *Knickerbocker News*.

That afternoon at the Automat, Bud Battersby had asked him to fill in for Mayflower as the *Knickerbocker*'s drama critic. This was the opening night of Ziegfeld's new musical revue, *Twenty-three Skidoo!*

Dorothy took her seat next to Benchley. She wore her best evening clothes—a midnight blue velveteen dress—and her hair up. She often accompanied Benchley to the theater in his professional capacity as a drama critic. And it was fun to play dress up—once in a while.

She opened up the *Playbill* and flipped through it. Something caught her eye. Staring up at her was the gaunt but smiling—almost leering—face of dapper old Leland Mayflower. His black-and-white picture stopped just below his chest, which gave the appearance that he sat at a high writing desk. In his hand, he prominently held a Saber fountain pen. At the top of the advertisement was the familiar Saber slogan. At the bottom of the ad was Mayflower's rollercoaster signature, with its high, narrow peaks, its wide, arcing loops, and its sharp, plunging depths.

Her eyes were drawn again to Mayflower's photo.

She couldn't stop staring at his taut, unwavering, imperturbable grin.

"Oh, dear," Benchley said.

"Yes, dear?" she said.

"Look here." Benchley leaned over and spread the tabloid newspaper for her to see. "It's all about the murder of Mayflower at the Algonquin."

Benchley read the headline and the deck line. "KNICK CRITIC KILLED! MAYFLOWER MURDERED AT ALGONQUIN ROUND TABLE."

She suddenly produced, as if by prestidigitation, a pair of horn-rimmed spectacles. She slid them on and scanned the headlines, the photographs and the tiny ten-point type. "It's not just about Mayflower," she said. "It's about each one of us. The Vicious Circle."

Dorothy and Benchley pored over the newspaper. It was a flimsy tabloid, only twenty-four pages, with more advertisements and pictures than text. And that text was largely taken up by screaming headlines. (She once offhandedly referred to the *Knickerbocker* as "nothing but ads and adverbs.") In this edition, the main body copy recounted the details of the murder, but several accompanying side articles reported the backgrounds of many of the Round Table members, even speculating about their animosities and disagreements with Mayflower.

Benchley scanned through the main article about the details of the murder—how, when and where Mayflower's body was found. Then he skipped past a few glowing biographical paragraphs about the deceased critic. The next few paragraphs caught Benchley's eye.

"Listen to this," he said, and read it aloud.

Imagine how simple it is for a great writer—
with the world at his (or her!) fingertips—to
cross out a word. Or, consider what a matter-
of-fact business it is for an influential editor—
flush with the power of his lofty position—to
strike out an entire paragraph, or whole pages

even. So, too, did this murderer rewrite New York history. It was as easy as this! A simple erasure. A blotting of ink. A word struck through with a line. This was how easy it was for a murderer to strike down the famous yet frail figure of Leland Mayflower.

"Who wrote this?" she said. She sought the byline. "*Bud Battersby?* That son of a bitch."

Benchley continued reading.

This coterie is the Vicious Circle, as the group "jokingly" refers to itself. Some joke! The name is apt, as was made clear when the group repaired to a nearby exclusive eatery, when their infamous Algonquin Round Table could no longer serve, and sat themselves comfortably down at the table—a regular rectangular one had to do. But did this inconvenience rain on their merry parade?

No! They were as gay as ever, with Mr. Benchley splitting their sides with an intemperate joke (which is unprintable in a family newspaper). The entire tragedy of their late colleague's death had fallen from their minds as quickly as the slightest of troubles!

Certainly, if one of their number should prove to be the murderer—and the New York Police Force, with its aggressive interrogation of the members of the Vicious Circle, seems to indicate that this is so—then that soul shall not sleep easy tonight, especially if Conscience (that old-fashioned thing!) has anything to say about it.

"How do you like that?" Benchley said, sinking in his velvet upholstered seat. "Someone stabs Mayflower in the chest. Then Battersby shows up and stabs the rest of us in the back. But you have to admit it. Battersby has a way with words, wouldn't you say?"

"A way up his ass, that's what I'd say." She considered a moment. "But there was no mention of Billy Faulkner and that suspicious man he described. Did you say something to Battersby? Tell him not to put the light on Billy?"

"No. Did you?"

"No. But it's a good thing Battersby avoided it. No sense getting Billy any further mixed up in this."

"The answer is simple," Benchley said after a pause. "Billy Faulkner is a nobody. The man Billy described is a phantom. Nobodies and phantoms don't make for juicy headlines. They *interfere* with juicy headlines."

"Are you defending that skunk Battersby?" She narrowed her eyes. "Do you like having your name in the paper, not so subtly accused of murder?"

"Well, it's not that. Battersby is a publisher—although now he seems to be the editor, the reporter and the newspaper boy, too, for all we know. Since Mayflower can no longer spin those sordid tales, it falls into Battersby's lap. What else can he do, with no obvious suspects, but point the finger at the people closest at hand—us?"

"You're just happy Battersby wrote that you were splitting everyone's sides."

Benchley conceded a smile. "Guilty as charged."

"At least Battersby seemed to let the both of us off easy," she said, pointing to the open pages. "Woollcott gets the worst of it. There's half a page devoted to him and his rivalry with Mayflower."

A murmur rippled through the audience. Benchley and Dorothy turned to look up the aisle. Floating toward them, in his usual broad-brimmed hat and opera cape, was Woollcott.

"Reading the newspaper in the theater, Robert? Tut-tut," Woollcott snorted, settling into his seat across the aisle from Benchley and Dorothy. "What is that, the

Knickknack News? I'd call it rubbish, but that would be an insult to rubbish."

Dorothy looked again at the tabloid, scanning for a mention of the name Dachshund. She worried that Battersby had described the man Faulkner said he saw in the lobby. If the police read about that, Faulkner would be in even deeper trouble for not reporting it to them. But she could find no mention of it.

"And Benchley!" Woollcott suddenly bellowed. "How could you take a job from that yellow rag and that scheming silver-spooned Battersby? How can you sit in the seat so recently occupied by my nemesis? What a callous, cold heart you have, Robert."

Benchley wasn't bothered by Woollcott's tirade. He was agitated for other reasons. "I'm not happy about the job either, Aleck. When Battersby asked me at the Automat to substitute for Mayflower tonight, I thought I was doing the *Knickerbocker* a good turn. I didn't know Battersby would do me a bad turn by vilifying our group."

"When you sit down with the dog, you get up with the fleas," Woollcott said with a knowing look to Benchley and Dorothy. "That's something *each* of you should remember."

The house lights dimmed, the conductor stood and the theater and the audience were engulfed in darkness as the orchestra thundered into the overture.

As the stage lights brightened, Dorothy barely paid attention. For one, she preferred serious drama to this song-and-dance revue. For another, her mind wandered to the strange young Southern man once again hiding out in her apartment.

Despite the bright lights and gaudiness onstage, and despite the blaring orchestra and the dancers' tapping feet—a clamor like a team of old horses crossing a rickety wooden bridge—she drifted into a fitful doze.

Dorothy awoke to an urgent whisper. *"Mrs. Parker."*

She was still in her velvet-upholstered seat next to

Benchley. The conflagration onstage and the cacophony in the orchestra pit were still in full swing. She felt a tug at her sleeve, and again someone whispered her name.

William Faulkner crouched by her side in the aisle. Rain had drenched his battered old hat, his thin scraggly beard and his oversized threadbare trench coat.

"Billy! What are you doing here? I told you to stay hidden at my apartment."

"I wish I had, Mrs. Parker. I wish I had."

Across the aisle, Woollcott peered at them. "By Jupiter!" he grumbled. "Put the pooch back in his kennel and let the rest of us watch the show."

She grabbed Faulkner's hand, and with an apologetic look to Benchley, who now saw what was going on, she led Faulkner up the darkened aisle and through the double doors into the brightly lit, ornate theater lobby.

She was prepared to give the young man a piece of her mind and set him straight. But when she got a better look at his bedraggled appearance and the hapless, even frightened, look in his eyes, she softened.

"What happened? Why did you come here?"

He sighed. "I came to New York because—"

"No, I didn't ask why you came to New York. I asked why you came to the theater when I told you to stay put—"

"I'm getting to that. I came to New York to experience life, not to hide myself away. So I was sitting in your apartment at the Algonquin, and I was thinking, even if it is a bit dangerous, even if the police are looking for me, I should take the chance and go out. Why not? There are good experiences and bad experiences, but in any case, I need to have *some* experiences. Otherwise, why did I bother to leave Mississippi?"

"Experience?" She frowned. "You know what I think? Writers are like fry cooks in a greasy spoon. No experience necessary. You know what else I think? You ought to listen to me."

"Well, I wish I had, because that's only part of it."

"What's the rest?"

He looked over his shoulder, then stepped closer. "On my way here, I was followed."

"Followed? By whom? The police?"

He shook his head. "The man I saw at the Algonquin this morning. The one who probably killed Mayflower."

At that, the music within the theater swelled and came to a noisy end. The audience applauded mildly, very mildly. In a moment, the double doors opened and the theater patrons swarmed into the lobby.

"Intermission," she said, and pulled Faulkner by the elbow and drew him toward the far wall, out of the way of the emerging flow of well-heeled theatergoers. Many in the burgeoning crowd lit up cigarettes and cigars and sipped surreptitiously from hip flasks.

Dorothy, a full foot shorter than most of the crowd, looked anxiously for Benchley, but instead she picked out another Algonquin member from the throng.

"Heywood!" she called. "Heywood Broun. Come here."

A bear of a man approached them. Despite his rumpled tuxedo, or perhaps because of it, he looked like a big pile of unwashed laundry.

"Heywood, you remember Mr. Dachshund from this afternoon, of course?"

"Of course!" said the man. His big paw shook Faulkner's delicate hand. "Heywood Broun. Sportswriter for the *New York Tribune*."

She said, "I wonder if you could do us a favor or two, Heywood."

"Of course!"

"Wonderful. First, do you have your flask?"

"As always." He winked and reached in his jacket for a well-worn silver army flask, which he handed to her. She unscrewed the flask's cap.

"Second, do you think you could escort us back to the Algonquin?"

She tipped the flask to her lips. Then she frowned. She held the flask upside down and shook it. Not a drop came out.

"Sorry about that," Broun said, reclaiming the flask. "I needed a little help to enjoy the show. Not bad so far, don't you think?"

"I've seen better productions in a chamber pot," she said. "Now, can you walk with us back to the Algonquin?"

Broun shook his head. "Sorry about that, too. I told my wife I'd meet her at the Cotton Club up in Harlem right after the show."

"Oh, never mind, then. Thanks just the same."

"It was nothing," he said, and disappeared into the crowd.

She watched him go. "You can say that again."

"Mrs. Parker! Mr. Dachshund!" Benchley fought his way through the crowd. "There you are. What's all the fuss about?"

"Mr. Benchley, where have you been?" she said. "Billy thinks he was followed by the man he saw at the Algonquin this morning."

"Really?" Benchley said. "Did you get a good look at him?"

"I think so," Faulkner said. "It looked like him."

"Dear me," Benchley said, and fumbled in his pocket for his pipe and pouch of tobacco.

She snatched something out of his hand. "What's this?"

"Oh, just a notepad," Benchley said, artificially casual, dumping much of his tobacco onto the floor instead of into the bowl of his pipe.

She looked at the notebook closely. It was small, the size of a deck of cards, and bound in black leather. Its pale blue pages were trimmed in gold. On the cover were monogrammed initials, also in gold.

"L.M.," she said. "*Leland Mayflower!* Fred, where did you get this?"

"Not so loud." Benchley coughed as he lit his pipe. "I found it on the table when Detective Orangutan took me to identify the body."

She flipped through it. The first page had been torn

out. The next few pages were filled with Benchley's handwriting in pencil.

He said, "You know how I'm always losing the darned things and I never have one when I need one. So I picked it up. Came in handy, too. I took notes of the show for my review, see?"

She read aloud: "'I am not overwhelmed. I am not underwhelmed. I am merely whelmed.'" She handed it back to him. "Well, I agree with you there, but I disagree with your actions. I never pictured you for a grave robber, Mr. Benchley."

"It was a thoughtless whim, not grave robbing," he said. "What's the opposite of grave robbing? *Comical* robbing? *Trivial* theft?"

Faulkner leaned into their huddle. "Petty larceny?"

"Yes," Benchley said. "That's all it was. I'll return it to Mayflower's widow, if it makes you feel better."

"He wasn't married," she said.

"His mistress, then."

She frowned. "Shouldn't you be toddling off?"

Now Benchley frowned. "I suppose I should."

"Toddling off?" Faulkner said. "Where are you going?"

"I have to review another opening play," Benchley said. "This is what we drama critics do in a busy season. We attend the first half of one play, then hustle down Broadway to see the second half of another. Mrs. Parker, as she often does, will take notes for me. Won't you, Dottie?"

"Mental notes," she said. "I don't need a filched notebook."

Faulkner said anxiously, "But what about the man who followed me here? He could be waiting outside."

Benchley scratched his chin. "Take my seat for the second half. Then when you leave, stick with the crowd and stay on Broadway. He wouldn't be likely to do anything to you under the bright lights with a thousand people around. Hail a cab, and I'll meet you afterward at Tony's."

"Tony's?" Faulkner said. "Who is Tony?"

But Benchley had already left. Pipe in his mouth, he waded through the crowd in the smoky lobby, and then he was gone. The lights flickered and the orchestra began tuning up. Intermission was over.

"Tony Soma's is a speakeasy," she said. "Everyone goes there. What do you say we go there now? I could really use a cup of tea."

Chapter 8

"A cup of tea?" Faulkner said.

"Yes, wouldn't you like a nice, strong cup of tea?" Dorothy said, taking his hand. "Look at you, you poor wretch. You're as wet as a dog's nose and just as cold."

She pulled him toward the exit.

He protested weakly, "Mr. Benchley said we should join the crowd after—"

But she ignored him. Gripping his cold, slender hand, she weaved through the crowd on her way toward the exit. Faulkner dutifully followed, fighting against the tide of theatergoers rushing back to their seats. Finally, they burst through the twin brass doors and into the cold, damp night air.

The rain had tapered to a foggy drizzle. The puddles on the sidewalk mirrored the dizzying glow of the lights of Broadway, as though a subterranean world of buildings and marquees grew downward like stalactites and could be glimpsed only through holes in the sidewalk. These lights also reflected upward, casting a ghostly illumination that reversed the shadows on the raincoats and faces of passersby. The wail of car horns and the screech of elevated trains, mimicking the shrieks and cries of unseen birds of prey, echoed through the thin fog and the cold night air.

She sensed Faulkner's reluctance to leave the well-lit radiance underneath the theater marquee. She sensed this in herself, too.

"How far is this speakeasy?" he asked.

"It's only on Forty-ninth, just a few short blocks away." She pulled up the collar of her jacket to cover her neck. "But perhaps we should take a taxi in case it suddenly starts to pour again."

"That's a good idea." He moved toward the curb, raised his arm to hail a cab but then lowered it abruptly.

"What's the matter?" she said.

"I don't think I have enough money for a taxi ride."

"Me either. Not one thin dime. Or a fat one, for that matter."

"How did you expect us to pay for tea?"

"Tony extends me a line of credit," she said. "Currently, that line extends from Manhattan up through the Hudson Valley, over the Adirondacks, and is now threatening to cross the border into Canada."

He glanced about nervously. "Then we'll walk?"

"Of course," she said with a confidence she didn't quite feel. She linked her arm through his and started walking. "There are hordes of people around. We're safe as houses."

They strolled to the end of the block and turned up Seventh Avenue. She had been right, of course, she told herself. People of all kinds—many dressed in formal clothes for the theater—filled the sidewalks. The crowds became even thicker as they approached Times Square. The theater lights were so bright and dazzling, they could have been on a Sunday stroll on a sunny June afternoon. But the night was cold. She cursed herself for forgetting her gloves.

"How many theaters are there in New York?" Faulkner said. He gazed upward as they walked into the bright pool of light under yet another theater marquee.

"Dozens. Maybe seventy-five or so legitimate theaters."

"*Legitimate* theaters?"

"Theaters that show dramatic plays or glitzy musical

revues, like that Ziegfeld piece of tripe. Then you have scads of other places for entertainment, such as the vaudeville houses and cabarets, the girlie shows and the minstrel shows." A sudden thought struck her. "Come to think of it, how did you get into the theater without a ticket, anyway?"

Faulkner looked guilty. "I fibbed. I told the usher that there was a certain doctor in the audience, a brain specialist, and the hospital sent me to fetch him."

"A brain specialist?" She laughed. "You're quite a fibber, aren't you?"

"No," he said quickly. "I mean, yes, sometimes. I mean, no, I'm not a fibber really. But it's true; sometimes I do tell stories to people for fun. I mean, a writer of fiction has to be something of a fibber, doesn't he? To make up an imaginary world, filled with imaginary people, he's got to be a counterfeiter. A prevaricator. A storyteller. A fictionalist."

"In other words, a liar. Guess that's why most of the great writers are men."

He chuckled. "I guess so. Can I tell you a secret?"

"By all means!" She loved secrets. "Can I tell you I'm not good at keeping them?"

"That's all right. During the war, I tried to run off and enlist. But I came too late. They declared armistice before I ever took up arms. Then, when I went back home, I—" He hesitated.

"Go on."

"I pretended I had fought. I walked around town in a uniform. With a limp. I even adopted a British accent, believe it or not."

She was both amused and appalled. "Oh, Billy. Pretending to be a soldier won't get you far with my crowd. Most of them—except for Mr. Benchley and Mr. Connelly—were behind the lines, either fighting or reporting. Perhaps I will keep your secret after all."

They continued arm in arm along the crowded sidewalk.

"Still, you're probably right that a writer has to be

something of a liar," she sighed. "But I've always been told the opposite. Be brutally honest, they said. Don't write one word that rings false, they said. Write as if you're stark naked, they said. I tried writing stark naked once. It didn't work."

"Why not?"

"All the other writers in the bull pen gave me funny looks, and I caught a nasty chill. But for you, I think you're right to be a storyteller, a fictionalist, a fibber."

"I hope so. But few people who've seen my writing think much of it."

"Is that why you came to New York? To have your voice heard?" She tried not to sound discouraging as she said it, but the motherly part of her mind wanted to discourage him, to shoo him back to the South, where, she imagined, he'd be safe and warm.

"Yes. Well, no. Not to have my voice heard. More like, to hear my voice for myself."

"To find your voice?"

"Yes, exactly." He seemed relieved. "I've filled notebooks with poems and sketches, but something's lacking."

"Did I tell you I read the pages you gave me? I liked what you wrote. You clearly have scads of talent. But it's a bit scattershot right now. All you need to do is to focus it—to find your own specific way of saying it."

He sighed, "I've got words rattling around my head like pennies in a tin can, but try as I might, it just comes out sounding like noise. As you say, I need to find my voice."

She squeezed his hand and bit her tongue. She wanted to say something tart and incisive, tell him his sensitive southern voice didn't belong in nasty New York. Give him a little bitter medicine that would be for his own good.

But she couldn't bring herself to hurt him, even if it would have helped him. He seemed so earnest and hopeful. *Writers are frail, vain creatures,* she thought. *And this boy still needs some mothering.* Mayflower's murder must have made her soft in the head to feel this way, she thought.

"You want to find your voice?" she asked. "Keep writing. Your voice will find you."

"You think so?"

"And don't stop reading. As a writer, I love to read."

"Me, too. What's your favorite thing to read?"

"The signature on a paycheck. Too bad I don't get to read it more often."

Faulkner chuckled, then stopped abruptly. His face froze. She looked at him and noticed an angry-looking man in a wide-brimmed hat standing close behind Faulkner.

"Stop right here," the man growled to Faulkner. Then he looked at Dorothy. "Don't move. I have a gun."

She didn't move. But she looked at the man closely. He wore a very long, dark gray wool coat. His eyes were in shadow beneath the wide brim of his dark gray hat. But she could see his mouth—his lips were bisected vertically by a leathery scar that ran from the right side of his nose to the left side of his chin.

The man turned away and raised his arm toward the street.

Faulkner whispered urgently, "It's the man from the Algonquin lobby. He followed us here."

In an instant, a taxicab pulled up.

"Get in," the man said. "We're going for a ride."

"Leave her—" Faulkner began.

"Shut up. Your mommy's coming with us. Now, get in."

Dorothy hopped forward. "Ladies first," she chirped, and jumped into the open door. She slid along the seat to make room.

Faulkner reluctantly clambered in, looking at her as if she were crazy. As the man with the gun sat down, she reached across Faulkner and across the man and quickly pulled shut his door.

"What the—" the man snarled.

She pulled herself back, then turned and yanked open the door on her side and quickly got out. As she did, she grabbed Faulkner's arm.

"Billy, come on!"

Faulkner was stunned, confused, but went with her because of the force of her momentum.

She heard, as she'd predicted, a roar of rage and frustration from the man inside the car. She had shut his door on his long, expensive wool coat. She had stopped him—for the moment—and he wasn't happy about it.

She pulled Faulkner in between the cars, trucks, buses and trolley cars moving through Times Square. Fortunately, the heavy traffic moved slowly—but horns honked at them. And at one point she narrowly got them out of the way of an oncoming trolley.

"Perhaps we were safer in the taxi," Faulkner said, only half joking.

The reached the sidewalk on the other side of Times Square and took a moment to catch their breath, as though they had forded a raging river.

"Look," Faulkner said. "He's coming after us."

She could see the man weaving through the midst of the traffic. He was moving quickly, heading right toward them.

She thought a moment.

"He can't come after both of us if we split up. Come on."

A few paces away, a green metal structure could be seen above the passersby. Its white glass dome glowed with light from within.

"What is it?" Faulkner asked, running after her.

"The subway. Do you have a nickel for each of us?"

A blast of hot air, a low rumble and a high-pitched metallic screech hit them as they descended the stairway. They dropped their coins in the turnstiles and hurried toward the platform. An uptown train had just pulled in.

"Get on it," she said, shoving him into the train's open door. "Meet me at Tony Soma's. Ask any cabdriver where it is."

"But you can come with me," he protested.

"He's after you, not me. I'll lure him away so you'll be safe. Don't argue."

Faulkner opened his mouth to do just that. But the conductor blew his whistle and the doors slammed shut.

The subway train lurched forward slowly; then all of a sudden it sped away with a whoosh and left behind a surprising hollow silence.

She looked around the dim, nearly empty platform. No other trains were in sight. Besides her, only a handful of people stood waiting.

The man with the scar would arrive any moment. Should she ask someone for help? That would certainly be the sensible thing to do. But getting someone else involved might put that person in danger, too.

Then she spotted a uniformed policeman at the far end of the platform. He stood with his wide back to her, twirling his baton, rocking on his heels. For once—*for once!*—luck was on her side. She hurried to him.

As she approached, she slowed her pace, noticing the policeman's white hair.

He turned to face her and smiled.

Her hopeful spirits sank. The portly old man was seventy-five if he was a day. He had the rheumy-eyed, slightly vacant expression that she associated with old age and senility.

Behind the elderly policeman was the pitlike darkness of the subway tracks. The man with the scar could shove this old cop down there with one little push.

She looked over her shoulder. There he was, fifty feet away. The man was running down the steps, his long coat flapping behind him. He reached the platform and looked around.

She turned away, but she could feel that he had spotted her, could feel that he was now stalking quickly after her.

"Evening, miss," the policeman said. "Everything all right?"

"Everything's just jake." She smiled and walked on.

She didn't want to give the man with the scar any reason to hurt the old cop.

Just beyond was another stairway, leading back up to the center of Times Square. She scurried up the steps.

Back on the busy sidewalk, she looked around. Above her were glowing signs and flashing billboards advertising Arrow Shirt Collars, Maxwell House Coffee, Squibb's Dental Cream, Camel Cigarettes, Chevrolet, Coca-Cola, and countless others. The illuminated marquees of the multitude of theaters and dozens of hotels blazed at her. People called Broadway the Great White Way because of the millions of bright lights that turned the dark city night into day. But all that light only served to make Dorothy feel more conspicuous. She glanced around, looking for somewhere to hide. To disappear.

Should she duck into one of the big theaters? If so, which one? The Rialto? The Bijou? The Lyric? The Gaiety? Or should she sneak into one of the small burlesque revues?

Should she run into that all-night Automat? Or up those stairs to a smoky pool hall? At the next doorway, a huckster tempted tourists into a dance hall where men paid a dime per dance to women with tight dresses and loose morals. Over there was a corner cigar store she'd accompanied Benchley into a few times. Or she could scurry into that soda fountain and hide behind the magazine racks.

She was paralyzed with so many ways to turn—and none offered any guarantee of safety.

Then, above the din of traffic, she heard the whinny of a horse. An open carriage stood in front of the Hotel Astor. A happy-looking young couple was climbing in.

Dorothy darted toward them. She sized up the young couple quickly: honeymooning out-of-towners, probably midwesterners, in New York for the first time.

She hurried toward the carriage and climbed up after them. She plopped down and found herself sitting next to the startled husband. On his other side, the young bride looked surprised but not alarmed.

"Welcome," Dorothy said brightly. "I'm from the Manhattan Tourist Bureau. First time in New York?"

"Y-yes," stammered the young woman happily. The young man was too taken aback to answer.

On the high bench seat in front, the driver, in a top hat and velvet cape, looked back at them.

"Let's be off, my good man," Dorothy said.

He turned around indifferently and snapped the reins. The old horse heaved forward and the carriage moved into traffic.

"Just married?" Dorothy said.

The young woman nodded eagerly. She smiled from ear to ear and squeezed the young man's arm. "My better half! I can't let him go for a moment."

There was a sudden jolt and the carriage stopped abruptly. Dorothy looked down and saw the man with the scar standing angrily beside the carriage.

"Get out now!" he snarled at her.

Dorothy turned to the young woman. "That's my lesser half. He won't let *me* go for a moment."

The woman looked shocked. "Oh, you poor thing."

"Out. Now!" The man reached into the pocket of his long coat.

The driver cracked his whip. "Begone, you!"

The man with the scar jerked away. His hand flew to his cheek and he staggered backward.

The crack of the whip goaded the horse. The carriage jolted forward and moved at a brisk trot.

Smiling, Dorothy turned back to the young bride as though nothing had happened. "On your honeymoon?"

"Oh, yes." The woman nodded eagerly. "We're so happy."

"Ah, marriage," Dorothy said, easing herself back in her seat. "What a wonderful institution."

"Isn't it?" the young woman agreed.

"Certainly," Dorothy said drily, "if you want to be institutionalized."

Chapter 9

Inside Tony Soma's speakeasy, Dorothy elbowed through the crowd and finally stood at the bar. The chase through Times Square had frazzled her nerves. She caught the eye of Carlos, the bartender.

"What are you having, Mrs. Parker?"

"Not much fun."

"The usual, then?"

She nodded. Carlos turned to the rows of bottles behind the bar, selected the three-sided bottle of Haig & Haig scotch, and deftly poured two fingers into a teacup. She held up three fingers and Carlos poured a little bit more.

He handed her the drink with a kindly nod. She cupped it in her hands as if it was warm and took a long sip.

"Ah, now, that's a nice, strong cup of tea," she said to herself.

She looked over the rim of her teacup and surveyed the familiar speakeasy. The room was narrow, with the bar on the left side and several booths on the right. It had once been the large front room of the brownstone. For a living room, it would have been large. But as a bar, the room was small. And it was jammed with drinkers and clogged with smoke. She hadn't seen either Benchley or Faulkner, but then, her short stature had her at a disadvantage. After another warming sip, she ventured forward again, cautiously navigating her way through the booze-swilling crowd.

Revelers of all kinds peopled the room. Glamorous showgirls and society matrons mingled cheek by jowl with bespectacled professors and slick politicos. To one side, a newly famous baseball player chatted with a grande dame of the social register. To the other side, a long-legged, loosely dressed flapper debated with a long-bearded rabbi. All clutched delicate teacups or stout coffee mugs of their favorite top-shelf liquor—sipping, swigging and gulping them down.

She overheard a familiar woman's voice and turned to see an acquaintance, the poet Edna St. Vincent Millay, talking animatedly to a powerfully built man. She had wavy, auburn hair, a pale, elliptical face, and wintry green eyes that were locked on the man's face. He had a thick shock of dark hair and wore an immaculate white wool overcoat. He had a face as square and hard as a block of ice, but he looked around, as though searching for a means of escape.

"Please don't be coy," Millay said, her green eyes flashing. "Tell me what it's like to pummel another man. I'm disgusted and thrilled by the very idea. Is there a lot of blood?"

"Nope, it's not like that at all," the man said, still looking about evasively. "It's not like I go in there and club the guy to death. Those days of boxing are history."

"But you're notorious for knockouts in the first round," Millay said, her eyes traveling over the man's broad shoulders. "You must be terribly strong."

"You got it all wrong," the man groused. "It's a thinking man's sport. It's a science. You prepare and you practice and you prepare some more. Then when you get in front of the crowd, it looks effortless. But it ain't."

Millay laughed at him. "A *thinking man's* sport? A *science*? I know a lot of thinking men and a few scientists, and they're nothing like *you*." She grabbed his arm, nearly spilling his drink. "Now, stop all this folderol and tell me about how you destroyed Georges Carpentier, the pride of France."

The man—Dorothy now recognized him as the heavyweight champion Jack Dempsey—recoiled from the woman's grasp. Still, Millay, almost drooling, continued to pepper him with questions. Dorothy couldn't help herself. She had to rescue the poor man.

"Well, hello," she said, stepping between them. "If it isn't the Poet of Greenwich Village! What are you doing up here, *Edna*?"

She knew that Edna St. Vincent Millay demanded everyone call her Vincent.

"Oh, hello, *Mrs. Parker*," Millay said, eyeing her suspiciously. "Mr. Dempsey and I were just having a cozy chat. You don't look so well, Mrs. Parker. And you seem to be missing your right hand."

"My right hand?"

"Mr. Benchley, of course," Millay trilled haughtily.

"Of course." She eyed Millay's hand on Dempsey's arm. "But then again, it's best not to let your left hand know what your right hand is doing, don't you find?"

Millay frowned and released her grip on Dempsey.

Dorothy continued, "I don't mean to disturb you two, but Horace Liveright just arrived. He's your publisher, isn't he, Edna? He said he was looking for you. Something about you owing him a manuscript in return for a large advance."

Millay looked as if a millipede had just crawled up her back. This information was well-known in the publishing community.

Dorothy spoke conspiratorially. "This place has a back door, if you want to give Liveright the slip. Mum's the word."

Millay nodded. With a longing look at Dempsey, she sneaked away.

Dempsey visibly relaxed. "Whew, that gal was tougher to shake than Billy Miske."

"Oh, she's just busy burning her candle at both ends. I take it she was bending your cauliflower ear?"

"You could say that. Is that Liveright guy really here?"

"I sure hope not. The only better way to kill the party would be a police raid."

Dempsey smiled. "Do I know you from somewhere?"

She told him her name, extending her hand.

"Yeah, I've heard of you." His palms were rough, but his handshake was surprisingly gentle. "The newspapers print the funny things you say. How does that one line go? 'Men seldom make passes at girls—'"

"With fat asses?" *Oh, brother,* she thought. She worked for months on perfecting a single poem or short story, but all anyone seemed to know was that stupid, off-the-cuff rhyme that took her all of four seconds to compose. Oh, well, at least this palooka knew who she was.

"'Who wear glasses.'" His smile dimpled his rugged face. "They say you have a wit sharper than a serpent's tooth, or something like that. I guess they're right."

"No, no. That's not me at all. Well, not tonight anyhow. My poison found an antidote."

"Well, you got rid of that goony poet lady for me. That's something. I owe you one."

"Forget about it. I'm forever rescuing puppies and pugilists. All in a night's work. And any other night, I'd be lining up right behind her to throw myself at you."

"Maybe some other night, then." He smiled and handed her a small card. "I gotta shake a leg, but here's my telephone number. I owe you one for getting rid of that gasbag. You ever need a favor, or anything"—he gave her a meaningful wink—"you just give me a call, okay? Bring your glasses."

Before she could reply, he had turned away, weaving through the crowd toward the door.

She mumbled sorrowfully to herself, "There goes another one. He'll probably be kissing the canvas before ever kissing me."

She took a long pull from her teacup and emptied it. She began to thread her way back toward the bar, now keeping a sharper eye out for Faulkner and Benchley. Despite the scotch, she was growing anxious. Faulkner should have arrived by now.

Then she felt a familiar tug on her sleeve.

"There you are," she said, expecting to see young Faulkner. But she found she was facing Benchley. "Oh, Fred, it's just you."

His smile withered. "Weren't you expecting me?"

"Of course I was. But I'm worried about Billy."

Benchley's merry eyes now grew concerned. "But isn't he with you?"

She felt a pang of guilt, remembering that Benchley had told them to leave the theater among the safety of the crowd. "Billy was right. There really is someone following him. A big, mean thug."

"What?"

"Billy and I separated in Times Square and I got the man to follow me instead of Billy. At least, I thought I did. But Billy hasn't appeared yet."

Benchley scratched his head. "I'm sure he'll be fine. Billy seems to be a clever and resourceful young man, probably not nearly as helpless as he appears."

"That's what I keep telling myself, too. But somehow I have a hard time believing it."

Benchley looked thoughtful. "However ... if there really is a man following him, that changes everything."

"How do you mean, that changes everything?"

Benchley looked into her empty teacup. "Let's get some drinks first, Mrs. Parker. Then we'll talk. Maybe Faulkner will show up in the meanwhile and all will be fine."

He guided her to the bar, where Carlos refilled her cup with scotch and gave Benchley a whiskey sour in a coffee mug.

"Come on." Benchley drew her to a less crowded corner of the room. "Let's talk over here."

They clinked cups. "God bless Tony's," Benchley said. And they drank. She felt the warmth of the scotch as before, but it did nothing to soothe her.

She said, "What did you mean just now? *What* changes everything?"

"The man following Faulkner. I suppose I really hadn't thought it through before."

"Didn't you believe Billy when he told you he saw such a man?"

"I believed that *he* believed it. But whether that man is the one who murdered Mayflower, I wasn't so sure."

"So how does that change anything?"

"Well, don't you see?" he said, smiling. "If there really was some gangster at the Algonquin this morning, and he was the one who killed Mayflower, then that proves the murderer isn't someone from inside the Vicious Circle!"

She looked shocked. "Has there ever been a doubt about that?"

"That's not what Bud Battersby and the *Knickerbocker News* would have the city believe." He pulled the rumpled newspaper from the deep pocket of his overcoat. "Look, these articles make it seem as if each member of our Round Table is a suspect, without a mention of anybody else. So, you see, if this threatening man was actually following Billy and even chasing him, we know that this fellow wasn't just some random suspicious character in the lobby this morning. If this man has a reason to hunt Billy down, then it means this man must indeed be the killer."

Her shoulders sagged. "But how does that change *anything*? It's the same thing that Aleck Woollcott said, that someone from outside our group murdered Mayflower. Only the murderer mistook Mayflower for one of us, or Mayflower somehow got in the way."

"Well, yes . . . ," he said weakly.

"That still leaves the rest of us in danger. And now Billy is in even greater danger, because this man clearly realizes that Billy noticed him this morning and can identify him. That's why the man is following him. To make quite sure—dead sure—that Billy won't identify him."

She could almost see Benchley's spirit sinking. He gulped his drink, saying, "And we thought we were protecting Billy by keeping the police from questioning him. If Billy had described the man to Detective Orangutan, the police would have had something to go on—a means to finding the murderer. But now if this man catches Billy—"

"You mean if this man *kills* Billy?"

"Then," he continued, rattled, "there won't be anyone alive who can identify the man."

"Only me," she said softly. "I saw him, too, remember."

"So you're in as much danger as Billy is."

"Birds of a feather. Flocked together."

Benchley gulped his whiskey sour. "You're flocked, all right."

Chapter 10

An hour later, which also meant several rounds of drinks later, Dorothy and Benchley had not forgotten about Billy Faulkner, but their troubles had for the moment abated.

"Well, what an evening," Benchley said. He wasn't yet slurring his words, Dorothy noticed, but he was extending his vowels. An *eee-ven-iing*, Benchley had said.

Finally, he added, "I think it's time to toddle along. I have two drama reviews to write tonight. And a train to catch."

She frowned. "I wonder where Billy wound up. I do hope he's all right."

"Not to worry." Benchley helped her put on her coat. "He's probably curled up on your davenport with your dog, both of them snoozing like lambs."

They made their way to the door. When Dorothy opened the door, the chilly night air made her catch her breath. She stopped. Suddenly there was movement, startling her. Someone—a man—was there outside the door, now before her, face-to-face with her, his face hidden in the dark.

"Oh, Mrs. Parker, finally!" His southern voice muttered through clenched teeth. "I've been waiting out here in the cold for three-quarters of an hour."

She grabbed Faulkner and hugged him.

"Wh-why, Mrs. Parker—"

"Billy, you silly boy, I'm overjoyed to see you. Oh, I'm over the moon! But why didn't you come inside and have a nice warm cup of tea? We've been worried sick."

She could feel that Faulkner's threadbare trench coat was still wet and icy cold from the evening's rain.

His teeth chattered. "The man at the door wouldn't let me in. I told him I was to meet you here and he laughed. He told me to 'vamoose.' But I stayed right here waiting for you."

She rubbed his sleeves. "You poor old thing. And all this time, we were inside, cozy and warm and having fun. Well, not much fun."

"No, not much fun," Benchley said. "We'd hoped you'd gone back to Mrs. Parker's suite at the 'Gonk."

"I couldn't. I couldn't move," Faulkner said. "I don't think I'm alone."

"Not anymore you're not."

"That's not what I mean," Faulkner said, casting a glance along the dark, quiet street of brownstone homes. "I think he's out there somewhere, waiting."

"You mean—"

"The man we saw earlier. The one I saw in the lobby before Mayflower was murdered."

"Well, there are three of us now," she said. "Safety in numbers, though I don't think one of us could harm a fly if put into a corner. Still, Mr. Benchley can escort us back to the Algonquin, and then we'll pour him into a cab so he can catch his train back to his family in Scarsdale."

She tried, as always, to keep the slight tone of jealousy out of her voice. She thought she succeeded.

Faulkner looked up. "F-family? Y-you're married, Mr. Benchley?"

"Naturally," she said before Benchley could answer. "Mr. Benchley has a wife and two little boys. He lives in a tidy little house in the suburbs. He rides the train from

Scarsdale every morning and home again every night. Is that such a surprise?"

Faulkner's stare ping-ponged from her face to Benchley's and back again. She kept her expression as neutral as she could.

"No, no surprise indeed," Faulkner said finally.

"Let's get going, then," Benchley said jovially, leading the way. "The Algonquin is only a few blocks away."

Despite this purposeful and well-intentioned objective, they moved forward slowly. Faulkner was frozen stiff from standing in the cold doorway for so long, and Dorothy and Benchley were both rather intoxicated. Not stumbling drunk, she considered, just pleasantly pickled so that one's thoughts were somehow only remotely connected with one's movements, such that it was something of a delightful surprise to find yourself walking when the thought of doing so seemed to have originated quite a while ago. In this manner, it felt like forever to approach the end of this long, quiet block of Forty-ninth Street, where they would turn south onto Sixth Avenue.

Shortly before reaching the corner, she stopped abruptly. This caused Faulkner and Benchley to stagger to a halt as well. A shiny object on the wet pavement had caught her eye. It was a silver dollar. She was never the kind of fortunate soul who just happened to find silver dollars lying about on the pavement. She stooped to pick it up.

"Isn't this my lucky day!" she said.

A cold, raspy voice answered, "Your luck just ran out, lady."

Chapter 11

Dorothy rose slowly, the silver dollar in her hand. First, she saw the man's expensive leather shoes. Then, she noticed his long, loose wool coat. One flap of the coat was pointing at her—inside the pocket, the man apparently clasped a pistol. Then she noticed the sparkling gold chain of his pocket watch and saw for the first time the single bone white tooth dangling there like a miniature skeleton swinging in a noose.

The man's eyes were in shadow beneath the brim of his hat. But she could see the leathery scar that bisected his mouth.

He had emerged from a tiny, dark alleyway—a narrow, coffin-sized opening—between two of the brownstone houses. His voice was like a nail file scraped across a tin can.

"Give me back my dollar."

"Easy come, easy go," she sighed, her hand outstretched. "Men and money simply slip through my fingers."

"Shut up." The man snatched the silver dollar from her palm. "Shut up and give me the rest of your money. This has to look like a stickup."

Benchley coughed. "I really don't think—"

"I don't care what you think." The man pulled the

pistol from his pocket. "Dead or alive, I'm taking your money. Hand it over. Now."

Faulkner and Benchley reluctantly dug in their pockets.

"You didn't hear me, lady?" the man said, raising the gun. "Hand it over."

"I'm afraid I'm in an awkward position," she said. "I don't carry any money."

There was a pause.

"All right. Where you're going, you won't need it anyway."

Faulkner held out a handful of change. "If you're just going to kill us anyway, what does it matter if we hand you our money or you simply steal it from our cold and lifeless bodies?"

The man seemed to consider this.

"You're right." Then he snatched the money from Faulkner's hand. "Get in that alleyway. It's time you went to sleep. Shut your goddamn mouths for good."

Faulkner hesitated. In one quick motion, the man stepped forward and put the barrel of the pistol to Faulkner's temple. "Go. Now."

Faulkner stepped into the inky darkness of the alleyway.

The man pointed the pistol at Dorothy. "Get in there."

"First Dempsey and now you," she said lightly. "Two lady-killers in one night. Lucky me."

The man's cold, raspy voice perked up. "You met Jack Dempsey?"

She felt a spark of hope. "Yes, I certainly did."

"I lost a bundle betting against that asshole Dempsey. Get in the alley."

She went in the dark, narrow alley. She could sense rather than see Faulkner in front of her. She stood against him and reached for his hand.

Benchley held out his money clip and his silver tiepin. "Just take it."

"Those cuff links," the man said. "They gold? Give me them, too."

"These were a present from my wife."

"I said, give me—"

"With pleasure," Benchley said brightly, unbuttoning the cuff links. "I can't stand the things. You'll be doing me a favor."

"Hold on. What's that?"

"Cuff links, my man. What do you think they are, gold teeth?"

"No, in your other hand. Is that a notebook? Is that *Mayflower's* notebook? How the hell did you get that?"

Benchley had taken the small notebook out of his pocket when he withdrew his other possessions. Dorothy saw the glint of the gold filigree monogram on the cover—*L.M.* The man reached to grab it. Instinctively, Benchley pulled away.

"You some kind of jackass?" the man said. "Give me that. Right now."

"I'm terribly sorry, but it has my notes in it. I'm afraid I can't let you have it."

The man raised the gun. "Hand it over or I'll let *you* have it."

Benchley shook his head, adamant now. "No, sorry, old man. I need it."

The man's voice grew louder. "Like I told the other jackass, where you're going, you won't need it. Hand it over right now or I splatter your brains all over the pavement."

Dorothy had rarely seen Benchley angry. Now he spoke petulantly, like a ten-year-old boy denied his dessert. "Fine, then. Take it!"

Benchley belligerently flipped the book in the air, in the direction of the man's head.

The man jerked backward, and the wide brim of his hat flicked the book farther upward. He reached up for it, but his one hand held the gun and his other held Benchley's valuables. The notebook bounced off the man's fingertips, fluttering upward like a thick paper moth in the night air. He reached again, now attempting to clap the book between his hands, but it fumbled out of his grasp and rebounded off his forearm.

Dorothy scurried forward out of the alley. The man didn't see her coming—he was looking down now as the notebook tumbled to the ground. She stomped her heel hard on the toe of his shiny shoe. The man howled.

Suddenly, Faulkner lunged forward and hurled the man to the hard pavement. Dorothy saw a glint of something white—the tooth from the watch chain—skitter sideways across the concrete sidewalk. With a swift kick, Faulkner knocked the pistol from the man's hand and into the gutter. The gun fired with an earsplitting blast. The bullet shattered the windshield of a parked Packard across the street.

With one hand, Dorothy grabbed Faulkner's coat sleeve. With the other hand, she clutched Benchley's wrist. "Shall we go, gentlemen?" she said breathlessly. "Party's over." She pulled them quickly toward the corner of Sixth Avenue, glancing over her shoulder. The man was moving slowly, groggily, to his knees, and began searching in the gutter for his gun.

"The notebook!" Benchley cried.

But she dragged them forward. They rounded the corner. Suddenly, they were on the busy, well-lit avenue. Automobiles and trolley cars trundled by. Well-heeled, bundled-up city folk hurried past in the chilly dark to get home. Workmen wearing heavy denim coats and carrying lunch buckets lumbered along on their way to the night shift. Dorothy, Benchley and Faulkner paused momentarily, as if surprised to find themselves back in their own bright and bustling world.

Then Dorothy quickly scurried forward, this time toward the street, nipping lightly onto the platform of a passing streetcar.

Benchley and Faulkner exchanged an astonished glance, both amazed to be alive. Then they ran to catch up with her.

Chapter 12

$\mathcal{B}$ack safely in her apartment at the Algonquin, Dorothy sat on her sofa while Woodrow Wilson lolled belly up on her lap. The dog's eyes were closed in contentment; his short legs splayed in the air; his tongue hung limply from his open mouth. She absentmindedly scratched his fat belly with one hand. With the other hand, she sipped a scotch highball and puffed a cigarette.

She turned her gaze to the clock. It was ten minutes past two in the morning.

Benchley loosened his collar and tie. His tuxedo was rumpled. His fingers stabbed the keys of her dilapidated Royal typewriter, a plain black economy model as battered and as functional as an old tortoise. He was growing increasingly frustrated with it. He slugged down his gin martini, growing increasingly inebriated. He glowered at her. "Mrs. Parker," he observed, "your dog is dead."

She glanced down at the motionless dog in her lap. "What makes you say that?"

"The smell."

"Nonsense. All dogs are going to heaven, and all dogs are going to smell."

She stopped rubbing the dog's belly to take a drink,

then a smoke. The dog opened his eyes and impatiently cocked up his head. She resumed grazing his belly with her fingernails. The dog's head dropped again to her lap.

Benchley clacked slowly on the typewriter. The dull little bell signaled the end of the line, and he swung the carriage back for the return. The handle came off in his hand.

After a moment of silent fury, he blurted, "How do you write with this infernal device?"

"Poorly," she said. "Don't worry. The handle goes back into place."

He harrumphed, then fitted the handle back onto the carriage and undertook typing the second line of the review of the first of the two plays he had seen earlier that night, before the gunman accosted them.

Benchley grunted again. The handle of the typewriter carriage had come loose in his hand for the second time.

"Pretend it's a woman," she said, closing her eyes, taking another drink, leaning her head back. "Treat her gently and she'll respond to your every command."

"It's not a woman. It's a machine. I could bang on it all night and it still won't—" He stopped himself. "Never mind."

But he didn't resume typing. She kept her eyes shut, imagining him sitting there, fuming.

Finally, she said, "Ignore it, then, and hope the problem fixes itself. Then again, that *is* how you treat a woman."

As soon as she had said it, she regretted it. They had unspoken rules, and one of the unspoken rules was not to speak about things like that.

Benchley didn't respond. She felt her face blush. Finally, she opened her eyes.

He wasn't there.

She felt a quick, cool wave of relief. Why should she be angry with him, anyhow? He had chosen to stay in the city tonight rather than go home to his family in Scarsdale. On theater nights, and after a few drinks, he often slept on her couch. Now it was two a.m., the height of the night. Let tomorrow take care of tomorrow. She lifted the dog off her lap and onto the couch, and raised herself slowly to her feet, careful not to spill her drink.

She found both men in the small bathroom. They were chatting quietly. Faulkner was curled in the tub, using it for a bed. He was covered in a wool blanket. Benchley leaned against the wall, sipping his martini.

He said, "I thought you had fallen asleep."

She shook her head. "I've been up talking to myself. The good part is that I'm rarely interrupted. What are you pigeons cooing over?"

Faulkner said, "We were just discussing Mr. Benchley's reviews."

"You should be writing them, not talking about them," she said. "Or just forget all about them. Your deadline was two hours ago."

Benchley frowned. "I hate to leave Bud Battersby in the lurch. First, his star drama critic is murdered in broad daylight. Then, after he asked me nicely to fill in, I fail to deliver the goods."

"Don't forget that little incident of nearly being murdered," she said. "I think there might be an escape clause for that. And did you forget this afternoon's edition of the *Knickerbocker*? The articles that made all the members of our little lunch circle look like suspects in Mayflower's murder?"

Benchley shrugged, unconvinced.

"It's too late anyhow," she said. "The morning edition goes out at six. That's only four hours from now."

"I could telephone the reviews in," Benchley said. "If only I could write the damn things down. Mrs. Parker, that contraption is a monster."

"Don't be silly. First of all, it's only a typewriter, Mr. Benchley. Mechanical devices are your enemy only because you make them so. Second, as you already know,

I don't own a telephone for you to call in your reviews. You'll have to go down to the lobby to place a call."

He didn't answer. He merely fumed at the thought of the typewriter.

She sighed. "Okay, then. Let's all have another drink. And, if you absolutely must do those reviews, we'll get you through them together."

This, at last, brought a slow, twinkling smile to Benchley's face. They returned to the parlor. While Benchley joked and made them laugh, she poured each of them a glass of bootleg bourbon. Then they had another.

It was three o'clock before Benchley finally fell into the chair and tried again to type. Dorothy and Faulkner sat on the couch, the dog lying between them.

"For Pete's sake!" Benchley cried. "Now the keys are malfunctioning. I typed a whole sentence. It came out gibberish."

"Are your fingers on the right keys?" she said.

Very slowly, very deliberately, Benchley lowered his head to look at his fingers on the typewriter keys.

"Well, would you look at that?" he mumbled.

Then his arms fell to his sides and his head dropped to the typewriter with a dull thud. After the briefest interval, he began snoring softly.

She said, "Well, I guess the party's over at last." She turned her unsteady gaze to Faulkner. "It's time for bed. You can sleep here on the couch. Looks like Mr. Benchley won't be using it."

Faulkner looked down at the stained, smelly, grubby couch. It was covered with a fine layer of vomit-colored dog hair.

"I think I'll go back to the bathtub," he said.

Chapter 13

The lobby of the Algonquin Hotel was crowded when Dorothy Parker went down for lunch the next day. People were everywhere. Every chair and every banquette in the lobby was occupied. A number of people meandered around aimlessly. They loitered at the entrance and the front desk as if waiting for something to happen.

On her way to the Rose Room, Dorothy encountered Robert Sherwood, who had pulled down his straw boater as if to hide his long face. Instinctively, she linked her arm through his. The bystanders gawked at them, and she sensed that this was not simply because she was very small and he was very tall.

"So, what fresh hell is this?" she muttered.

Sherwood leaned down and whispered, "They're a bunch of scandalmongers—that's what. They read all about the murder of Leland Mayflower, how he was found under our table and how any one of us might have stabbed him in cold blood. If you read it in the newspapers, *certainly* it must be true. Now they want to have a look for themselves."

She shrugged in response. She had woken up just an hour before with a terrible hangover. She had done what she could to brighten her appearance, with a green dress and a bit of pancake makeup. But, having caught her reflection, she decided she looked like a thin, dried-out pickle topped with a smudge of flour.

Georges, the maitre d', stood holding back a small crowd at the entrance to the dining room. He waved Dorothy and Sherwood through. The gaggle of wide-eyed onlookers watched them pass, some of them whispering conspiratorially to one another.

The dining room was packed and noisy. Every seat at every table—except at the Round Table in the center—was filled. The ruckus quieted momentarily as Dorothy and Sherwood entered and all eyes turned toward them. Then the loud chatter resumed with renewed gusto as the diners conferred about the new arrivals.

At the Round Table, Alexander Woollcott sat looking pleased with himself. He had a fresh lily in the lapel of his snugly fitted, black worsted wool jacket. He smiled broadly as Dorothy and Sherwood approached. His beetle eyes glittered behind his owllike glasses. Also seated at the table as usual were Franklin Adams, George Kaufman, Marc Connelly, Harold Ross and Heywood Broun.

"Mrs. Parker," Woollcott trilled in his high, nasal voice. "How perfectly delightful to see you. You look like you've been hit by a trolley car. And you, Mr. Sherwood, you look as elongated as always."

She wasn't usually bothered by this typical greeting from Woollcott. On any other day she would have ignored it or made a nonchalant but witty response. But this day Woollcott was preening for the onlookers, basking in their sidelong glances. She couldn't help herself from sniping in return.

"And what makes you so happy and gay today?" she snapped. "Another one of your competitors turn up dead?"

George Kaufman, a perpetually nervous and sensitive person, winced at this remark.

"Tut-tut, Dottie," Woollcott said, raising a cup of tea,

disappointed in her rudimentary riposte. "If I am shining like a sunbeam today, it is due in no small part to Mr. Benchley's reviews in this morning's *Knickerbocker*. The old cutup had me chuckling all morning. Now, tell us, where is that rogue writer? That man of letters? I must confer my accolades."

These weren't words of praise, she knew. This was Woollcott sharpening his claws.

"Once again, Aleck, you have it wrong," she said. "Mr. Benchley didn't submit his reviews. He didn't even write them. He fell asleep before he finished the first paragraph."

Now Franklin Adams spoke up, removing the cigar from his anteater face. "And you—*ahem*—have an intimate knowledge of his sleeping habits?"

Some of the others at the table chuckled wryly, though Adams and Sherwood kept stony expressions.

"No," she said. "I have an intimate knowledge of his *working* habits."

She felt cooler now. She wanted to divulge the dangerous events of the night before, how they had been held at gunpoint and nearly killed. It would knock their damned socks off. But, on the elevator ride down, she'd decided to let Benchley tell this tale. He'd get a great deal of enjoyment in telling it, and he would make it funnier, more absurd, than she could. (His talent was in making the ridiculous sublime, she knew, while hers was in making the bitter taste sweet and the sweet taste bitter.)

Woollcott said, "If these reviews are what Benchley considers work, then I'd suggest he retire forthwith. In any case, where is the jovial jackanapes?"

Reviews? Benchley had slept with his head on her typewriter all night. How could he have submitted his reviews? She didn't let her face betray her puzzlement.

"He went up to Doug Fairbanks' penthouse to borrow a change of clothes," she said. "Well, here's the proud peacock now."

Robert Benchley, beaming widely, strode into the dining room. He wore a well-tailored expensive-looking blue suit, a crisp white shirt, a florid pink tie and a matching pocket handkerchief. He wore it with a casual, care-free confidence, even though it was at least a full size too small. The pants displayed his stockinged ankles; his jacket sleeves ended midway between his elbows and wrists. As he crossed the room, he acted unaware of both the shortcomings of his borrowed suit and the stares focused on him by the room's scandal-hungry spec-tators.

"Good day to you all," he chimed, seating himself next to Dorothy. "No dead writers joining us today, I trust? No skewered critics on the bill of fare, I hope?"

Gasps emanated from a nearby table. Seated there were two dowdy, middle-aged, eavesdropping women. No one at the Round Table paid them any mind.

Woollcott grinned mirthlessly. "The only critic that should be skewered is you, old chum."

Benchley's eyes twinkled as he tugged at his cuffs. "In that case, waiter, give me a skewdriver. I'm parched. Come now, why are you all looking at me like that? Something amiss?"

Benchley expected to be taken to task for wearing the undersized suit. He had clearly intended it. Dorothy could almost see a clever response waiting at the corner of his upturned mouth. But Benchley didn't know that Woollcott had something else in mind, and she didn't know how to alert him to this.

"Something amiss?" Woollcott purred. "Nothing much. Only your writing. It's more than amiss. It's a mess."

Benchley's smile didn't falter, but he stopped adjust-ing his cuffs. "My writing, you say? Or my wardrobe?"

"Today," Woollcott said, driving the point home, "you come up short on both."

With delicate, disdainful fingers, Woollcott slid the morning edition of the *Knickerbocker News* across the table. He had folded it so that the drama page faced up. Benchley didn't pick it up at first. Then, suddenly, as if spotting his own obituary, he seized it and inspected it closely.

Dorothy leaned over his arm to look. He read aloud. "A DARK DAY FOR BROADWAY, BY ROBERT BENCHLEY, SPECIAL TO THE DRAMA PAGE." He looked up. "But I never submitted this piece. I never even finished it. Barely got it started."

Woollcott smirked. "Please continue."

Benchley read the article aloud:

> There are many new shows on Broadway, and I can say with confidence that *Twenty-three Skidoo!*, produced by Florenz Ziegfeld, is certainly one of them.

Marc Connelly nodded. "Sounds like your writing."

"Yes, I did write that," Benchley muttered, as if to himself. "And that's all I wrote. I had an argument with Mrs. Parker's typewriter, and the typewriter won. So I stopped there. But the review continues—" He read on.

> Leland Mayflower, rest his soul, isn't the only deadweight on Broadway—

"Oh, dear." Benchley frowned.

> *Twenty-three Skidoo!* is the familiar kind of musical revue we've seen time and again, featuring yet another spanking new ingenue, plucked fresh from the chorus line, with more looks than talent. The evening's entertainment ends when the opening curtain rises; it's all downhill from there, with a supply of musical numbers gathered from the refuse of Tin Pan Alley.
>
> This is the same dead horse that Mr. Ziegfeld has been flogging for years. And this dead horse stinks. I had to brush the flies

aside to get a good look at Dulcea McCrae,
the show's ingenue. When I finally did see
her, and heard her, I stopped swatting. The
flies made a more pleasant noise—

"But I didn't write this," Benchley said. "How did
Bud Battersby print this?"

Woollcott said nothing; he merely scooped a spoonful
of butterscotch pudding into his widely grinning mouth.

Franklin Adams narrowed his eyes. "Maybe Battersby
wrote it himself. When you didn't hand in the reviews as
promised, maybe he went ahead without you."

Benchley looked perplexed. "But . . ."

Woollcott said, "Please, Robert, continue to indulge us."

Benchley scanned the article, jumping to the second
review.

Meanwhile, down the street at the Shel-
drake Theater, Bibi Bibelot and Carl Worthy starred in the debut of Cornell Clyde's
The Winter of Our Marriage. I won't quip
that this *Marriage* should be annulled. It's
not significant enough for that. It's not significant for much of anything, really. This
lifeless bedroom drama is the apex of mediocrity, if mediocrity indeed has a high point.
And if it does, then mediocrity must have
a low point also. Interestingly enough—and
this is the only interesting thing about this
play—*The Winter of Our Marriage* man-
ages to be the rock bottom of mediocrity as
well.

Benchley stopped reading.

Connelly said, "That review sounds like you, too."

"It sounds like what Benchley might *say*," Sherwood
remarked. "Not what he would *write*. Not what he'd put
into *print*."

Woollcott said shrewdly, "Are those indeed your words?"

"Well, yes." Benchley allowed himself a sly smile. "But I never actually wrote them."

"Then how, pray tell, did they appear in the *Knickerbocker News*?" Woollcott said. "Not that it matters now. What's done is done."

"Aha!" Benchley grinned. "I think *you* wrote them. You were at both plays, too. I think you're putting one over on me."

"Would that I had such talent!" Woollcott replied drily. "No, my boy, I could not possibly write my two excellent reviews for the *New York Times* and also write your ridiculous reviews for the *Knickerbocker*. I'm flattered that you think I'm capable of such."

Adams spoke, this time not removing his cigar. "Maybe that's not all you're capable of."

Woollcott drew his marshmallow body as erect as he could. "What are you implying?"

"You know what," Adams said, leaning forward. "You've got a mean streak as wide and as dirty as the Hudson River. You had it in for Mayflower. Now you have it in for Benchley. Watch your back, Robert."

Woollcott's white face turned a bright, mottled red. "Withdraw that accusation immediately!"

"Prove me wrong," said Adams, always the journalist.

Woollcott responded with a blustery retort . . . but Dorothy stopped listening. Her hangover nagged at her, and she was tired of their arguing. She was hungry, too. She leaned toward Benchley and spoke quietly.

"What a handsome suit," she said, "for a ventriloquist's dummy."

"Why, thank you," Benchley said, smiling, tugging again at his short sleeves. "I'll pass your compliments on to our friend and movie star Doug Fairbanks."

She took a roll from the bread basket. "Pass the butter instead."

Benchley handed her the butter dish. "So—*ahem*—

where is our friend Billy? He has an odd habit of turning up at the strangest of times, and in the strangest of places, and in the strangest of ways."

She looked up from her plate and her heart sank. "You're right about that. Speak of the devil."

William Faulkner stood silently at the entrance to the dining room.

Chapter 14

Seeing Faulkner standing there, Dorothy felt both sorry for him and sorry that he had shown up.

Faulkner looked like he hadn't slept. His loose, tattered coat hung awkwardly from his narrow shoulders. His face was pale and hollow. His thin, scruffy beard was unkempt. His necktie, same one as yesterday, was slightly askew. He approached the table hesitantly.

"Look what the tide dragged in," Woollcott sneered.

Dorothy jabbed an elbow into Heywood Broun to move to the next seat over. She waved Faulkner to sit down next to her.

"Leave him be," she said. "He had quite a night."

"Didn't we all?" Woollcott said. "I myself was out making merry until the wee morning light. But you don't see me dragging myself around like I'm the ghost of Hamlet's father."

"Of course not," Benchley said. "No one would mistake you for a ghost, much less a father."

Woollcott ignored him. He addressed Faulkner. "Look here, young man—Mr. Dachshund or whatever your name is. This suffering-artist appearance that you're cultivating is beyond the pale. It's an effrontery. Your disheveled bohemian costume might find you friends with *les artistes* down in Greenwich Village or on the Left

Bank of Paris, but the rest of the world won't give you the time of day."

"The time of day is lunchtime," Dorothy said. "Not time for dressing down Mr. Dachshund because he doesn't dress up."

Woollcott waved a hand in the air. "Mr. Dachshund can dress like Puss in Boots, for all I care. I'm talking about his approach to life from the inside out. It's an insult to this table, to this room, to this time. Your dingy *déshabillé*, Mr. Dachshund, clearly displays your dour disposition."

"My *dissa*—What?" Faulkner said.

"If clothes make the man, then you're a sad sack, indeed," Woollcott continued. "Your depressing dress is an insult to this gay room. To this celestial sunny spring day. To this magnificent, merry time we live in. Cast off those rainy-day raiments, Mr. Dachshund! Lose that bird's-nest beard. Divest yourself of that derelict's overcoat. And for God's sake, rid yourself of that rain cloud over your head."

Faulkner didn't—couldn't—respond.

"You're asking him to change his entire outlook," said George Kaufman, often a downbeat person himself. "You might as well ask him to change his skin, or change his soul."

"Exactly! That's exactly what I'm asking him—no, begging him—to do," Woollcott said. "You're cheating yourself, Dachshund. You're a young man, just starting out in the world. Do you want to go out there shackled with sadness?"

Faulkner didn't even attempt to reply.

Woollcott spread his arms wide. "Take your unhappy head out of your navel and look at the bright world around you. By scorning gaiety, you give a black eye to the glorious age in which we live. There's a party going on, and you're missing it."

"Not at the moment, he isn't," Dorothy said. "He's here, isn't he? Not that this place is much of a party these days. Used to be people would drink themselves under the table. Now they're found dead there."

"True," Woollcott persisted, "times aren't always grand. The past decade has dished out the worst that Fate could throw in our path. There was the Great War. A hundred thousand young men killed and twice as many wounded. We saw the theater of war firsthand—Adams, Harold Ross and myself. We wrote and edited the soldiers' newspaper, the *Stars and Stripes*. We reported it all. We saw men dismembered. Gunned down. Gassed."

"Now who's being a wet blanket?" Dorothy said.

Woollcott ignored her and continued to lecture Faulkner. "And my esteemed colleague Mr. Sherwood here was in the trenches. On the front lines, he fell into a so-called German bear trap and took shrapnel in the legs. But does he drag his troubles around like a ragman drags his cart?"

Sherwood shifted in his seat. His long legs still gave him difficulty.

Woollcott kept talking. "And just when the war was barely won, we had the influenza epidemic, the Spanish flu. More than half a million Americans dead. But there was one tragedy yet to come, more pervasive than war or plague."

Benchley nodded his head. "The Volstead Act."

"The Volstead Act!" Woollcott wailed. "The Eighteenth Amendment. The prohibition of intoxicating liquors. But did we flagellate ourselves with our misfortune?" He slapped both hands on the table. "No, sir. *That* was the nail in the coffin of our misery. We had had enough. America gave a collective yell and threw the rule book out the window!"

"Can I get an amen?" Marc Connelly said sarcastically.

"Bad times were banned," Woollcott said. "And thank God! Cold funeral dirges gave way to hot jazz. Necklines plunged and hemlines rose. Booze is now found in every bathtub. And the world is roaring back to life. The stock market is booming. The music is gay. Skyscrapers are touching the heavens and so should we. Eat, drink and be merry, for tomorrow we may die!"

Dorothy held her aching head. "Alas, we never do."

Broun cracked an easy smile. "Eat, drink and be merry. I'll drink to that." He produced his silver flask, unscrewed the cap and dribbled a measure of whiskey into his coffee cup. He passed the flask to Faulkner, who hesitated to take it, then cautiously poured a few drops into his cup. Faulkner passed it to Dorothy, who looked at the flask as if it was a skunk. She shrugged and poured a healthy shot into her orange juice.

"That's the spirit," Woollcott said. "What's Prohibition? Prohibition is the pitiless schoolmaster that compels the pupils to truancy. There's never been a better time to drink."

"Hear, hear," Benchley said. Then he gestured to Dorothy to pass him the flask. "I mean, here. Here."

Woollcott continued, "Since they shut the saloons down, every back room and every back pocket has a bottle in it. It merely proves my point."

"And what point is that?" Dorothy said.

"Man should live while the living's good, and if he's smart, he'll find a way to do it," Woollcott said. "What's the point to life if not to live? Gather ye rosebuds while ye may, I say." He ended with a flourish of his fork, popping a piece of popover in his mouth. "Now, what do *you* say, Mr. Dachshund?"

Faulkner didn't respond. His forehead wrinkled as he gathered his troubled thoughts.

In the absence of Faulkner's response, Benchley said, "The devil take me for agreeing with Mr. Woollcott, but damned if I don't. Matter of fact, I'll go you one better, Aleck."

"That'll be the day," Woollcott said snidely.

"Hear me out, now," Benchley said, raising a hand. "To expand upon your argument, not only should we live each day to the fullest—we should live every second to the fullest. Drink every last drop of it, I say. Seize the day, yes—and live in the moment."

"As Mr. Benchley says, drink every last drop of it!" Woollcott cried, pouring the last trickle of liquor into his cup. Then he handed the empty flask to Kaufman, who tipped it over his cup without result.

They all clinked their cups and glasses and congratulated one another on this idea. Except Faulkner.

As they drained their cups, Faulkner cleared his throat, then ventured to speak. "I respectfully disagree with you, Mr. Benchley, Mr. Woollcott. I don't think that's right. That *can't* be right."

"He speaks!" Woollcott said. "Can't be right, eh? What's your view, then?"

"Man must be more than that," Faulkner began softly, then gathered steam. "He must be more than the sum of his experiences. He must be more than a gatherer of ephemeral events, like a fat toad sunning himself on a log, flicking his tongue at flies and then forgetting them as soon as they're swallowed, the way you speak of consuming life's experiences. Man has a soul burning like a lantern that fickle winds can't blow out. Man is surely more than just a lowly creature that lives purely for the moment."

Dorothy sucked on her cigarette and looked at him with pity. "No, Billy, man is indeed just such a lowly creature," she exhaled. "Now, woman on the other hand—"

"Hold that thought, Dottie," Woollcott said. His words dripped cold and clear, like water dropping from an icicle. "Though I am but a mere gatherer of ephemeral events, I must ask you a question, Mr. Dachshund."

Faulkner nodded uncertainly.

"Was the lantern of your soul burning the midnight oil to enable you to put Mr. Benchley's name on the drama reviews you wrote," Woollcott said, "and forthwith submitted to the *Knickerbocker News*?"

All eyes turned to Faulkner. He sat motionless and

silent, pointedly avoiding the gaze of Dorothy to his left and Benchley on her other side.

So Faulkner had written Benchley's reviews?

"Is that true, Billy?" she heard herself say. "Did you come to New York to find your own voice—or to use Mr. Benchley's?"

She immediately wished she hadn't said it. She hadn't intended to, but she'd hurt him, she knew. Why did she sometimes say such vicious things? As she considered an apology, she heard Benchley mutter that it was okay— that he wasn't using his own voice anyway.

But then a looming shadow fell over her. A large hand clasped Faulkner's shoulder.

"Dachshund, you old dog," said Detective O'Rannigan. "Been looking for you everywhere. Where've you been keeping yourself?"

Faulkner's face turned even paler.

O'Rannigan's smirk disappeared. He grabbed the back of Faulkner's chair.

"Get up," he growled. "Let's go for a ride."

Chapter 15

Benchley helped Dorothy put on her coat.

Woollcott sneered from his seat, "Where do you think you two are going?"

"After him, of course," she said.

Detective O'Rannigan had marched out Faulkner only moments before.

Sherwood stood also. "I'll come along, if you two don't mind."

"Now everyone's going?" Woollcott said. "The party's over? Just like that?"

Still seated, Adams, Kaufman, Broun and Ross looked at one another with expressions of insult and incredulity.

Woollcott buoyed himself out of his seat. "Well, if you must go, you can drop me off at the Times Building on your way."

He hustled past them and sauntered through the lobby and out the door. They finished putting on their coats and met him in front of the hotel.

Out on the sidewalk, Woollcott busied himself with inserting a Lucky Strike into his cigarette holder.

"Benchley," he said, lighting the cigarette, "be a good boy and have the doorman call us a cab." He indicated a uniformed man in front of them. The man wore a visored cap and a long coat with gold-braided epaulets on his shoulders. The man was elderly and sported a trim white mustache.

"Good day, sir," Benchley said. "Would you call us a taxi, please?"

"I'm not a doorman!" he barked. "I'm a rear admiral in the United States Navy!"

"In that case"—Benchley smiled pleasantly—"can you call us a battleship?"

As he said this, a cab pulled to the curb. The old navy officer seized the handle and yanked open the door. But before he could get inside, Benchley ushered in Dorothy, Woollcott and Sherwood. Benchley was halfway inside the door himself as he shoved a quarter into the astonished admiral's gloved hand.

"This will not do!" the admiral huffed.

"Beg your pardon." Benchley slipped another quarter into the admiral's hand. "Much obliged."

He slammed the door and the cab sped off, leaving the navy officer on the sidewalk in a cloud of exhaust and exasperation.

Inside the cab, Woollcott and Benchley sat with Dorothy in between them, while Sherwood sat on the fold-down jump seat at the side, extending his long legs in front of theirs.

Woollcott smirked. "I suppose your Mr. Dachshund is going up the river now. What do you possibly think you can do for him?"

Dorothy said, "Your ability to distinguish an innocent man from a guilty man is as good as your skill in distinguishing a military man from a doorman."

"The police don't seem to think he's so innocent," Woollcott said.

"They will once they hear about the man Billy saw in the lobby," she said.

"What proof does Dachshund have that such a man exists?" Woollcott cried. "This mystery man is no more real than the bogeyman."

"He's real, all right," Benchley said jovially. "The gun-man tried to rob and kill the three of us—Mrs. Parker, Mr. Dachshund and myself—last night."

Woollcott drew in a sharp breath. His eyes bulged. He loved hearing about the crises and misfortunes of others.

"Rob you and kill you?" he said breathlessly. "Last night?"

"Exactly," Benchley said matter-of-factly. He tried to put on a pair of moleskin gloves he found in Fairbanks' suit pocket. But, like the suit, the gloves were also too small.

"Don't stop there, man," Woollcott sputtered. "Tell us more."

Sherwood also stared back and forth at Dorothy and Benchley in astonishment.

Benchley blankly returned their stares, as if surprised they'd want to hear about such a trifling matter. He looked to Woollcott. "Are you going to finish that ciga-rette? It's nearly kaput."

"Damn the cigarette!" Woollcott cried. "Tell us about the gunman. Who was he? When was this? *Where* was this? Why did he try to kill you?"

Benchley smiled, as if comprehending. "Well, Mrs. Parker had his silver dollar, you see." He stopped there, as if that cleared up the matter.

Woollcott turned pink. "No, I don't see," his nasal voice whined. His small, round, gloved fists pounded the air. "Explain yourself. Commence at the beginning and relate the events in chronological order. Can you do that?"

But Benchley couldn't. As he meandered his way through his telling of the encounter, and as the cab plod-ded its way through midday traffic, Dorothy watched with amusement. Benchley's face was blank, innocent. But she knew he was having fun taunting Woollcott.

"And that's when Mrs. Parker stomped on the man's toes. He fell down, and we got away," Benchley said.

Woollcott looked at her, his mouth agape. "You toppled this murderous brigand by means of stomping your little shoe on his toes?"

"No, no, certainly not," Benchley said. "Dachshund launched himself from the alleyway, tackling the man. That's when his tooth went flying."

Woollcott gasped, "Dachshund lost a tooth in this fracas?"

"Of course not. It was the gunman's tooth."

"Dachshund knocked out the gunman's tooth?"

Now Benchley appeared frustrated. "No. The gunman's tooth was on his watch chain."

"The gunman's watch chain pulled out his tooth?"

Benchley shook his head. "The tooth was a fob on the chain. But this is when the windshield shattered, and we left the notebook behind."

Woollcott rested his head in his hands. His nasal voice came muffled between his thick fingers. "I believe that's enough. I think I get the gist. You've had your fun, Benchley. Thank you for your story."

Benchley was sorry to see it end. "Then Dachshund wound up in the tub. And, as I explained, that's how he wrote the reviews."

Woollcott lowered his hands. His beetle eyes were slits behind his owlish glasses. "That will do, Robert." His voice was solemn, his tiny eyes sincere now, even to the point of tears. "Indeed, Mr. Dachshund talks like a Mississippi mammy and dresses like a ragamuffin bohemian poet from Greenwich Village, but he's nothing less than an all-American hero."

Dorothy turned to Woollcott. This was typical of him—a mercurial change of opinion. But something else had been nagging at her mind since they left the Algonquin.

"Aleck, how did you guess that Billy wrote Mr. Benchley's reviews?"

"Elementary, my dear Dottie," he sniffed. "Mr. Benchley, by his own admission, did not submit the reviews.

And you said he was with you last night, and we all know you don't care a fig about deadlines. And you wouldn't use his name in vain regardless, even as a prank."

She nodded.

He continued, "That leaves us with one would-be writer trying to impress his newfound literary friends. But what he lacks in the written word, he has made up for in valiant deeds." Woollcott laid a white-gloved hand on her sleeve. "He saved your lives, my dear comrades. And for that, he has my earnest and heartfelt esteem. I shall immortalize his heroics in my next column in the *Times*. Ah, here we are."

The cab pulled up in front of the New York Times Building.

Dorothy said, "Aleck, this is one can of worms you might want to keep a lid on."

He either ignored her or didn't hear her. He swept up his cape and flung it over his shoulder. "Thankfully not for the last time, *mes amis*, I bid you *adieu*." And he quickly went out the door.

The cab rolled on.

Sherwood said, "Like you two, I took a liking to Billy from the start. But if your encounter last night happened as you say, then Billy—what's his real name again?"

"Faulkner," she said.

"Then Billy Faulkner has jumped in my esteem, too," Sherwood said. "Still . . ."

"Still something leaves you wondering?" she said, voicing her own hidden doubts.

"I'm wondering, if he did write those reviews, how did he do it? Did he have help? I mean, is there more to Billy Faulkner than we know?"

She quickly detailed for Sherwood what she knew: Billy lived in a hallway apartment far uptown, that he had come up from the South several weeks beforehand, that he had apparently been working in the bookstore at Lord & Taylor until recently, that he aspired to be a writer, and that he came to New York to find his voice.

Sherwood nodded slowly. "He seems a decent fellow on the whole. But then again, there's something about him. Something—"

"Peculiar?" Dorothy said.

"Precisely," Sherwood said.

Benchley said, "I chalked that up to artistic temperament."

"I don't know about artistic temperament," Sherwood said. "But I do know this. Many great artists are merely lunatics with talent."

Benchley smiled. "I guess that leaves me out on both counts."

Dorothy thought about Faulkner's other admission that, after the war, he had pretended to be a wounded veteran. What did that make him, an artist or a lunatic?

Chapter 16

"Dachshund?" said Detective O'Rannigan. His small brown derby tilted forward over his big sweaty forehead. "We grilled him, and how. Which is probably what we shoulda done to you. Why didn't you tell us right from the get-go that he saw the Sandman? You coulda saved everybody, including your boy Dachshund, a bunch a trouble."

Dorothy, Benchley and Sherwood spoke in unison. "Who's the Sandman?"

"I thought you're newspaper people," he sniggered. "You don't read the papers? You don't know who the Sandman is?"

"We're magazine people," Dorothy said. "We don't fold as easily as newspaper people and we have staples in our middles. So enlighten us."

O'Rannigan leaned his wide backside against the low wooden balustrade that divided the entrance hall of the police station between a foyerlike common area and a bustling police-only receiving area. All around them, brass-buttoned officers strode purposefully. People of all stripes and classes stood about as they waited for their bit of justice to be served.

But the detective chatted casually as though this was

nothing more than a friendly conversation among old friends.

"The Sandman, otherwise known as Knut Sanderson," O'Rannigan said. "Sanderson used to be known as the Sinister Swede. That was back in his nicer days, before the war, when all he'd do was deliver a little love note by breaking your kneecaps or chopping off a couple of fingers. Now everybody just calls him the Sandman. You know why, don't you?"

"Let me guess," she said drily. "He puts people to sleep?"

"Puts 'em to sleep, but for good. We've been looking to nail him for a while. We know he works as a gunman for bootleggers. You're lucky. I never heard of anybody getting the best of the Sandman. You have your pal Dachshund to thank for that, sounds like. Yup, Dachshund told us all about it."

Benchley said, "So if this Sandman is your man, why don't you let Billy go?"

"What, are you my boss now?" O'Rannigan said, his color rising. "Anyways, we did. Just got the release order. Took him a little while, though. Dachshund yapped and yapped about all kinds o' hooptedoodle. Finally he coughs up a description we can hang our hat on—the vertical scar down Sanderson's mouth and the tooth on his watch chain. That's the Sandman, all right. Once we heard that, we knew your boy Dachshund was nothing more than just a dopey schnook. Mayflower's killer wasn't Dachshund. It was Sanderson. So we let Dachshund go."

They simultaneously shot questions at O'Rannigan.

"You let Billy go?" Dorothy said.

"Where is he?" Benchley said.

"Why would Sanderson kill Mayflower?" Sherwood said.

Before the detective could answer, a uniformed policeman hurried by.

"Watch out, sir," the policeman said. "Captain's looking for you, and he don't look happy."

O'Rannigan straightened up and twisted his head around like a barn owl. A tall man with the somber face of an undertaker moved slowly toward them. The man wore a gray suit. His right pant leg was cuffed just below the knee, and below this was a wooden stump in place of his lower leg.

"C-Captain," O'Rannigan said. "You needed to see me?"

The man spoke in a low monotone. "Where is William Dachshund?"

"Dachshund? He's released. Just like you ordered."

The man didn't say a word. O'Rannigan began to fidget.

Finally, the man said, "Did you read the order?"

"Of course, sir, I—" He grabbed at a sheaf of papers on a nearby desk. "I have it right here. Here's—no, wait. That's the release order for Dunkelmann. Here it is, the order for Dachshund. It says—" O'Rannigan went pale. "For cripes sake."

The captain turned away. "Find Dachshund. Get him back in custody. And release *Dunkelmann*, as ordered."

O'Rannigan muttered to himself, "Goddamn German names!"

Chapter 17

It was half past eleven o'clock the next morning—
Friday morning—by the time Dorothy Parker hooked
the leash onto Woodrow Wilson's collar to take him for
a morning walk.

She had intended to get up early. But a pound of intention is worth an ounce of chores, she acknowledged.
She had been up late the night before, just floundering
in her apartment alone, hoping for Faulkner to return.
She nearly worried herself sick. She had a drink and a
cigarette to soothe herself and to while away the time,
and one led to another and another. Still, Faulkner never
knocked on her door.

Now, this morning, instead of waiting around for Faulkner to show his face, she would find him. She and her
dog were on the hunt through the streets of Manhattan.

Benchley, that other stiff, had taken a train back to
the suburbs yesterday afternoon. He had finally tired of
the stunt of wearing Douglas Fairbanks' short suit, so he
had gone home to take it off and to put on the mantle
of father and husband, since he hadn't seen his wife and
family for nearly two days.

And, she thought, *why shouldn't he? Why not indeed?*
She realized she was suddenly walking faster, nearly

stepping on poor little Woody's stubby tail. She slowed her pace and took a deep breath, and shoved aside the thought of Benchley in the bosom of his family.

Never mind; she would see him tonight at Tony Soma's.

She lightly tugged the leash to prompt the dog to turn up busy Fifth Avenue. Faulkner had told her where he worked, at the Doubleday bookstore inside the Lord & Taylor department store.

Was he still working there? She wasn't sure. Faulkner had been unclear, and she hadn't pushed him for answers. Whether or not he had a steady job hadn't seemed important before. And if, for whatever reason, he no longer had the job, and was trying to avoid the embarrassment of explaining this, that hadn't mattered either. She knew plenty of people who flitted from one job to another much like bumblebees meandering from flower to flower.

But now ... Now that Faulkner was missing, there was something about his evasiveness—about his job, about where he lived, about where he came from, even about his ambitions of being a writer—that bothered her. It itched at the back of her mind. So she wanted to see for herself—where he worked, where he was living and what, if anything, he was doing here in New York.

She had intended to set out earlier. Now she would miss lunch at the Algonquin. Ah well, Benchley wouldn't be there in any case. And he would have refused to join her on this little errand anyway.

"I can't bear to enter a bookshop," he always said, his mustache drooping. "To see all those thousands of brightly bound volumes, each with its author's dreams and hopes and passions tucked tightly inside, like thousands of dear little mummies entombed, waiting in vain to be set free." Fortunately, as soon as talk of bookshops ended, so, too, did Benchley's melancholy.

Her mind turned back to Faulkner. She worried that he could be anywhere out on the street, in danger of being captured by Detective O'Rannigan—or worse, the one they called the Sandman.

Then she brightened. Maybe Faulkner was safe (a relative term, she conceded) in police custody. Better yet, maybe the Sandman was in custody. Fear—or at least caution—had been another reason she had stayed in last night.

O'Rannigan, after that curt reprimand by his superior, had had a big bee in his bonnet when they left the police station yesterday afternoon.

"If you see that Dachshund, you turn him in but quick, understand? Or, by God, I'll lock the bunch of you stuck-up snobs into cuffs and toss you all into the Tombs!"

By *the Tombs*, she knew, O'Rannigan meant the medieval Manhattan House of Detention. So Dorothy, Benchley and Sherwood made a hasty departure. Outside, on the steps of the police station, whom should they bump into but Bud Battersby.

"Well, if it isn't the publisher, editor and now ace reporter for the *Knickerbocker News*," Sherwood said. "Where *do* you find time to give people the old screw, Bud? Because you're doing a bang-up job of it."

Battersby's boyish face looked wounded.

Sherwood persisted, as though in a vaudeville act. "Say, Mr. Benchley?"

Benchley, always game for a joke, replied, "Yes, Mr. Sherwood?"

"Mr. Benchley, how do you make a small fortune in the publishing business?"

"I can't say, Mr. Sherwood. How *do* you make a small fortune in the publishing business?"

"Start out with a *large* fortune, and buy a printing press." Sherwood guffawed.

Battersby's lips tightened; his face reddened.

"What's the matter?" Sherwood taunted. "Silver spoon got your tongue? You have plenty to say about us in your tabloid rag of a newspaper. Too scared to say it to our faces?"

Battersby scanned each of their faces in turn and pleaded to the only one that seemed at all sympathetic.

"Mr. Benchley," he said, struck by a new thought, "I gave the money for your reviews to the man who delivered them. I trust he passed the cash along to you. The amount was acceptable, I hope?"

Benchley considered this. "Yes, I guess so. Certainly, the amount of money I received corresponded to the amount of work I put forth. Tell me, though, was the man who delivered the reviews the same one who sat at our table at the Automat? Thin, young, scruffy fellow with a hangdog look and an unsuccessful beard?"

"Oh, yes," Battersby said. "Was there any question? Fellow had a funny name—Mr. Dachshund. He called in the reviews by telephone in the middle of the night. Then he came in yesterday afternoon to collect the payment. I assumed it was the same man."

"Oh, I'm certain it was," Benchley said wryly. "Lovely fellow, Mr. Dachshund. Have you seen him lately, by any chance?"

During this conversation, Sherwood stood simmering.

"Benchley, that's enough. How can you even be civil to this man? You of all people. One minute he's begging you to write drama reviews for him. The next minute, he's scandalizing all of us in the very same ratty newspaper."

Battersby sighed, his face perplexed and his voice defeated. "Sherwood, you know how it is. You're in the business. Mayflower was the best attraction I could have. Now what do I do? I have to sell newspapers. The police have nothing to tell me. And Mayflower was found under *your* Round Table. Of course I have to write about you and your friends. It pains me to do it, honestly. But I have to follow the story. I have to give the people what they want. You understand that, don't you?"

Sherwood was livid. His large hands darted into the air like bats fleeing a belfry. "The hell I do! The news isn't a commodity, to be sold for mass enjoyment like candy bars and Cracker Jack. You can't simply give the people what they *want* to know. You have to give people what they *ought* to know. Newspapers have a sacred covenant to educate, not to placate. Don't you understand *that*?"

Battersby shook his head. "I understand the notion. That's what got me into this business. But people just do not read to be educated. That's a fact. A newspaper isn't a Princeton education for a few pennies. Now, sleaze and slaughter—that's the news they want. Bullets, blood, sex and booze. That's what they want. And you can't tell me different, because I learned it the hard way."

"Sensationalism!" Sherwood cried. "That's another thing. Your headlines are positively explosive. They shout at passersby from the newsstand. Let me sum up the problem in four words. Too! Many! Exclamation! Points!"

"Sherwood is right, Bud," Benchley said. "The *Knickerbocker* puts the 'yell' in yellow journalism."

"Is that why you're here?" Dorothy said. "Chasing down another screaming headline?"

"I could ask you the same thing," Battersby said, the journalistic gleam returning to his eye. "That pal of yours, Dachshund? I hear he's now in custody for Leland Mayflower's murder." He looked at Benchley. "I wish I'd known that when he came to my office at the paper. Still, I guess the wheels of justice move fast in this town." He moved up the stone steps toward the door of the police station.

"The wheels move faster than you can follow," she said.

Battersby halted. "How do you mean?"

"Mr. Dachshund has been released. The police have posted an all-points bulletin for the man who tried to kill us—Mr. Dachshund, Mr. Benchley and myself—last night. The police think that this gangster, the Sandman, is the one who cut down Mayflower in the full bloom of his life. But you can read all about that in tomorrow's

New York Times. Look for it in Alexander Woollcott's column."

They turned and walked away, leaving a gape-mouthed Battersby on the steps of the police station.

"You should talk to Detective Orangutan," Benchley called over his shoulder. "Lovely fellow. He'd be happy to answer all of your questions. Tell him we sent you."

Dorothy and Woodrow Wilson approached the entrance to the behemoth of a building that was the Lord & Taylor department store. An explosive boom suddenly drowned out the din of the midday traffic. Woody hunched down like a frightened toad. Dorothy spun around to see a sooty black cloud of exhaust belch from the tailpipe of a nearby double-decker bus. Its engine, she gathered, had just backfired.

"There, there." She picked up the dog, cuddled it in her arms and pushed open the large glass-and-brass door of the department store. As she walked past the cosmetics counter, she caught sight of her gaunt reflection in a mirror.

Nowadays, women of all kinds wore lipstick and rouge. *The cosmetic industry should invent something for the bags under one's eyes,* she thought. *I could carry my groceries in these.*

She consulted the directory and found the bookstore. She didn't consider bookstores heartrending, as Benchley did. Then again, she didn't find them magical or wondrous, as Faulkner seemed to. To her, a bookstore was the equivalent of a hardware store—a place to obtain one's necessary tools, equipment and supplies.

Once inside the bookstore, she stopped an aproned salesclerk and asked him to point out the manager. The clerk, with an odd look in his eye, directed her to the back of the store.

At first, Dorothy assumed the clerk reacted strangely because she carried a dog—and not a very handsome dog, she conceded—in her arms. Then, when she spotted the bookstore manager, she understood the clerk's surprise, for she had the same reaction.

The manager looked almost exactly like her. The woman was about the same age and height as she. The woman had dark, bobbed hair and wore horn-rimmed glasses. Dorothy's hair wasn't quite a bob, and she wore her glasses only for reading. Still . . . the main difference between them: The woman wore a crimson dress, while Dorothy's dress was dark blue.

Also, the woman held a pen and clipboard in her hands, not a gargoyle-like Boston terrier.

Dorothy approached her. "Pardon me."

The woman turned. She had a sober, discriminating face, which tightened when she saw the dog.

"Customers are not to bring dogs into the store. I'm sorry." She didn't seem sorry in the least.

"I'm not a customer," Dorothy said. "I'm a friend of one of your employees, William Faulkner."

The woman's face softened. She forgot about the dog.

"William? He gave his notice all of a sudden a few days ago. Is he all right?"

"I was hoping you could tell me."

"I haven't seen him. I was very sorry to say good-bye. Not a very earnest worker, I'm afraid. But he's a dear boy, isn't he? I felt I had taken him under my wing."

Dorothy was surprised to feel a sting of jealousy. As they talked further, she learned this woman's name, Elizabeth Prall.

She also learned that Ms. Prall had no idea where Faulkner lived. He had his personal mail sent in care of the store, which was against the rules. Several times, packages and letters from Mississippi arrived, along with stern admonishments from one of the department store's directors. To these admonishments, Faulkner paid no heed, as Ms. Prall recalled with a wistful smile.

"Did he explain why he gave notice?" Dorothy said.

"He said he could no longer sell books that other

people wrote. He wanted to sell books that he wrote. He wanted to find his voice as a writer."

"That sounds like our Billy. Well, if you hear from him, would you please contact me at the Algonquin Hotel?"

"Certainly, and may I trouble you to contact me likewise?"

Dorothy politely, albeit rather unwillingly, said she would, and bid Ms. Prall good-bye.

Back outside the store, she unloaded Woodrow Wilson to the sidewalk. The dog hesitated and sat cowering at her feet, apparently recalling the bang of the bus's backfire from before. She goaded him along.

But, like the dog, she felt an anxious twinge, too. She had come to a dead end. She didn't know how to locate Faulkner. She didn't even have the hope of knowing how to find him, and she worried where he might be. Maybe he was held against his will in some dank basement. Maybe he'd been tied up and plunked like a potato sack into the East River. Maybe . . .

But then she reconsidered. If she couldn't find Faulkner, perhaps others couldn't find him either. Neither the police nor that Sandman thug knew his real last name. They'd have been looking for William Dachshund. She allowed herself a smile; she'd thoughtfully provided him with an alias—it just might save his life.

After all, the Sandman was a well-known criminal. *He* couldn't hide for long. The police would track down his hideouts. Or one of his partners in crime would rat him out. Soon, once the gunman was locked up, Faulkner could show his innocent face again.

Innocent. *Innocent?* It gave her pause. She literally stopped in her tracks. Woody jerked to a halt at the end of his leash. Passersby grumbled as they maneuvered around her. But she didn't take notice.

If Faulkner was indeed innocent—if he had told the police all he knew—why did they need him anymore? Why had that police captain wanted to keep him in custody? Why did they so desperately want him *back* in custody?

This was too much for her. This was more worry than she had ever expected when she first took the bedraggled young man under her wing just a few days ago.

Mr. Benchley was right, she realized. She had to stop picking up strays.

Chapter 18

Late that night, Dorothy Parker stood alone amid the crowd inside Tony Soma's speakeasy and waited for Mr. Benchley to arrive. Then, like a genie, he materialized at her side, with his pipe in his mouth contributing to the haze of smoke.

"Good evening, Mrs. Parker."

He handed her a teacup, which held two fingers of good hard scotch.

"Fred, I've been waiting for you for a dog's age. What do you have to say for yourself?"

He merely smiled, raised his coffee mug and clinked it with hers, and they drank.

"There are a lot of jokes going around," Benchley finally said. "Did you hear the one about Leland Mayflower?" He paused. "One of the Round Tablers took a pen and wrote him off."

She frowned, offended more by the joke's lack of wit than by its lack of truth.

"Here's another one," he said. "What do the Pilgrims and the notoriety of the Vicious Circle have in common?" Again he paused. "They all rode in on the *Mayflower*."

"Is that the best that people can do?" she said sourly. "Wit and scandal make strange bedfellows and lousy jokes."

Despite her frown, she was glad to see Benchley again. After her fruitless visit to the bookstore, she had dutifully spent the afternoon at her desk at the offices of *Vanity Fair*, but she performed as little work as possible.

Her editor, Frank Crowninshield, had given her a book to review. Her mind was distracted, and she wasn't willing to commit herself to writing the full review just yet. She merely jotted some notes, her first impressions of the book.

You simply cannot put this book down, she wrote, *fast enough.*

But you can put this book down by other means: It's boring, it's repetitive, and it uses words in ways not found in Webster's. *I could construct other put-downs, but they involve the kind of colorful expletives not permitted in this publication.*

That's a start, she thought.

She left the office at the stroke of five o'clock. Then she spent the early part of the evening restlessly lingering in her apartment, hoping once again that Faulkner might appear, safe and sound, at her door. She knew that Mr. Benchley was busy with an assignment to review a Broadway play and wouldn't be available until later. And now, finally, that hour had arrived.

And here he was, his cheerful grin and merry wink in place, as reliable as Christmas. The scotch made her feel warm, and she wanted to hug him.

Of course, she did not.

"How was the play?" she asked blandly.

"Just dandy," he said. "It was a romantic comedy about Eskimos. You could half shut your eyes and almost kid yourself into believing you were at the North Pole. Then again, you could entirely shut your eyes and almost kid yourself into believing that you were counting sheep. I opted for the latter."

"Benchley's two-word review," she said. "'Very restful.'"

"And did you have an equally productive day?"

She recounted her largely uninformative expedition to the bookstore, her futile afternoon at the office and her wasted evening at home.

"Fear not for young Faulkner," Benchley said. "Think about this. Now that Detective O'Tannenbaum and the other Keystone Kops know that this Sanderson fellow is at the heart of the mystery, they'll forget all about Billy. Some other explanation is bound to come out. Likely, Mayflower had some long-standing gambling debts with some dicey characters. And that elderly ninny probably thought that no gangster would ever so much as lay a hand on the sleeve of his old-fashioned topcoat. So, Lucky Lou or Diamond Harry called in some muscle in the form of the Sandman."

"And?"

"*And* Mayflower probably sneezed on the fellow. Or jabbed him with a barbed quip. The thug responded the only way his kind knows how, with violence. That's probably the story in a nutshell."

"In a nutshell?" she said. "That's where your story belongs. If the man is a real gangster, why would he stab Mayflower in the heart with a fountain pen? Why not use a gun, or at least a knife? And why do this at our Round Table in the middle of the day? Why would this gunman not handle such a task at his typical time and in his typical element—a silent, darkened alley in the middle of the night, pistol in hand?"

But to these questions Benchley had no answer. He thought for a moment, and he brightened.

"Have you read the latest restaurant review of the Algonquin?" he said finally. "They say the food won't kill you, but the customers might."

The following afternoon, Dorothy sat in a plush lounge chair in the Algonquin lobby. In front of her, on the low coffee table, was a bell. It was the silver half-dome type with a button on top. When rung, it would summon a waiter. She had the urgent desire to slam the bell repeatedly. She resisted the maddening urge to kick the damn thing right off the table.

But the bell, she realized, was not at fault. It sat there innocent, squat and silent. Rather, it was the open newspaper in her lap—the *Knickerbocker*—that had raised her anger.

The cover headline blared, POLICE HUNT MISSING "DACHSHUND"! Inside, the main article described William Dachshund as a "morose, sullen, disaffected itinerant—his face half-hidden by an unkempt beard—who apparently hails from the deepest regions of the South, although this is uncertain, as Mr. Dachshund is also reputed to be a charlatan and compulsive liar."

The article went on to say that "Dachshund is wanted desperately by the police in regard to the dastardly and cowardly murder of the *Knickerbocker*'s own esteemed drama critic and columnist, Leland Mayflower."

The article glossed over how Faulkner had been released, even implying that he had as good as escaped. "Through an inadvertent administrative error, the suspect was temporarily given leave of police custody. That was when Mr. Dachshund, as any guilty party would, took the first opportunity to slip free and hied away immediately, disappearing into the anonymity of the city streets. But he won't remain anonymous for long."

The article continued, providing a detailed description of Faulkner's physical appearance and manner of dress, and assuring readers that the public could soon rest easy thanks to the "dogged pursuit and eventual swift capture" by Detective O'Rannigan. Although this was annoying enough, what really enraged Dorothy was that Battersby (for his byline was on the article) never once mentioned that the reason why the police brought in "Dachshund" in the first place was to provide a description of the gunman. Indeed, the article included no mention of the gangster, nor the name Knut Sanderson, nor even the more sensational sobriquet of Sandman.

That this was Saturday—the day of the week that newspapers receive the least readership—was no consolation to her. Neither was the article in the *New York Times*, authoritatively penned by Alexander Woollcott, that described in detail the nearly fatal encounter that she, Benchley and "Dachshund" had had with the Sandman.

It was some time before she realized that three of the members of the Vicious Circle had dropped into the other chairs around the coffee table.

"Dottie, did you even hear me?" said Marc Connelly, sitting at her left. Directly opposite her, George Kaufman sat slumped in his chair. To her right sat Harold Ross.

Connelly and Kaufman were a successful playwriting duo. Connelly was a fast-talking showboat. He had sharp features and a round, bald head. Kaufman, his opposite, was a sly sourpuss. The mournful eyes under Kaufman's knitted brows tended to gaze over his spectacles. Where Connelly was energetic, Kaufman was laconic. They were something like the quibbling but inseparable old married couple often depicted in the kind of conventional Broadway plays that they themselves satirized in their own plays.

"Did you hear what I just said?" Connelly repeated.

Dorothy looked quizzically at him. "Did you say something worth hearing?"

"Ross has been beating our ears about this new magazine he wants to launch," Connelly said. "Tell her about it, Ross. Let's see what she thinks."

Harold Ross (everyone simply called him Ross) was the black sheep of the Round Table, or perhaps the dark horse. He didn't speak in quick wisecracks or enlightened insights. Just the opposite. He was often slow to catch on to the joke or understand an esoteric reference. But he absorbed all they said, and he was a hell of an audience for them.

Ross had the face of a gap-toothed gargoyle and a

spiky head of hair like an upturned shoeshine brush. Despite his homely appearance, he had a discerning, even wry gleam to his eye.

"Okay, here's the idea." Ross leaned forward on the edge of his seat, elbows on his knees, his jacket sleeves hitched up to his forearms. "I know I'm just the editor for *American Legion Weekly*. But I think—goddamn it, *I know*—there's room for a smart, high-class magazine that covers all the goings-on in New York. It will be *by* New Yorkers and *for* New Yorkers. The hell with the old lady in Dubuque; this won't be for her. And the hell with *Vanity Fair* and *Collier's* and the *American Mercury*. This magazine won't have an article about pets, or ladies' fashions, or lawyers. It'll have some news articles, some fiction, some poems, some cartoons. . . . It won't be snobbish or arty or high-minded, but God damm it, it'll be smart. What do you think?"

"I'm impressed. I'm all for it. I'm sure it will be a huge success," she said. "And I'm the Queen of Romania."

Ross frowned; his shoulders drooped.

"See?" Connelly cackled. "Your magazine will fly when pigs do. Now, never mind that nonsense. How about a game of cribbage? We have a foursome right here. We'll play teams."

Connelly drew a deck of cards from his jacket pocket and dealt them. Dorothy folded up the *Knickerbocker News* and picked up her hand. Cribbage was just a warm-up for these boys, of course. The main event for them was the poker game that night.

The game flew by, and Kaufman and Connelly wound up winning. They were playing another game (with Dorothy and Ross in the lead) when Frank Case strolled by. The genteel and solicitous hotel manager said politely, "Looks like great fun." They understood immediately what he meant: Please don't play cards in the lobby of my hotel.

Connelly picked up the deck of cards and cribbage board. "Boy, cribbage works up a man's thirst."

They migrated to the usual room on the second floor. Heywood Broun was there by the door, setting up bottles of gin, scotch and beer. Alexander Woollcott sat ensconced behind the round table (not *the* Round Table). He shuffled the cards and stacked up poker chips.

Dorothy stopped in the doorway and watched what they were doing. "You boys sure know how to treat a woman," she said. "Liquor in the front and poker in the rear."

Within an hour, a dozen players had arrived, and more were coming. The room was soon filled with smoke, the clink of whiskey and martini glasses, the clatter of poker chips and a barrage of insults and excuses as the stakes of the game rose.

This was the less public gathering of the Round Table members and many of its ancillary members and regular guests. The weekly Saturday night poker game (or the Thanatopsis Pleasure and Inside Straight Club, as it was more formally called) had been going on for as long as the daily Round Table lunches. Longer even, as it had originated with Woollcott, Ross and Adams from their *Stars and Stripes* days covering the war in France. It was more like a party in a fraternity house than a star-studded gathering of New York's intelligentsia.

At the poker table, Woollcott had squared off against the stage comic Harpo Marx, who was nearly unrecognizable offstage without his trademark curly wig. Next to Harpo slouched Ross, who flung his cards down. "Son of a bitch."

Harpo looked at his hand. "Don't you know when to call a spade a spade?"

Next to Ross sat the yeast tycoon Raoul Fleischmann, who laid down his perfect hand of cards with a sheepish grin. Seated next to him, cigar-chomping Franklin Adams threw down his useless hand. "Who do you think you are? Royal Flushmann?"

The others at the table—Connelly, Kaufman, Heywood Broun and publicist John Peter Toohey—cursed and tossed down their cards as well. Standing behind the table to observe the game were Robert Sherwood and Dorothy Parker.

"Why don't you play a round, Mrs. Parker?" Sherwood said.

"I do play around," she said. "And just like in poker, I always wind up losing my shirt."

Several others—the hugely successful novelist Edna Ferber, the magazine illustrator Neysa McMein and the Broadway composer Irving Berlin—loitered about the room. They all smoked. They all drank. They all cracked jokes and cracked peanuts, letting witticisms and shells drop to the floor.

"I have a legal question," said Robert Benchley as he emerged from the bathroom with a glass of gin and orange juice. "If an illegal drink, such as this orange blossom, makes me an outlaw, then does a legal substance, such as tea, make me an in-law?"

The door flew open and Luigi burst in. The waiter's breathless, heavily accented voice was barely intelligible.

"The police—they are here! Dump your liquor. It's a raid!"

Everyone jumped up and rushed to the bathroom to pour the contents of their glasses, cups and bottles down the sink or into the toilet.

Detective O'Rannigan strode through the door of the suite with hotel manager Frank Case in tow.

The room was empty. The chairs and poker table were deserted. A half-eaten pastrami sandwich teetered on the edge of a side table. In ashtrays, the cigarettes and cigars released ribbons of smoke that curled upward to meld with the gloom of the empty room.

O'Rannigan tipped back his tiny brown derby and scratched his big round head. "What kind of nonsense is this?"

He looked into the bathroom. More than a dozen

people were crammed inside, silently, expectantly peeking out at the police detective.

"Where's Robert Benchley?" O'Rannigan yelled. "Get out here now. You're coming with me."

Due to the crush of bodies, Benchley was pressed like a pancake against the far wall of the bathroom. Fortunately, he did not even have room to quake or quiver because, if he'd had the room, that was exactly what he would have done.

Chapter 19

Benchley and Dorothy sat in a small, cold, colorless room on the second floor of the dingy, crumbling stone Sixteenth Precinct Station on West Forty-seventh Street. The floor of the narrow little room was bare gray wood and speckled with stains of varying types and colors—tobacco juice certainly, urine likely, and blood possibly. They sat in hard wooden chairs and faced a battered maple table. They waited.

Some Saturday night this turned out to be, Dorothy thought.

She should not have been there. At the Algonquin, Detective O'Rannigan had demanded only Benchley accompany him. The detective refused her request to come along. So she kicked him in the shins.

Now, despite her devotion to Mr. Benchley, she realized she may have made a mistake.

He seemed to read her thoughts. He smiled warmly. "Kicking that cop in the leg—that was the greatest act of friendship I have ever seen. Thanks for coming along."

She almost choked up. She clasped her hand in his. All she could say was, "Forget about it." Then she cleared the lump in her throat. "There's no one in the world with whom I'd rather be trapped in a police interrogation room than—"

The door behind them opened with a creak. They heard a soft thump and dropped each other's hand. Entering the room was the thin, solemn man with the natty suit and the wooden stump. Detective O'Rannigan trailed behind him like a humble caboose.

"I am Police Captain Philip Church," the man said. His voice was as cold and flavorless as ice water. With a certain mechanical grace and precision, Captain Church sat down in a chair on the opposite side of the table. "Mr. Robert Benchley, do you know why you are here?"

"No."

"Can you tell us why your writings were found in a notebook in the possession of Knut Sanderson, also known as the Sandman?"

Benchley swallowed. "My *writings*? How could Sanderson—"

He stopped to reconsider.... *The notebook,* he thought. Leland Mayflower's notebook. Benchley's notes for his drama reviews were in Mayflower's notebook.

Dorothy said, "What makes you so sure that it's Mr. Benchley's writing?"

Church opened a large envelope and pulled out the small black notebook. He held the book open for them to see. Benchley's signature was written a dozen times on a single page.

Benchley looked sheepish.

"Practicing your autograph?" she said to him.

"Never know when you'll be called upon to sign a tax form or a Magna Carta or something."

Church said, "We found this notebook hidden on Sanderson's person. Can you explain its presence there?"

"Well, I guess you could say that Sanderson stole the notebook from me, the night he attacked us. I was under the impression that Mr. Dachshund gave Detective Orangutan a full description of the evening's events." Benchley looked up at O'Rannigan, who grimaced.

"Dachshund never mentioned any notebook," the detective muttered.

"Sanderson stole the notebook from you?" Church repeated. "And where did you get the notebook in the first place?"

O'Rannigan's grin was a gloating one.

Benchley swallowed. "I must have picked it up from the Round Table, when the good detective here asked me to identify Mayflower's body."

Church's voice remained flat. "So you took an item of police evidence from a murder scene? Is that correct?"

Benchley bit his fingernail, thinking.

Dorothy spoke quickly. "Since you have the notebook from the Sandman in your possession, that must mean you have the Sandman, too?"

Church's level gaze shifted to her. "Yes, we have him."

"We have him, and how," O'Rannigan said.

"That's marvelous," she said. "You already know, or at least you strongly suspect, that he was the one who killed Leland Mayflower. Now all you have to do is give him your famous third degree, or what have you, and make him confess. Right?"

"A confession is not necessary," the captain said. "We found Knut Sanderson's fingerprints on the fountain pen lodged in Mr. Mayflower's chest. We found Mr. Mayflower's notebook, albeit with your notes in it, inside Sanderson's pocket."

"Then it's all wrapped up," Benchley said, rather gleefully. "Let the State of New York put the Sandman to sleep, if it must."

O'Rannigan leaned back. "Too late. Sanderson took care of that himself."

"I don't understand," Dorothy said.

"He's dead," O'Rannigan said.

She nearly gasped, but she held it in.

Captain Church explained, "Sanderson switched residences frequently, so we have had trouble finding exactly where he lives. Finally, earlier today, police officers found his body in a tony Park Avenue apartment, dead of apparent suicide. He had his head in the oven, and the apartment was full of gas."

"Funny," she said. "I would have figured him to choose a Smith and Wesson over a Westinghouse."

"Funny?" O'Rannigan sneered. "What's so funny about it? It's nuts—that's what it is. A raving animal like the Sandman doesn't up and commit suicide."

Captain Church, a very patient, methodical man, didn't directly contradict O'Rannigan. Church didn't even look at him. "Let us stick to the facts, since they are all we have at this point. The facts indicate that Sanderson committed suicide. This much we believe to be so. Let us test this theory as a scientist tests his theories, by attempting to disprove it."

Dorothy was thinking of Faulkner. She reasoned that if everyone believed that the Sandman indeed murdered Mayflower, then Faulkner would be free.

"Disprove it?" she said. "What's the use? Let sleeping dogs lie."

"Dead dogs, too," Benchley added.

Captain Church's thin mouth tightened. His pale eyes stared at them. She wondered whether Church was about to throw them in the hoosegow and throw away the key. Then the captain said something odd.

"Detective, in the bottom drawer of my desk is a paper bag. My wife packed me a midnight snack. Please get it for me."

O'Rannigan left the room without a word.

Church's glare never wavered. "I know you, you know."

Out of the sides of their eyes, Dorothy and Benchley glanced at each other.

"You know us? You know *of* us?" she said. "You've read the drivel we've written in magazines?"

Church shook his head, almost imperceptibly. He stared at Benchley. "I know you from Harvard. I was a year above you."

Benchley shifted uncomfortably in his chair. Dorothy

thought she understood why: Church looked many years older than Benchley, and Benchley certainly hadn't recognized him.

The police captain continued, "I know your antics from your performances in the Hasty Pudding club, and your writing in the *Harvard Lampoon.* That is where you learned you could make a living out of clowning around. But this is no time for funny business. One cannot cut his way out of a mess like this with a sharp little joke."

Benchley, a very sensitive man, didn't answer right away. He thought this through.

"I think you misunderstand," Dorothy said. "A joke isn't a sword. It's a shield."

"Yes," Benchley said. "We laugh to keep from crying. It's a constant battle."

"Battle?" Church's taut mouth compressed into a short frown. "I gather you did not fight in the war."

"I don't believe in war," Benchley said simply.

For the first time, Church displayed naked emotion. His face screwed up in disgust.

"You don't believe in war?" he spat. "War is not Santa Claus or the Tooth Fairy. You cannot choose to believe in it or not. War is a fact. It happened."

Now Benchley looked emotional. "I lost my older brother in the Spanish-American War. I was nine."

"All the more reason to fight," Church said. "Thousands of boys lost life, limb and sanity in the war. That doesn't give *you* the option to choose to not believe in war, as though it doesn't exist."

Benchley reddened. "Obviously, I know it exists—"

Detective O'Rannigan came bustling through the door. He placed a small brown paper sack on the table in front of the captain. Church unrolled the top of the paper bag, dipped his hand inside and pulled out an egg. This process seemed to have a calming effect on him.

"See this egg?" he said evenly. "Do you think something like this could start a war?"

They didn't answer.

Church then placed the egg upright on the table and spun it like a top. Dorothy knew the egg must be hard-boiled. (This was her principal meal at the Algonquin, as it was just about all she could typically afford.) An uncooked egg spins wobbly. This egg, like the captain himself, she thought, was hard-boiled.

Church said, "As a boy, did you ever throw an egg at a comic in a bad vaudeville show?"

Benchley admitted a guilty grin.

Church said, "Imagine you threw an egg or two, and it started a war, a war that killed tens of thousands. Things like this happen all the time."

"An egg that started a war?" Dorothy said. "If that happened even once, I think we might have heard about it."

Church's mouth tightened again. He reached for something below the table and laid it on the tabletop with a thump. It was a dull gray metal service revolver. It was extremely large, Dorothy thought. The barrel pointed almost directly at her chest, which made her decidedly uneasy. She tried not to show it.

"Unload a cartridge from the barrel," Church said to her.

She looked down at the heavy pistol. "No, thank you."

Captain Church didn't move. He stared at her.

"I mean, I don't know how," she said.

Church picked up the gun and snapped it open. He dug one of the cartridges out of the barrel and then tossed it at her. Benchley jumped like a housewife from a rat, but Dorothy sat frozen as the cartridge landed in her lap.

"Pick it up," Church said.

She didn't like being told what to do. But it was pointless to try to assert herself at this moment. She picked up the cartridge. It was less than an inch and a half long, with a dull lead bullet poking out of the shiny brass cartridge jacket. It was heavier than it looked.

"Now hold this." Church lobbed the egg at her. Instinctively, she caught it.

"Weigh them in your hands," he said. "What do you conclude?"

She compared the bullet in one hand against the egg in the other. "I suppose they weigh about the same." She placed them gently on the table.

"The same," he said, picking them up. "Now maybe you understand my point. Something the weight of an egg can start a war. Look at this bullet. It is small. Much smaller than an egg. But just a few of these little things, shot by a Serbian terrorist into the body of Archduke Ferdinand, set off the spark that ignited the Great War. Every time I load this gun, I think about that."

As he spoke, he removed the shell from the egg. Then he popped it whole into his mouth. He continued to stare at them with his hard eyes, though his cheeks bulged with the egg. Dorothy found this action to be grotesque, even somehow obscene. It was as though he intended to entirely swallow up every protestation or defense she and Benchley might raise, without acknowledgment or consideration. She realized it was an exhibition intended to disarm her, to make her feel defenseless. She was annoyed that it succeeded in doing just that.

The egg was gone in two gulps, and Church's long, thin face returned to its tombstone solidity.

"Now," he said, "shall we continue? I assume you have heard of the bootlegger Michael Finnegan?"

Chapter 20

Dorothy and Benchley shook their heads. No, they had never heard of a bootlegger by the name of Michael Finnegan. Even if they had, they wouldn't admit it to Captain Church.

Church continued, "Michael Finnegan is a major underworld crime figure. He is a bootlegger, a racketeer and the leader of a large, notorious gang of confidence men, extortionists, thieves, violent criminals and petty swindlers."

O'Rannigan, still standing, appeared to be growing restless. He shifted from foot to foot.

"Mickey Finn!" O'Rannigan blurted. "Everyone calls him Mickey Finn."

"Oh . . . ," said Dorothy and Benchley together.

They knew about Mickey Finn, of course. They'd never met him or even seen him, but they knew that Finn supplied Tony Soma's and many other good speakeasies with top-shelf European liquor smuggled down from Canada.

"The Sandman worked for Mickey Finn," O'Rannigan continued quickly. He was like a bottle uncorked—his words poured out. "Finn used him for muscle and, we think, for the occasional murder. But we've never been able to nail Sanderson or Finn for anything. Witnesses keep changing their stories or disappearing, often turning up dead."

"So, you think the Sandman killed Leland Mayflower on Mickey Finn's orders?" Dorothy said. "Gambling debts, something like that?"

Church shook his head. "We were able to secure an interview with Finnegan—not an interrogation exactly. Finnegan is too canny for that. He was genuinely surprised when we told him that we believed Sanderson had killed Mayflower, and he was positively shocked when we informed him that Sanderson was dead."

"Shocked doesn't cover it," O'Rannigan said. "He hit the roof. I thought he might explode on the spot."

"Finnegan is a very volatile individual, definitely," Church said.

"Let's see if I have this right," Benchley said. "Mickey Finn ordered the Sandman to do his dirty work, threatening and even killing snitches and welshers and such."

The streetwise words sounded silly coming out of Benchley's mouth, Dorothy thought. The conspicuous way he said *snitches* and *welshers*, he might as well have been talking about pixies and unicorns.

"But," Benchley continued, "Finn *did not* send Sanderson to kill Mayflower. Didn't even know about it. So, the question is, who did order the Sandman to murder Mayflower?"

"That," said Church, "is what we hope you can tell us."

They stared stupefied at the police captain for a long moment. Apparently, he was serious.

Finally, Dorothy said, "How the hell can we tell you that? We don't know ourselves."

"You may help us determine the killer's motive—the real killer, that is, as Sanderson was apparently only an instrument in this whole affair," Church said. "Let us approach the question methodically. To perpetrate a crime, a criminal usually possesses three things: means, motive and opportunity. With Sanderson providing both the means and the opportunity, that leaves us with motive. Someone else—the one who hired or otherwise contracted with Sanderson—supplied the motive. Now—"

"How can you be so sure that there was someone else involved?" Dorothy said. "How do you know it wasn't a personal matter between the Sandman and Mayflower? For all we know, little old Mayflower may have been puttering along Sixth Avenue when he accidentally poked the Sandman with his walking stick. Perhaps the Sandman followed Mayflower into the Algonquin, saw that Mayflower was alone in the dining room and took the opportunity to take revenge the only way he knows how."

"Indeed," Church said simply, "that cannot be ruled out. And the crime certainly points to a hurried, improvised execution. Sanderson killed Mayflower by stabbing, yet Sanderson's implement of choice was usually a handgun. He not only stabbed Mayflower; he used Mayflower's own fountain pen, and he did it in broad daylight, so to speak, where observation of the crime and subsequent capture were all the more likely, even probable."

"There you have it," said Dorothy. "Means, motive and opportunity."

"Only one problem," O'Rannigan snorted. "The Sandman suddenly turned up dead. But there's no way the Sandman would commit suicide, because he didn't have a conscience. It ain't likely that all of a sudden he felt so sorry for what he did that he had to go and stick his head in the oven. Naw, somebody else was involved. Somebody who wanted Sanderson to keep his mouth shut, and for good."

"But who?" said Benchley.

"Again," said Church, "that is where you may help us."

"Help how?" said Dorothy.

"Help us understand the motives of the members of your Round Table."

Dorothy and Benchley both sat up in their chairs. The idea of reporting on their friends to the police was detestable.

"Say that we don't want to help you?" she said.

O'Rannigan growled, "Then say that we charge you with assaulting an officer, withholding evidence and harboring a fugitive?"

"Go right ahead," she said. "While you're at it, charge me with harboring impure thoughts and coveting my neighbor's oxen."

They looked to Benchley. By unspoken agreement, it seemed his response would break some tacit deadlock.

"Don't bother charging me," he said finally. "My credit rating is lousy."

Dorothy smirked. O'Rannigan lurched forward as if to throttle them both. Captain Church, like a traffic cop, calmly held up a hand. O'Rannigan stopped in his tracks.

"Shall we look at it this way?" Church said. "By providing an understanding of your associates' motives and whereabouts, you will be exonerating them from blame and helping to prove their innocence. By doing so, you will bring us closer to the real killer. That is what we all want."

Dorothy remained silent. Under the shadow of her dark bangs, her eyes were hard and her face was sullen. Benchley sat smiling politely and didn't say a word.

"Let me add this," Church continued. "We have already spoken to some of your associates. We have formed opinions and are in possession of certain pertinent facts. Your perspective will certainly do them no harm and could do them a world of good."

"And if you don't talk," O'Rannigan snarled, "we charge you and toss you in the Tombs."

Church stared at them patiently. This time, he did not contradict O'Rannigan.

She looked out at the darkened window. It was long after midnight. An icy drizzle spattered the glass panes. She thought of Faulkner. He was out there, somewhere, waiting.

She exhaled softly. "All right. What do you want to know?"

*   *   *

Before resuming the interrogation, Church sent O'Rannigan to get a drink of water for Dorothy and Benchley.

"He's a very ... *persistent* fellow, that Detective Orangutan," Benchley observed.

"Say his name correctly, please," Church replied. "Still, you are right. He is persistent. But you say *persistent* as if that is a character flaw, or a euphemism for being shortsighted or stupid. Believe me, what the detective lacks in imagination, he makes up for in determination. Unlike what they print in those detective magazines, most police work comes down to simple dogged tenacity. Knocking on door after door. Asking the same questions over and over. Getting evasive variations on the same answer. Detective O'Rannigan is very good at his job. You would be unwise to underestimate him."

The door opened and O'Rannigan entered awkwardly. He held a paper cup in each hand, his face intent to avoid splattering the water as he hip checked the door to open it wider. Red faced and pugnacious, he gingerly set the cups down on the table in front of Dorothy and Benchley without spilling a drop.

"Let us proceed methodically," Church said, drawing forward a sheet of paper with several names typed neatly on it. "I have here a short list of about a dozen people whom you probably know. These people were acquainted with Mayflower in one way or another. Just tell us anything that may be significant, anything at all, regarding the relationship between these individuals and Leland Mayflower."

"All right," Dorothy said, taking a sip of water. It tasted peculiar. She wondered whether O'Rannigan had spit in it. Or worse.

"The list is alphabetical by last name," Church said. "Let us begin at the top. . . . Merton Battersby."

"Bud Battersby?" Benchley said. "He's the owner and editor in chief of the *Knickerbocker News*. Surely you can't suspect him?"

"We suspect everybody," Church said.

"But Mayflower was the prizewinning horse in Battersby's stable, just about the only horse in his stable," Benchley said. "Without Mayflower, the *Knickerbocker* is falling to pieces. And so, it seems, is Battersby."

Detective O'Rannigan leaned forward. "All the more reason to get rid of him. Maybe Mayflower did something Battersby didn't like. And Battersby called in a favor from the Sandman, or maybe Battersby just paid the Sandman cold, hard cash. Battersby has lots of it, right?"

Dorothy said, "Battersby is a rich kid whose hobby is running a tawdry little tabloid. He'd be about as likely to hire a gangster to kill his best employee as you would be to hire a dressmaker to make you a gown for the policeman's ball. And I'm afraid that's all we can tell you about the motives of Bud Battersby."

"Fine," Church said. "Robert Benchley, you are next."

Benchley chuckled. "Oh, I know Mayflower like I know the back of your hand. In other words, hardly at all."

"But you are a drama critic, and Mayflower was a drama critic. There must have been some professional rivalry."

"Mayflower wrote for a newspaper. I write for a magazine. The only time our paths crossed was on our way out the door after some lousy play."

"But you replaced Mayflower as the drama critic in the *Knickerbocker*," Church said shrewdly. "The articles appeared just one day after Mayflower was killed."

"What do you take me for?" Benchley said. "See here, I could never fill Mayflower's shoes. For one, he had feet like a little girl. For another, Battersby begged me to write those reviews. It was a onetime assignment. And I never even got the money."

He stopped short of explaining that Faulkner not only had written the reviews, but also had apparently pocketed the money.

Church recorded a short note against his list of names. His penmanship was small, and he pressed his pencil hard against the paper. Dorothy, try as she might, could not make out what he wrote.

"Moving on," Church said. "Heywood Broun."

"Broun is a sportswriter and essayist for the *New York Tribune*," Benchley said. "He had nothing in common with Mayflower."

"Nothing in common is putting it mildly. They're opposites," said Dorothy. "Mayflower was a shallow, snobbish dandy. Broun is an intellectual but down-to-earth slob."

"Mr. Broun is a very large and perhaps very strong fellow—"

"Stop right there. Heywood is a pussycat. He wouldn't swat a fly."

"I've seen it," Benchley said. "Flies swarm him in the summer. He doesn't even flinch."

Church looked at the next name on the list. "Frank Case, the manager of the Algonquin Hotel."

O'Rannigan muttered, "Slippery eel."

Benchley and Dorothy both smiled at the thought of this very proper, very friendly, very kind man. Dorothy's smile broadened at the thought of him as a slippery eel. Frank Case, she thought, could make a reprimand seem like a compliment, though he seldom reprimanded. He loved his residents and his guests. He cultivated the Algonquin as a haven for writers, actors, musicians and artists. He actually favored this motley and often impecunious clientele over well-paying, respectable businessmen.

Indeed, this was the reputation that he strived for. It was almost conceivable—she grinned even wider—that Case could have somehow encouraged or even arranged Mayflower's murder just for the notoriety.

She half turned to Benchley and realized by his curious smile that he was thinking the same thing.

"Well?" Church said.

"Nothing," she said. "Frank Case is an angel."

Church looked at her sternly. "If I find you are withholding vital information—"

Benchley spoke hurriedly. "Mr. Case didn't even recognize Leland Mayflower. Remember? He was the one who suggested I identify the body."

"True." O'Rannigan nodded. "That's true."

"See?" Benchley said. "True and true are four."

O'Rannigan seemed to suddenly dislike siding with Benchley. "But then again," he growled, "maybe Case was just playing dumb, to throw us off the scent. And maybe—"

Uncharacteristically, Church yawned, which caused O'Rannigan to forget what he was saying.

"Why would a hotel manager murder a man in his own dining room?" said the captain. "Shall we move on? Marc Connelly."

Dorothy shrugged. "I'm sure you've heard of him. Marc Connelly and George Kaufman have written three smash Broadway comedies in as many years. I seem to recall that Leland Mayflower wrote glowing reviews about each of them. Neither Connelly nor Kaufman had anything against Mayflower. They probably loved him— professionally speaking, that is."

Church narrowed his eyes. "What do you mean, 'professionally speaking'?"

"Just that on a professional level, they probably all admired one another quite a bit," she said.

"But on a personal level, they did not?" Church said.

"I didn't say that."

Church nodded slowly and inscribed more notes against his list of names. He looked up. "William Dachshund."

She said, "Mr. Dachshund never met, never even knew Leland Mayflower."

Captain Church opened a manila folder. "That is what he told us, too. The interesting thing about William Dachshund is that there appears to be no William Dachshund."

Dorothy compelled herself to keep still, to show no anxiety. "Well, I've met him. You interviewed him. Are you saying we all imagined him?"

Church reviewed the information in the folder. "There is no William Dachshund in the city directory. No New York tax records ever filed by a William Dachshund. No William Dachshund from the town of Jefferson, Mississippi. As a matter of fact, there is no town of Jefferson, Mississippi."

"He's a writer," she said. "Perhaps Dachshund is his nom de plume."

Church slowly shook his head. "Detective O'Rannigan looked it up. There are no books by a William Dachshund listed in the Library of Congress, and in the last ten years no articles written by a William Dachshund in the Index of Periodicals."

Benchley said, "Be that as it may, Mr. Dachshund had no axe to grind with Leland Mayflower."

"According to Dachshund's own account," Church said, "he was in the lobby at the same time as Sanderson. Perhaps Dachshund was working in conjunction with Sanderson. That would be conspiracy to commit murder."

"Impossible," Benchley said.

"It's silly, is what it is," Dorothy said. "You met Dachshund. Not only has he no motive—he has no backbone and no stomach for such things. He's as tough as a wet autumn leaf."

"And as slippery," O'Rannigan interjected. "As for being tough, you said yourselves how he knocked down the Sandman. Of course, once the Sandman bumped Mayflower off, Dachshund wanted Sanderson out of the way, too. Dachshund set you up to think he was innocent, that the Sandman had you in his sights. But all the time, Dachshund was working to get rid of the Sandman and make himself look like nothing more than the monkey caught in the middle."

Dorothy bit her lip. Could there be any truth to this? In her heart, she felt Dachshund was innocent. But the boy was certainly an odd little duck, and he did some inexplicable things. And it was a strange coincidence that he showed up on the same morning that Mayflower was murdered. . . .

She pushed the thought away. Whatever Faulkner was up to, it certainly wasn't murder. It just *couldn't* be.

She said, "You asked us here to help you supply any possible motives, to help prove our friends' innocence. Well, the long and short of it is this: Dachshund is innocent. He had no motive against Mayflower whatsoever."

"So you say," Church said. "Let us move on, then."

"Just a moment," she said. "Are you absolutely positive that the Sandman is dead?"

"Dead?" Captain Church looked perplexed. "What do you mean? Absolutely he is dead."

"I mean, are you sure it's Sanderson? Are you sure it's his body you found headfirst in his oven?"

Church sighed and spoke as if reassuring a child about the boogeyman. "We have the body in the morgue. There is no question that it is Sanderson."

"He's got the scar through the lips, all right. It's him," O'Rannigan said.

"Shall we proceed, then?" Church said. "We have several more of your acquaintances to discuss."

She nodded begrudgingly.

"Continuing alphabetically, the next on the list is Michael Finnegan, also known as Mickey Finn. I believe we have discussed his involvement as far as we could, at least insofar as your input is concerned."

"And he's not, as you say, one of our acquaintances," Benchley said.

Church ignored him. "Next is George S. Kaufman."

Benchley said, "We've discussed Kaufman's involvement, or lack thereof, when we discussed Marc Connelly. At least insofar as our input is concerned."

Church stared at Benchley, and Dorothy felt that they were edging closer to imprisonment yet again. She said, "So who's next on the list?"

The captain slowly drew his glare away from Benchley and consulted his list. "Aloysius Neeley."

Dorothy and Benchley glanced at each other.

"Who is Aloysius Neeley?" she said.

"He is . . . ," Church stumbled, looking uncomfortable. "He is . . ."

Dorothy and Benchley glanced at each other again.

"He was Mayflower's boyfriend," O'Rannigan said, with a mixture of menace and glee. "Mayflower was an old fairy. Or didn't you know that?"

Of course they knew that, she thought. Everyone knew that. Even if you somehow didn't know it, you could have seen it a mile away. It was so obvious, and so clearly a part of Mayflower's persona, that everyone simply took it as a matter of course.

"So he was queer," she said. "What does that have to do with the price of tea in China?"

Church opened his mouth to respond, then hesitated as if suddenly unsure what to say.

O'Rannigan spoke instead. "Neeley is a Broadway chorus boy, and Mayflower was his sugar daddy. They probably had a screaming catfight or something. You know how emotional these fairies are."

Benchley shrugged. "Whether he was Mayflower's boyfriend or not, we don't know this Neeley fellow."

Church straightened in his chair, apparently eager to move on. "Very well. Next, then . . . Dorothy Parker."

He leveled his eyes at her. She looked up at the ceiling.

"Mrs. Parker," Church said. "Where is *Mr.* Parker?"

Her eyes were fixed on the ceiling. "He fell down a coal chute. Two or three years ago. Haven't seen him since."

"Mrs. Parker?"

She continued looking up.

"Mrs. Parker."

Finally, she lowered her eyes and met the captain's gaze.

"Tell me again," she said. "Are you absolutely sure that the Sandman is dead?"

Captain Church sat back in his chair. He spoke resignedly, "Would you like to go to the morgue and see for yourself?"

"Yes!" she said brightly. "Oh, yes, let's go."

Chapter 21

Detective O'Rannigan sat behind the wheel of a large black Buick sedan. Captain Church sat next to him in the passenger seat. Dorothy Parker and Robert Benchley sat on the wide bench seat in the back.

The car was noisy, drafty and cold. Outside in the dark night, the black rain pelted the metal car roof and leaked through the tops of the windows. O'Rannigan's lead-foot driving was exasperating—he hit the gas too hard, then hit the brakes even harder.

They hurtled their way to the city morgue, located deep in the basement of Bellevue Hospital. The hospital, Dorothy knew, was at the easternmost side of Manhattan, where Twenty-sixth Street met the East River—a desolate and mournful place even in daytime, much less in the dead of night.

The pale face of an illuminated clock in the tower of a church momentarily shone through the gloom. It was just after three in the morning. Soon, she thought, they would be in the depths of the cold morgue to view the corpse of a killer.

She continued to gaze out at the dark city passing swiftly by, and she reached for Benchley's hand. He gave her hand a reassuring squeeze. They did not look at each other.

"Well, isn't this a jolly Sunday drive?" she said cheerfully. "Did anyone think to bring a picnic basket for lunch?"

Church turned around to face them. She quickly let go of Benchley's hand.

"Mrs. Parker," Church said, "let me ask you again: where is *Mr.* Parker?"

"I left him at the corner store," she said. "I exchanged him for a can of beans and a box of oyster crackers."

"Mrs. Parker—"

Benchley spoke softly. "Mr. Parker went off to the war soon after they were married. He had a tough time of it. He was an ambulance driver and was trapped for three harrowing days when the ambulance fell into a mortar crater. There he was, buried alive with several dead and dying men, never to know if he'd be rescued. Finally, he was, but he was not the same man. Shortly after that, he crawled into a morphine bottle and never really emerged, even after he returned home."

Church looked at her. "Is all that correct?"

She was furious at Benchley. How dared he tell the truth? It made her feel naked and vulnerable. Of her many sore spots, it was nearly the sorest.

But . . . she told herself to get over it. Church would have pestered her anyway until she had to tell the story herself, and she didn't want to do that. Better that Benchley tell it, if it must come out.

"So you are Mrs. Parker in name only?" Church said.

"And what a nice, clean name it is," she said. "It was the best thing that Edwin Parker ever gave me."

She noticed that Church still had his list of suspects in his hand.

"And what association did you have with Mr. Mayflower?"

"That old game?" she said. "Can't we play a round of something else? Russian roulette, maybe."

Church stared at her, waiting.

"Fine," she said. "I once removed a thorn from his paw. He was so grateful, he chose not to maul me to death."

Church frowned. "Is that some kind of metaphor?"

"No. Do you want to know the boring, old truth? I didn't know Mayflower at all. I mean, I knew him by sight and I knew how callous and unfair his drama reviews could be. But I never met him personally. Is that really what you want to hear?"

Church exhaled in another rare moment of candor. "This does not seem to be getting us anywhere," he muttered, looking down at his list. "Still, the last few names here are the most promising. The next one is Franklin Pierce Adams."

She said, "If you're working alphabetically, his last name is not Pierce Adams, just Adams. Pierce is his middle name—"

The car jolted to a halt.

O'Rannigan, who had slammed on the brake, howled, "You should scratch him from that list, Captain. Mr. Adams is the most respected newspaperman in the country. He couldn't possibly have anything to do with the murder of that old twinkle toes."

"Yes, you read his column every morning, Detective. You used to read his column in the *Stars and Stripes* in the war," Church said, turning to face Dorothy and Benchley. "What I want to know is, what was his relationship to Mayflower?"

"Didn't you read the articles in the *Knickerbocker News*?" she said. "Adams said Mayflower owed him fifty dollars from some old poker game. That's as much as he told us, and I believe him."

"Because, like Woollcott said of himself, Adams also would rather mete out his justice in print than in person?" Church said.

"No, if Adams stabbed Mayflower in the heart with a fountain pen, he'd happily tell you about it. He'd sit you down and gleefully relate every detail. Adams is tight with a buck, but he'll spend countless hours telling you about himself."

"Why, you little—" O'Rannigan glared at her. "Mr. Adams said your poetry was just the cat's pajamas and then you turn around and say—"

"Don't get me wrong," she said. "I love old Frank Adams dearly. He raised me from a couplet. I've cried on his shoulder so many times that he puts on a raincoat when he sees me coming. But did he kill Mayflower? Not a chance."

Church reluctantly returned to his list. "Harold Ross."

Dorothy and Benchley laughed explosively.

Church spoke wearily, "What is so amusing about Harold Ross?"

"Ross?" she chortled. "Ross might accidentally bump someone out a window as he bends over to tie his shoe. But murder? Not in a million years."

"Ross won't shut up about this absurd idea he has for a new magazine for New Yorkers," Benchley snickered. "Perhaps he could exasperate a man to take his own life. But not murder."

"Please stick to the facts," Church said. "How did Ross know Mayflower?"

"Oh, please. An African pygmy knows more about Broadway than Ross does," she said. "Ross thinks Ibsen's *A Doll's House* is something you buy in Gimbels' toy department. He wouldn't know a Broadway darling like Mayflower from a . . . Well, from an African pygmy."

Even in the darkness inside the car, Church's frown was obvious. "Next, Robert Sherwood."

O'Rannigan grunted. "The guy on stilts. He and Mayflower had a beef."

Church perked up. "Is that so?"

Benchley spoke first. "Mr. Sherwood is a gentleman in the true sense of the word—a gentle man. If he had an argument with Mayflower, he'd settle it honorably. Pistols at dawn perhaps."

"Is that how he settles arguments?" Church said.

"Of course not," Dorothy said. "Mr. Benchley was obviously embellishing to make a point. The only killing Mr. Sherwood ever possibly did was in the war, as I'm sure you'd understand. And even at that, I'm sure he did so reluctantly."

Church's voice was low. "You understand what it is to kill a man? Even in war, even on the most gruesome battlefield, killing another man brings at the very least a small sense of elation, that you are glad to be the one who remains alive."

"I'm quite sure that Mr. Sherwood took no such joy," she said.

"You are quite sure, are you?"

"Quite."

O'Rannigan, his eyes on the road, called over his shoulder. "Battersby said Sherwood threatened him."

"What?" Dorothy and Benchley both said.

"On the steps of the station. I had just let you yahoos go. Then Battersby comes in two minutes later sweating like a whore in church, and he says he had a run-in with you and you." With a twist of his head, he indicated Benchley and Dorothy. "And that skyscraper Sherwood, too. Battersby says Sherwood turned blue and violent just because Battersby was telling it like it is in the *Knickerbocker*."

"Telling it like it is?" she said.

"Now, that's embellishing," Benchley said. "Embullishing, even."

"It is worth noting," Church said. "But return to how Robert Sherwood knew Leland Mayflower."

"Not personally," she said. "Mr. Sherwood's first play premiered last year. Mayflower's review slaughtered it. That's as close as they ever got."

Church turned to O'Rannigan. "I want to question this Sherwood. Tomorrow."

O'Rannigan checked his watch. "You mean later today?"

"All right, then. Today." Church consulted his list again. "Lastly, Alexander Woollcott."

Dorothy groaned. She was exhausted trying—apparently in vain—to vindicate all her friends.

"He did it," she said. "Woollcott did it. Now can we stop?"

"I do not appreciate your sarcasm. Besides professional rivalry, what other association did Alexander Woollcott have with Leland Mayflower?"

Benchley was equally exhausted. He tried not to let it show. "Now, stop me if you've heard this one before. But Woollcott freely admits that he would only murder Mayflower in print, not in person."

"Precisely," Church said. "Sanderson was the one who murdered Mayflower in person. The real murderer—the one who hired Sanderson—is someone too timid to do the deed in person."

"There are many unflattering adjectives that describe Woollcott," Dorothy said. "But timid is not one of them."

Benchley spoke. "I believe you said one needs three things to perpetrate a crime: motive, means and opportunity. That leaves out method. Even if Woollcott had a motive, he certainly would not have chosen actual murder as his method. What's that Chinese form of execution? Death by a thousand cuts? Woollcott would employ—and occasionally does—death by a thousand cutting remarks."

"Return to motive, then," Church said.

"What motive?" she said.

"Money."

"Ha, Woollcott has it pouring in."

"Perhaps Mayflower had more," Church said. "He stole a lucrative endorsement contract from Woollcott. For Saber fountain pens, the very pen stuck into Mayflower's body."

"Hogwash," she said. "Woollcott shills for Chevrolet and for Chesterfield cigarettes, and he doesn't drive a

Chevrolet and he doesn't smoke Chesterfields. He probably considered fountain pens beneath him, and the company went to Mayflower as second-best."

O'Rannigan jerked his head around. "Nope, we talked to the Saber people. Mayflower pulled a fast one on Woollcott. They told us so themselves. He hung Woollcott out to dry."

She couldn't answer. This took her by surprise. But before she could summon some halfhearted response, the car came to an abrupt stop. She looked out into the darkness to see the black shadow of the immense, imposing brick structure of Bellevue Hospital.

"We're here," O'Rannigan said. "City morgue."

Chapter 22

The light was so bright that it hurt Dorothy's eyes. She paused in the doorway.

They had descended a short flight of stone stairs and were about to enter the hospital's basement through a pair of heavy wooden double doors.

Detective O'Rannigan held the door. "What, are you scared now? Go ahead."

She stepped past him through the door and entered the hallway. The walls were covered in brilliant white tiles. The flagstone floor was sprinkled with sawdust, which stuck to her wet shoes like glue.

The bright light was bothersome, but the smell was sickening: the damp, permeating stink of a butcher's shop, with the added odors of formaldehyde, bleach and urine. She was glad to have Benchley beside her. When she looked up at him, he gave her a reassuring wink.

Behind them, Captain Church's peg leg thumped on the flagstones, causing a dull echo in the chilly hallway.

"This way," he said, pointing toward an archway that opened to a large chamber.

Brass pendant lamps with green glass shades hung from the low ceiling, casting pools of light on the marble slab tables spaced throughout the wide room. Silent, immobile bodies, covered in gray sheets, lay on most of the slabs. At the far end of the room, a bearded man leaned over one of the tables. He had his arms elbows deep inside the abdomen of a naked male corpse.

"Dr. Norris?" Church said.

The large, bearded man straightened up, looked at them a moment, grabbed a nearby towel and wiped his hands clean of blood. He approached them slowly. His shirtsleeves were rolled up above his elbows, he had a briar pipe in his mouth and he wore a bloodied canvas apron. He chucked the towel into a bin, set his fists on his hips and scrutinized each of them with his deep-set gray eyes.

"Well?"

"Some visitors to see the remains of Knut Sanderson," Church said. "Mrs. Parker, Mr. Benchley, this is Dr. Charles Norris, chief medical examiner."

The doctor's voice was gruff, businesslike. "Welcome." He extended his hand, still slightly bloodstained.

Dorothy looked at his hand. "It won't kill you to wash before you take a lady's hand."

He looked at her sternly, though she detected a twinkle of amusement. "It won't kill you to shake it."

She shook it.

Church stepped forward. He didn't seem to like this banter. "Mrs. Parker and Mr. Benchley are here to settle their minds about the suicide death of Knut Sanderson."

"I see. You want to be absolutely certain he's dead?" Dr. Norris said. "I'm sure you're not the only ones. Over here."

He walked them to one of the marble slab tables, on which lay a long body draped in gray. He pulled back the sheet. Dorothy and the others moved forward.

It was the Sandman, all right. He didn't look the same as the last time she'd seen him. The man's dark eyes were closed and his skin was an odd cherry pink color. But there was no mistaking the hard, menacing face and the scar that bisected his mouth.

"He's dead," Dr. Norris said, his pipe jutting up from his mouth.

"Dead?" Benchley said. "He's in the pink."

Dr. Norris grunted. "Carbon monoxide poisoning. Even if we didn't know that his apartment was full of gas, the pink skin coloration would be a dead giveaway. Feel better now?"

Both Dorothy and Benchley nodded.

"Only one problem," Dr. Norris said. "He wasn't a suicide."

O'Rannigan nearly jumped. "I knew it!"

Church cleared his throat, ignoring the detective. "How did you come to that conclusion?"

Dr. Norris grabbed the body with two hands. "Help me turn him over," he said to Church.

They rolled the body facedown.

"Look here," Dr. Norris said. "Can you see the lividity, that slightly purplish color along his back? That indicates where the blood and bodily fluids settled. That means he died lying on his back and then continued to lie there a good long time."

"But he was found with his head in his oven," Church said. "His apartment was full of gas."

"No doubt the gas killed him, but I bet he was lying asleep in bed at the time. Someone came along later and stuffed the body in the oven to make it look like a suicide."

They rolled the body so that it faced them again.

"That confirms our suspicions," Church said. "But it brings us no closer to the real killer."

Dr. Norris said, "You mean that the person who hired Sanderson to kill Mayflower is also the person who then killed Sanderson?"

"In all likelihood," Church said. "But we shall stick to the facts for now. And the facts show us that we have two murdered bodies in our possession, but no murderer."

Shortly after this, they said good-bye to Dr. Norris. As he shook Dorothy's hand, he smiled warmly. "Very pleased to meet you."

"Likewise," she said.

His smile widened; his hand lingered in hers. "Hope to see you again soon."

She smiled sweetly in return. "Over my dead body."

They got back in the car and drove in silence to the police station. On the pavement in front of the station, Church and O'Rannigan—each in his own way—left them with stern warnings to immediately report any information or any sign of William Dachshund.

Without another word, the policemen turned and entered the building, leaving Dorothy and Benchley at four o'clock in the morning with no means to get home. They stood there a moment, very tired and unsure what to do next.

Benchley finally spoke. "So our peg-legged police captain seems quite baffled."

"Oh, yes." She couldn't resist. "Now he's really stumped."

They stood a moment longer.

"Do you think Tony Soma's is still open?" Benchley said. "I could use a drink after seeing all those dead bodies."

"Sure," she said. "What's another stiff one?"

Chapter 23

But the speakeasy was closed. They banged on the door repeatedly, but no one answered.

"The smart thing to do would be to call it a night," Dorothy said.

"Well, then?" Benchley said.

"Then, let's get a cup of coffee."

They walked up the empty street, hurrying quietly past the dark alley entrance where they had last met the Sandman. They turned the corner to the bright lights of Sixth Avenue. They walked a few blocks farther until they found a place that was open—an all-night greasy spoon.

The bell on the door tinkled as they entered. The small place was empty. Along one wall were a few narrow booths. Along the other wall was a long mirror, fronted by a linoleum counter and a few stools. No one stood behind the counter.

They sat down in the last booth in the rear. A fat cook in a stained white T-shirt came out of a doorway at the back.

"What'll it be?" he said.

"Coffee?" Benchley asked cautiously.

"Coffee," the cook said. "Anything else?"

"What do you suggest?" Benchley said politely.

"Special of the day is liver and onions."

"Just the coffee, I think," Benchley said. Dorothy nodded in agreement.

"Suit yourself." The cook turned to a battered metal urn behind the counter and filled two mugs. He came over and plunked the cups on their table.

"Lemme know if you need something else." Then he disappeared through the doorway to the back.

She glanced down into her mug. The coffee looked watery and smelled burned. She pushed it aside.

"I confess I'm as stumped as Captain Church," she said. "First of all, why *would* anyone really want to murder silly old Leland Mayflower? Second, if someone did want to kill him, why use a hired gunman? Third, why kill him in broad daylight in a well-known public place—and with a fountain pen, of all things? Lastly, why then kill the man who killed Mayflower?"

"The last one is obvious," Benchley said. He took a sip of the coffee, winced, then put the cup down with finality. "Whoever killed the Sandman wanted to make sure the Sandman stayed quiet. As a hired gun, the Sandman could very likely be paid or otherwise convinced to talk. But dead men tell no tales."

"And madmen smell toenails. But do you believe what Church said—"

The bell tinkled softly as the door opened. A man in a long trench coat and a wide-brimmed hat entered and sat down on a stool at the counter. The man didn't even glance at them.

She continued, speaking in a whisper. "Do you believe what Church said about Woollcott? That Mayflower went behind his back to land that Saber pen contract?"

"I doubt it. But then again, Woollcott might indeed be tight-lipped about Mayflower making such a coup de grâce under his upturned nose. It would bother Woollcott to no end, and he'd know we'd rib him for it."

The bell rang again, and two more men entered. They sat down in the booth closest to the door.

The fat cook came out from the back and approached the man sitting at the counter. "What'll it be, bub?"

"Seltzer."

The cook called to the two men at the booth. "How about you fellas?"

"Give me a seltzer, too."

"Orange juice," said the other man.

As he grabbed a seltzer bottle and some glasses, the cook addressed the man sitting at the counter.

"Something to eat?"

"What do you have?"

"How about some nice liver and onions?"

"Nah. Just the seltzer."

Dorothy and Benchley resumed their conversation as the cook went through the same rigmarole with the two men in the booth, who also turned down the chef's special.

She said, "I don't like the way that Captain Church talked about our little pal Mr. Sherwood. We'll have to warn Sherwood that they're looking to bring him in for a round of twenty questions."

"Agreed," Benchley said. "Constable Orangutan made it sound like Mr. Sherwood physically threatened Bud Battersby on the steps of the station house. It was nothing of the sort."

"Bob Sherwood wouldn't lay a hand on Battersby," she said. "I don't care how many Germans he killed in the war."

Her statement hung in the air a moment.

"Besides," she said quickly, "even if Sherwood is a bloodthirsty killer, as the captain and the detective seem to suggest, then he wouldn't bother with a hired gun, would he? He'd do the job himself."

"Now you're talking sense."

"But what worries me is Billy Faulkner. If he doesn't turn up soon, I'll really start to worry. Then again—"

"Then again, if he does turn up and we don't inform

the police, as they very clearly told us to do, then we'll all be in some very serious hot water."

The bell on the door jingled yet again, and another pair of men entered. They didn't look at the other men, and they didn't look at Dorothy and Benchley. They didn't linger in the doorway either, but sat down right away beside the first man at the counter, like schoolchildren late for class.

"Now, what fresh hell is this?" Dorothy whispered. She looked at a grimy electric clock on the wall. It was nearly four-thirty in the morning.

The fat cook waddled along behind the counter. "Evening, boys. Would you like to hear about our special of the day?"

"Just coffee, thanks."

"Me, too."

The cook frowned and shuffled once more toward the battered coffee urn.

After observing this short exchange, Benchley turned back around to face Dorothy.

"Popular place all of a sudden," he murmured. "What do you say we go somewhere a little less crowded, like a downtown bus at rush hour?"

"Now you're talking sense," she said. But as she began to slide out of the booth, one of the men looked at her. His expression was ominous. She sensed that the other men were suddenly alert, like a flock of birds ready to take flight.

She stopped. She turned toward the cook behind the counter.

"Can I trouble you for some cream for the coffee?" she said.

The cook handed her a tiny ceramic pitcher filled with thick white cream. She sat back down in the booth, intentionally not looking at the men. She poured the cream in her coffee and stirred it. She lifted it to her lips, but she didn't drink it.

Over the cup, she whispered, "I'm in no mood for any more questions and arguments, are you?"

Benchley understood. "No, indeed. It's both too late and too early for any more of that."

Unobtrusively, she reached into her coat pocket for something. She placed it on the table.

"Can you ask our worthy innkeeper if you could use his telephone?" she said. "Dial that number. Tell the man who answers to come here. Tell him I want to see him now."

Benchley glanced at the slip of paper. He stood up. The man who had glared at her now stared menacingly at Benchley.

At that moment, the bell tinkled and the door opened. Two more men in long dark coats entered. They halted and looked intently at Benchley. For a long moment, no one moved.

Finally, Benchley timidly turned to the cook. "Excuse me. Can I use your . . . your water closet?"

"In the back, on the left," the cook said.

Benchley went through the doorway in the back.

The two men who had just entered now glanced at Dorothy. They seemed to be sizing her up. Despite their stony faces, she could almost tell what they were thinking: This little lady wouldn't go anywhere without her gentleman escort, and the escort was too much of a gentleman to leave without her. Slowly, they sat down in the only open seats—in the booth adjoining hers.

The fat cook had finally realized that there was something odd about having a full house at half-past four in the morning. He addressed everyone in the place. "What is this? A trench coat convention or something?"

The men ignored him.

The cook spoke to the two men who had just sat down. "Let me guess. You'll have a glass of water and a plate of nothing."

"Root beer."

"Me, too."

"Fine," the cook said, exasperated. "Two root beers, coming up."

"On second thought," Dorothy spoke, and her voice sounded high and tremulous to her own ears. The cook and the other men seemed frozen in expectation. "On second thought, give us a couple plates of the liver and onions after all. We're not going anywhere for a while."

She sensed that this had a calming—or at least a delaying—effect on the seven menacing men. But it had the opposite effect on the cook. He was ecstatic.

"You will?" He beamed. "Two plates?"

She nodded. He nearly danced his way to the griddle behind the counter and seemed to bop to a silent jitterbug as he warmed it up.

Benchley returned and sat down.

"What did I miss?"

"I ordered us the liver and onions. I hope you have some money."

"I wouldn't worry about paying," he muttered. "If this gang of thugs doesn't get us—"

"Then the liver and onions will. Very funny. So, were you able to place the call?"

"Yes, but it was a bad connection. I'm not sure if he understood what I was saying, and I didn't want to raise my voice, of course."

"Of course," she said. "So I guess we'll wait and see."

Several long minutes ticked by as they waited. The men at the counter and in the booths occasionally shot them dark glances but otherwise did nothing. The men didn't even talk. Dorothy and Benchley found this unnerving.

Benchley decided to break the silence.

"My niece informs me," he said loudly, "that a friend of hers at Yale ran off with the track coach."

"Sounds like she put her heart before the course," Dorothy obligingly replied. Then she added, "Well, that's a Yale girl for you. If all those sweet young things were laid end to end, I wouldn't be at all surprised."

One of the men in the next booth tittered, and he clapped his hand to his mouth. She could see his shoulders silently shudder as he tried to keep from laughing.

"That's one good thing about a girl who goes to college," Benchley continued. "She has an open mind."

"Sure," Dorothy replied, "her mind is so open, the wind whistles through it."

Now the other men strained to keep from laughing. The strain to keep silent, she knew, made them want to laugh all the harder.

Benchley changed the subject. "So, that was quite a visit we had earlier."

"What visit?"

"We met a police captain with one leg named Church."

"Oh, yes," she said. "But what was the name of his other leg?"

Two of the men laughed openly. A few of the others bit their tongues and hissed in exhalation as they tried to hold it in. Benchley surely guessed that they knew of Captain Church. A joke at the policeman's expense was the final straw.

"Here you are," the cook said, carrying two plates to their table. "Special of the day."

Benchley looked at the leathery slice of liver and the pungent, greasy onions. "If this is the special, I'd hate to see the average."

Dorothy said, "I'd hate to see the sick horse this liver came from."

"Don't look a sick horse in the mouth," Benchley said.

"In the mouth? I can't even look at it on my plate."

"Hey," the cook yelled from behind the counter, "take that back."

She held up her plate. "Only if you return the favor."

The men laughed again. Above the laughter, the bell rang once more.

A sharp voice called out, "What's so damn funny?"

The men went silent immediately. At the door stood a very handsome man. He wore a fur-collared coat and a top hat on his head. He had a walking stick—a knobby, silver-tipped shillelagh—in his hand and an angry scowl on his face. He strode forward and his face brightened, but his voice still held menace.

"I like a funny joke." The man had a faint Irish brogue, but it was more guttural than lilting. "Tell me, now. What's so funny?"

The other men didn't respond. They looked away—at one another, at their shoes, at the clock—they looked anywhere but at the newcomer. The man now grinned maliciously, his ice blue eyes alight, gazing sideways at Dorothy and Benchley as he came closer. This was certainly not who Benchley had called, Dorothy thought.

"You telling jokes, are you? Go on, tell us a joke, then."

He took off the top hat. His hair was ginger red. Now he stood over their table. The man was devilishly handsome, Dorothy thought, except for his teeth, which were yellow, crooked and foul. Looking into his mouth was like looking into a rusty can filled with a jumble of old, ivory mah-jongg tiles. Even his gums receded, as if to get away from those decrepit teeth.

"Go on." He grinned, his eyes flashing. "Tell us a joke."

Benchley said the first thing that came to mind. "What's black and white and red all over?"

"Hmph," the man said, disappointed. "A newspaper."

"Nope," Benchley said. "A zebra with eczema."

The man's smile disintegrated. "I said I like a *funny* joke."

"Try the liver," Dorothy said. "You'll feel funny in no time."

The red-haired man smiled. "Now, that's a joke. So, let's say you two come with us. We'll have a drink, share some more laughs, and have a nice little chat."

"Chat about what?" she said.

"Your friend Mr. Dachshund. I hear you've been talking about him to the police. They're looking for him, I know. But I want to find him first."

She didn't like his smile. She had a sinking feeling in her stomach, and it wasn't from the liver.

"Thanks for the invitation," she said, "but it's late, and we each have liver to eat."

"It wasn't an invitation. Let's go. Or you'll have lead to eat."

"What if we put up a fight?"

He threw his head back and erupted in laughter. "Put up a fight? Oh, now, that is funny. You are too funny, miss. Put up a fight, will you?" Tears rolled down his cheeks as his laughter subsided. The menace returned to his eyes and his voice. "You and what army?"

The bell tinkled again.

She exclaimed, "Well, if it isn't my old friend Jack Dempsey! And you brought some friends!"

The square-shouldered boxer entered calmly, confidently. Behind him, extending out the door, was a gang of a dozen other tough-looking men. Probably fellow boxers or cornermen, Dorothy thought.

"Mrs. Parker," Dempsey said, ignoring the red-haired man as he stepped by him. "Ain't that a kick in the head to see you here. Talk about a coincidence. Why, my pals here were just walking by on our way to find a cocktail. Would you like to join us?"

"Delighted," she said, scrambling out of the booth.

The redheaded man stepped forward, his blue eyes raging. "Why don't you make plans to meet Mr. Dempsey later? It's not healthy to eat and run, don't you know?"

Benchley shoved away his plate. "It's not healthy to eat in here, period."

"Hey, take that back, too," the cook yelled from behind the counter. Everyone ignored him.

Dorothy wouldn't be intimidated. She started toward the door.

The red-haired man stood in her way, holding the shillelagh to block her path. He spoke between his clenched yellow teeth. "I'm telling you, it's not good for your health. You'll live longer if you take your time."

"I'll take my chances."

She brushed by him. Dempsey stepped aside to let her pass, and although she wanted to run, she calmly strolled out the door, followed by Dempsey's gang of boxers. Benchley jumped up, threw a few bills on the table, and quickly joined the group.

Outside, it was still dark on the nearly deserted city street. Dempsey walked beside her.

"That was pretty gutsy of you," he said.

"Gutsy of me?" she gushed. "You came to our rescue."

"Don't sweat it. That hoodlum wouldn't touch me, especially with my chums here. But he could knock down your door anytime, and there's not much I can do about it unless I just happen to be nearby, like I was tonight when your friend Mr. Benchley called."

"Strange men knocking down my door?" she said. "Sounds like an average Saturday night."

Dempsey placed his large hand on her sleeve. "Hold on, now. You do know who that was back there, don't you? Only one of the most ruthless gangsters in the city."

"Was it? I confess I didn't catch his name."

"That was Mickey Finn."

Chapter 24

The Sunday afternoon sun slanted through her bedroom window and warmed her face. She sat up in bed. The sunlight felt good, and she realized she felt good. She felt alert and ready to go.

This was unusual. Most Sunday afternoons, she woke up hungover and irritable.

The good feeling was short-lived, though, as she recalled the night before . . . the long grilling by Captain Church and Detective O'Rannigan. The close call at the greasy spoon with Mickey Finn and his henchmen. Then Jack Dempsey had informed her that he wasn't really up late drinking cocktails. He was up early and on his way to the gym. He said he hoped to see her again; then he and his pals left. Benchley had walked her back to the Algonquin; then he, too, toddled off to the train station to spend the day with his family.

She kicked the blankets off. She lit a cigarette and exhaled fiercely. The hell with all those men!

Woodrow Wilson hopped up on her bed and nuzzled under her arm. The poor dog needed a walk, she knew. But would she be safe if she took the dog for a stroll by herself? She imagined a long black limousine pulling up alongside her, a pack of men in long coats jumping out, grabbing her, dragging her inside.

The dog laid its head on her lap.

The hell with Mickey Finn! Who was he to cage her up on such a brilliant, sunny day?

"Come on, Woody. Let's go for a walk."

The dog jumped down from the bed with a bark. He seemed to make a playful bow. His forelegs stretched out, his backside went up in the air, his stubby tail wagged expectantly and his snout curled almost in a grin.

While she got dressed, she tried to catch the thread of a nagging thought. Several things about the previous night bothered her, but there was something in particular. Something about someone Church had asked about . . .

Was it something about Frank Case? Could the hotel manager have murdered someone in his own hotel to make headlines? That bothered her, true, but that wasn't it.

Was it something about Robert Sherwood? Sherwood had certainly killed men in the war; that was a fact. But Sherwood, even if pushed far enough to kill, wouldn't have murdered Mayflower in so cowardly a fashion. No, her mind was certain about Sherwood. But, she remembered something else. Church and O'Rannigan wanted to pull Sherwood in for questioning. She'd have to warn him. But, still, this wasn't the thread she was trying to get hold of.

Was it something about Woollcott? Perhaps. O'Rannigan had said Mayflower went behind Woollcott's back to land the Saber fountain pen endorsement contract. That had surprised her. Had Woollcott seriously wanted that endorsement deal? Would it compel him to murder with the very item in question? Hmm. Something didn't add up there. Mayflower had been appearing in the Saber ads for months now. But on the day he was murdered, Mayflower had contacted Woollcott to brag about some *new* accomplishment.

That wasn't quite it, but that was closer to the thought she was trying to recollect. Something about Mayflower. Something else that she didn't know—

Yes, that was it! Mayflower had a lover. Everyone seemed so desperate to catch Mayflower's killer, yet no one seemed to give a damn about Mayflower himself. Perhaps she could go talk to the man—what was his name? Aloysius Neeley; that was it. Perhaps she could go talk to Mr. Neeley to learn a little bit more about Mayflower. Maybe, somehow, she'd learn of a connection between Mayflower and the Sandman. Maybe this would get the cops and the gangsters off her back, which in turn might bring Faulkner out of hiding, and then the whole lousy mess would be over with. Maybe.

Hell, it was worth a shot.

She was starting to feel better again. In the elevator, she cheerfully greeted old Maurice. "Good morning!"

"It's afternoon," he grumbled.

"Says you." She smiled.

She walked the dog through the lobby. Sunday afternoons were always quiet. She realized she was hungry, but it was well past lunchtime. The Vicious Circle did not gather for lunch on Sundays.

"Oh, Dottie," called a sultry female voice.

She turned around. Neysa McMein approached her, looking considerably worse for wear. Neysa wore the same slim black dress she had worn when Dorothy saw her at last night's poker game. Neysa's beautiful half-lidded eyes drooped more than usual.

"What happened to you last night?" Neysa said.

"I could ask the same of you," Dorothy said.

"The last we saw, that grizzly bear of a policeman dragged you and Mr. Benchley out the door. We thought you might be in for a spell at Sing Sing."

"I sang-sang, all right. I sang like a bird. The police questioned us all night."

She explained to Neysa how Captain Church had a long list of suspects and how she and Benchley had to answer for each one.

"How detestable," Neysa said. "On a brighter note,

I'm having a little get-together at my studio on Thursday night. Can you make it?"

For these "little get-togethers," Neysa threw open the door of her spacious artist's studio, and anyone and everyone was likely to walk in. While the party went on, Neysa continued to paint. These huge gatherings were often the oddest and most interesting parties that Dorothy attended.

"Can I make it?" she said. "Try and stop me."

She said good-bye to Neysa and steered the dog away. She hadn't gone more than a few paces when she saw the tall figure of Robert Sherwood approaching.

"What happened to you last night?" he said.

As she had explained to Neysa, Dorothy repeated the events of the previous night.

"And that's not all," she added. "Captain Church said he wanted to bring you in for questioning, too. I'm sorry if I said anything to get you into hot water."

"It's not your fault. That's what I get for tormenting Bud Battersby. Next time, I'll watch my temper."

She paused, thinking.

"What's the matter?" he asked.

"Nothing," she said. "How many men did you kill in the war?"

"Not many, I don't think. I don't know, really. Why?"

"Would you kill a man for revenge?"

"Honestly, Mrs. Parker." He pretended to be insulted, but there was an amused grin behind his shocked grimace. "Leland Mayflower, do you mean? First of all, why would I wait a year after his malicious drama review to get my revenge? And second of all, to answer your question, no, I don't think I could kill a man out of revenge, even at my worst. And third, even if I could, I wouldn't hire some devious thug to do the deed for me."

"That's what I thought." She felt relieved, even though she'd known how he would answer. "By the way, have you ever heard anyone mention Mayflower's boyfriend, Aloysius Neeley?"

"No, though I always had the impression Mayflower skulked around with some sequin-shirted chorus boy. Did you check the obvious sources?"

"The theater guild, you mean? It's Sunday. They're closed."

"Some detective you'd be," he said. "I meant the city directory."

She said good-bye to Sherwood and made her way to the hotel's front desk. She asked to see the city directory.

A suave voice purred in her ear. "What happened to you last night?"

"Everyone keeps asking me that," she said, turning to greet the Algonquin's manager, Frank Case. Having explained what happened twice in just the past ten minutes, she didn't feel like going over it again. "Let me ask you a question instead. Would you kill a man for the publicity?"

Case considered this. "In my own hotel? Do you think that's the kind of publicity I really want? Dead men lying about in our restaurant? Not very appetizing, I'd venture to say."

She felt ashamed to even consider that he might find such notoriety appealing.

Case continued, "So, do you imagine that Leland Mayflower was murdered for the sake of publicity?"

"Not his own, certainly," she said.

"Then for whose?"

Yes, indeed, she thought, *for whose?*

Aloysius Neeley was not what she had expected. She had pictured Neeley as an ostentatiously pretty young playboy, his grin too wide and his hair artificially blackened, wearing a flashy tie and an expensive suit, living in a ridiculously extravagant apartment overlooking Central Park, squandering away his trust fund or living off Mayflower's generosity.

But the city directory informed her that Neeley

lived on West Forty-eighth Street, not a far walk but far enough from Central Park. Neeley's apartment was in an unremarkable building in a modest neighborhood. Dorothy stood in the April sunshine and stared up at the building. She finished off the little roast beef sandwich that Frank Case had fetched (or more precisely, that Luigi the waiter had fetched) for her, and tossed the last bite to Woodrow Wilson, who chomped it down in one gulp.

The doorman admitted her and directed her to Neeley's apartment. She knocked. A middle-aged man in horn-rimmed glasses (much like her own) opened the door. She immediately assumed it must be Neeley's father.

"Is Aloysius Neeley at home?"

"I'm Aloysius Neeley, but you can call me Lou. Can I help you?"

The man wore a camel's hair sweater over a cream-colored shirt. His hair seemed to be colored, but it was brown, not glossy black. His shoes—the same color as his hair—were in need of a polish. He was trim, but his apparently once-handsome rectangular face had softened with age, like a favorite old suitcase.

Without asking her permission, the man bent to scratch the dog behind the ears. She liked Lou Neeley immediately.

"Can I help you?" he repeated. He had a soft, mellifluous voice.

"My name is Dorothy Parker. I'd like to talk to you about Leland Mayflower."

Chapter 25

They sat on the sofa. Lou Neeley handed her a cup of hot black tea.

"What would you like to know about merry old Mayflower?" he said. His expression was one of sadness mixed with fondness.

"I'm curious to know who might have wanted him dead."

Neeley pondered this a moment. "Well, at first, the newspapers said that one of the members of your famous Round Table probably killed him. That's where he was found, right? Then the police came around again—trying to be intimidating, and a very good show they put on, too—and they told me some gangster killed him. I really don't know who to believe. I'm just sorry the cranky old fool is gone."

The man's eyes clouded with mixed emotions again. She pretended not to notice. She looked around at what had been, until recently, a cozy little apartment. But boxes, bags and suitcases were piled in heaps. Pictures had been taken off the walls. A cabinet stood with its empty drawers agape.

"Moving out?" she said.

Neeley surveyed the room, as if trying to recall old

memories. "I can't afford the place anymore. I have a modest income as a sales clerk at Brooks Brothers."

"So you're not a chorus boy?"

"Not by a long shot," he snorted. "Oh, once upon a time, about a hundred years ago, I was in the chorus on Broadway for a few golden years. Then I got tired of starving for a living. So, I went from working for peanuts on Broadway to working for pennies on Fifth Avenue."

"That's where you met Mayflower."

"Yes. One thing led to another. The years flew by, and here I am. All alone in an apartment I can't afford. Leland paid half the rent. He practically lived here, but he insisted on keeping his own fancy apartment for appearance's sake."

His eyes traveled over a few of his things—a Tiffany lamp, a Persian carpet, an amber ashtray fixed in a brass stand.

"Leland bought many of these things. But that horse's ass always spent more than he had coming in, so he put everything on credit. Now what isn't being repossessed is being auctioned. Whatever is left over, I'm selling off. Would you like to buy a cut-glass pitcher in the shape of a trout?"

"Thanks, but I already own one." She smiled. "Did Mr. Mayflower owe a lot of people money?"

"Did he ever. He owed the Chinese laundry twelve dollars. He owed the barber who cut his hair ten dollars. He owed the man who blocked his hats fourteen dollars. He owed the landlord almost fifty dollars—"

"I mean—"

"Oh, I know what you meant. You meant, did he have any large debts? Like hundreds or thousands of dollars? Specifically, you mean, was he in debt to any loan sharks or underworld gangsters? Don't look so surprised. The policemen asked me this over and over."

"Well, was he?"

"Of course not," Neeley said. He plunked down his

teacup, stood up and moved toward a narrow liquor cabinet. "How about something a little stronger than Earl Grey?"

Dorothy took this as a cue to light a cigarette. She held up her empty teacup, and Neeley poured her a large splash of brandy. He poured himself an even larger splash. He sat down, lit a cigarette as well, crossed his legs and leaned back. The dog crawled up and curled in his lap. He scratched the dog's ears absentmindedly.

"If you saw Leland," he continued, "then you saw that he wore his silk gloves almost all the time. He was so dainty about those hands of his. He never washed a dish or picked up a broom. So, tell me, do you think he'd get his hands dirty by dealing with some loan sharks or crooks who just crawled out of the gutter? Oh, yes, he owed money. But not *that* kind of money, and not to those kinds of people."

"On the day that he died, he had sent Alexander Woollcott a note saying that he had some big news to share. Do you know what that was all about?"

"Leland always had some new scheme, some new big deal. He told me his ship was coming in next week. But he told me that every week."

"Anything in particular?"

"Oh, let's see," Neeley said. "There was something about importing vanilla beans. That didn't pan out. Well, he did go see a lawyer recently. You see, Leland had always talked about writing his memoirs. And so recently he met with a lawyer about it. I don't really understand what that had to do with writing his memoirs, but he certainly seemed over the moon about whatever the lawyer told him. Then again, as I said, he'd talked about writing his memoirs for a long time, but I never really paid him much mind."

"Do you remember the name of this lawyer?"

Neeley shook his head.

"Did you tell the police about this?"

"No, they didn't ask about Leland's work. Just a lot

of prying questions about his personal relationships, of course. And if he owed any money to gangsters. As if I didn't have enough people to answer to!"

As Neeley raised his voice, the dog crawled off his lap.

"Now I'm stuck paying off his piddling debts. I'm getting kicked out of the apartment we couldn't afford to begin with. And, somehow, I've got to come up with the money for his funeral. He's still at the morgue, for heaven's sake. I can't claim his body because I can't pay for the burial."

He sank his head in his hands. "I have to take care of him. He'd never forgive me if I didn't take care of him."

She wondered whether Mayflower had been in the large underground room in Bellevue Hospital where she had seen the Sandman's body. The thought of Mayflower's body in the same room with his murderer's corpse gave her a chill.

Neeley sat up and composed himself.

"The worst of it," he said, "is that I'll never see him again. I wouldn't wish this feeling on my worst enemy. I'm in love with someone who's just out of reach. And I've got my whole life ahead of me, and I know I'll still feel this way until my own dying day. You've no idea what it's like."

"Oh, brother, don't I?" she said. "I know what it's like, and how."

"You do? Well, then, I'm sorry for you."

"I'll drink to that." She drained her cup.

They sat in silence a moment.

She spoke softly. "I tell myself that loving someone out of reach is better than having no love at all."

He smiled weakly. "I'll give that a try."

She had an idea. "There's a party Thursday night at Neysa McMein's studio. Do you know her? She's a good illustrator, but she outshines herself the way she throws a party. Everyone is there. Would it be all right if we passed the hat around to help you cover the funeral expenses?"

"Oh, no!"

"No?"

"I mean, oh, no, your dog just peed on the rug."

She turned and saw the evidence and the guilty party. "Oh, Woody."

"Never mind about it," Neeley said with an impish smile. "It's being repossessed. As for passing the hat, Mayflower would roll over in his grave. But since he's not in his grave yet, I think it would be a wonderful gesture. A tribute, even. Thank you. And people say you've got a wicked streak. Why, you're not wicked at all."

"If your taste in mates ran in a different direction, my boy, I could prove you wrong on that score."

Chapter 26

Dorothy waited to speak until Alexander Woollcott had raised a spoonful of tomato soup to his lips.

"Aleck," she said, "why did you lie to us about Leland Mayflower?"

He choked and coughed as he tried to swallow the soup. He couldn't speak. She waited.

It was lunchtime on Monday. The Vicious Circle was gathered again at their Round Table. Only Robert Sherwood was absent. Dorothy could have questioned Woollcott when he first arrived for lunch. She had decided to wait until the right moment.

"Never," he sputtered breathlessly. "Never did I lie."

"Mr. Benchley and I spent a good portion of Saturday night and early Sunday morning defending your good name. Then we learned that you didn't tell us the truth."

Woollcott had recovered his poise. "The truth? What, that I murdered Mayflower? There's no truth in that, as everyone knows. You could have saved your breath."

"You never told us that Mayflower went behind your back to land the Saber fountain pen contract. That's tantamount to lying."

Marc Connelly turned to Robert Benchley. "She's pithy. More so when she's angry."

"Yes, she's full of pith and vinegar," Benchley replied.

Woollcott rose from his chair. "If you will indulge me, I'd prefer to speak to you two in the lobby."

Dorothy and Benchley followed Woollcott. When he reached the enormous old grandfather clock in the center of the lobby, he stopped and turned to them. His nasally voice was quiet but stern.

"It's so very impolite to talk about one's business affairs in such an open forum," he said. "My business is just that. *My* business."

She said, "When *your* business has us answering questions at the police station in the wee hours of the morning, it ceases to be merely *your* business. Now, tell us the truth."

Woollcott looked peevish. He pursed his lips. "Well, I admit it. Mayflower got one over on me. There you have it. Are you happy now?"

"I'm feeling slightly better," she said. "Tell us more."

Woollcott pumped his fists like a petulant child. "I had that Saber pen contract all sewn up. I almost had the money in the palm of my hand. Mayflower knew it. He knew we were both up for consideration."

"So, he went behind your back?"

"Yes, he went behind my back! He proposed a better deal, that crusty old turd. Instead of receiving a large lump sum, which they would have given me, Mayflower offered to take a very small percentage."

"A percentage?"

"He got almost nothing up front, but he got a very small piece of the profit for every pen sold. The Saber people thought it was a great advantage for them, and they took him up on it."

She found herself silently admiring Mayflower. She wondered whether Lou Neeley, who undoubtedly worked on commission at Brooks Brothers, had even suggested the idea to Mayflower.

"But that was about a year ago. I didn't bother with

sour grapes then," Woollcott continued, again looking superior. "Why would I wait so long to get revenge on him, and in such a callow fashion?"

Dorothy played devil's advocate. "To throw off suspicion. Revenge is a dish best served cold, they say."

"What do *they* know?" Woollcott replied coolly. "If I wanted revenge, I couldn't wait a year. Instant gratification is not soon enough for me."

"Then why did Mayflower want to see you? Why did he send you that note?"

Woollcott looked at them squarely. "I honestly don't know. May God strike me down if I lie."

"Don't bother Him now," she said. "He'll get around to you in His own time."

When they returned to the table, Robert Sherwood was there. He was explaining to everyone how he had just come from the police station, where he was questioned by Captain Church and Detective O'Rannigan.

"They're completely in the dark," Sherwood said sourly. "They asked me the very same questions they asked Mrs. Parker and Mr. Benchley. One minute, they asked whether one of us had a reason for revenge. The next minute, they asked whether Mayflower was in debt to gangsters. How should I know whether Mayflower owed money to Mickey Finn? They kept asking about my military service, though."

"Ah, yes," Benchley said. "Captain Church has a soft spot for hard artillery. And hard-boiled eggs."

"He and that buffoon of a detective kept trying to get me riled. They were deliberately trying to anger me, just to provoke me. Perhaps they thought I might let the cat out of the bag if I lost my temper. But I wouldn't fall into that trap. I kept my head. Thanks for tipping me off about that, Mrs. Parker."

"Keep your head and you'll save your neck," she said. "Those nitwits are out for someone's blood. Anyone who even closely fits the bill."

"Speaking of keeping my head, I ran into Bud Battersby again on the steps of the police station. He tried to give me his old song and dance that we're all in the same game, all on the same side of the fence. That he just has his job to do and I have mine. I wanted to say that my job doesn't involve dragging the names of good people through the mud. But again, I kept my head. I didn't want to give him any fodder for his dishrag of a newspaper."

"Smartly done," Benchley said.

"More timely than smart," Sherwood said. "That was before I saw today's *Knickerbocker News*. Out of curiosity, I bought a copy after I ran into Battersby. I wouldn't have been so . . . charitable with him had I read this first."

He handed the tabloid newspaper to Benchley, whose sunny face went cloudy. Dorothy leaned against him to read it.

"Well, spit it out, then," Woollcott said impatiently. "What does it say?"

"This is disastrous," Benchley said.

Woollcott's voice rose. "What's it say?"

Benchley spoke solemnly. "Harvard lost to Princeton. Fourteen to zip. And the shortstop sprained his ankle."

"Go ahead," Dorothy said. "Read it."

Benchley looked hurt. "I had two dollars on that game."

"Knock it off, Fred. Read it."

Benchley shrugged. "Here's the headline: POLICE GRILL FAMOUS WRITERS IN MAYFLOWER MURDER."

"Keep going," she said.

Benchley read the article:

> Late Saturday night, police officials appre-
> hended two writers from the celebrated Algon-
> quin Round Table. Police detectives detained
> Mrs. Dorothy Parker and Mr. Robert Bench-
> ley for questioning until nearly four o'clock
> Sunday morning about the cold-blooded mur-

der of *Knickerbocker News* columnist Leland Mayflower.

Police Det. Albert O'Rannigan tracked down Mrs. Parker and Mr. Benchley at a smoke-filled, booze-fueled secret card game at the famed Algonquin Hotel, 59 W. 44th St., where the two are members of the well-known Algonquin Round Table, an exclusive clique of intellectual writers, editors and other assorted literati, who were discussed in depth in last week's editions of this newspaper.

After a short but violent scuffle, in which Mrs. Parker deliberately assaulted Det. O'Rannigan (who later reported he suffered no lasting ill effects—nor ill will!—from Mrs. Parker's beatings), Det. O'Rannigan transported the two famed writers to the 16th Precinct Station House, 345 W. 47th St. Once there, Mrs. Parker and Mr. Benchley were questioned intensely about their involvement in the murder of Mr. Mayflower.

The *Knickerbocker*'s own Leland Mayflower, as all New York now knows, was found stabbed dead last Wednesday directly underneath the famed Round Table. The murder instrument was, of all things, a fountain pen. Rampant rumor—as well as common sense—suggests that one (or more) of the members of the Round Table committed the crime. (They call themselves the Vicious Circle, after all!) But police have yet to determine the cold-blooded killer.

To that end, Police Capt. Phillip Church and Det. O'Rannigan exhaustively questioned Mrs. Parker and Mr. Benchley about their motives and those of their wordsmithing compatriots. Police could not reveal the results of the questioning, but much controversy swirls

around a shadowy figure named William
Dachshund, a name that may be fictitious. Indeed, Mr. Dachshund, whose whereabouts are
unknown, as described in Saturday's edition
of this newspaper, apparently bills himself as
a fiction writer, and is also apparently a newly
appointed member of the Vicious Circ—

"Give me that." Dorothy grabbed the newspaper
from Benchley's hands. She rapidly scanned the remain-
ing few paragraphs of the article, then hurriedly flipped
through the pages of the paper.

"Damn that bastard," she said.

"Damn who?" Benchley said. "Dachshund?"

"No. Damn that Battersby! He goes on and on about
the Round Table and about Billy. But again he makes
no mention of Knut Sanderson. He doesn't bother to
say that the reason we were questioned was because the
Sandman had Mayflower's notebook with your notes in
it. He doesn't say that the Sandman tried to kill us. He
doesn't mention that we went to get a good, close look
at the Sandman's dead body. Nothing. Battersby only
wants to paint the picture that one of us or Billy Faulk—
Billy Dachshund was behind Mayflower's murder."

Franklin Pierce Adams leaned back in his chair, his
cigar in his mouth. "So, what are you going to do about
it? Take it lying down?"

"Isn't that the way you deal with most men?" Woollcott sneered before she could answer.

"Not this time," she said with a smirk. "Time to stand
up for the truth. Let's pay Bud Battersby a little visit."

Chapter 27

The *Knickerbocker News* was housed in a gigantic, dingy industrial building in Lower Manhattan, within spitting distance of the docks on the Hudson River.

Dorothy Parker and Robert Benchley approached the large, battered, wooden front door. A small, old tin sign read: NEW AMSTERDAM SUPPLY CATALOGUES AND CALENDARS, INC.

"Is this the right place?" Benchley said, looking cheerfully doubtful. "It makes the newspaper buildings on Publishers' Row look like palaces."

Dorothy held the copy of the *Knickerbocker News* that Robert Sherwood had given to her. In tiny print on the second-to-last page was the newspaper's masthead. She read the address again.

"Seventy-five Clarkson Street. If you can believe what the *Knickerbocker* prints, then this must be the place."

"Isn't the whole point why we're here is that you *don't* believe what the *Knickerbocker* prints?"

"Don't confuse me by making sense. Anyhow, that's not the point we're here."

"It's not?"

"No. It's only the side point."

"What's the main point? The one on Battersby's head?"

"Mayflower visited a lawyer for some unknown reason. We need Battersby to tell us the name of that lawyer. That's the point."

"Point taken," Benchley said. "Point, set and match."

"Thanks for playing," she said. "Now, the door. Don't try it until you knock it."

Benchley knocked on the wide door. They waited, but there was no answer. Then he tried the knob. The door swung open to reveal a narrow, shadowy, marble-floored entranceway. A woman was crossing the foyer. She wore an ink-stained leather apron, and her hair was pulled back in a kerchief. She stopped abruptly at the sight of the two visitors.

Dorothy stepped forward. "We're here to see Mr. Battersby."

The woman frowned and made a hollow, hoarse sound.

Dorothy turned her head to her companion. "What do you make of that?"

"I'd say that means 'no dice' in whatever language she speaks."

Benchley then stepped forward, speaking loudly and slowly. "Where is Mr. Battersby? It is very important that we speak to him."

The aproned woman shook her head and responded with a throaty bark. She pointed to her head. Then she pointed toward the door, as if shooing them away.

Benchley said to Dorothy, "Maybe this isn't the right place after all."

"One more try," Dorothy said. She unfolded the newspaper and located the masthead again. She scanned the short list of names. She showed the woman the newspaper and pointed at Battersby's name at the top.

The woman grunted in assent and turned back the way she had come. Dorothy and Benchley glanced at each other, then followed the woman along a dark, dusty hallway. They heard a deep, distant, thunderous sound, as though several chugging steam locomotives were hurtling full speed somewhere inside the build-ing. Through their shoes, they felt thrumming vibrations come up through the wooden floor of the hallway. But the sound didn't die away as the sound of a steam train does as it passes by. It only became louder.

The woman yanked open another door and went through it without looking back. Dorothy and Benchley followed. Now they were in a wider corridor, not quite as dark. Here the rumbling sound was even louder, and it grew louder still as they walked farther into the building. It was a pounding, grating, chattering sound. Dorothy could feel the vibrations in her stomach and in her teeth. The corridor ended at an archway, and they entered a cavernous room. The sound was almost deafening.

This was the main floor of the printing plant. The space was three stories high and a football field long. Three enormous printing presses, each as large as, though lon-ger than, a steam locomotive, were chugging and bang-ing away. Enormous rolls of white paper, as long as tree trunks and twice as wide, spooled out faster than Doro-thy's eyes could follow. Within the printing press, this endless ribbon of paper zipped in and out of a dozen or more pairs of gigantic, barrel-thick metal rollers.

A web of stairs and catwalks covered each printing press in a latticework of metal. Little men (they ap-peared to be miniature in comparison, anyway) scurried up and down the stairs and along the catwalks. They tended to the machines—pulling levers, adjusting con-trols, squirting tiny cans of oil—like Lilliputians who had roped down a giant.

The aproned woman was already several paces away from them, moving quickly along the length of the near-est press.

In that direction, at the far end of the room, Dorothy could see the paper being slit and divided, like a sluiced river, then slid into slabs, which were cut in quick suc-cession by a long guillotine-like blade. These pages were whisked along to be folded, then folded again, and spit

out onto a conveyor belt. More men, their forearms
darkened by newsprint, grabbed the newspapers and
piled them into bundles on wide metal tables. They
stacked the bundles on pallets; then other men carted
them away.

She wanted to hold Benchley's hand. Instead she
merely linked her arm through his. He stared at the
immense machines with a mixture of awe and apprehension, as though he gazed upon a terrible wonder of
nature, like an earthquake or Niagara Falls.

At the far end of the room, the aproned woman ascended a well-worn wooden staircase. Dorothy and Benchley hurried to catch up with her. At the top of the staircase,
the woman entered a room that jutted like a wide balcony
over the printing-room floor. They followed her in.

The room was just as noisy inside. Three of the four
walls of the large room were nothing but windows that
looked out over the printing presses, eye level with
the catwalks. Inside the room, a dozen or so men and
women worked at tables and desks. It was the typesetting room, Dorothy realized. The men and women—
each in an ink-stained apron, like the woman they had
followed—darted from a desk, where they gathered up
lead letters, to a table, where they inserted their letters
into a frame. This frame eventually became a printing
plate for the newspaper. At the back of the room were
three tall Linotype machines, each manned by an operator at a keyboard. The Linotype machine looked like a
hissing, clacking hybrid of a pipe organ and a steam shirt
press. It formed molten lead into lines of type that were
attached onto a large cylinder, which was used to print
pages on the printing press.

Dorothy made a mental note to remember these
people the next time she felt like complaining about her
lousy job.

She saw that the woman they had followed now approached a man who stood staring out through the glass
to the printing floor. The woman tapped the man on the

shoulder. The man turned around, and Dorothy was somehow surprised to see it was Battersby, even though they had come specifically to talk to him. It was just that when she had seen the timid fellow before, he seemed to be nothing more than a newspaperman whom everyone just called 'Bud.' But here, he was the captain of the ship, the chief of an enormous operation.

Battersby approached them sheepishly. He had to yell to be heard above the cacophony of the printing presses.

"Mr. Benchley, Mrs. Parker, what brings you here?"

"We'd like a word with you," she yelled. "Can we talk somewhere more private?"

"Private?" Battersby looked around at the typesetters. "Don't worry about them. They're all deaf. That's why I hire them. Say what you want. They won't hear a thing."

She glanced at the workers. If she didn't get out of this room quickly, she'd soon be deaf, too.

"I mean," she yelled, "can we talk somewhere more quiet?"

"Ohhh," Battersby said. "Come with me."

They followed Battersby to a huge basement room just under the printing presses. Here, three massive boilers generated the steam to power the presses. Not only was this room even louder—as if that were possible—it was hellishly hot. Three burly men covered in soot shoveled coal into the roaring, insatiable, infernolike mouths of the boilers.

They kept walking. Battersby led them down to yet another subterranean level. It was much quieter here, much cooler, too.

"I take it from your expressions that you've never seen a large press operation before," Battersby said, leading them onward.

It was true that although they'd both been involved in publishing for several years, neither she nor Benchley had seen such an enormous machine, much less three of them going full tilt side by side. But for what? To print a crappy tabloid newspaper.

"It's not the size that matters," she said. "It's what you do with it."

Battersby opened a vaultlike door to a series of offices. The first was a wide, windowless newsroom, with some two dozen desks stationed in rows as though it was an enormous classroom. However, only three or four unknown reporters (unknown to Dorothy and Benchley, anyhow) were in the room, seated behind typewriters or talking on phones.

Battersby opened another door and entered a small, nondescript office. Dorothy assumed this was Battersby's secretary's office; then Battersby dropped into the wooden swivel chair behind the desk.

"Have a seat," he said.

But there were no other seats in the room.

"Where, exactly?" she said.

Benchley dropped to the floor and sat cross-legged.

Battersby hustled from around his desk. "I beg your pardon," he said, extending a hand to Benchley to pull him up off the painted-concrete floor.

"If you want to beg our pardon," Dorothy began, "you can start by apologizing for the flaying you gave us in today's edition of your newspaper."

"Ah, that's what brought you down here, is it?" Battersby said with an anxious look.

"No, you brought us down here," Benchley said. "How many leagues beneath the surface are we?"

"Maybe we'd be more comfortable in Mr. Mayflower's office," Battersby said. "Please follow me."

Dorothy was tired of touring around this place. It took something of an effort to remain righteously angry, and all this walking about was taking the piss right out of her.

Battersby opened a large, well-varnished wooden door and stepped aside to let them enter. The other side of the door was upholstered in cranberry red leather. The inside of the room held a great deal of red leather furniture to match—several armchairs, a chaise longue and a couch or two.

Ornate brass lamps sat glowing on either end of the monstrous mahogany desk, which squatted like a hippopotamus at the far end of the large room. A large brass chandelier, with burning gas jets, hung from the tiled ceiling. A plush Turkish carpet covered the floor. The walls were paneled in chestnut. A brick fireplace, unlit, took up half of the wall to the right.

Battersby closed the door, and the last faint sound of the printing presses faded out. Dorothy could feel only the faintest vibration, and once she sat down in a comfortable leather armchair, even that feeling disappeared.

She noticed that on the big wooden desk was a leather cup that held a handful of Saber fountain pens—the same as the one found lodged in Mayflower's heart.

Battersby didn't sit behind the big desk. He dragged a chair to a halfway spot in front of Benchley and Dorothy, as if to be put on the spot.

"So you came here to give me what for about the article in today's *Knickerbocker*?" He crouched in his chair, almost wincing, like a dog expecting a smack on the nose for punishment.

It's easy to give hell to an arrogant jackass, Dorothy thought. *Why couldn't Battersby be an arrogant jackass, instead of this timid, nearly middle-aged man who seemed as wide-eyed as a child?*

"This was Leland Mayflower's office?" Benchley said incredulously.

"Yes," Battersby said.

"And that nondescript little room out there, the one desperately lacking in chairs—that's *your* office?"

"Yes."

"I see. Yes, that's as clear as mud. Now, indulge me— why did Mayflower have this luxurious room while you continue to use a dank antechamber without sufficient furniture?"

"Let me explain.... Do you have children, Mr. Benchley?"

"Yes, two or three. I lose count now and again. And you?"

"Unfortunately, I'm not married, unless you count this." He gestured with both hands to encompass the building, the newspaper, his enterprise. "Nor have I been blessed with children. Unless you count my workers as my children. And if you do, then Mayflower would have been my highly favored son—my prodigal son, for whom I'd slaughter the fatted calf."

Battersby leaned forward and continued. "I would have done anything to keep him happy. When I bought the *Knickerbocker* a few years ago, no one read the darn thing. The circulation was in the toilet. Then I lured Mayflower over from the *Daily News* to be my star columnist. He was a spoiled so-and-so, no question. But he gave the *Knickerbocker* a recognizable name, a recognizable style. Sure, it can be an acerbic, corrosive style— call it what you will—but it set us apart. It gave us an identity. Circulation went up. People took notice. Now Mayflower's gone, and I'm doing my best to carry on without him."

His chin sank into his hands. "I'm running around, trying to write most of the stories and edit the rest, but I also oversee the printing and advertising, and the day-to-day operation of this entire plant—the accounts, the bills, the inventory, the employees. It's a kick, I'll tell you. I love it all. But it's killing me. It's just killing me."

Here they were to tear the guy to shreds, Dorothy thought, and he was doing it for them. How could she slap his wrist when she felt the need to pat his hand?

"We can see that this place isn't King Solomon's mines," she said, "but can't you afford to hire a few more people, at least temporarily?"

Battersby brightened. "Oh, you're mistaken. It's extremely profitable. I'm bringing it in hand over fist. The *Knickerbocker*, my pride and joy, does little more than break even. That's true. But most of my business is industrial catalogues, seed catalogues, several trade publications, company and commercial directories, hymnals and religious tracts. We do a big calendar business that keeps growing every year. Those printing presses are running around the clock. We can barely keep up. The money is practically pouring in."

"Then, for heaven's sake, hire some people! Why do everything yourself?"

Battersby shook his head. "There's no replacing Mayflower. I see that now." He spread his hands, palms up. "I try to do what he did, but it's falling to pieces. Circulation is still up, thank God, but that's mostly due to the continuing news of Mayflower's own murder. He's still carrying me, bless him. What do I do when his story is over?"

She couldn't hold her tongue any longer. "Is that why you've done such a shitty job covering it?"

Battersby looked wounded. "What do you mean?"

"You imply—no, no, you directly point your finger at the members of the Round Table for Mayflower's murder. You're telling people that Mr. Benchley or I or Aleck Woollcott or Bob Sherwood murdered Mayflower. To top it off, you hardly bother to mention that the police know—and know full well—that a gangster called the Sandman did the murder. All the other newspapers have reported that. Why hasn't yours?"

Battersby looked away. He spoke without enthusiasm. "A gangster committed the murder? That just seems so conventional. So typical." His eyes lit up. "But if a member of the Round Table is a murderer, now, that's a story!"

"A fictional story, yes. You can't simply ignore the facts to write a load of sensational bullshit. That's libel."

"I'm not trying to ignore the facts," Battersby said weakly. "I'm just . . . trying to sell my newspaper. The only way I know how."

Dorothy sensed an opening and spoke quickly, like a boy who hastily springs a rabbit trap. "Speaking of libel, did Mayflower mention seeing a lawyer recently?"

"No," Battersby said, his mind still on his own train of thought. "Not that I recall. Something important?"

"No. Never mind."

Battersby roused himself. He looked at the enormous pendulum clock on the wall. "Shoot, is that the time? I'm sorry, but I have loads to do. I have an ink shipment that's supposed to be delivered in a few minutes. If there's more you want to talk about, can we continue this another time?" He walked them toward the leather-padded door. "I must say, though, it's good to take a few minutes to chew the fat with some fellow journalists."

"Keep it up," she said, "and maybe you'll grow up to be one yourself someday."

Chapter 28

It was lunchtime the following day when Dorothy Parker and Robert Benchley entered the spacious lobby of the Algonquin Hotel. She didn't have much of an appetite. And the crowd of nosybodies in the lobby didn't raise her spirits one bit.

She and Benchley had spent more than two unproductive hours that morning at the offices of *Vanity Fair*. They tried to get at least a little bit of their work done. But, since their desks were side by side, they mostly chatted about that morning's edition of the *Knickerbocker News*.

Battersby had written yet another article about Dorothy and Benchley. This was based on their conversation in Mayflower's office the previous afternoon, except Battersby had altered much of what had happened. The article implied that Dorothy and Benchley had been confrontational, insulting, almost threatening. Battersby painted her as an irrational hothead and Benchley as a mealymouthed sycophant.

The article said that Mrs. Parker had demanded that the *Knickerbocker* retract its previous stories about the members of the Round Table. But it also said she had insisted that the *Knickerbocker* report that William Dachshund had seen the Sandman in the Algonquin's lobby the morning of Mayflower's murder. The article even implied that she was doing this to fashion an alibi for Dachshund, for herself and for the other members of the Round Table. The article made it clear that Dachshund was nowhere to be found.

Dorothy was frustrated with this but even more annoyed that the article never mentioned the one thing that she really did try to convey to Battersby—that the police knew full well that the Sandman had killed Mayflower. Battersby evidently wanted to keep that question unanswered.

"So he can keep beating up on us," Benchley had said.

"And keep the story of Mayflower's murder going, so he can keep up the sales of his crappy newspaper," Dorothy said.

Apparently, the *Knickerbocker*'s readership was high indeed, because the lobby of the Algonquin was once again crowded with loiterers, interlopers and busybodies hoping to catch a glimpse of the members of the Round Table or overhear a snippet of their conversation. All eyes turned toward them as they crossed the lobby. It was an uncomfortable feeling for both of them, since Dorothy preferred to be inconspicuous and Benchley wanted attention only when he told a joke.

"Mrs. Parker!" called Alfred, who manned the front desk. "There's a telegram here for you."

She and Benchley angled their way through the people toward the front desk. She unfolded the yellow telegram sheet that Alfred handed her. She turned in toward Benchley to read it so no one could look over her shoulder.

"It's from Lou Neeley, Mayflower's beau," she whispered to Benchley. "He remembered the name of the lawyer: Wallace Ramshackle. His office is on Seventh Avenue."

"I take it you want to strike out immediately?"

She looked around at the people milling about the

lobby. "And miss lunch with a hundred of our newest, closest friends?"

But she knew that Benchley enjoyed the camaraderie of lunch at the Round Table—eavesdroppers or no eavesdroppers.

"Perhaps I'll go see him myself," she said. "Give the others my regards. Except for Woollcott. Give him my—"

"Mrs. Parker?"

An errand boy, about the age of thirteen, stood beside her. He had on a blue uniform with gold piping and gold buttons. He was as tall as she. "Are you Mrs. Parker?"

"Yes," she said.

"There's a man outside. He says he has a surprise for you."

"Right now?"

The boy nodded.

"Is that all?" she asked.

The boy nodded again. Benchley handed him a quarter and the boy disappeared.

"You go have lunch, Fred," she said. "I'll let you know what transpires."

She could see him wavering. She was relieved when he didn't go. Good old Benchley.

"Perhaps I'll tag along, if you don't mind," he said. "We can have lunch later. Besides, I love surprises."

They moved toward the entrance. Again she wanted to hold his hand. But in this crowd, she didn't even dare put her arm through his—

"Pssst!"

She almost didn't see him. Had she not caught a movement out of the corner of her eye, had she not turned her head, she wouldn't have seen him—a familiar face peeking through the fronds of a large potted plant, tucked away in an alcove.

She grabbed Benchley's arm and dragged him with her.

The face was thin and pale, the eyes still droopy. But

the scraggly beard was gone. Now, below the birdlike nose, there was just a wispy, light brown mustache, like a moth about to flutter away.

"Billy," she said softly. "What are you doing here? Where have you been?"

"I've been staying up in New Haven with a friend of my family," Faulkner said. "But I couldn't stay away forever."

She tried not to draw attention. She didn't want to be any more conspicuous than she already was, both for her sake and for Faulkner's.

She said, "Did you just send that messenger boy? An unsigned telegram would have done the trick."

"Messenger boy?"

If Faulkner hadn't sent the message to meet outside, who had?

"Forget it," she said. "We can't talk here. Go upstairs to my apartment. Lock the door and wait for us there. We'll be back soon." She slipped him a key.

Not looking back, she and Benchley moved quickly toward the hotel's entrance. Once outside, on the sidewalk, she turned to him. "What do you make of that?"

"That Billy is a strange bird," Benchley said, looking up and down the street. "Speaking of strange, there seems to be no one here waiting— Look out!"

Tires screeched. A horse whinnied. A car horn blared. To her left, a truck was suddenly rushing at her. It jumped the curb. The front end smashed apart the back corner of a horse cart. Shards of wood flew everywhere. Then the truck was on the sidewalk, almost on top of her before she could even move.

Arms grabbed her. She saw the truck's grille zip just inches in front of her eyes. Then she was pulled into the door of an automobile. The door swung closed. The car lurched forward.

She sat up. She heard a loud clang. She looked out the car's window to see that the truck had struck the light pole in front of the Algonquin. On the side of the truck's cargo panel was printed in large letters: NEW CANAAN BIBLE CO.

Benchley, who was sitting in the car beside her, looked out the window, too.

"I've heard of Bible-thumping," he said, "but that's taking it too far."

As the car pulled away, she could see the truck slowly reverse. The truck lurched forward, puttered off the curb and merged back into traffic. Then the car turned the corner and the truck was lost from view.

"What do you make of that?" Benchley asked her.

"Divine intervention?" she said.

"A Holy Roller?"

"The Ford of Gideon?"

One of the men in the seat facing them said, "You came close to meeting your Maker, sure. I think we saved your souls."

The man seated across from her wore a hat and a long coat. The man sitting next to him wore the same.

"The biggest piggy bank in the world couldn't save my soul," Dorothy said.

She recognized them as Mickey Finn's men from the greasy spoon. They were inside what appeared to be a long limousine. Another man in a similar hat drove the car.

"Well, it's not your soul we're interested in anyway," the man said. "But lucky for us, and for you, we showed up when we did."

"Lucky?" Benchley said. "You mean that wasn't one of your boys behind the wheel of that truck?"

The man looked at Benchley as if he were stupid.

Dorothy explained, "A messenger boy just came for us. He said there was a man waiting outside with a surprise. Certainly that was your trick to kidnap us. You used the truck to scare us so you could grab us like a pair of frightened rabbits."

"Scare you?" the man said. "Lady, whoever was driving that truck wanted to do more than scare you. If we hadn't come along when we did, you'd be rabbit stew by now."

"So it wasn't you who sent the messenger boy? It wasn't one of your fellows who drove that truck?"

"Course not," the man said. "If we don't bring you to Mr. Finn like he wants, see, we'd be the ones meeting our Maker."

She turned to Benchley. "Then, who sent the messenger boy?"

"That's easy," the other man said. "It was whoever drove the truck."

"And the message is," Benchley said, "drop dead."

Chapter 29

The limousine rolled through a part of the city that Dorothy Parker and Robert Benchley didn't know well. She figured they were in some corner of the Bowery. The few folks on the street looked down-at-the-heel. Many of the storefronts were dilapidated, their windows dark or broken.

The car slowed down in front of what appeared to be a large abandoned brewery building. The front door was boarded up. Across the boards, someone had painted in whitewash, *Prohibition, go to hell!*

The limousine slowly rounded the corner. On this street was a short row of derelict stores, backed up against the brewery. Only one of the stores still appeared to be in business. The car came to a stop in front of it: PROF. ODDBALL'S MAGIC & NOVELTY EMPORIUM.

One of the men swung open the car door and stepped out. He held the door open. "Get out."

"A magic shop?" Benchley said to Dorothy.

"This is how they make people disappear," she said, then took her time getting out of the car. Benchley followed. The other man got out, and then the car drove away. Dorothy was surprised to realize it was not a long black limousine, but a long white one.

"Get inside," said the first man.

The windows of the magic shop were filled with tricks, props and curiosities. Magic rings. Magic boxes. A crystal ball. Sneezing powder. Itching powder. An assortment of colored silks. A monkey's paw. An upturned top hat with a glassy-eyed, stuffed rabbit peeking out. All the things were covered in a thin gray layer of dust.

Dorothy opened the door and stepped inside, with Benchley and the two men close behind her. The place was dark and smelled musty. The shelves were filled with all kinds of cheap novelties, games, toys and magic tricks. But they all appeared untouched, as if no one had bought anything here in a long time. An enormous, ornate cash register sat on the counter, with nobody behind it. No one was running the store.

"In the back," said the man.

She went along a narrow aisle toward the back of the little shop. She saw a figure in the dimness coming toward her. As she approached the figure, she could make out that it was a woman. The woman was abnormally tall, with a dark blue coat and a brimless cloche. Shadows of other people appeared to be behind the woman. But when Dorothy slowed her step, the woman hesitated, too.

That was when she realized she was looking at her own reflection. It wasn't a regular mirror, though. It was a fun house mirror that elongated her shape. No wonder she didn't recognize herself in the dark. She moved forward confidently. She didn't want Finn's men to think she had been fooled by such a dumb trick.

She went right up to the mirror and looked at her seven-foot-high reflection. So that's what she would look like if she were as tall as Robert Sherwood. Maybe being petite was not so bad after all, she thought.

"I must stop working so hard," she said.

"Why do you say that?" Benchley kindly responded.

"Look at me. I've stretched myself way too thin."

Behind them, one of the men shuffled impatiently. "Shove it, lady."

"Pardon me?" she said. "*You* shove it, pal."

"The mirror. Shove it forward."

She faced the mirror and placed her hands on it, meeting the lengthened reflection of her own hands. She pushed.

Silently, the mirror glided away from her.

It was a secret door. She looked inside at what must have once been a storeroom. The room was dark and empty, but on the far side of the room was an open doorway. Bright light, music and laughter came through that doorway.

"Go on," the man said. "Mr. Finn is waiting for you."

As they stepped into the large, brightly lit room, Mickey Finn jumped up. His yellow, polluted grin spread across his handsome face. The sounds of fiddle and piano came from somewhere.

"Hail! Hail! The gang's all here," he sang, prancing toward them with a sideways, crablike jig. "We've been waiting for you. Couldn't start the party without you."

He was in his shirtsleeves, his jacket draped over a chair. He had a glass mug of beer in one hand and a large cigar in the other.

"You and you," he called to two men slouched in armchairs. "Get up. Give 'em a place to sit."

They were in a bar as big as a cafeteria. Dorothy realized it was the employee tavern inside the brewery building. Before Prohibition, such a room would have served as the lunchroom as well as the after-hours hangout for the brewery workers, she knew. Now it was the private hideaway for Mickey Finn and his gang.

Most of the bar tables and benches had been removed or pushed to the walls. In their place were armchairs and a few couches. About ten or so of Finn's men sat or milled about. A white-haired old man with furry black eyebrows stood behind the long bar. A trio of statuesque women in flashy dresses—low cut and high hemmed—stood poised on a makeshift stage at the far end of the room. One of the women (a real beauty, Dorothy had to admit, despite the streetwalker dress) alighted from the stage and came forward with a bewitching grace.

"Now, listen," Mickey Finn said, steering them into seats. "I want to apologize for the other night. I wasn't acting like myself. I'm a likable guy, really. You'll see. I'll prove it to you. How about a cigar for the gentleman? A cigarette for the lady?"

He hooked his fingers, and one of his men jumped up with a wooden box full of cigars. The beautiful woman produced a silver cigarette case. Someone shoved a cigar into Benchley's mouth and a cigarette into Dorothy's. Finn snapped a match on his thumbnail, and the flame danced in his hand. With a fluid motion, he lit her cigarette and Benchley's cigar. Benchley didn't notice the cigar. He was gawking at the stunning harlot.

"Let's get these two swell folks something to wet their whistle. How about a goblet of choice wine for the lady? And a mug of fresh beer for the gentleman?"

Benchley's attention was momentarily distracted away from the woman. "A mug of fresh . . . *beer*?"

Beer had never been Benchley's drink, Dorothy knew. But since Prohibition had gone into effect, good beer had been nearly impossible to acquire. Liquor could be smuggled in, but casks of beer? That was unheard of. The current saying went: "Prohibition succeeded in replacing good beer with bad gin."

"Lucy, fetch this estimable man a mug of our finest. Do you know my Miss Lucy?" Finn said as the woman sashayed toward the bar. "Ah, I can see the gentleman does."

Dorothy leaned toward Benchley, who was transfixed by the woman's posterior.

"Who is she?"

"Lucy Goosey, the famous stripper," Benchley mumbled. "Or . . . so I've heard."

"A striptease *artist*," Finn corrected affably. "She's an artist."

"Oh, right," Dorothy said. "I've seen her oeuvre in the Louvre."

"Aye," Finn said with a wink. "She has quite a body of work."

The woman returned with a mug of beer, a glass of red wine and a smirk on her face. "Here you are."

Benchley fumbled taking the mug from her hand, nearly spilling it. He raised the mug in a sort of toast to her; then he took a long drink and smacked his lips. His mustache was coated in foam.

Dorothy did not feel the same about the wine. "Have anything stronger?"

"You name it," Finn said hospitably.

"Haig and Haig?"

"Yes and yes."

Finn snapped his fingers and yet another man jumped up and quickly returned with a highball glass full of scotch.

"Now," said Finn, dropping into a chair opposite them and taking a long pull on his cigar. "You are probably wondering why I called you here to my little sanctum sanctorum."

"I couldn't hazard a guess," Dorothy said.

"I could hazard one," Benchley said. "But my doctor told me to stop. Hazardous to my health."

"We wouldn't want that, sure." Finn smiled. "Like I say, I'm a likable fella. Everyone likes me." He turned to his gang with a shout. "Everyone likes me. Don't they?"

Like a chorus, they sang his praises.

"Absolutely, boss."

"You bet."

"One hunnert percent!"

Only Lucy Goosey remained silent, like a beautiful statue. Finn turned to her, waiting. He seemed to want her approval most of all. "Everyone likes me. Don't they, doll?"

She gave him a reluctant smile. "What's not to like?"

Satisfied, Finn turned his wide yellow grin to Dorothy and Benchley. "There you are, see? We're all friends now. Just like that." He snapped his fingers. "So, tell me, where's our other friend, Mr. Dachshund? Wouldn't it be great if he could join us?"

"That would be dandy," Dorothy said. "If we only knew where he was."

Finn cackled a knowing laugh. "Aye, that's the thing, isn't it?" He changed tack. "There was an article about you in the newspaper today. Did you happen to read it?"

"In the *Knickerbocker*?" she said. "The only place for that newspaper is the bottom of a birdcage."

Finn ignored this. "Seems our friend Dachshund might need something of an alibi. And you two want to prove that Dachshund's alibi is all tied up with my very old friend Knut Sanderson." He leaned forward with a fist on each knee. "Now, here I am—I've got my new friend Dachshund on the right hand and my old friend Sanderson on the left. And these two friends of mine were apparently working on some business together. That pretty much makes it my business, too."

"I don't understand," she said. "Didn't the Sandman work for you?"

"Here and there, he did, sure."

"Here and there?" she said. "So he didn't work *only* for you? He was a freelancer?"

"A freelancer?" Finn cackled again. "You could say that. Only most of the lancing he did was for me. And it wasn't free. I'll assure you of that."

"So who's to say you didn't hire him to kill Mayflower?"

He smiled. "Ah, but if I did, we wouldn't be having this nice little get-together, now, would we?"

"Then who else did he work for?"

"Whoever might pay. Certainly none of my competitors, though. He was smart not to do that. But he did . . . other types of things. Like what he did for our friend Dachshund."

"Dachshund didn't hire Sanderson to kill Mayflower," she said. "Don't be stupid."

Everyone in the room suddenly froze.

Finn turned red. "Stupid? You just said I'm stupid?"

"I didn't say you were stupid," she muttered quickly. "I meant you shouldn't believe a bunch of stupid lies from a newspaper that's only interested in selling more newspapers. What I mean to say is, how can you be so sure it was Dachshund who hired the Sandman?"

Finn no longer appeared on the verge of fury, but he spoke sharply. "Knut had a fancy Park Avenue apartment in the Reginald. He worked out of there, you could say. Well, after we heard he was dead, we went through every inch of that place. Couldn't find a trace of who he was working for. But he was smart, you see. Not sloppy. He wasn't the type to leave names and numbers lying around. He never slipped up."

"At least once he did," she said. "We gave him the slip."

Finn leaned back thoughtfully, exhaling cigar smoke. "Aye, that you did. And that's the nail in the coffin. Knut Sanderson was always careful not to get caught. But, just like a Swede, he was also careful about getting paid. He wouldn't kill the goose that laid the golden eggs, you see, unless he had a good reason."

"Have you seen Dachshund?" she said. "He's not a goose who lays golden eggs."

"Unfortunately, I haven't had the pleasure." Finn smiled. "But I believe Dachshund did employ Sanderson, and at the time when the three of you met him, Dachshund hadn't yet paid him. Maybe in the space between wanting to kill Dachshund and wanting to get paid, Sanderson let his guard down a little and you three were able to slip through."

"Still doesn't make sense," she said. "Why would Dachshund want to kill Mayflower?"

"How in blazes should I know?" Finn jumped up out of his armchair. "All I know is Sanderson did it. And Dachshund was the one who put him up to it."

She sighed. This was the same dumb argument she'd had with Captain Church and Detective O'Rannigan. She looked to Benchley for support, but Benchley's eyes were drinking in Lucy Goosey as his mouth was drinking in beer.

"You'll hate yourself in the morning," she muttered to him.

"It's just one beer," he said.

"That's not what I'm talking about." She turned back to Mickey Finn. "You admit that the Sandman murdered Leland Mayflower."

"Sure he did. And Dachshund hired him to do it."

"Did the Sandman usually use such things as fountain pens to murder people? I guess a bobby pin wasn't at hand."

Finn dropped back into his chair. He frowned at this insult to his memory of Sanderson. But apparently, this question bothered him, too.

Lucy Goosey slid onto the arm of Finn's chair. "It's obvious," she said. "Whoever wanted to kill Mayflower wanted to send a message. You reap what you sow. You know, Mick, like when that two-timing fella who owned that concrete business turned up at the bottom of the Hudson, his stomach and mouth filled up with concre—"

"Nah, that's not it," Finn said sourly. "Knut Sanderson didn't deal in poetic justice, like some of us do. I think there's another reason why he used that fountain pen."

"Why?" Benchley said.

With a thoughtful expression, Finn tapped the ash off his cigar. "I'm not ready to say why just yet. That's why I need to talk to Dachshund. You bring him to me. By this Friday. Or else."

Dorothy laughed. "Or else what? We'll wind up at the bottom of the Hudson?"

Finn leaned forward with a wink. "Even that wouldn't shut you up, I'm sure. No, I'm thinking you do me a favor, and I'll do you a favor. I know a lot of people, and I know a lot of things. For instance, I know you go to Tony Soma's speakeasy. I supply Tony with his liquor. So it's simple. You get me Dachshund by Friday, and I make sure Tony's supply doesn't run dry."

Benchley, empty glass in hand, turned white. "You wouldn't."

Dorothy had a stiff backbone. But she knew even she couldn't suffer the loss of Tony's.

"See?" Finn said with a wide yellow grin, arms wide. "I want you to like me. We're friends. This is how friends do things for each other."

Benchley's voice wavered. "But you're threatening to take away our booze. How can you say we're friends?"

"Take away your booze?" Finn was genuinely shocked and hurt. "Not at all. I'll make certain you and Tony keep getting it, as long as you do what I need. We help each other out, see?"

Dorothy muttered into her glass, "If this is how you treat your friends, I'd certainly hate to see how you treat your enemies."

"Yes," Lucy Goosey said, leaning forward. "You certainly would."

Chapter 30

Several hours later, cold and drenched from the rain, Robert Benchley shivered in the dark under the awning of the Reginald. This had been Sanderson's apartment building; Mickey Finn had said so that very afternoon. But now that he was here, staring through the glass door to the little lobby, Benchley wondered why he had even thought up this idea—to break into and search the Sandman's apartment for *any* clue about who had hired the Sandman to kill Mayflower. Now that he was here, he didn't want to go through with it.

But he had told Dorothy Parker he would do it, and now there was nothing to do but go ahead with the wrong-headed plan.

Benchley's first obstacle was the doorman. The heavy-lidded, slack-jawed, uniformed brute sat slouched behind a narrow desk just inside the lobby. Not only did Benchley have to get past the doorman, but he also had to somehow wheedle out of him the Sandman's room number.

Sanderson wasn't listed in the city directory, of course. Benchley had at least determined that first. And Benchley could see there was no posted list of residents anywhere in the lobby.

What could he do? Could he trick the doorman into telling him Sanderson's apartment number? Maybe Benchley could say he was a friend of Sanderson's, that Sanderson had borrowed a book and he needed to get it back? Well, it was worth a try.

Benchley opened the door and entered. To be sure he had the doorman's full attention and sympathy, he shook himself, flinging rain droplets everywhere. A few drops landed on the doorman's jacket. The man frowned.

"Ah, good evening, good sir." Benchley approached him. "An acquaintance of mine by the name of Knut Sanderson lives here. I don't believe he's at home right now. But he borrowed a book of mine. Perhaps you'd be so kind as to show me into his apartment."

"Sorry," the doorman said without a touch of actual sorrow. "Can't let you in."

Oh, forget it, Benchley thought. He'd just have to do this the old-fashioned way. He pulled out his wallet and laid a five-dollar bill on the table.

"Well," Benchley said awkwardly, "you don't have to actually show me his apartment. Perhaps you could simply walk me up there and unlock the door? I'll take it from there."

The doorman pocketed the bill. "Sorry. Can't leave my post."

Benchley laid another five on the table. "In that case, could you loan me your skeleton key?"

The bill disappeared. "Sorry. Can't do that."

Benchley shook his head as if to clear it. The man would have to give in soon, out of sheer indebtedness.

He put down another five. His voice was impatient. "Can you at least tell me which apartment he's in?"

"Sorry. Can't do that either."

Benchley exhaled sharply. "This is my last five dollars. What *can* you do for me?"

He threw down the bill. The doorman snatched it up.

"Nothing, mister. The doorman who was on shift before me accidentally went home with both the master key and the apartment directory. I couldn't help you if you forked over a million."

Benchley was exasperated. "Well, why didn't you tell me that ten bucks ago?"

Across town, Dorothy Parker and William Faulkner huddled together under an umbrella, walking quickly and discussing their plan. Since Mickey Finn and the police and who knew who else were looking for Faulkner, he needed a new place to stay. Their goal was to move Faulkner into Alexander Woollcott's apartment and move Woollcott into Dorothy's apartment.

She wasn't quite sure how to accomplish this.

"We're at Wit's End," she said.

"That we are," Faulkner agreed.

"No, that's what I call Woollcott's place—Wit's End."

The apartment building was at the very end of Fifty-second Street, overlooking the East River. They entered the building, went up the elevator and arrived before Woollcott's door.

He answered in a red silk Oriental robe. Gold-embroidered dragons crawled up along his paunch as though scaling a mountain. His beady eyes examined them through his owllike glasses.

"Look what washed up from the rain," his nasal voice sneered.

Before Dorothy could speak, Woollcott turned argumentative. He poked a chubby finger at Faulkner.

"What do you mean by bringing this known fugitive to my quiet quarters?"

"Fugitive? The other day, you called him an all-American hero," she said. "This hero needs a place to stay."

"Why darken my doorstep? Have him stay at your lovely abode, your haven for wayward boys."

"He can't," she said. "The thing is, the police *are* looking for him." She didn't mention that Mickey Finn was looking for him, too. "Perhaps he could stay the night here."

"I certainly don't want him here. And even if I did,

which I don't, there's no room. There's hardly enough room for me."

"That's the other thing. I need to stay here, too."

Woollcott rolled his eyes. "There most certainly is not enough room for three."

"Right," she said pleasantly. "So you could stay at my apartment at the 'Gonk."

"Now you're talking bald-faced balderdash."

"Why not?"

"Well, for one, I lunch there every day."

"So?"

"So, have you heard that genteel old aphorism 'Don't shit where you eat'?"

She shrugged. "So go shit someplace else."

"Knut Sanderson," Benchley repeated. "Does that ring a bell?"

"Beats me," the doorman said. "I just started yesterday."

"I'm sure that someone must have told you that hordes and fleets of policemen have been tramping through here. Which room did they go to?"

"The police? Because this guy borrowed your lousy book?"

Benchley thought a moment. He was stumped.

"The mail," he said finally. "Have any tenants not picked up their mail in a while?"

"I dunno. Mail room's over there. Take a peek for yourself."

Benchley rounded the doorman's desk and peered behind a wall of mailboxes. He scanned the cubbyholes. Four or five were packed full of mail. He looked at the names pasted above each of these compartments. On the third try, he found it. At the top of this particular pile was a copy of *American Legion Weekly*, the servicemen's magazine that Harold Ross edited. On the mailing label was "K. Sanderson. Apt. 1027."

Benchley thanked the doorman and took the eleva-

tor up to the tenth floor. Halfway down the hallway he
found number 1027. The door was locked. How could
he get in?

He knocked on the door of the adjacent apartment.

A young, affluent-looking couple answered the door.
The husband had a cocktail glass in his hand.

"Hello, I'm the window inspector," Benchley said of-
ficiously. "I'm here to check your windows."

"At eight o'clock at night?"

"Windows never close, nor do we," Benchley said and
hurried past the couple. He went to the back bedroom
and opened the window. He looked down. There was a
narrow ledge about twelve inches wide. Beyond that, in
the darkness far below, he could see the headlamps of
cars crawling along the street. About ten feet to his left
was a window to Sanderson's apartment.

Better not think too much about this part, he told himself. *Better to climb out there immediately. Ready, set . . .*
He couldn't move.

"Can I assist you?" came the young husband's voice.

Benchley spun around. The young man stood wide-
eyed and wondering.

"Matter of fact, you can," Benchley said. He grabbed
the man's cocktail glass and drained it. "A Manhattan.
Delightful."

Benchley turned back to the window. He stepped
out onto the ledge and teetered momentarily before
clutching to the wall behind him. With his back against
the wall, he sidestepped to the left, inching along to the
Sandman's apartment.

It was much colder up here than on the sidewalk. The
wind and rain tore at his coat and pulled his hat right
off his head. Instinctively, he grabbed for it and nearly
pitched forward. He flattened himself against the rain-
soaked wall, his heart pounding furiously. The hat disappeared into the darkness.

What was he doing out on this slippery ledge? He
had volunteered to be here. This was his idea. *We can't*

let Tony Soma's be shut down, he had said to Dorothy. We need to do something—anything—to link the Sandman to the real killer, to get Mickey Finn off the scent. The only place to look is the Sandman's apartment.

Dorothy had said something about exonerating Billy Faulkner. Yes, that was important, too, Benchley had replied. *But Tony's cannot close!*

Now his thoughts about Tony's were literally up in the air. Maybe, just maybe, could they get by without Tony's?

Then he thought better of it. So what if he fell to his death? Death was preferable, after all, if living meant going without a steady and reliable supply of liquor and good times.

The rain stung his face. It was a lot windier than he had expected. A sudden gust of wind grabbed him. It felt like it could pull him right off the ledge. The wind whipped the tails of his coat around his legs, and he felt that his feet might slip out from under him, flinging him out into the night air, only to fall into the dark street more than a hundred feet down. His fingers scrabbled at any indentation in the solid brick wall.

"Hello," the young man cried, leaning out the window. "Do you want to get into the apartment next door? Is that why you're out there?"

Benchley didn't—couldn't—answer. He was too petrified to speak.

"We have a key, you know," the young man said.

Benchley's clenched teeth chattered. "Well, w-why didn't you t-t-tell me that t-t-ten floors ago?"

Woollcott, cloaked in his Oriental silk robe, his arms folded over his wide body, appeared as immovable as a big brass Buddha. There was no chance he would let them stay.

Dorothy stepped toward Woollcott and whispered, "What about our little secret?"

Woollcott's eyes zeroed in on hers. "What secret?"

"You know."

"Oh, yes," he muttered conspiratorially. "You're squandering your talent on poems about ponies, peonies and petty heartbreak? It's not such a secret. The word is out."

The insufferable windbag!

She forced herself to be calm. "No, the one about how Mayflower hoodwinked you to land that Saber fountain pen endorsement."

He cinched his robe tighter and pointed his pinched little nose in the air. "Go ahead. Tell everyone. It's water under the bridge to me."

Just the day before, Woollcott had nearly thrown a tantrum when she had forced him to explain Mayflower's gambit. Now he acted as if he didn't care?

Finally, she made her weakest appeal of all—to his compassion.

"Have a heart," she said. "Where's your sense of charity? You can't turn the poor boy out on the street."

"I'm not turning him out on the street. If he needs a place to stay, there are many fine hotel rooms in this cosmopolitan metropolis. Now, kindly remove your Dachshund from my doorstep. Good night."

This was impossible. She was indeed at Wit's End, literally and figuratively.

Faulkner, apparently giving up, began his retreat. Dorothy heard cellophane crinkling in his pocket.

"Hold on," she said to Woollcott. "Let me sweeten the deal."

She gestured to Faulkner to hand over the wrapped box. Faulkner, not comprehending at first, finally drew the flat box from the deep pocket of his long coat. It was a box of liquor-filled chocolate cordials. She handed it to Woollcott.

His eyes widened. He panted. "Chocolate . . . *and* liquor? Where did you get these?"

Truth was, Mickey Finn had pressed it into her hands on their way out of his bootlegger's den. She had refused the token gift at first, but Finn was insistent—it was just easier to accept it. Later, she had carelessly handed it to Faulkner to carry. How surprising that she found a use for such a gift so quickly.

"Oh, do you like them?" she said indifferently. "I have a whole crate of them back at my apartment."

This, unfortunately for Woollcott, was not true.

But Woollcott was suddenly a one-man beehive of activity. He pirouetted away, calling over his shoulder, "Well, as you say, one must be charitable. One can't turn a poor boy out in the street. I'll pack my valise—just for one night, of course."

Benchley slid the borrowed key into the door of the Sandman's apartment.

After he had come back in from the ledge and into the neighbors' apartment, he had joined them for another Manhattan or two. What nice people they were. He didn't have the heart to confess that he was not really a window inspector. But perhaps they had figured that out.

In the course of conversation, they told him that having Sanderson next door had frightened them. When Sanderson had first moved in, he hadn't bothered to change the locks. The nice couple still had the key that the previous neighbor had given them in case of emergency. But they were too intimidated by Sanderson to offer to return the key. So they kept it.

When the Sandman was found dead, the couple didn't know whom to give the key to. It was a hot potato, they said. They were happy to hand it over to Benchley. They gave him one more Manhattan "for the road."

Benchley had not yet had dinner. And he had had only beer for lunch, courtesy of Mickey Finn. So the cocktails were working their magic. He had some trouble finding the light switch, but eventually he flicked it on. One bare overhead bulb illuminated the room.

The Sandman's large studio apartment would have

been elegant, had anyone bothered to decorate the place. There were a few very expensive, very ostentatious items of furniture—a bamboo bar and stools, an oxblood leather sofa, a walnut gun cabinet. The rest was junk—a card table in the kitchen, a wooden orange crate for a makeshift shoe rack (which was filled with fancy shoes and boots) and a cast-iron bed that looked like an army cot. It was as though the Sandman had had the money and desire to buy a few items he considered valuable and either didn't know or didn't care to fix up the rest of the place to match.

Benchley didn't really know what to look for. What might connect the Sandman to Mayflower? Or, what missing link might connect the Sandman to the real killer—the one who hired the Sandman . . . the one who then killed the Sandman in this very room?

Benchley wandered around the room. Old newspapers and a few wax paper sandwich wrappers littered the card table. The kitchen cabinets held nothing but cans of beans and sardines. The door of the oven, where the Sandman's body had been found, gaped open. Benchley hurriedly turned away.

In a far corner, he saw another orange crate and went over and crouched down to inspect it. The crate was stuffed with playing cards, poker chips, some handcuffs, a blackjack, a rope, a lead pipe and other miscellaneous junk. Nothing.

Benchley scratched his head. Mickey Finn and his boys had already searched the place and found nothing. What could he hope to find?

Benchley stood up quickly—too quickly—and the room started to swim. He braced himself against the wall. His eyes came to rest on the only picture in the apartment. It was a large black-and-white photograph, about a foot and a half wide. The photo was of some fifty men in army uniforms, posing in rows for the picture. A few men in the bottom row held a sign: THE FIGHTIN' THIRD: 3RD NEW YORK INFANTRY, 108TH INFANTRY REGIMENT, 54TH

BRIGADE, 27TH DIVISION. BELLICOURT, AISNE, FRANCE. OCTO-
BER 1918.

So, Sanderson had fought in France. . . . Benchley
scanned the cheerless gray faces for a young, doughboy
version of the Sandman. But doing this made Benchley's head swim again.

There was a sound. Someone was at the door. On
blind instinct—rare for him—Benchley switched out the
light and turned to hide in the darkness.

As soon as he did this, he silently cursed himself for a
fool. It was probably just that nice young couple coming
over to check on him.

He shuffled to where he thought he had switched off
the light, but he couldn't find the switch, couldn't even
find the wall. Now he was stuck, and he cursed himself
again for acting so rashly.

Then he heard a metallic squeak—someone was test-
ing the doorknob. Something told him it wasn't the nice
couple. Had he locked the door behind him? He didn't
think so. Of course he'd left it unlocked so that any murderous stranger could come in and strangle him in the
pitch dark.

He turned around and banged his leg against something hard. It was the cast-iron bed. As quickly and quietly as he could, he dropped to the floor and slid under
the bed.

The door opened. The light clicked on. Someone
stood in the doorway. Under the bed, Benchley could
see only a nondescript pair of men's black shoes and
men's dark trousers. The shoes didn't move for a very
long time. The man, whoever he was, seemed to suspect
there was someone else in the room, Benchley thought.

Almost imperceptibly at first, Benchley began to
feel a tingling sensation. His face had been against the
floor for only a few moments. Could his cheek be falling asleep already? The tingling turned into a prickling
sensation, an unsettling feeling of movement along his
skin. Then there seemed to be a shadow in his vision. He

realized he was staring into the eyes and antennae of a large brown cockroach perched on his cheek.

It took every last ounce of courage and nerve for Benchley not to scream and flail about like a six-year-old girl.

Woollcott seemed almost giddy as he climbed into a taxi with Dorothy and Faulkner bound for the Algonquin Hotel. He reevaluated Faulkner with approval, chattering ridiculously.

"You've certainly cleaned yourself up, my lad," Woollcott said. "You've shaved. You've lost that bohemian coat. Good for you, young man. Writing is a business, after all, and one must dress for business, don't you agree? That isn't to say that one should lack style or go without a measure of artistic flair. . . ."

Dorothy's mind wandered. She was feeling guilty about letting Benchley go to the Sandman's apartment alone. Still, the Sandman was dead. And as long as there was nothing mechanical there for Benchley to get entangled with, he should be fine.

Woollcott and Faulkner were hitting it off, talking about their favorite books—Woollcott doing most of the talking while gobbling up the liquor-filled chocolates.

Soon, they arrived at the Algonquin. Woollcott bounded out the door, leaving the empty box of chocolates on the seat. Dorothy looked at Faulkner apologetically.

"I don't have a dime to pay the fare."

Faulkner pulled out a carefully folded bill. "It's my bottom dollar." He handed it to the taxi driver, received a dime in change, and they got out.

Upstairs, Dorothy unlocked the door to her small suite. The room, as usual, smelled like dog. Woodrow Wilson jumped off the couch and trotted over. She scratched the dog behind the ears, feeling guilty and sorry for the third time in almost as many minutes. Here she was, about to leave the poor pooch all alone with Woollcott. And how did Woody respond to her treachery? With a cheery little four-step dance and a frenetically wagging tail. How she adored and envied the boundless optimism of dogs!

Woollcott, for his part, was staggering around nearly half-drunk and looking out of the corner of his eyes for more of the as-promised booze-filled chocolates.

"Perhaps you might have something a man could eat?" he said, not so obliquely.

She ignored him and hurried to her bedroom, quickly stuffing clothes in an overnight bag. She cursed herself for not thinking of doing this beforehand.

She slung the bag over her shoulder and went back into the living room. She patted Woody—now looking puzzled—on the head. Then she turned to Woollcott.

"Now, I have your word that you won't mention to anyone where we are, right?" she said.

"As a man of many words," he said, "you may rest assured that your secret is safe with me."

She motioned to Faulkner that it was time to go.

Woollcott followed them to the door. "One other thing . . . You had mentioned that carton of chocolates—"

"Oh, look around," she said. "It's here somewhere. Unless the dog ate them all."

She left Woody and Woollcott sizing each other up as she closed the door.

The pair of shoes crossed the hardwood floor of Knut Sanderson's nearly empty apartment. Under the cover of the sound of the clacking shoes, Benchley slapped the cockroach off his face.

The man went to the far wall and stopped.

The cockroach landed beside Benchley's ear. He could feel its hairy legs flutter beside his earlobe. The sensation—its presence—was intolerable.

The man in the shoes was doing something—pulling something, disrupting something—Benchley didn't know what.

Benchley knew he should pay attention to what the

man was doing, but the cockroach was driving him mad. It quivered and clawed at his hair, his scalp, chilling him and making his skin crawl.

That was it. He couldn't take it anymore. He clutched at the cockroach and flung it away. The huge brown insect skittered across the polished wood floor, skidding to a stop in the dead center of the room.

The man in the shoes spun around. The shoes raced across the floor—the clattering, thumping sound reverberated in Benchley's ear like thunder. The man stopped just before the cockroach. Benchley could see the bug helpless on its back, its tiny clawlike legs grasping and flailing desperately. The man raised one shoe and stomped the bug without hesitation.

Benchley held his breath. Did the man know he was under the bed? The man stood still a moment, as though looking around. Then the man came toward the bed. The shoes were inches from Benchley's face. The man raised the shoe that had stomped the cockroach—Benchley could see its liquefied, flattened body on the sole—and wiped the bottom of the shoe against the edge of the mattress. The shoe came down. The cockroach was gone.

The shoes moved toward the door. The light went out. The door closed with a bang.

Dorothy and Faulkner had settled in nicely at Woollcott's apartment. They were lounging on his sofa, wearing his robes, smoking his cigarettes and sipping his hidden stash of brandy.

"I wonder how Aleck is holding up right now at the Algonquin," she said lazily, although she was more concerned about Woody than Woollcott.

"What's next?" Faulkner asked. "Are you any closer to finding who killed Mayflower—that is, who killed the Sandman?"

"In a word, yes. And no."

She described how she and Benchley had almost

been flattened by the Bible truck. "So we hit a nerve with someone. We just don't know which nerve we hit."

"Or who the someone is."

"As for finding the someone, we have until Friday. Otherwise, Finn will put an end to Tony Soma's."

And put an end to Faulkner, too, but she didn't mention that. She merely described to him how Mickey Finn had shaken them down for some answers and had given them the Friday deadline.

"What will you do between now and then?"

She shrugged and sucked her cigarette.

"What about that Bible truck?" he said.

"What about it?"

"Did you look up the company?"

"The New Canaan Bible Company? It wasn't in the directory. Heywood Broun has a friend at the *Wall Street Journal*. Tomorrow I'll ask him to call his friend to track the company down."

"And what if he can't?"

"Oh, don't worry." She sipped the brandy. "Something will emerge."

Benchley poked his head out from underneath the bed and exhaled. Before this, he had waited a moment to be sure that the man was gone. It seemed he had been holding his breath for an eternity. Finally, he crawled out from under the bed before any more cockroaches decided to use his face for a playground.

He stumbled toward the wall and flicked on the light.

He looked around the room. Something was different.

Then he figured it out. The far wall was bare.

The Sandman's army photograph was gone.

Chapter 31

Wallace Ramshackle, Esquire, had a face like an Easter ham: round, plump and pink. His oily gray hair was parted neatly down the middle. He gazed at Dorothy over half-moon glasses.

"You'd like what?" he croaked.

She shifted in her chair. She wore the closest thing she had to a formal suit, a slender wool serge ensemble in gray with a black felt cloche. She felt fairly present-able and, having had an excellent night's sleep in Woollcott's plush feather bed, she felt fairly confident for this morning's meeting with this aging attorney.

"I'd like to see your contract with Leland Mayflower. I was an acquaintance of his."

"Out of the question. That's an outright violation of the attorney-client privilege."

She batted her eyelashes. "I was under the impression that, since the party of the first part has departed, then the attorney-client relationship would no longer apply."

"You are under a misapprehension, Miss—"

"Apprehension?"

"No, your name. Miss—"

"Parker," she said. "*Mrs.* Parker, actually."

"Mrs. Parker," Ramshackle said, rising from his chair,

"I cannot divulge any business of another client, living or deceased. Now, if you'll excuse me, I have other business to attend to."

"So," she said, "you haven't discussed Mr. Mayflower's contract with anyone? Even the police?"

"Not without a court order."

"The police haven't even contacted you?"

"No, they have not. Now, if you would excuse me, I have many other clients—"

That was good, she thought. From what Lou Neeley had told her—that Mayflower had visited this lawyer shortly before his murder—she felt certain that Mayflower's death was tied to his business with Ramshackle. Even the police hadn't figured this out yet. Somehow, that seemed like a good sign for Faulkner. She felt closer to proving his innocence and having this whole business done with.

Ramshackle hobbled around the desk and stood over her. He smelled of hair tonic and cough lozenges. "I said, I have many other clients, Mrs. Parker. Good day."

"But that's why I'm here. I'd like to be a client. A *paying* client."

Despite's Ramshackle's self-importance, she had noticed that his vest needed mending, his carpet was well-worn, and his office seemed less frequented than it probably had once been. His gruff manner changed immediately.

"Well." He beamed. "Why didn't you say so? Now what sort of legal representation do you require?"

She hesitated. How should she put this?

"Ah, I see," Ramshackle said, settling again into his desk chair. "You needn't worry. I am discreet—the absolute apex of discretion. So it is a divorce, then?"

Her jaw dropped. Did she look like a divorcée? Was that the first thought that came into a person's mind?

"These things can be messy, of course," he continued, smiling, "but lucrative. Oh, yes, you needn't subsist on a pittance as spinsters did in the old days."

"No, no, no," she blurted. "I'm not getting a divorce.

I want what Mayflower had. Just write me up one of those."

His Easter ham face reddened. "You want indemnity for libel?"

Indemnity for libel?

Ramshackle stammered, "B-but Mr. Mayflower was a writer—a famous columnist—working on his memoirs. He had reason to be cautious about being sued for libel. I-I take it you are just a housewife, are you not?"

Now it was her turn to be indignant. "Just a housewife? I'm a writer. A goddamn writer for *Vanity Fair*! And a goddamn poet, too. People quote me. Franklin Pierce Adams quotes me in the goddamn *New York World*."

Ramshackle was flustered. He grabbed a handful of papers to busy himself with. "Forgive me; please forgive me. I read only legal journals and—and occasionally *Reader's Digest*. My humblest apologies." He shuffled the papers. "Now, let me see, let me see. Yes, here we are. To protect you from libel—"

She stood up. "No, thank you. I think I'll seek representation elsewhere."

She had learned what she wanted to learn about Mayflower. That was good enough.

But she had also embarrassed herself, and she wanted to leave quickly. What bothered her wasn't that Ramshackle didn't recognize her name. (Well, that bothered her a little.) But what really bothered her was that she had stooped to boasting. *People quote me. Franklin Pierce Adams quotes me in the goddamn* New York World.

How shameful. She was thankful Benchley hadn't accompanied her to hear her talk like that. She could barely look at the lawyer as she turned to leave.

Wallace Ramshackle, for his part, was dumbfounded. He pushed his half-moon glasses up his nose.

"Please come again," he mumbled.

She closed the door.

Chapter 32

"Dottie!" The sultry voice of Neysa McMein called from across the lobby of the Algonquin.

Dorothy turned to see Neysa ambling toward her. Neysa wore a red plaid wool *jaquette* over a white silk blouse and a long, charcoal gray wool skirt. Faded streaks of colored pastel dust were visible on the cuffs of her blouse.

"You'll be at the little gathering at my studio tonight, won't you?" Neysa said.

"I wouldn't miss it if my hair was on fire."

"No need to put on the dog," Neysa said. "It's come as you are."

It was lunchtime. They turned and walked together toward the dining room.

"So, where were you yesterday?" Neysa said. "You missed lunch."

After the embarrassing meeting with Wallace Ramshackle the previous morning, Dorothy hadn't felt like joining the Vicious Circle for lunch that day.

"My yacht sprung a leak," she replied breezily. "Had to take it in for repairs."

In truth, she had spent the rest of yesterday afternoon hiding out in Woollcott's lavish apartment, playing cards and talking about books with Billy Faulkner.

They entered the Rose Room and found Robert Benchley holding court at the Round Table. He was in the midst of recounting his peculiar adventure in the Sandman's apartment.

"So I found myself out on a wet, slippery ledge, in the dark, quite drunk, and the wind threatened to whisk me off to my fast-approaching doom."

"A drunk daredevil in a driving wind," said Franklin Pierce Adams, chomping on his cigar.

"Yes," said Benchley, "I was literally three sheets to the wind. Fortunately, just then, the young husband leaned his head out his window to offer his help."

"What kind of help?" Marc Connelly said. "A trapeze?"

"Another drink," Benchley said. "And I decided it would be inhospitable to decline his offer. One way or the other, I was facing a wet Manhattan. I decided on the one that comes in a cocktail glass. So I crawled back in his window. . . ."

Dorothy was reminded of something that Benchley occasionally said—something that many of their group took to heart—"Never let the truth get in the way of a good story." Benchley had called her at Woollcott's apartment the night before to recount the story without embellishment.

She and Neysa said quick hellos to everyone and sat down. She noticed that Woollcott was absent. As Benchley continued his story, she wondered about this, about the truth and a good story. What was the truth to this whole mess? Which part was the made-up story? She had to get to the bottom of it soon. Tomorrow was Friday—Mickey Finn's deadline.

She picked up a popover—which was complimentary—and nibbled at it while she mulled this over.

Benchley was coming to the end of his story, concluding how the unseen intruder had stolen the Sandman's army photograph.

Neysa said, "Why would anyone want to break into this gangster's apartment to steal an old military photo?"

"It's obvious," said Robert Sherwood. "No doubt Sanderson was in the photo and so was his killer. Whoever killed Sanderson knew him from his days in the war. Benchley told us that neither he nor Mickey Finn could find in Sanderson's apartment any evidence of a connection between the Sandman and his killer. That photo is the connection."

George Kaufman, always skeptical, said, "But how would the killer even know that the Sandman had such a photo?"

"Don't forget," Dorothy said, "that whoever killed the Sandman did it in his apartment. He turned on the gas oven while the Sandman was sleeping. Then he must have come back later and stuffed the Sandman in the oven to make it seem like the Sandman committed suicide. So he was in the apartment at least twice already."

"So why didn't he take the photo then?" Kaufman said doubtfully, peering at her over his glasses.

"He probably didn't put two and two together at the time," she said. "It was only later, after he had time to think about it, that the killer must have realized that his appearance in the photograph could link him to the Sandman's death. So he came back to remove it—unfortunately it happened to be at the same time Mr. Benchley was there, too."

"Maybe all is not lost," said Adams, puffing on his cigar. "Benchley, you said you read the sign that the soldiers were holding. What did it say?"

"Well," Benchley gulped. "Let's see. Something with a three, I think. The Fighting Three? And there was a twenty-seven, I think. The twenty-seventh infantry, perhaps."

"And the town in which they took the photo?" Adams said.

"Bellicose, I believe," Benchley said. "That sticks with me because it reminds me of war."

"So what do you say, Ross?" Adams said, removing his cigar.

Everyone turned to look at Harold Ross, who was in the middle of a mouthful of stuffed cabbage. "Hmph?"

"Yeah, what do you say, Ross?" Dorothy said. "Can you track down the names of the soldiers in this troop? You edit that American Legion magazine. You were the editor for the *Stars and Stripes* during the war. You could call your pals in the War Department and find out who else was in the Sandman's regiment."

"Goddamn it," Ross muttered, gulping down his meal. "Is that all I'm good for? Nobody wants to help me with my idea for a smart magazine for New Yorkers. But how about calling up the War Department with hardly any idea of the name or number of the regiment, and Ross is your man?"

"Yes," she said. "Exactly."

Ross threw down his napkin. "You people will have me in the bughouse. I guess I'll go make a telephone call. What was the regiment again, and the town?"

"Three," Benchley said. "Or, perhaps, twenty-seven? I'm sure the town was Bellicose, France. I think."

"Goddamn it," Ross muttered as he stood up and stalked away from the table, headed toward the lobby.

"Speaking of making phone calls," Dorothy said, turning to the rumpled figure of Heywood Broun, "did you get my telegram yesterday? Did you talk to your colleague at the *Wall Street Journal*?"

"I did receive it, and I did talk to him." Broun scratched his disheveled hair. "But he couldn't find any trace of the New Canaan Bible Company. It doesn't exist."

"It exists, all right," she said. "Their truck nearly killed us. Your friend didn't look hard enough."

Broun frowned, shifting his massive bulk in his chair. "He looked plenty. He checked all the companies listed on the stock exchange. He checked all the companies incorporated in New York and in all of New England.

He checked to see if the company ever filed a federal tax return. Nothing. The company—on paper at least—doesn't exist."

"How could it not exist?" she asked. "That's impossible."

"I'm a sportswriter." Broun shrugged. "I can't explain all the whys and wherefores. What he told me was that it's probably owned by some other company but doesn't use the same name."

"Like a pseudonym," Benchley said. "A pen name."

"Something like that," Broun said.

They sat silently a moment, eating their lunch and thinking.

"Mrs. Parker." Adams put down his cigar and picked up his cup of tea. "Mr. Benchley tells us you visited Leland Mayflower's lawyer yesterday morning. Did you learn anything of interest?"

"As a matter of fact, I did," she said.

She told them how she had learned that Mayflower was apparently protecting himself against a libel suit that might arise from his memoir. (She did not mention how she had lost her head and boasted to Ramshackle.)

"I don't understand," Neysa said. "Mayflower was afraid someone would sue him for something he was going to write in his memoir? If Mayflower planned to write his own memories, how could anyone say that's libelous?"

"It's all in what you say and how you say it," Adams replied. "If you write something that someone else can prove is both damaging and untrue, then that's libel."

"The question is," said Sherwood, "who didn't want Mayflower to publish his memoir?"

"His boon companion, perhaps?" Adams said.

"Lou Neeley?" Dorothy said. "I doubt it. He was the one who told me Mayflower was writing his memoir in the first place. Besides, he was such a nice man. And he was totally devoted to Mayflower."

"And too old to be in the war, wasn't he?" Benchley said.

"If not him, then who?" Adams said.

"Someone who was in the war," Dorothy said slowly and thoughtfully. "Someone who was in Knut Sanderson's troop—or regiment or division or whatever. Someone who had it in for Mayflower."

They all looked at one another a moment.

Finally, Dorothy said, "So where the hell is Woollcott?"

A moment after Dorothy said this, Frank Case, the hotel manager, glided into the dining room. He carried a yellow envelope.

"Good day to you all," Case said smoothly. "I have a telegram for you."

"For who?" Adams said.

"All of you," Case said. "It's addressed to 'The Vicious Circle.'"

"I'll take it," Dorothy said. Case handed her the envelope.

Suddenly there was a clamor at the entrance. The group turned to see Alexander Woollcott burst into the dining room, with Bud Battersby following closely on his coattails.

"Leave me be, you pestilential parasite!" Woollcott cried. He scurried toward the Round Table, then halted suddenly—Battersby nearly collided with him—and thrust a chubby finger at Dorothy.

"You! I have been your prisoner for nigh on a day and a half. I will tolerate it no longer. I want out of—"

"Stop right there," she said to him, her eyes darting to Battersby. "You said I had your word you wouldn't speak about this."

"That word was given to a friend," he said haughtily. "And certainly my word is as good as gold—"

"Glad to hear it," she said.

"But some friend you turned out to be," Woollcott huffed. "There are no chocolates, as you led me to believe. And the—" He sought another way to refer to her dog. "The *former president* is simply intolerable."

Battersby's glance followed their conversation at first. But the quizzical look on his face was fading. He appeared slightly puzzled, but he seemed to think that this squabble was nothing interesting—nothing worth reporting, Dorothy surmised. She watched his glance roam over the faces of the other members of the group.

Woollcott now looked around as well. "And no chair for me! Now, this is the last straw." He glared at Frank Case. "If this is how you choose to run your hotel, my worthy innkeeper, your license should be revoked."

Case smiled warmly. "I shall make certain that Luigi finds you a chair—before I lose my license." He turned away in search of the waiter.

"Take Ross' chair, Aleck," said Heywood Broun. "Who knows when he'll be back?"

Woollcott observed the half-eaten plate of stuffed cabbage at Ross' seat. He turned his nose away.

"I'd rather stand for now," he said.

"Let him stand on principle. Let him walk on egg-shells," Benchley said. "Me, I'm sitting on the edge of my seat! What's in that telegram?" He pointed excitedly to the yellow envelope in Dorothy's hand.

By this time, Frank Case had returned, followed by Luigi, who carried a chair for Woollcott. But Woollcott was peering over her shoulder. So was Bud Battersby. The others seemed to lean forward as well.

Dorothy ripped open the envelope and unfolded the telegram. She read the message aloud. "MAYFLOWER HAS BEEN PLUCKED. SANDMAN WENT TO SLEEP. ROUND TABLE YOUR TIME HAS COME FULL CIRCLE. PREPARE FOR TRIAL BY FIRE."

"Trial by fire?" Benchley said.

"Threats at lunchtime?" Woollcott cried. "This is the very last straw!"

"Who would send such a thing?" Sherwood asked.

"We know it isn't from a rival writer," Dorothy said.

"How do you know?" said Bud Battersby.

They ignored him.

"How do you know?" echoed Neysa McMein.

"Because it's so poorly and unimaginatively written," Dorothy said.

"It sounds like the work of a half-literate anarchist," Adams said.

"It sounds like the work of a half-witted amateur," Woollcott said. "My money's on Dachshund. You call off your hound right now, Dorothy. Enough of these pranks."

Her eyes flashed to Battersby, who had pulled out his notebook and pencil. "Billy had nothing to do with this," she said firmly.

"Are you so sure?" Woollcott sneered. "Do you watch his every move? Can you read his murky thoughts? I say we have an enemy in our midst. A thorn in our side."

"A fly in our soup," Benchley said.

"Calm down, Aleck," she said, glancing again at Battersby, who was scribbling notes. "Instead of mixing your metaphors, go mix yourself a drink and cool off."

"Cool off?" Woollcott's eyebrows rose ever higher. His face turned pink. "I will not cool off! How dare you! You trespass on my goodwill. You lie to me about the chocolates. You take my honored seat at the table—"

"I didn't take your seat," she said.

Woollcott ignored her. "Now we have this maleficent missive from a Mississippi misanthrope! This shot across the bow from a southern sociopath! It is all too much. I cannot take any more. This is *absolutely* the last straw." His hands fluttered in the air. "I'm going to the Plaza for lunch, and the hell with Dachshund! And the hell with all of you!"

He paused for effect, but no one said a word or made a move to stop him. With a harrumph, he turned on his heel and bustled out of the dining room. They watched him go.

Now the only sound was Battersby's pencil scratching in his notebook. He looked up. "Is Mr. Woollcott always—"

Ignoring Battersby, Dorothy waved the telegram. "What do you think it all means?"

"Read it again," Adams said, inhaling thoughtfully on his cigar.

She read, "Mayflower has been plucked. Sandman went to sleep—"

"That's clear enough," Broun said. "It means both of them were murdered."

They all nodded in agreement.

She continued, "Round Table your time has come full circle. Prepare for trial by fire."

"Our time has come full circle?" Benchley repeated.

"I don't think that's any kind of riddle," said Adams, who loved word games. "I think we can simply take it at face value—our time is up."

"So what's the trial by fire?" Dorothy said.

They stared at one another a moment.

"A courtroom in candlelight?" Benchley offered.

"A hearthside hazing?" Sherwood smiled.

"Go ahead and joke all you like," Adams said. "But I'm with Woollcott in one respect—I've had enough of the gloomy shadow casting its pall over our little circle here. This telegram just makes it worse. It's time to cut to the chase."

Dorothy sat up. "What do you suggest we do?"

"Whoever sent the telegram wrote that we need to prepare for trial by fire," Adams said, jamming his cigar back in his mouth. "I say, let's fight fire with fire."

"I'm with you in spirit," she said. "But how?"

"We write a reply that says: Go to hell!"

"But to whom?" Benchley said, plucking the telegram from Dorothy's grasp. "There's no name on the telegram to send a reply."

"I never said we'd send a telegram," Adams said, smiling craftily.

"Now I get it," Dorothy said. "We all know that two out of three New Yorkers read our esteemed Mr.

Adams' daily column in the *New York World*. If we want to send a message—"

Benchley said, "Adams can write it in his column, and all of New York will be able to read it."

Battersby, still standing, continued to scribble everything they said in his notepad.

"Sure," Dorothy said drily. "If they don't read about it in Adams' column in the *World*, they can read it sitting on the john before using the *Knickerbocker* as toilet paper."

Battersby's face reddened, but he didn't look up. He just kept jotting notes.

"You can quote me on that," she said to him, and turned back to Adams. "Now, what will you write?"

"I'll write a short description of what happened here today, and then the exact contents of the telegram, and then our response."

"Fine," she said, surveying the group around the table. "How should we respond?"

"I have it," Benchley said. "This telegram pricked the ears and innocent soul of Alexander Woollcott. 'Come and get me,' he boldly stated."

"No adverbs," she said.

Benchley continued, "'Come and get me,' Mr. Woollcott said, actually throwing down his glove. 'I shall be at the Algonquin as usual at lunchtime tomorrow. If you want to show your face, you murderous coward, you can find me there.'"

"Sounds just like Woollcott," Adams nodded, writing it down in a notebook. "That should draw out our murderer."

"That should draw quite a crowd, too," said Frank Case, tapping a finger to his chin. "I'll have to order more food and put another cook on duty."

He hurried away busily. Luigi, the waiter, his shoulders sagging, followed him.

"It's a plan," Dorothy said. "Whoever shows up tomorrow will be our killer. Tomorrow, ladies and gents, we unmask a murderer."

Chapter 33

"It's a plan, Mrs. Parker," Benchley said. "But . . . isn't it a rather silly plan?"

"Bite your tongue, Mr. Benchley," she said, a little hurt. "It's a fine plan."

"It's *silly*?" Robert Sherwood said. "How do you mean?"

The three of them had spent an uneventful—and unproductive—afternoon at the offices of *Vanity Fair*. Now they strolled from Forty-fourth Street up Park Avenue on their way to Wit's End to pick up Billy Faulkner and to make their way to Neysa's party.

The evening was mild for April. Somewhere behind the tall buildings, the sun was setting in a rosy glow. The pleasant weather, combined with the feeling that this sordid murder business was nearly concluded *and* that they were on their way to a lively party, put them in a happy mood.

Indeed, many of their fellow New Yorkers seemed to be enjoying themselves, too. Businessmen ambled along instead of running for their taxis or trains. Even the traffic on Park Avenue seemed to be taking its time. As they turned east onto Fifty-second Street, Benchley paused a moment to wave at a smiling infant in a baby carriage pushed by a matronly nanny.

To get his attention, Sherwood repeated, "How do you mean the plan is silly?"

Benchley, falling back into step, said casually, "I mean that this man—whoever he is—is a cold-blooded killer. An actual murderer. And we've just invited him to lunch. Does that sound very sensible to you?"

"As long as he pays his part of the check, who's going to quibble?" Dorothy said.

But perhaps Benchley had a point. She wasn't so concerned about her own safety. She was much more concerned about Billy Faulkner. He was still in danger.

Then again, now that Billy had shaved his scraggly beard and traded in his bohemian rags for a dapper dress suit, would the killer even recognize him?

"Besides," she said, expressing her thoughts aloud, "there's safety in numbers. You heard what Frank Case said. The Algonquin will be packed. The crowd will be phenomenal. There's nothing to worry about."

"But with such a crowd," Sherwood said, "do you think our murderer will show up? Won't he be scared away?"

"Nope, he'll be there," she said. "The offer is too tempting for him to resist. Oh, he might pretend he's just one of the spectators. We might have to draw him out somehow. But he'll show his hand eventually. I'm sure of it. Like I said, there's nothing to worry about."

There was very little traffic along this quiet stretch near Wit's End. So it was a surprise that as they stepped off the sidewalk to cross First Avenue, a white limousine pulled up abruptly and blocked their way. A man in a long coat hopped out of the passenger seat and opened the rear door. Mickey Finn stepped out of the limousine, followed by Lucy Goosey. They were dressed in evening clothes. He wore a top hat and a long black overcoat over his tuxedo. She wore a white fox fur wrap over a clingy, pale green, emerald-studded evening dress.

"I'll be," said Dorothy. "If it isn't a loosey goose and a dandy gander."

"'Tis indeed." Mickey Finn grinned his yellow, crooked smile. "I've been looking for you."

"And why is that?" she asked.

"Once again, you've gone and got me in a bother. And I'm not a man easily bothered."

Dorothy noticed that both Benchley and Sherwood had their eyes fixed on Lucy Goosey.

"Then we'll bother you no longer," she said, and started forward.

"Hold on, there," Finn said, swinging his silver-capped shillelagh to bar her way. "Let's not get confrontational. We're friends, are we not? Let's have a drink and talk about it. As friends." He gestured with the stick toward the car.

"We're not going anywhere with you, even for a drink," she said.

"No need to travel," he said. "My car has a fully stocked bar."

"A saloon car!" Benchley said, tearing his gaze from the striptease artist. He nearly jumped into the limo.

Dorothy and Sherwood exchanged glances, then followed him in.

Inside the spacious automobile, Benchley was already mixing drinks—splashing expensive Irish whiskey and spritzing the seltzer bottle. They slid in and sat beside him. He handed each of them a highball glass of whiskey and soda. Mickey Finn and Lucy Goosey climbed into the car and sat in the rear-facing seats opposite them. They already had drinks, which they raised in a toast.

"To you and your health," Mickey Finn said.

"And never the twain shall meet," Benchley said, and they all clinked glasses and drank.

After clinking glasses again, and drinking again, Dorothy sat forward.

"This is a jolly little get-together, but let's talk turkey," she said. "What did you want to see us about?"

"I read Mr. Woollcott's ultimatum," Finn said, picking up a newspaper. "And, bless me, but I think it stinks."

Now they all sat forward, giving Finn their full attention. How had he read Frank Adams' article? It wouldn't be printed in the *World* until the next morning. Then they realized that Finn was holding a copy of the *Knickerbocker News*.

Dorothy grabbed the tabloid. An old file photo of the Algonquin Hotel was on the cover. The headline screamed, ROUND TABLE SAYS "COME AND GET US!"

She gritted her teeth. Bud Battersby must have rushed back to his printing plant and quickly thrown together an extra afternoon edition. He had scooped Frank Adams by more than half a day!

"It stinks, I say!" Finn repeated.

"For once, I agree with you," she said.

"You tell your Mr. Woollcott to keep his trap shut."

"Easier said than done," she said. "Have you ever met Mr. Woollcott?"

"Can't say I've ever had the pleasure of his acquaintance."

"Nor have we," Benchley said, "and we've known him for years."

Finn leaned back, his hands resting on his knees. "I have a few deeply held beliefs. You want to hear 'em?"

They didn't respond. What choice did they have?

Finn's ice blue eyes were cold. "I believe you know where Mr. Dachshund is. I believe you're hiding him. I believe if the cops grab him tomorrow at your little lunchtime pantomime show, then I believe you'll have considerably more to worry about than your lousy little neighborhood speakeasy going dry. I believe I need to get my hands on your Mr. Dachshund myself."

She looked back and forth to Benchley and Sherwood. "You believe the nerve of this guy?"

"This is no joke, Mrs. Parker," Finn said, his yellow teeth clenched.

"I believe you," she said.

"I tried to be friends. I asked for your help, but you

don't seem to want to help me. From now on, I'll help myself. You understand?"

Again they didn't respond. What could they say?

Finn pointed toward the door. "Now, put down your drinks and get the hell out of my car."

Cautiously, as if facing a wild animal, they put down their drinks. Sherwood opened the door and unfolded his long body to step out. Dorothy slid across the seat to follow.

But Benchley paused. His expression was quizzical but amused, like he was solving a crossword puzzle. He looked directly at Lucy Goosey. "What is it you see in this man?"

Dorothy could guess the answer. What really bothered her was that Benchley had wanted to ask the question.

Lucy Goosey said, "A bottle of buttermilk has a longer shelf life than a stripper in this town. I need all the good friends I can get." She looked to Finn and smiled. Finn smiled back at her. "And Mickey is a very good friend."

Benchley nodded, while Finn, though smiling, didn't seem entirely reassured by her answer. Dorothy noticed this. But she didn't really care. She was angry with Benchley. She got the hell out of the car, with Benchley following close behind.

Then a thought occurred to her. She poked her head back inside the limo. Finn sat back in stunned surprise.

"Since we're such good old friends and everything," she said, "would you happen to have another box of those chocolates with the booze inside?"

Finn looked at Lucy Goosey. "You believe the nerve of this gal?"

As they walked the rest of the way to Woollcott's apartment, the three of them debated whether to bring Faulkner to Neysa McMein's party after all.

"Let's just let Billy decide for himself," Dorothy said finally.

Faulkner, who hadn't left Woollcott's extravagant apartment in almost two days, couldn't wait to get out to the party.

Neysa's artist studio was in a dark building on a busy, noisy corner of Fifty-seventh Street, across from Carnegie Hall. Inside the high-ceilinged studio, it was just as busy and noisy, but the scene was alive with bright lights, laughter and liquor.

In the center of the big, crowded, smoky room, Neysa stood (as she always did) at her easel, paying almost no heed to the party going on around her. On the easel was a half-finished painting of a beautiful woman (who looked suspiciously similar to Neysa herself) dressed in a jaunty sailor's outfit—the cover illustration for the next issue of *Collier's* magazine.

Neysa looked up from her painting as Dorothy, Benchley, Sherwood and Faulkner entered. Neysa didn't come to greet them but gave a leisurely wave, as though this was a typical day at the office for her.

"Gin's in the bathtub," she called. "Have fun."

Then she continued painting—and continued ignoring the man chatting next to her. He was another, less illustrious illustrator—a hanger-on, a third-rate Norman Rockwell by the name of Ernie MacGuffin. He kept up his patter, unaware or indifferent that she wasn't paying attention.

Over in a brightly lit corner, surrounded by a small throng, Irving Berlin sat at the upright piano, his nimble fingers fluttering merrily up and down the keys. On either side of him were the beautiful Billie Burke—a stage and movie actress *and* the wife of Broadway impresario Florenz Ziegfeld—and Ed McNamara, the so-called singing policeman, a former New Jersey cop with a booming opera singer's voice.

Together, they wailed out "Oh! How I Hate to Get

Up in the Morning," a tune that Berlin had written in his army days during the war. Joyfully, they sang,

> Someday I'm going to murder the bugler,
> Someday they're going to find him dead;
> I'll amputate his reveille
> And step upon it heavily,
> And spend the rest of my life in bed.

In the opposite corner, in front of the bookshelves, Alexander Woollcott sat huddled with Harpo Marx, who was autographing each volume of the complete works of William Shakespeare.

Strolling by was Douglas Fairbanks arm in arm with Helen Hayes, a pretty young actress—just a girl, really—who was making a splash on Broadway.

"Going to nab Mayflower's murderer tomorrow?" Fairbanks asked, not slowing his pace. "Break a leg!" He escorted the young actress through the crowd and toward the open door to the balcony.

Benchley smiled, taking in the scene. Then he turned to Faulkner. "So, it's your night on the town, *Mr. Dachshund*. How about a little hair of the dog?"

"Most certainly," Faulkner said.

"Make that two," Sherwood added.

"Make it three," Dorothy said.

Benchley gave a little bow, turning halfway toward the bathroom. "You'll have it in a trice."

"I'd prefer it in a glass," she said, "but any port in a storm."

"It's not port," Benchley said, calling over his shoulder. "It's gin."

As Benchley went off to get the drinks, Dorothy remembered her promise to Lou Neeley, that she'd take up a collection to help him pay for Leland Mayflower's funeral. She took off her hat and handed it to Sherwood.

He was perplexed. "What's this for?"

"A good deed for a bad seed," she said, then explained Neeley's predicament. Sherwood looked skeptical until she told him how Mayflower's body was likely in the same morgue with that of the Sandman.

"Okay, I'll pass it around," Sherwood said. "It's funny how things turn inside out. It was only a few days ago that you called Mayflower a 'malevolent old shit.'"

"I'm not so concerned for the dead as for the living," she said. "Why should poor Lou Neeley have to suffer any further? He already lost Mayflower. His only fault was falling in love with the wrong man. That's heartbreak enough."

Sherwood leaned toward her. "And what would you know about that?" he asked with a knowing wink, as Benchley returned, carefully balancing four martini glasses in his hands.

Sherwood grabbed a glass from Benchley and moved off into the crowd, her hat in his other hand.

Benchley handed them each a glass of gin. She sniffed hers. It smelled like turpentine.

"Here's to laughter," Benchley said, raising his glass.

"Here's to luck," Faulkner said.

"Here's two years off your life," she said.

They clinked glasses and drank. She was still angry with Benchley. He didn't even seem to notice.

Over the rim of her glass, she saw Sherwood approaching Harold Ross and his wife, Jane Grant, who were talking heatedly with the yeast magnate (and sometime poker player) Raoul Fleischmann. Undoubtedly, she thought, Ross and his wife were trying to get Fleischmann to put his money into their magazine idea. Hopefully, Sherwood would have better luck getting a few dollars out of Fleischmann than Ross and Grant.

Suddenly, a nasal voice wailed like a siren in her ear. "What do you think you're doing?"

She turned to see Woollcott's round face pinched with rage and disgust. Behind him, Harpo Marx silently mimicked Woollcott's expression.

"Drinking turpentine," she responded blandly. "What does it look like we're doing?"

"You're feeding that hack Battersby quotes that I never said!" Woollcott cried.

He explained that "some liquored-up loudmouth" had just approached him and praised him for "throwing down the gauntlet" in the *Knickerbocker News*.

"Apparently," Woollcott continued, "said gauntlet was thrown at lunch today at the Algonquin. That bird-brained Bud Battersby doesn't have the imagination— or the impudence—to fabricate phrases I never uttered. So I know those words could only have one origin." He jutted a stubby finger at her.

She watched Harpo silently mouth Woollcott's words, and she couldn't help but smile. Woollcott, who was wearing his silly opera cape, turned around theatrically. Harpo's expression went blank. Woollcott turned back to face her.

"I don't know what you're talking about," she said.

"Tell the truth," Woollcott said. "Do you have a copy of that *Knickerbocker* rag?"

Faulkner gulped his drink and turned away slightly. In his jacket pocket was the copy of the newspaper that Mickey Finn had given to them.

"I need to go to the bathroom," Faulkner said.

She glanced at his empty glass. "Going for a refill?"

"Oh, yeah, that, too," Faulkner said. He slinked away sideways.

"If there was any justice in this world, you'd be drawn and quartered," Woollcott continued. "You'd hang by your thumbs—"

Woollcott's beady-eyed, bespectacled gaze shifted to someone behind her. Dorothy turned around, expecting to see Harpo Marx playing some prank.

Instead, she faced Detective O'Rannigan and Captain Church. Benchley yelped, and she almost spilled her drink.

Chapter 34

"Providence be praised!" Woollcott cried. "Officers, arrest these two."

"Maybe we'll arrest the whole lot of you for violation of the Volstead Act," O'Rannigan sneered, tipping his tiny brown derby forward on his fat forehead. He grabbed Dorothy's glass, sniffed it and winced.

"You can arrest them anytime for that," Woollcott said. "This time, they've used my name in vain. They bore false witness against me."

"Go cry someplace else," O'Rannigan said. "We got business to talk with these two. So scram, fattypants."

Harpo laughed loudly at this. Woollcott, O'Rannigan and Church all looked at him angrily. Harpo shut up. Woollcott grabbed Harpo's arm and pulled him away.

O'Rannigan shoved the glass back into her hands. Benchley looked nervously at his own glass, as if unsure how he had acquired it.

"So is this a raid?" she asked. "Are you going to run us all in?"

"Drink yourselves blind for all we care," O'Rannigan said. "But you're going to cooperate."

"Cooperate?"

Captain Church finally spoke. "Show us the telegram you received this afternoon."

She looked to Benchley. He had pocketed it after lunch. He glanced about for a place to set down his drink. He handed the glass to O'Rannigan; then he fumbled in his jacket pockets for the telegram. He grabbed his drink from O'Rannigan's hand and replaced it with the crumpled telegram.

The detective gave Benchley an angry look, then carefully unfolded the telegram and handed it to Church. While the police captain inspected it, O'Rannigan said, "Why didn't you bring this to our attention right away, instead of giving it to the first reporter you could find—and then holding on to it? We had to read about it in the tabloid, for Pete's sake."

"You're a big fan of Franklin Adams' column in the *World*, right?" Benchley said. "Wait until you read about it in there."

Church grimaced. "For the hundredth time, Mr. Benchley, stop treating this like some joke." He held up the telegram. "This is evidence."

"Not only that," O'Rannigan said. "Your little prank about challenging the murderer to appear tomorrow could interfere with our investigation. You call it off."

"That was Woollcott who said that—," she began.

"Knock it off," O'Rannigan said, leaning over her. "We know that was you two. Your chubby buddy Woollcott just told us as much."

"We are very close to capturing this killer," Church said. "We have an excellent idea of his identity. Your imbecilic charade tomorrow puts that in jeopardy."

"Speakin' of stupid," O'Rannigan said, glancing at the faces of partygoers around the room. "You wouldn't be stupid enough to have brought Dachshund here, would you?"

"Sure, we're stupid enough," she said. "Look up there. He's swinging on the chandelier."

O'Rannigan and Church automatically looked up to the ceiling high above. Not only was there no Faulkner; there was no chandelier.

While they were momentarily distracted, she glanced toward the bathroom to see Faulkner coming out. He held three martini glasses. She shook her head, and he quickly ducked back in.

"So you still think this is funny—," Church said. Then he was suddenly distracted. His expression changed from seething rage to shameless rapture. "Is that who I think it is?"

She followed his gaze to the small crowd around the piano.

"Why, certainly. It's Irving Berlin, the Broadway composer."

"No," Church said, mesmerized. "Standing next to him!"

"Oh, of course," she said. "Surely you know him. That's Ed McNamara, the singing policeman."

Church groaned. "Not him either. *Her!* That's Billie Burke, the actress."

"Ah, yes, the great Ziegfeld's wife."

Church—and O'Rannigan, too—couldn't take their eyes off the red-haired beauty. Dorothy Parker glanced slyly at Benchley.

Benchley's eyes lit up. "Would you like me to introduce you to her?"

Church could scarcely look away from the actress. "Do you know her?"

"Well," Benchley said, rocking back on his heels, "I know Irv Berlin. He could introduce you. Come on, let's go!" Eagerly, Church and O'Rannigan followed Benchley toward the trio at the piano.

Then Woollcott came bobbing up from the other direction, looking even more angry. His hands were flailing; his cape was flapping.

Jeez, Dorothy thought, what a swell party this was turning out to be.

"Does your brazenness know no bounds?" Woollcott cried.

"I refuse to bind my brazens," she said. "So what has *your* brazens in a bind now?"

"You're passing the hat for Mayflower!" Woollcott cried. "Why not just slap me in the face?"

"How tempting. And how inconsiderate of me to take up a collection."

"It's inconsiderate to almost everyone here. To honor Mayflower's name is an insult to the good working folk gathered around us."

She momentarily considered explaining Lou Neeley's plight, as she had to Sherwood. But she didn't get the chance.

"And speaking of insults," he continued, "I insist you hand over that tabloid rag in which you besmirched my good name. I know you have a copy on your person."

"My person has no such thing, and neither do I." She saw Sherwood approaching and caught his eye. "I gave it to Mr. Sherwood, here."

"Is that so?" Woollcott turned as Sherwood joined them. "Today's *Knock-kneed News*, do you have it?"

"Oh," Sherwood said, catching on. "I handed it to Harold Ross. You can find him on the balcony, smoking a Camel."

Woollcott sensed a trick. "Why would he go out to the balcony to smoke a cigarette?"

"Because it's a lovely night," Sherwood said.

"And because it's a real camel," she said. "Couldn't fit it in the studio. Now, go."

Woollcott departed reluctantly, glancing suspiciously over his shoulder. But Dorothy didn't yet breathe a sigh of relief. William Faulkner was now approaching, nearly staggering with the three martini glasses in his hands. She gave a quick glance toward the piano—Billie Burke had O'Rannigan and especially Church enthralled. Benchley winked his assurance.

"Now, this is the literary life," Faulkner said, his smile beaming, nearly spilling the drinks as he handed them to her and to Sherwood. "This is what I always thought a writer's life would be like in New York."

Faulkner wasn't quite three sheets to the wind, she thought, but his foresail and his mainsail were clearly loose and flapping in the breeze, and his mizzen sail was threatening to come untied.

She glanced to Sherwood. "He's been around that bathtub too long already."

Then she saw Benchley covertly waving to her from across the room. Billie Burke had been momentarily diverted by, of all people, Jack Dempsey. Even from this distance, she could tell the cops didn't like being brushed off and were getting ready to give up if Dempsey didn't walk away soon.

In front of her, Faulkner simply stood there with a bemused smile.

"Take him back to the bathtub and dry him out," she said to Sherwood.

Sherwood shielded Faulkner from the policemen's view as he escorted him back to the bathroom.

"What's Woollcott's problem?" A familiar midwestern voice spoke beside her.

She turned to see Harold Ross, with a cigarette dangling from his down-turned mouth.

"Where do I begin?" she said. She was amazed to see that Ross' cigarette was indeed a Camel.

"Woollcott said you told him that I had a copy of today's *Knickerbocker News.* Now, why would you say—"

She tuned Ross out. The policemen were moving. Church and O'Rannigan had given up on the red-haired actress. Now, as they turned to go, their eyes locked on Dorothy.

"I don't even read the lousy *Knickerbocker,*" Ross was saying. "I haven't bought a copy in years—"

Church and O'Rannigan marched past on their way toward the door, their gaze still holding hers.

"Watch out tomorrow," the detective snarled at her. Then he followed the police captain out the door.

She sighed once they were gone. That was at least one problem finished with for the night.

Benchley had been a few paces behind the policemen. Now he came over. She then realized that Ross was still grousing at her.

"Say, Ross," she interrupted. "Did you ever get any answers from your pals at the army board? Did they provide the names of the Sandman's troop—or his regiment, or whatever?"

"Not yet," Ross grunted. "They'll wire me a list tomorrow." He turned to Benchley. "You didn't make it easy. Third something or other of the twenty-seventh or so infantry . . . And there's no town of Bellicose in France, by the way."

Benchley was shocked to hear this. "Well, there should be."

"You two figure that out," she said. "I have to go save a Dachshund drowning deep in drink."

In the bathroom, she found Faulkner sitting on the edge of the tub. Sherwood stood leaning against the sink.

Faulkner looked up as she entered. His gaze floated all around her but couldn't quite make a landing.

"Why, hello," he said. "Our hostess—what is her name?"

"Ms. McMein."

"Ms. McMein. Oh, yes. Look at how elegantly she sherves—she serves her guests." Faulkner gestured to the tub. The drink sloshed in his hand. "Unlike the backwoods boys I've met down South, Ms. McMein doesn't distill her own gin. She must buy the grain alcohol in quantity. Then she pours it in this gargantuan glass punch bowl here and sets it ever so nicely in her ice-filled tub—it's so much more hygienic and appealing than actually using the tub itself—"

"Billy—," she said.

"And inside the punch bowl, the alcohol steeps in juniper berries, oil of coriander and orange peel. But look, you can add your own juniper berries." He picked up a tiny blue-black berry from a small silver bowl, squished it between his fingers and let it fall—*plop!*—into his glass. "Delightful."

"Billy—"

He raised the glass and slurped it down, juniper berry and all.

She looked at Sherwood, who was grinning, his eyes half lidded. He looked like he might slide off the sink at any moment.

"You were supposed to cut him off," she said.

"Don't you worry." Sherwood waved his hand. "This boy can hold his liquor."

"Yes, he's now holding a glass of it in each hand," she said, and grabbed one of the glasses from Faulkner. Faulkner used the free hand to steady himself on the edge of the tub.

Benchley entered, took one look around the small room, then stepped forward and dipped his martini glass into the big punch bowl. Contentedly, he sat down on the edge of the tub next to Faulkner.

"Oh, well," Dorothy sighed, giving up. Then she, too, filled her glass. "No one frolics like we alcoholics."

She sat down on the edge of the tub on the other side of Faulkner. She took out a cigarette, which prompted Faulkner and Sherwood to light up cigarettes as well, and Benchley took out his pipe.

They sat contentedly smoking and drinking for only a moment when Woollcott suddenly stood in the doorway.

"What the deuce is going on in here?" Woollcott glared at each of them in turn. His eyes nearly popped out when he looked at Faulkner. "Is that my tie, young man?" He turned to Dorothy. "Is he wearing my necktie?"

Woollcott fluttered forward, his cape flapping behind him. He stood over Faulkner and Dorothy. "You two overtake my humble abode for who knows how long!

You hold out the promise of chocolates that never existed! You besmirch my good name by fabricating lies and deceit in a lowly tabloid! And you solicit funds for my foe's funeral! To top it off, you purloin my most treasured necktie! I won't stand for this!"

"Then, take a seat," she said calmly, pointing at the toilet. "The john is unoccupied."

Woollcott ignored her. He continued his tirade, now demanding that Faulkner take off the tie. Then Woollcott demanded that Faulkner and Dorothy never return to his apartment.

Dorothy noticed Neysa McMein standing in the bathroom doorway, seemingly indifferent to Woollcott's temper tantrum. In her hands, she held Dorothy's upturned cloche. Neysa came forward, handed the hat to her, shrugged, then left the room.

Dorothy looked into the hat. It was almost as empty as when she had taken it off earlier. At the bottom were a few wadded-up dollar bills, a handful of loose change, a couple cigarette butts and a gum wrapper.

Well, what had she expected, after all? Did she think she could help Neeley pay for Mayflower's entire funeral expenses by passing around a hat at a party of his rivals?

Still, she was disappointed just the same. She sucked away the last of her cigarette and tossed the butt into the hat with the others.

"Hold on, now, just a minute," Faulkner was saying. Unsteadily, with the assistance of Benchley, he rose to his feet, inches from Woollcott's pinched nose. "Maybe I can make up this to you, sir."

Faulkner fumbled in his pockets and finally withdrew a shiny object. "Here!"

He dropped it into Woollcott's open palm. Woollcott actually jumped when he realized what it was: the tooth from the Sandman's watch chain.

Woollcott's upper lip curled in disgust. His chubby fingers could scarcely hold the thing.

Benchley clapped Faulkner on the shoulder. "Well done, my lad! How did you find it?"

Faulkner smiled; his eyes tried to meet Benchley's but couldn't quite make it. "Simple. I went looking for it the following morning. There it was in the gutter, covered by a leaf."

"Take this *thing* away!" Woollcott cried. He held it at arm's length.

Faulkner shook his head. "No, please, you keep it. You've been so gener—"

Woollcott was nearly shaking. His doughy face was pale. "I won't be insulted like this!"

Faulkner smiled again. He didn't seem to understand. "Think nothing of it."

Dorothy stood. It was time to use the secret weapon. "Billy," she said, "give him the thing in your other pocket."

She had to repeat it, and even so, it took a moment for Faulkner to comprehend. Finally, from his other jacket pocket, Faulkner removed the box of liquor-filled chocolates. He looked at it and his jaw dropped. He was seemingly unaware of how it had gotten there, as though he had just pulled a rabbit out of his pocket.

Woollcott stopped shaking. His whole demeanor changed. "Now, that's more like it—"

Then, with stunned surprise still etched on his face, Faulkner passed out. He fell forward, collapsing directly into Woollcott, tearing his cape and landing facedown on the bathroom floor, crushing the box of chocolates beneath him.

For once, Woollcott was speechless. For a long moment, no one said a word. They just stared at Faulkner lying on the floor.

"Alcohol," Dorothy said. "The life—and the death— of the party."

Chapter 35

Dorothy rolled over and fell to the floor. Her head pounded furiously. She stared at the carpet. It was not her carpet. It was much nicer. She slowly turned her head and looked at the sofa on which, until just a moment ago, she had been sleeping. It was not her sofa. It was much nicer. She realized it was Woollcott's sofa, and she wondered for a moment how Woollcott's carpet and sofa had found their way into her apartment. Then she realized it was not her apartment. It was much nicer. It was Woollcott's apartment.

Then, still lying on the floor, she began to piece together the final events of the night before.

Faulkner had passed out on the floor of Neysa McMein's bathroom. She remembered that very clearly. Woollcott, who had been indignant a moment before, suddenly changed his tune and became devilishly merry. He abruptly bid them good night, saying he was returning, as planned, to Dorothy's apartment at the Algonquin.

Forget it, she had told him. The ruse is no longer necessary. He could have Wit's End back.

Wouldn't think of it, Woollcott had said. A deal's a deal.

She realized he was doing this just to spite her—the

distance to Woollcott's apartment was several blocks farther away than the distance to the Algonquin, which would make transporting Faulkner that much more difficult.

But before she could protest, Woollcott had turned and was gone with a swish of his torn opera cape.

Eventually, Benchley and Sherwood pulled Faulkner to his feet and managed to walk him out to the street and fold him into a taxi. Fortunately, getting Faulkner to Wit's End wasn't much different from getting him to the Algonquin, just an extra few blocks in the taxi. Again, Benchley and Sherwood lugged him out and into Woollcott's apartment building, and up the elevator to the apartment, and dumped him onto Woollcott's bed.

To celebrate getting Faulkner back safely, they decided to empty Woollcott's liquor cabinet. They plopped down on the sofa and managed to empty half a bottle of brandy before they gave up at around three o'clock in the morning.

One thing Dorothy remembered clearly: After Sherwood excused himself for a minute, Benchley turned to her.

"Is there anything at all the matter?" he asked casually. "You've been giving me that evil eye of yours all night."

"As a matter of fact"—she couldn't stop herself—"I'm annoyed how you talked to that Goosey woman. You already have a woman who loves you. You shouldn't need to look at and talk to that harlot that way."

His smile faded. "I know my wife loves me." The words stung her. "But I can't help but notice that stripper. She's like an eye-catching billboard or a rare animal in a zoo. One's attention is attracted to such spectacles. As for talking to her—"

"Yes, did you *have to* inquire about her romance with Mickey Finn? 'What do you see in this man?' That was shameful."

Benchley considered this. "I was merely curious

about her welfare in a very small way, much the same way you've been a mother hen to our little Billy. I wasn't looking to rescue her or—heaven forbid!—fall in love with her, if that's what you mean. My, my, Mrs. Parker, I had no idea you were such a slave to propriety," he teased.

She realized she felt relieved. "I'm no slave to propriety." She leaned toward him and held out her empty glass. "Nor to sobriety. Fill 'er up, Mr. Benchley."

Later, she had a vague recollection of Sherwood and Benchley saying good night. She recalled that Sherwood had offered Benchley his couch. She also seemed to remember that Sherwood had given her a hug, which made her feel warm, and Benchley had kissed her forehead, which made her stomach flutter.

Had she dreamed that? The members of the Vicious Circle didn't hug. They certainly didn't kiss.

Must have been a dream, she decided.

But having decided this, she felt sad. And that got her thinking about other sad things. She felt sad that she had been able to collect only a few dollars for Lou Neeley. She felt sad that she had allowed Faulkner to get stone drunk, as if she had misled him somehow, as if this whole sordid affair was somehow her fault and she had dragged him into it. She knew that wasn't how it really was, but she couldn't help but feel it.

She also felt sad for poor Woodrow Wilson, who had been cooped up with Woollcott for three days, and she hadn't even visited him to take him for a walk or pat him on the head. She assumed Woollcott would have it in his heart to care for the poor dog.

Her thoughts turned back to Benchley, and now she felt sad for herself. But she silently cursed herself for feeling this way. What right did she have to feel sad for herself when she caused so much trouble for everyone else? She curled up on the carpet and put her hands over her eyes.

Still, she wanted to see Benchley. She felt at loose

ends now, but seeing him—being around him, with his easygoing, cockeyed confidence—would make her feel like herself again.

Well, she would see him soon. She would see him at the 'Gonk for lunch—

Oh, shit!

She sat up and looked around for the clock.

Oh, shit!

It was ten minutes past noon! They gathered for lunch at one o'clock.

She dragged herself up off the floor, her head swimming. She staggered into the bathroom to splash some cold water on her face.

Today of all days! she thought. Today, when everybody would be there as she and Benchley would—somehow—bring forth Mayflower's murderer....

She hurried into the bedroom. Faulkner was still out cold on the bed.

Let sleeping dogs lie, she thought.

She tore open the closet door, hoping she had brought at least one decent dress that was something close to clean and unwrinkled....

"Is it time to get up?" Faulkner muttered. He lay still, one eye open.

"Not for you," she said. "You stay put."

She had only two outfits to choose from. One of the two she had worn the day before, so she picked the other—a violet frock with a matching belt. She also grabbed her black cloche.

"Where are you going?" he mumbled.

"Lunch at the Algonquin. Today's the big day. Will you be all right here alone?"

He cocked his head to look at her. "I won't be."

"You won't be all right?"

"I won't be alone." He sat up and winced. "I'm going with you."

"Forget it. You won't be able to hold your lunch,

much less hold your end of a conversation. Just sleep it off." She went back into the bathroom to get changed.

By the time she came back out, Faulkner stood swaying by the front door. He had changed his jacket and had put on another one of Woollcott's florid neckties. She went over to him and straightened it. His eyes were sunken and his skin was pasty. She felt ill just looking at him.

"I don't think this is a good idea," she said.

"I need to be there."

She was too tired, and in too much of a hurry, to argue with him. "It's your funeral."

She took his arm, opened the door and pulled him out.

On the street, they realized that neither of them had any money for a taxi or even five cents each for the subway. So they began to walk the sixteen blocks to the Algonquin Hotel.

It was warm outside, especially for April, and beads of sweat trickled down Faulkner's face. They didn't speak much, each one lost in thought. About halfway along, Faulkner turned to her.

"Is this a typical Friday morning for an average writer in New York City?"

"I wouldn't know," she said. "I don't know any average writers. Why do you ask?"

His heavily lidded eyes fluttered. "I'm beginning to think New York is not for me."

She looked at him. His skin was fish-belly white. "Nonsense. You fit right in. Just don't think of yourself as average, no matter where you go. Come on. We're almost there."

She pulled him along. Faulkner's skin was so pale that he was almost green. And her head was pounding.

They reached the Algonquin just after one o'clock. A small crowd had gathered under the awning at the hotel's front door. As she and Faulkner approached, the cluster of people turned to stare. Dorothy took a deep breath, gripped Faulkner's arm and pulled him through the knot of onlookers and in the door.

Inside—instead of the usual welcoming cool, dark and quiet atmosphere—the lobby was now crowded, loud and brightly lit. Undaunted, she elbowed her way forward, her hand clutching tightly to Faulkner to keep from losing him in the crowd. Expectant faces that she didn't recognize turned to look at her.

A hand tapped her shoulder. She spun around, ready to launch a nasty remark.

But it was Benchley, smiling as ever. As reliable as Christmas. She would have hugged him—but it was too crowded, of course.

"Afternoon, Mrs. Parker," he said brightly, nearly shouting above the din. "How are you today?"

"Just dreadful," she said brightly, although this time it was true. "And you?"

"Couldn't be worse, Mrs. Parker," he said merrily. "Couldn't be worse. Ready for lunch?"

Still holding on to Faulkner with her right hand, she reached for Benchley with her left. Benchley led the way, and they shuffled like a little train through the crowd toward the dining room.

At the partition, Georges, the maitre d', held back the horde of people from entering the Rose Room. When he saw Dorothy, Benchley and Faulkner, Georges stepped aside with a curt little nod to let them pass.

In the dining room, Frank Case stood like a traffic cop, directing waiters and busboys with unflappable efficiency. Every table was full, and several people stood along the walls, each holding a glass or a little plate of something to eat.

Dorothy recognized almost everyone. In the center of the room, of course, the members of the Vicious Circle gathered at the Round Table. Robert Sherwood sat upright, as though afraid he might topple. (She could almost sense his hangover. It was the same as hers.) Next to Sherwood, Heywood Broun, disheveled as ever, fiddled not so surreptitiously with his silver flask. This he passed to Marc Connelly and George Kaufman, who had their respective bald and pompadoured heads together in some spirited discussion. Next to these two, Harold Ross was holding a match to light Franklin Adams' cigar.

Adams settled back and puffed the cigar. He seemed to radiate a kind of magnanimous, self-satisfied air—then Dorothy remembered that his column, in which they had issued their challenge to the murderer, must have appeared this morning. Clearly, Adams felt empowered that his article had drawn such a crowd.

Next to Adams, Ross looked up and caught her eye. Ross wore his typical perturbed expression—like he was sitting on his keys or some other uncomfortable thing—but he also seemed to want to talk to her.

Next to Ross were four empty chairs—one each for her, Benchley, Faulkner and . . . Woollcott! No doubt the big, stuffed turkey was waiting to make a grand entrance. They had made it seem as though Woollcott was the one, in print at least, who threw down the gauntlet. Now, she thought, Woollcott would no doubt rise to the occasion—but on his terms and in his typical bombastic style.

As she rounded the table to take her seat, her gaze took in the many other familiar faces in the room. There was nothing like the possibility of public humiliation to bring in the crowds, she thought. But who were they hoping to see humiliated? The murderer? Or the members of the Round Table?

In the corner, poised like a pack of vultures, stood Bud Battersby and a few other second-string reporters. Battersby looked on edge, overworked and out of place, and Dorothy couldn't resist indulging in a fleeting moment of gratification to see the muckraker so bedraggled.

Her smile traveled to the table nearest to the Round

Table. There sat Douglas Fairbanks and Helen Hayes across from Florenz Ziegfeld and his wife, Billie Burke. At another table, Harpo Marx, who was a frequent guest at the Round Table, sat with Irving Berlin and a couple other Broadway entertainers. At a table for two, Neysa McMein was being bored to tears by that would-be painter Ernie MacGuffin. At the next two-person table was the lawyer Wallace Ramshackle, looking uncomfortable, and Lou Neeley, apparently just getting acquainted. In another corner, Jack Dempsey and some of his boxing pals were ignoring the hell out of Edna St. Vincent Millay.

Many others were there as well. Raoul Fleischmann sat at a table with some white-haired Wall Street businessmen. And there was Billy Faulkner's manager from the bookstore, the prim Elizabeth Prall. She did a double take when she saw Faulkner, now well tailored, beardless and pasty white. And among the people standing along the wall was Dr. Charles Norris from the Bellevue morgue. He gave Dorothy a smile and a wink, both of which she ignored. Even old Maurice the elevator operator was peering from around the partition to see what was going on.

All their eyes were looking toward her and the Round Table. Some were looking slyly, others staring outright. But the sensation of everyone looking at her was like physical pressure. . . . She felt uncomfortably warm. Her head was pounding. She sank into the chair next to Harold Ross. Faulkner eased down next to her, and Benchley sat next to him. She reached for her water glass and took a big drink.

"Dottie, Bob," Ross was saying, "I have that list of names you wanted." He held out a telegram.

Benchley was talking, too. "Everyone's waiting. Should we get started?"

Ross held the telegram right before her face. She snatched it away. But she didn't read it. She would have to put on her glasses to read it, and she didn't want to do that with all those eyes on her. More important—

"I need a drink first," she said. She nodded to Luigi, who hurried over. She ordered an orange juice for herself and a tomato juice for Faulkner, whose complexion was still frog-belly white. Benchley ordered coffee.

Now that they were sitting, a hush fell over the room.

Frank Adams leaned forward. "Your audience awaits."

"They waited this long," she muttered. "Let 'em wait a little longer."

Luigi returned with the drinks. She considered asking Heywood Broun for his flask but decided against it. She took a big gulp. Faulkner picked up his glass with trembling hands and just barely raised it to his lips without spilling.

Marc Connelly, with a mischievous wink in his eye, reclined in his chair. "Well," he sighed, "we probably *should* wait for Woollcott anyhow."

That, and the juice, galvanized her. *To hell with Woollcott,* she thought. Although she didn't really want to be the ringmaster, she also didn't want Woollcott to swoop in and steal the show. She sat up in her chair and addressed the others at the table. "Let's get this show on the road."

Benchley smiled with bemusement. "Now, how exactly do we do that?"

Good question, she thought. *How* do *we do that?*

All the eyes of the Round Table—even Faulkner's woozy eyes—were on her.

She turned in her chair to address the dining room at large. Everyone was now looking at her. The room was smotheringly quiet.

"Well, murderer extraordinaire, we know who you are," she shouted. "Come forward and explain yourself!"

No one moved. No one spoke. For a long moment— a very long, very quiet, very expectant moment— absolutely nothing happened.

Then, slowly at first, their eyes glanced at one another. Was the murderer here? Was he someone in this very room? Was he about to reveal himself?

Still, no one said a word. But now they were looking at one another openly. For a just moment, they had felt a thrilling expectation, a fearful wonder. Now there was doubt. And now that doubt was mutating into something else, Dorothy could sense it. It was turning into skepticism, which she knew would soon become derision and ridicule. She felt her face flush, and it had nothing to do with her hangover.

Then, gasps and shouts of surprise came from the lobby. The people gathered at the dining room's entrance whirled in surprise. They jumped aside. A fleeting, dark blur shot forward out of the throng of onlookers.

Chapter 36

The dark blur rocketed forward, low to the ground. It zigzagged between the tables, aiming unerringly for the Round Table. Like a bolt of lightning, it launched into the air directly toward Dorothy, nearly knocking the wind out of her.

Dorothy found herself holding her little dog, Woodrow Wilson, who was panting hard.

Everyone in the room laughed—partly in amusement, partly in relief.

"Oh, my little man," she said, embracing the dog. Its eyes bulged in panic; its batlike ears flattened against its head; its tongue lolled out of the side of its mouth. "What happened to you? Why, you're wheezing like an old horse. You're quivering like a bowl of jelly."

She held the dog close and petted it reassuringly.

Benchley leaned across the table. "How did he get loose?"

She frowned. "Old Aleck Windbag, no doubt. Probably terrorized the poor thing for the past few days." She cupped the dog's face in her hands. "I'm so sorry, my little man. Dottie has you now. Don't worry."

Although the dog still quivered with anxiety, the mood had changed in the room. People were chattering, laughing and joking. The dog had broken the ice.

Douglas Fairbanks made some remark about the dog revealing himself to be the murderer.

"Maybe he had a bone to pick with old Mayflower," responded Harpo Marx, and everyone erupted in laughter.

Next to her, Faulkner clutched a hand to his stomach.

"Are you all right?" she whispered to him.

He spoke slowly, as though from a distance. "If anyone's looking for me, I'll be in the men's room. Please excuse me."

She watched him get up unsteadily and shuffle away.

"Dottie," Adams said, drawing her attention. "Maybe now is the time to resume, while your audience is amicable."

Her audience? Again she flinched from the idea of being the ringleader of this circus. She glanced at Benchley. He had been looking at her. His smile widened; his eyes creased in merriment. He understood. Then he stood.

"Everyone, your attention, please." He clinked his fork against his coffee cup, and conversation hushed to a low murmur. "Undoubtedly, you read Mr. Adams' column in this morning's *World*. And a fine *World* it is, and a fine world we live in. That being said, you certainly read about the . . . well, the threats made to this little group of writers and editors who sit at this table. And no doubt you read Aleck Woollcott's bold and provocative response—"

Out of the corner of her eye, she saw Battersby shift from foot to foot. She was pleased Benchley didn't mention the article in the *Knickerbocker*.

"Where is Woollcott anyway?" Harpo yelled. "He should speak for himself."

Adams shot Harpo a nasty look. "Children are best seen, not heard."

That shut Harpo up.

"Heh-heh," Benchley laughed awkwardly. "Yes, well, I'm sure Mr. Woollcott will arrive pleasantly—I mean *presently*. Mr. Woollcott is clearly not pleasant—I mean *present*!"

Yes, where is *he?* Dorothy wondered. One of Woollcott's few positive traits was punctuality.

"If Mr. Woollcott were present," Benchley continued, "I'm sure he would ask the same thing that's teetering on the tip of all our lips—and I'm not talking about a silver hip flask. He would say, 'Oh, murderer, oh, murderer, won't you come out to prey?'"

No one laughed at the joke. Benchley stood in the awful silence that followed it, one hand hesitatingly touching the table. Still no one spoke. Clearly, Benchley wanted to give up and sit down, but he couldn't.

This half-assed plan wasn't working out at all, Dorothy thought. It was a disaster. She compelled her brain to say something funny, to break the ice again, get Benchley off the hook. But before she could speak, the people standing at the entrance to the dining room erupted into another commotion.

Adams leaned forward. "Tell me it's not another dog."

She shrugged.

Frank Case sailed into the room. He held a candlestick-style telephone. He walked calmly to the Round Table, plugged the telephone wire into an outlet in the floor and set the phone down on the table. He held the earpiece to his head and clicked the switch hook. "Go ahead, operator. Put the call through."

He handed the earpiece to Dorothy. "For you."

She accepted it tentatively. "Hello."

"Ah, there you are, Mrs. Parker." She recognized the faint Irish brogue immediately. "You're just in time."

"Time for what?"

"Time to listen to me kill your friend Mr. Dachshund," Mickey Finn said, his voice a mix of menace and mirth. "He won't admit he murdered my man Sanderson. Now I'm going to kill him—unless he spills his guts."

Her whole body went cold. Fear drained her of rational thought. Panic rose in her chest. Had Finn or his men grabbed sick, sad Faulkner in the men's room? The poor young thing—

Then rational thought returned. Something wasn't right.

"Where are you?" she said. "Where is Dachshund?"

"Dachshund? Why, he's right here. We're in my little sanctum sanctorum. You remember, now, don't you?"

She laughed. Faulkner had left only a minute ago. And Finn's hideout was at least two miles away.

"So what's so funny, my dear?" Finn said, his anger rising. "This is no joke, to be sure."

"If it is, the joke's on you," she said. "I don't know who you've got there, but it isn't Mr. Dachshund. Toodle-oo!"

She hung up.

The moment she did, she realized whom Finn held captive. She felt terrible for a moment; then she laughed out loud. Everyone looked at her.

"Well?" said Benchley, who was still standing. "What was that?"

"An Irish blessing," she laughed. "Mickey Finn is going to kill Woollcott."

Adams yanked the cigar out of his mouth. "Mickey Finn the gangster? You're not serious?"

"Don't worry," she said. "Finn said he'd kill him if he doesn't talk. Fat chance. He'll kill Woollcott just to shut him up!"

"He wouldn't!" Sherwood said.

"No, he wouldn't," she said. "Finn isn't that stupid. He'll figure out he has the wrong fellow. Woollcott is in no danger—well, not very much."

"Still, shouldn't we call the police?" asked George Kaufman, always the worrywart.

"Oh, I suppose—" She reached for the phone and clicked the switch hook. "Operator, get me the police."

Yet another commotion stirred the onlookers standing at the entrance to the dining room. Captain Church emerged though the crowd, followed closely by Detective O'Rannigan and two cops in uniform.

"Operator, you deserve a raise," she said into the phone, and hung up.

Church, O'Rannigan and the other cops swarmed toward the Round Table.

"Well?" Church said.

Woody started trembling again. She tried to soothe him. "Well what?"

O'Rannigan stepped forward. "We're parked across the street. We saw Finn and his gang walk out of here a half hour ago with fatty pants in his pajamas. They put him in a car and drove off."

"And you didn't stop them?" she cried.

Now Church spoke. "We believe we know who killed Mayflower and Sanderson, and it was not Mickey Finn or Alexander Woollcott. As far as we are concerned, they were doing nothing illegal and they are not part of this murder investigation."

"So who is?"

"Didn't you find out?" O'Rannigan sneered, cocking his little brown derby over his wide forehead. "Isn't that what this whole hullabaloo is all about?"

Church said, "Did anyone come forward?"

"No," she said. "Not yet."

Church turned to the two uniformed policemen. "Officers, block the exits. Make sure that no one leaves this building."

"Captain," Frank Case interjected, "you can't—"

Church ignored him. He turned to O'Rannigan. "Detective, you know who to look for. Arrest him."

The crowd in the room grew uneasy, anxious, alarmed.

It suddenly occurred to Dorothy that Billy Faulkner had been gone far too long.

She turned to Benchley, trying to keep her voice calm. "Fred, would you please go check on Billy? Right now?"

Benchley's smile wavered only a moment. "I'm sure he's fine. Probably just taking a nap on the bathroom floor, as usual." He turned and strolled purposefully toward the lobby.

Something else bothered her. Then she spotted the telegram on the table and snatched it up. It was the list of names in Sanderson's army regiment.

"I wondered when you'd get around to that," Ross muttered.

She searched in her purse for her horn-rimmed glasses. "Did you read it?"

"Looked it over," he said. "Nothing jumped out at me."

She put on her glasses and read the telegram.

"What's it say?" asked Sherwood.

"It says, PER YOUR REQUEST, HERE ARE NAMES OF FIFTY-TWO MEN IN THIRD NEW YORK INFANTRY, FIFTY-FOURTH BRIGADE, TWENTY-SEVENTH DIVISION, BELLICOURT, FRANCE. Then it lists the first initial and last name of each soldier."

"Do you recognize any?"

"Nope." She read aloud. "*G. Abbott . . . J. Albright . . . M. Andrews . . .*"

As she spoke, the telephone rang. Automatically, she picked it up. It was Mickey Finn.

"You hang up on me like that once more, and you'll be the next saint in heaven."

"Me in heaven? You called the wrong number."

"How many times do I have to tell you this isn't a joke, Mrs. Parker? Now, I'm going to put your friend Dachshund on, and you tell him to admit—"

"What makes you so sure that man is Dachshund?"

She could hear Woollcott's incessant, nasal voice in the background.

"He's Dachshund, all right. *Shut up, you!*" Woollcott's voice quieted. "We hoisted him from your apartment, didn't we? You've been lying to me, my dear lass. He's been hiding out there all this time. But the nail in the coffin was that he had Sanderson's gold tooth!"

As she listened, she continued to silently read the list of names. *N. Archer . . . T. Baker . . . C. Bartlett . . .*

"You might as well let him go. That man isn't Dachs—" She dropped the phone. "Holy shit!"

The dog on her lap jumped to the floor. She leaped to her feet. She scanned the faces in the room. She didn't see the face she was looking for.

Benchley ran back in. "Billy's gone."

"Shit!" She pointed to one of the names on the telegram. "It's Battersby! It's *Battersby*, damn it!"

"Battersby?" Now Benchley looked around the room. "Where the devil is he?"

"He's gone," she said. "And he took Billy!"

Chapter 37

Everyone in the room was now standing, shouting and hurling questions at one another.

"Hold on," O'Rannigan bellowed. "This is no time to panic."

"Are you kidding?" Dorothy cried, scooping up her dog. "This is *precisely* the time to panic!"

She turned on Harold Ross, her voice sharp. "You read the names on that list. Why didn't you tell us right away about Battersby?"

Ross looked stunned. He grabbed the telegram. "It says *M. Battersby*, damn it, not *B. Battersby*."

"His first name is *Merton*. 'Bud' is just a nickname. Everyone knows that."

Ross shrugged, helpless.

Kaufman spoke skeptically. "So Battersby was in France in the war? What does that prove?"

She handed Kaufman the telegram. "Look at everyone whose last name starts with *S*."

He read the names. "*K. Sanderson!* The Sandman."

"And Battersby, being a newspaperman, certainly knew what kind of business the Sandman did," Benchley said. "Battersby must have hired the Sandman to kill Mayflower."

"Never mind that now," she said. "He took Billy. We have to stop him."

"Not to worry." Captain Church spoke commandingly. "My men will have stopped him at the door of the hotel."

Marc Connelly scratched his bald head. "But what does Battersby want with Billy anyway?"

"Dachshund is the only one who can place Sanderson here at the scene of the crime," Church said. "Without Dachshund, we lose our link to Sanderson. And without Sanderson, we lose our link to Battersby. In *his* mind anyhow."

"But where are they?" she said.

Church looked toward the entrance. "Wait here." He hobbled away.

The dog squirmed in her arms. She let it go. Woody barked at the telephone on the floor. She picked it up. Finn was still cursing on the other end.

"Now, is that any way to talk to your 'friends'?" she said.

"What's going on there? What did I tell you about hanging up on me? As soon as I get finished with Dachshund, I'm coming for you!"

"Do what you like, but it's not Dachshund you want. It's Bud Battersby. Battersby killed your man Sanderson, after he ordered Sanderson to kill Mayflower."

"Battersby? The guy from the newspaper?"

"That's the one."

"So where the hell is he?"

Church, O'Rannigan and the two officers returned. Church's jaw was clenched. O'Rannigan's face was redder than usual. Battersby—and Faulkner—were not with them.

She looked at Church. "So where is he?"

"Gone. He and Dachshund must have left immediately after we arrived, before I could post my men at the door."

"I heard that," Finn roared on the phone. "Where did he go?"

"Good question," she said to Finn. "I have an idea. Hold the line."

"I *won't* hold the line!" Finn's voice shouted. "If you put down that phone, your life ain't worth spit."

"Well, I never did live up to expectorations." She put down the phone and turned to Church. "That telegram— the threatening one we received yesterday. Do you still have it?"

"No, not here."

O'Rannigan explained. "It's in the evidence locker, at the station."

Adams chuckled. "Don't you read the paper? I printed it word for word in my column today, remember?" He tossed a copy of the *World* across the table.

She snatched it up and ruffled through the pages. "Battersby undoubtedly sent us that telegram. He was trying to tell us something." She found Adams' column and read aloud, "'Mayflower has been plucked. Sandman went to sleep. Round Table your time has come full circle. Prepare for trial by fire.'"

"Trial by fire?" Benchley said, tugging at his bow tie. "I don't like the sound of that. What does it mean?"

"It's not just a trite metaphor," she said. "I think we can take it almost literally."

"But what kind of fire?"

Suddenly she knew.

"Oh, God," she gasped, clutching his arm. "Remember those steam furnaces in the basement of the *Knickerbocker* plant?"

Benchley's jaw dropped. "You don't think—"

"I do think. Those furnaces could burn up anything to cinders and leave no trace behind. That's where Battersby's taking Billy."

Church turned to O'Rannigan. "You heard what she said. Get the cars."

She stood in front of Church, blocking his way. "We're going with you."

He surprised her by not arguing. "Just you and Mr. Benchley. You might be of help."

Finn's voice shouted from the phone. "I heard all that!"

Church stopped and picked up the phone. "Do not interfere, Mr. Finnegan. This is your warning. And turn that Woollcott fellow loose."

They all heard Finn reply.

"Like hell I will! And we'll get there first, you damned peg-leg prick."

The line went dead.

Everyone stared at the police captain.

"What are you waiting for?" he thundered at Dorothy and Benchley. "Get in the car!"

Chapter 38

Dorothy scooped up Woodrow Wilson and shoved the dog into Sherwood's arms. She and Benchley raced through the crowd toward the front door. Captain Church followed quickly behind them.

Out on the street, an unmarked black Buick screeched to the curb. O'Rannigan jumped out. Immediately behind the sedan, a paddy wagon, manned by the two uniformed cops, pulled up.

O'Rannigan looked stunned to see the captain shepherding Dorothy and Benchley toward the sedan. They scrambled into the backseat. As Church climbed into the front passenger seat, O'Rannigan stared at them.

"They're coming along?"

Church ignored the question. "Go back inside. Call the Fourteenth Precinct. It's the closest one to the *Knickerbocker* plant. Get as many officers as possible on the scene."

"To intercept Battersby?"

"And to stop Finnegan. He aims to beat us there. Have them waiting for him."

One of the officers got out of the paddy wagon. "Where are we headed?"

"A printing plant near the West Village," O'Rannigan said.

"Where?"

"A block north of Houston. You take Seventh straight down. At Clarkson, Seventh doglegs and becomes Varick. Take a right at Clarkson 'til it dead-ends. The printing plant is right there."

The officer put his hands on his hips. "Nah, if it's on West Street, let's go straight down Eleventh 'til—"

The other officer leaned out the window. "You nuts? If you go down Eleventh, you gotta go all the way around the Gansevoort Meat Market—"

Dorothy watched Church growing impatient listening to this argument.

"So," she said, "what were you doing parked across the street out here while we were inside?"

Church turned around. "Waiting for you to spring your trap. We suspected Battersby all along, of course. That is why we let you cavort freely with Dachshund, instead of hauling Dachshund in. We were certain he was the linchpin to the whole works."

"So you were using us and Faulk—Dachshund as bait?"

"If you choose to look at it that way."

On the sidewalk, O'Rannigan continued to argue with the other officers.

She sighed. "I'm worried about Billy."

Benchley patted her hand. "Don't worry. Billy's not a weakling. Remember how he knocked down that Sandman fellow?"

"Billy couldn't knock down a sand castle right now."

Church, reaching the end of his patience, reached forward and turned the crank on the siren. O'Rannigan and the other two policemen jumped. O'Rannigan sprang toward the sedan, and the officers hopped back in the paddy wagon.

Climbing behind the wheel, O'Rannigan looked sheepishly at the captain. "We'll take Ninth. Straight down Ninth until it becomes Hudson, then—"

"Just *drive*!"

O'Rannigan gunned the engine, and the car leaped

forward. Church cranked the siren again. The paddy wagon followed, its siren now wailing, too. Pedestrians, cars, trucks and horse-drawn wagons scattered in all directions to clear the way.

O'Rannigan yanked the steering wheel. The sedan went up on two wheels as it banked sharply onto Fifth Avenue. Dorothy slid across the seat and slammed into Benchley, her hip pressed hard against his. He was pinned between her and the car door.

"I'm sorry, ma'am," Benchley gasped. "This seat is taken."

The car turned again onto Forty-third and raced headlong, all too quickly approaching the clog of traffic in Times Square.

Twenty feet ahead, a double-decker bus was slowly crossing Seventh, blocking their way through the busy intersection. Dorothy's hands flew to her eyes. O'Rannigan jerked the wheel. The sedan swerved in front of the bus, passing its front end by inches.

Once past the heavy traffic of Times Square, the police cars picked up even more speed. O'Rannigan pulled the wheel to the left, making a sharp turn onto Ninth. Benchley slid along the seat and collided into Dorothy, slamming her painfully against the side door.

"Try that again, mister," she said through gritted teeth, "and I'll call the usher and have you thrown out of the theater."

Benchley looked grief stricken. "Beg your pardon, Dottie dear!"

It was almost worth a pair of bruised shoulders and knees to hear him talk like that.

The cars roared down Ninth, the paddy wagon now leading the way. Above them, at second-story level, the tracks and girders of the elevated railway cast the street below in a latticework of dark shadows.

In the front seat, O'Rannigan hunched over the wheel. Beside him, Church continued to crank the wailing siren.

"Captain," Dorothy yelled over the siren's scream, "how did you figure out it was Battersby?"

Church turned slightly. "Good old-fashioned police work."

O'Rannigan barked a laugh. "Ha, that's exactly right." He didn't take his eyes off the road. "When we went to question Battersby the very first time, he showed us Mayflower's big, fancy office. But we insisted on talking to Battersby in his own little dinky office. Then, when he stepped outside for something or other, some papers—you know—fell out of his desk, like."

"They fell out all by themselves?" she asked.

Church shot O'Rannigan a stern look, but the detective didn't see it.

"They were Mayflower's papers. Seems he was writing a kind of autobiographical exposé, and a big chunk of it was about what a great big dummy his boss, Battersby, is. You know, rich kid who doesn't know nothing but thinks he can run the show? That was Mayflower's take."

"So that's why Mayflower went to Ramshackle. For libel insurance."

"Who?"

"Wallace Ramshackle. Mayflower's lawyer."

"Lawyer?" O'Rannigan turned and gave her a nasty look. "Why didn't you tell us Mayflower had a lawyer?"

"Why didn't you tell us you were using us as bait to trap Battersby?"

"Detective!" Church shouted. *"Look out!"*

O'Rannigan turned to see a traffic cop directly in front of the sedan. The cop held up a white-gloved hand; he blew furiously on his whistle; his face was red and panicked. O'Rannigan twisted the wheel to the left, directly into the path of an oncoming truck. Swerving around the traffic cop, O'Rannigan jerked the wheel back to the right. The truck raced by within inches of the sedan.

"Good heavens!" Benchley's hand went to his forehead.

"That was a close one, wasn't it?" Dorothy said.

"Not that," Benchley said peevishly.

"What?"

"I mean, good heavens, Detective Orangutan figured it out right from the first! Remember what he said during our nightlong Spanish Inquisition?"

"What'd he say?"

"Something to the effect that Mayflower had annoyed Battersby. And then Battersby called in a favor from the Sandman or somehow paid him to kill Mayflower. That was it. O'Tannenbaum deduced it."

"The de-deuce you say!"

"I told you," Church said. "Detective O'Rannigan is very good at his job. You would be unwise to underestimate him."

"He is, is he?" she said. "Say, *Detective*, something's been on my mind since we left the 'Gonk. Did you ever call the cops at the Fourteenth Precinct to intercept Battersby at the printing plant? Or were you too busy arguing over directions?"

The smug smile disappeared from O'Rannigan's face.

"Detective?" Church said.

"Well, I—" O'Rannigan began.

Church's voice was hard and cold. "Pull over now! A call box is right there, in front of the post office."

On the corner at Thirty-third was the colossal post office building, as solid and massive as a Greek temple. O'Rannigan slammed on the brakes and spun the wheel directly toward it. On the sidewalk, an organ grinder and his monkey barely jumped out of the way. O'Rannigan flung open the door and nearly leaped toward the police call box.

"And make it quick!" Church shouted after him. He turned to Dorothy. "Why did you wait until now to remind the detective to make that call?"

"I only thought of it now."

"At this rate, Finnegan will slaughter Battersby and

Dachshund, then make his escape before we even arrive."

"Then, let's go!" she cried, and jumped forward to crawl over the seat and get behind the wheel. But O'Rannigan, bursting into the car, pushed her back with one wide hand.

"Get outta here," he cried. "Do you even know how to drive?"

She landed back in her seat. "No, do you?"

All of a sudden, a long white limousine, followed by a white sedan, came hurtling around the corner, sped past the police sedan, and flew down Ninth. Dorothy thought she had seen Woollcott's terrified face staring out the window of the limo.

"Son of a gun!" O'Rannigan shouted, throwing the car into reverse. "It's Mickey Finn and his gang."

Chapter 39

The police car shot forward. In a moment, they had passed the paddy wagon, which struggled to catch up. But they couldn't catch up to Mickey Finn's limo and the car following it.

Dorothy closed her eyes and clutched her stomach.

"I never thought I'd get seasick in the middle of the island of Manhattan."

She couldn't decide which was more terrifying—keeping her eyes open or keeping them closed. She decided to keep them closed for a while to find out. Then the car screeched and lurched forward. She opened her eyes to see gunfire blazing out of the window of the white sedan.

Next to the white car—and directly in front of the police sedan—was a rickety coal truck. Small bursts of flame erupted in the open cargo bed as the bullets struck.

"They're shooting into the coal truck," O'Rannigan shouted. "It's catching fire!"

Pockets of flame now dotted the truck's load of black coal.

One of Finn's henchmen stuck his head and arm out of the window of the car. He reached forward, the top half of his body now struggling toward the tailgate of the coal truck.

In an instant, Church released the siren and clutched a snub-nosed pistol. Quickly, he rolled down his window—but not quickly enough.

The man grabbed the tailgate's latch and opened it. The tailgate disappeared under an avalanche of flaming coal that poured into the street, directly in front of the police sedan.

O'Rannigan wrestled with the wheel, but there was nowhere to go. To the left was a series of upright girders that supported the elevated train platform overhead. To the right was a milk wagon pulled by a horse.

At the sight of the oncoming pile of flaming coal, the horse reared in fright. The driver of the milk wagon held on for dear life.

O'Rannigan slammed the brakes. The car skidded on the first few chunks of coal. The oncoming pile was only thirty feet in front of them.

"The milk!" Dorothy shouted.

"What?" O'Rannigan yelled.

But Church understood immediately. He flung open his door and swung his wooden peg leg out into open space. He pivoted and, with dead accuracy, shot his leg out sideways like a bolt. It broke the pole that connected the horse's harness to the wagon. The driver released the reins. The horse ran free. But the wagon tilted on two wheels. It turned sharply—as Dorothy and Church saw it would—directly into the sedan's path.

The police car rammed straight into the broad side of the wagon, smashing the wooden cart to pieces. Pint-sized and quart-sized milk bottles exploded everywhere like fluid fireworks, spattering the sedan's windshield with a cataract of creamy liquid, white foam and chunks of glass.

Then the car smashed into the pile of coal like a fist pounding into a mound of sand, and lurched to a stop. Lumps of coal thunked and smudged the cracked, white-painted windshield, which shattered under the hailstorm of coal. Through the open window, they could see that the sedan's hood was buried nose deep in the heaping pile of wet coal. The milk had extinguished most of the flames.

They looked at one another, as if surprised to be alive.

"Hey, you lunatics!"

They turned to see the wagon driver shaking an angry fist. "You wrecked my wagon, spooked my horse and nearly killed me!"

"Ah, piffle," she said. "It's no use crying over spilled— oh, never mind. Let's clear out of here."

The paddy wagon screeched to a stop right behind the sedan. They clambered out of the car, stumbling and tripping over the lumps of wet coal.

"No room up front. Get in the back," O'Rannigan commanded Dorothy and Benchley, pointing to the prisoner compartment of the paddy wagon. The detective raced around and opened the back doors, clutching his small derby to his big head.

"Won't be the last time I ride in one of these, I'm sure," she said, and climbed in. Benchley, Church and O'Rannigan followed.

Chapter 40

In the back of the speeding paddy wagon, Dorothy—with her eyes squeezed shut—caught the scent of baking bread. She had read that this smell was the last thing you sense before dying. Was she now about to die? She could smell it. The rich, yeasty, sweet aroma of . . . cookies?

Her eyes popped open. Benchley wore his usual merry smile.

"Smell that?" He breathed in deeply. "Must be fattening to live in this neighborhood."

She glanced out the small window at the hulking red-brick North American Biscuit factory.

"Fig Newtons, I think," he said.

She shrugged. "Who gives a fig?"

"Officer!" Church yelled through the small window to the driver's cabin. "Do you have them in sight?"

"Yes, sir! About a block ahead. We're closing the distance."

"Faster, Officer. Faster!"

"Sir!"

Benchley leaned forward, a perplexed look on his face. He had to shout over the siren and the roar of the engine. "So, Captain, can you please explain something? If you had intended to use our lunch meeting today as bait for your trap, why did you come around to the party last night and tell us to call it off?"

"We have our methods," Church said.

O'Rannigan wore a self-satisfied smile. "Ain't you never heard of reverse psychology? We know how you smart alecks think. We tell you *not* to do something, and you go ahead and do it. We tell you to do something, you *don't* do it. So we wanted to make sure you went ahead with your cuckoo plan."

"You're a regular Dr. Freud," Benchley said drily.

"I'd say he's Jung at heart," she muttered.

Church ignored them. "Officer! Have you caught up yet?"

"Closing in, sir!"

Against her better judgment, Dorothy leaned forward again over Church's shoulder to peer through the little mesh window. She could see the white sedan just a short distance ahead and, beyond it, the long white limousine.

An intersection approached. The limo sped heedlessly through the tangle of traffic; the sedan followed.

She saw the elevated train tracks above the intersection. This must have been Greenwich Street again, where the Ninth Avenue El continued into Greenwich Village. The street fell into shadow under the train tracks as the paddy wagon sped into the intersection.

The police driver jumped in his seat. "Holy sh—"

Suddenly, a large white flash appeared directly in front of the paddy wagon. Dorothy saw the terrified eye and heard the frantic whinny. She and Church were jolted forward against the small window as the paddy wagon slammed hard, as if it had hit a wall.

Chapter 41

The paddy wagon stopped. The whinny turned into a keening wail, more shrill and earsplitting than the siren's wail. People screamed. Cars screeched to a halt.

"God, no!" Dorothy cried. "Was that a horse?"

The police driver looked back, horror-struck. "Came out of nowhere! I c-couldn't stop in time."

Church spoke calmly, almost coldly. "Never mind. Go around it. Continue after Finnegan."

The paddy wagon was still rocking up and down.

"Th-the horse is in the way. We're stuck. God, it's flailing!"

The other officer in the passenger seat looked back. "It's flopping around like a fish, Captain. It's nearly crushed."

O'Rannigan got up, withdrawing his large police pistol. "I'll take care of it."

Dorothy grabbed his sleeve. "Don't you dare—"

He didn't look at her. He shook his arm free and kicked open the back doors of the paddy wagon. He jumped out.

They couldn't see where he went, but they could imagine it. A stomach-churning moment passed, until the echoing gunshot ended the horse's wailing. The paddy wagon stopped rocking.

She buried her face in her hands.

The detective pulled himself back in. He closed the doors and sat down. "Let's go, Officer."

The paddy wagon lurched into reverse, disentangled itself from the body of the horse, then rolled forward haltingly.

"Can't you move this thing any faster?" O'Rannigan barked as the paddy wagon limped along.

"The whole front end is smashed in," the driver said. "We're lucky we're moving at all."

"Detective O'Rannigan?" Benchley said.

The detective didn't respond.

Benchley leaned forward, speaking louder. "Detective O'Rannigan?"

The detective didn't seem to hear him. "You're never gonna believe this," O'Rannigan said, his gaze and his voice distant. "It was the horse from the milk wagon. Must have kept running down Ninth, then took the dogleg at Greenwich. Damned thing was nearly in two pieces when I shot it."

Dorothy cringed.

"Detective O'Rannigan?" Benchley said tentatively.

The detective turned sharply. "Did you just call me O'Rannigan? Not O'Tannenbaum? Or Orangutan? Or Orient Express?"

"Yes, I did."

"Okay, Mr. Benchley. What?"

"I do believe you were right from the start," he said. "We should have taken Seventh Avenue."

Captain Church grimaced. "Officer," he snapped at the driver, "faster, now, faster!"

The paddy wagon hobbled forward without gaining much speed.

"What's the use?" Dorothy slumped in her seat. "There's no chance we can catch up now. Either by Battersby or by Finn, Billy's goose is cooked."

"Not so fast, Dottie." Benchley took her hand, which made her stomach—already upset—tremble. "Billy's resourceful. He's smart. And despite what you may wish to think, he's not a helpless little puppy. Furthermore, he wouldn't give up on you. So let's not yet give up on him, shall we?"

She sat up. His optimism, as always, took the edge off her despair. It didn't dispel it but made it somehow surmountable.

"Perhaps," she said.

"Certainly. Billy probably gave Battersby the slip, and at this very moment he's likely waiting at a bus stop somewhere to get back to the Algonquin. We'll all have a good laugh and a drink together when this is cleared up. You'll see."

"Nah."

"No?"

"He's got no bus fare. He's probably hitchhiking."

"See?" Benchley said, grinning. "What a resourceful fellow he is."

She suppressed a smile. Damned Benchley. Always ruining her bad moods.

She turned and peeked out the tiny back window. They were moving into the industrial part of town now. They puttered by an icehouse, small factories, warehouses, stables and a couple tumbledown hotels. Eventually, the paddy wagon turned onto a cobblestone street.

"There it is," the driver said.

On the left was the enormous St. John's Freight Terminal. The printing plant was on the right.

Finn's white limo and white sedan were parked half in the street, half on the sidewalk. Most of the car doors were still open—Finn and his men had been in a hurry.

"Go around the corner—to the loading dock," O'Rannigan ordered. "We'll sneak in the back door."

Around the corner, at the loading dock, stood a line of big trucks emblazoned with NEW AMSTERDAM SUPPLY CATALOGUES AND CALENDARS, INC.

A smaller truck was also haphazardly parked there. Its front end was severely dented in, and its front doors had been left open hurriedly, too. Printed on the side of the truck: NEW CANAAN BIBLE CO.

"So it was Battersby who tried to run us down," Benchley said.

The driver said over his shoulder, "That truck was parked behind the Algonquin Hotel today."

"It was?" O'Rannigan snapped. "Why didn't you say something?"

"I-I didn't think anything of it. How was I to know?"

O'Rannigan fumed but didn't have an answer. "Stop the car. Let's go!"

The paddy wagon skidded to a stop. They jumped out onto the cobblestone street. The two officers took the lead, O'Rannigan and Church next, followed by Dorothy and Benchley. They ran up the concrete steps to the loading dock.

O'Rannigan cursed. "Where the hell are the men from the Fourteenth Precinct?"

As if on cue, sirens sounded nearby.

O'Rannigan and Church, their guns drawn, paused to listen. The sirens came closer. Then they seemed to come to a stop around the corner, where Finn's cars were parked.

"Good," said Church. "Those officers will secure the front of the building. We have the rear. No one can escape."

"Let's go!" O'Rannigan roared, his pistol clutched in his meaty fist. He ran into the only open bay on the loading dock. The officers and the police captain followed him.

Dorothy and Benchley peered into the darkness through the open bay door. They could hear the loud locomotivelike chugging of the printing press.

Benchley raised his eyebrows. "Once more unto the breach, dear friend?"

She shrugged. "Lay on, MacDuff."

They turned and went inside.

Chapter 42

The large room was dark, but Dorothy and Benchley were able to make out the outlines of thick bundles of newspapers piled into six-foot-high mounds, ready to be loaded onto the trucks outside.

Ahead, they could see the figures of the policemen, shouting and running into the wide doorway that led to the printing floor. From that direction came the chugging of the enormous printing presses.

She tugged Benchley's sleeve. "The cops and the gangsters will keep each other busy. We have to find Billy and Battersby."

"Certainly. But where?"

"The boilers, of course. Let's find the stairs to the cellars."

Instead of following the policemen, they circled around the edge of the room, looking for a stairway. Finally, as they neared the wide doorway that opened to the printing room, they spotted a darkened stairway. Trotting down the dark stairs, they nearly collided with a portly figure.

"By Jupiter!" the man shrieked.

"Woollcott!" she yelled. "You just about scared the pants off us!"

Woollcott, in his silken Oriental pajamas, was nearly shaking.

"And it looks like someone scared the pants off you," Benchley said.

Woollcott composed himself quickly. "Those brigands. Those bootlegging fiends. Kidnapping a man out of his bed—"

"My bed, you mean," she said.

He ignored her. His tone changed from indignant to joyous. "But what loyal friends you are to come to my rescue! How can I repay you?"

"How?" she said, moving down the stairs. "You can stay here. We're looking for Billy. Have you seen him?"

"Well, no."

They turned and left him openmouthed at the top of the stairs and continued down into the darkness.

At the bottom of the stairs, they could smell rather than see the furnaces somewhere to their left. Someone was coming toward them. They heard the sound of pounding feet and heavy breathing. Benchley reached into his pocket and pulled out a box of matches, lighting one quickly with his thumbnail.

Three burly men, covered head to toe in soot, charged out of the darkness. Dorothy and Benchley flattened themselves against the wall. The three coal scuttlers grunted as they ran by, not even slowing down.

"Let's go," she said after they passed. "Battersby and Billy can't be far."

As they neared the end of the corridor, they could see the flicker of flames coming from the infernolike boiler furnaces. When they turned the corner, the heat hit them like a wave.

Ahead, silhouetted by the flickering light of the three boilers, the figure of Battersby pulled on the arm of Faulkner, who lay on the ground.

"Bud Battersby! Enough!" she yelled.

Battersby looked up. Then he turned away toward the boiler. He grabbed something—a shovelful of yellow hot coals. Twisting back around, he flung it—shovel and coals together—at her and Benchley. They jumped back into the corridor. The shovel landed at their feet with a clang. The glowing coals skittered across the floor.

After a moment's pause, she and Benchley peeked around the corner. Both Battersby and Faulkner were gone.

"Is he—" Benchley said. But Dorothy was already running for the nearest furnace. She was relieved she couldn't see Billy inside. She glanced at the floor.

"Look," she said. Something had been dragged away in the coal dust. "This way."

They ran ahead and soon came to the open door of the large newsroom. The room was empty. Two sets of dusty footprints went off in the direction of the executive offices at the far end of the room. They followed the footprints, which ended at the doorway to Battersby's spartan office.

An electric whirr came from the back wall. There was a small metal door set into the wall at about waist level. It looked like a tiny elevator.

"A dumbwaiter," she said, moving toward it. "It's going up."

On the floor, directly below the dumbwaiter, were a few scraps of paper.

"What are those?" she asked.

"Typesetter's instructions," Benchley said. "You suppose they somehow took this dumbwaiter up to the type-setting room?"

"So it would seem," she said. "Should we wait for this one to return, or take the stairs?"

They turned around and took the stairs.

Back up on the printing floor, the thunderous noise from the printing presses battered their ears. Looking around, they saw a knot of men at the far end of the gigantic room: Captain Church and several policemen stood guard over a few of Mickey Finn's men. But Finn himself, as well as Lucy Goosey, was noticeably absent.

As Dorothy and Benchley ascended the wooden staircase to the typesetting room, they noticed that the three enormous printing presses were going full steam, yet there were no workers tending to the great machines. Likely the police had evacuated them from the building.

So, it was a surprise to find the typesetters still working busily in the glass-enclosed room that overlooked the printing floor. The half dozen typesetters—speedily punching keys on the Linotype machines or filling up the printing plates—seemed unaware of, or unconcerned about, the mayhem going on below.

Benchley scanned the room to locate the dumbwaiter; then he tapped the shoulder of the nearest man, who turned with a start.

"Your boss?" Benchley enunciated loudly and slowly. "Mr. Battersby?" He pointed to the dumbwaiter.

The man frowned, seemingly annoyed by the interruption.

Dorothy grabbed some of the lead letters from the table and quickly put them in order. She waved to get the man's attention, then pointed at what she had spelled: *BatTerSby*.

The man nodded, smiling at her. He now casually glanced about the room, as if perhaps Battersby might very well be present. Then something caught the man's eye. He pointed out the plate-glass windows.

Below, skulking along the near wall, was Battersby. He dragged along Faulkner, whose hands were bound. Faulkner looked like he might collapse at any moment. Then the two of them disappeared through a high, narrow archway.

Benchley again enunciated loudly, "Where—does—that—doorway—lead—to?"

"Never mind. Let's just go," Dorothy shouted to Benchley. Then, with a quick shake of the man's hand, she ran from the room. Benchley followed on her heels.

They hurried down the stairs. At the far end of the printing-room floor, they could see that Church and the other policemen were not looking in their direction—

and they had not seen Battersby and Faulkner either; otherwise, at least a few of the cops would have come running.

"That dumbwaiter must have been a trick," Benchley yelled over the noise of the presses. "And we fell for it."

"Live and learn," she shouted. "I've fallen for dumb soldiers, dumb sailors and dumb writers. About time I was fooled by a dumb waiter."

"Beg your pardon?"

She didn't answer. They darted through the high archway and found themselves in another enormous room. They faced a forest of huge blank rolls of newsprint, all standing upright in neat rows, like columns of a Greek temple, but placed much closer together, just wide enough for a person to walk between. The paper rolls, hundreds of them, filled the room from one end to the other.

Dorothy detected movement out of the corner of her eye. At the far end of a long corridor, she saw Mickey Finn and a couple of his men racing toward her. They'd be in the room in a few moments.

"Well," she said to Benchley, "we know Battersby didn't go down *that* hallway. Shall we peruse this room for Battersby and Billy?"

"Indeed we shall," he said. "Why, I spy with my little eye . . . what do you call that walkway?"

He pointed up to a narrow metal catwalk that encircled the upper half of the room.

"An elevated sidewalk," she said. "Why don't you go up there and take a peek around? Perhaps you'll be able to spot our quarry from that lofty position."

"Perhaps I will. And perhaps you can stall Finn and his bootlegging brutes. You let that kind of riffraff in the place and it'll give this joint a bad name."

He jogged toward a nearby iron ladder and climbed it carefully to the catwalk. She turned toward the entrance to the corridor, but Finn and his men were already bursting into the room. Right behind them came Detective

O'Rannigan—huffing, puffing and sweating—and two brass-buttoned policemen.

"Hold it right there, Finn," O'Rannigan wheezed.

Finn didn't even hear him. He shouted at Dorothy. "Battersby! Where is he? We saw him come in here."

"There he is," Benchley yelled from the catwalk. He pointed toward the far end of the room. "He's dragging Billy like a dog on a leash."

Finn looked up at the sound of Benchley's voice. His eyes narrowed. He grabbed one of his henchmen by the shoulder. "Muldoon, look! See that crane up there? Get it working and drop it on Battersby's head. Now!"

Finn pointed to a large, medieval-looking mechanical device that drooped down from the rafters like an enormous rusty metal spider. Dorothy figured it must have been used to transport the giant rolls of newsprint in and out of the room. She traced its chains and wires back to a set of controls up on the catwalk, just a few feet from where Benchley stood.

The man named Muldoon threw off his hat and trench coat as he ran to the ladder.

"Stop in the name of the law," O'Rannigan wheezed. "Finn, you're under arrest, and that goes for your men, too."

Lucy Goosey had somehow appeared at Finn's side. She chuckled contemptuously at O'Rannigan, a low, throaty sound.

"Fred!" Dorothy yelled, pointing at the controls. "Don't let him use that crane."

Benchley spun around, unsure of what she pointed to. Then he saw the controls and his gaze followed the wires to the low-hanging crane.

Finn was smiling, but his voice was ruthless as he spoke to the detective. "I supply all the booze that your flatfoots sneak into the policeman's ball, not to mention the booze for the speakeasies that all you cops go to."

"I don't—" O'Rannigan began.

Finn cut him off. "You arrest me, I shut off the booze.

Then you'll have the whole New York police force down on your neck."

That gave O'Rannigan pause—just long enough for Muldoon to leap along the catwalk toward the controls of the crane. But Benchley got there first.

High above, the crane jolted to life.

"Ha!" O'Rannigan turned to Finn. "Who's got the last laugh now?"

"Oh, no," Dorothy said, realizing her mistake. "Mr. Benchley should not be allowed near mechanical things. Better that Mr. Muldoon—"

Too late. The head of the crane dipped sharply. Benchley wrestled with the controls. Muldoon was right behind him, reaching around him.

Like some kind of prehistoric beast, the head of the crane swooped down as if to strike. Dorothy, O'Rannigan, Lucy and even Finn and the other men crouched low to the ground. Dorothy felt a rush of wind as the thing swung over her head.

"Not at us!" Finn yelled. "Swing that damn thing at Battersby!"

Benchley nodded, seeming to finally understand how to work the machine. The arm of the crane twisted sharply to the left, colliding brutally with the top of a nearby roll of newsprint. As if in slow motion, it toppled like a chopped redwood, knocking down the next roll.

"Oh, no, Fred," Dorothy said, seeing what was about to happen.

The fall of the two paper rolls spread in a chain reaction. Like monolithic dominos falling, every roll of newsprint came crashing down in a slow but inexorable wave. The room rumbled like an earthquake. O'Rannigan pulled Dorothy back to the safety of the archway, where Finn and the others also stood.

As the crescendo of falling rolls of newsprint came to an end, a thin cloud of dust rose over the monstrous disarray. Then, from far across the room, she heard a yelp.

"There he goes," Benchley called from the catwalk. "It's Battersby."

"Is Billy with him?" she said.

"No, he was alone."

She filled her lungs and shouted as loud as she could. "*Billy!* Billy! Are you here?"

There was no answer.

"Let's go," Finn said to his men. "This way."

They turned and dashed out through the high, narrow archway. Lucy Goosey followed them at her own hip-swaying pace.

As Benchley came to Dorothy's side, she put a hand on his arm. "You go with them. Maybe Billy got out unobserved. But in case he didn't, I'll stay here and look for him."

Benchley squeezed her hand and rushed after them.

She cautiously approached the jumbled sea of fallen rolls of newsprint. "Billy? Billy!"

From somewhere deep within the room came a weak, nearly inaudible, response.

"Here . . . over here . . ."

Chapter 43

Benchley followed Finn and his men but quickly stopped. All this aimless running about seemed misguided.

A half dozen paces in front of him, the printing presses chugged and thumped along deafeningly. He felt the sound in his stomach. It vibrated up from his shoes.

He decided to think. What would he do if he were in Battersby's shoes? Battersby clearly wanted only one thing: to print his lousy newspaper. Above all, he'd want to make sure it continued uninterrupted. That's what all this was about, wasn't it?

Benchley looked up at the massive printing press, spitting out hundreds of those dreadful tabloid newspapers per minute. He searched the weblike network of ladders, stairs, catwalks and cables that covered the enormous machinery.

Now, he thought, *how do you turn the damn thing off?*

"Billy!" she shouted. "Billy, answer me. Where are you?"

A voice came from directly behind her. "Why, Mrs. Parker!"

She spun around. There stood Alexander Woollcott, still in his silk pajamas, his owllike glasses sliding down his pinched nose, a long, thin cigarette smoldering in his hand.

"Still looking for Dachshund?" he asked.

"Yes, of course I am."

"Can I help?"

"Help?" This took her aback. "Yes, you can help by shutting up and butting out."

Woollcott approached her slowly. "I certainly haven't been the boy's strongest champion, that's true. But that doesn't mean I want the boy to come to harm. This very day, I have seen for myself what kind of antipathy your Mr. Dachshund has been subject to. Allow me to make amends."

"Well, all right. A Dachshund is amends' best friend, after all." She turned back around and shouted, "Billy, where are you?"

From far away, the answer came softly. "I-I can't say exactly. It's very dark."

"Are you hurt?"

"I've had better days."

"Can you move?"

"No, I seemed to be pinned down."

"Start talking. We'll find you."

She moved forward into the maze of toppled paper rolls. She headed in the direction of his voice. One of the uniformed policemen—she learned that his name was Officer Compson—was at her side. Woollcott followed, shuffling in his slippers.

"Start talking?" came Faulkner's voice. "What shall I say?"

"You're a writer. Make up something."

Then he started speaking. For a moment, they were transfixed by his voice, which began weakly but quickly gained strength. "Battersby wanted his name to be known, not merely for accomplishment, not for fame, not for family pride, most certainly not for family pride, as he'd had enough of that, being that his affluent forebears bequeathed a family name that he indeed disdained, even as he sought to raise his own name in his own right by the quotidian accomplishment of a two-penny periodical—"

His words now tumbled over one another, rapid and diffuse.

Meanwhile, Dorothy, Woollcott and Officer Compson made slow progress, turning this way and that, like mice in a maze.

Faulkner rambled on. "And he labored and he worked and he toiled in quiet, dark silence, his hands ink stained with the fruit of his labor, and all the time he gave a platform for the vituperative voices of others, he standing well behind in the dark—"

Finally, they came to something of a small clearing. Faulkner's voice seemed to be coming from just beyond it. The logjam of newsprint rolls was too high to climb over, and there was no gap to squeeze under.

"This one," Compson said, pressing his shoulder against a roll. "If we can shove this one aside, we might be able to create an opening to crawl through."

She stood next to him, placed her hands on the roll and tried to anchor her tiny feet on the ground. Woollcott, imitating the officer, put his sloped shoulder uncertainly against the roll of newsprint.

"Ready?" Compson said. "Push!"

She pushed with all her might. The policeman grimaced. Woollcott groaned.

The roll didn't budge an inch.

They gave up, stood back and took another look at it.

While they stood there thinking, Faulkner's voice continued unabated. "And he vouchsafed this to me, his secret, his passion, his lament, his unfulfilled desire, as I listened, inebriated, incapacitated, bound and gagged, though not gagged with a gag but stunned into silence—"

Compson scratched his chin. "I saw a long iron crowbar, tall as you, back near the doorway. That could do the trick."

"Might as well," she sighed.

He turned and quickly disappeared in the maze.

Faulkner continued speaking without pause.

Woollcott whispered, "Why must he keep talking? Give the poor boy a break."

"I don't want him to think we've stopped. I don't want him to get discouraged," she said. "Besides, it gives him something to do."

Finally, Officer Compson returned. He carried the five-foot crowbar like a shepherd's staff. He wedged the flat end of it below the newsprint roll they had pushed against. Dorothy, wanting to help, also grabbed the crowbar. Woollcott merely watched.

With a mighty heave, Compson and Dorothy shoved the crowbar down. Slowly, the roll of newsprint inched up. Then, abruptly, it popped out of place and tumbled backward with a resounding thud.

They stood facing a blank brick wall.

Billy's voice had stopped.

"Billy?" she said. "Where are you?"

"I'm still here." His voice echoed off the wall in front of them, emanating from somewhere else in the room. "Is everything all right? What was that noise?"

She sighed. "Just keep talking. We're getting closer."

He continued where he'd left off. "And as he reached the apotheosis of his dissertation and his explanation and his confession all rolled into one, we arrived, as though in conjunction with his words, at the printing plant, which was the cranking and sputtering and blackened center of his irrevocable heart. . . ."

Benchley had climbed the metal stairs that were built on the side of the printing press. He then strolled along a narrow catwalk, scaled a ladder and found himself staring down into the belly of the beast. It was a churning, roiling river of black, white and gray—the newspaper sped by as fast as lightning, disappearing between massive rollers, yet continuing on and on and on.

The fleeting action and the noise made him dizzy and

nauseous. He tore his gaze away and looked around. There was no one to ask how to turn off the printing press.

Well, any lever, any wheel or any button is as good as another, he thought. He grabbed the largest lever he could find.

"Stop the presses!" he yelled. "I've always wanted to say that." Then he pulled as hard as he could.

As loud as the printing press was, this caused a noise that was even louder—a bloodcurdling metallic screech. The nearest set of rollers slowed to a stop, but the other rollers didn't stop. The steady stream of speeding newsprint kept spewing forth into the stopped rollers, piling up quickly. He smelled burning metal and saw smoke leaking out of the machinery. Then, finally, the whole thing began to shut down—some sort of emergency shutoff, he figured.

Like a locomotive pulling into a station, it took a few moments for the enormous printing press to click and whirr into silence. Benchley watched it come to a dead stop.

Then there was a hammering, but it wasn't coming from the now silent press. Benchley looked around him. Across the distance, almost at eye level, was Bud Battersby. He stood behind one of the large plate-glass windows of the typesetting room. His face was dismayed, his fists up against the window, hammering the glass so hard that Benchley was afraid it would shatter. Battersby mouthed something—curses, probably—but Benchley couldn't quite make it out.

"Hey, Battersby!"

Benchley looked down. There stood Mickey Finn, legs planted apart, his crooked yellow teeth grinning, his hands gripping a Thompson submachine gun.

"Battersby!" Finn yelled again, pointing the muzzle of the tommy gun directly up at Battersby. "The cops tell me that you killed my man Sanderson. You don't kill one of my best men and expect to walk away."

Rat-a-tat explosions of flame burst from the barrel of

the gun. Benchley looked up to see the plate-glass windows shatter into millions of glittering pieces. Battersby had disappeared.

Tiny shards of glass rained down on Benchley. He covered his head with his arms.

"Finnegan! Stop that immediately!" roared Captain Church, who appeared behind Finn. Church turned to the three uniformed policemen who were with him. "Go up there and see if Battersby is still alive. If he is, hand-cuff him and bring him down."

The policemen turned and ran up the wooden stairs toward the typesetting room.

"Me first," Finn yelled, and ran to overtake them. "Leave Battersby for me."

Benchley looked at the jagged empty windows of the typesetting room. Battersby's eyes peeked over the sill of the nearest broken window.

"Breaking news, Bud," Benchley called to him. "Mickey Finn and a handful of cops are on their way up."

Battersby immediately stepped to the window ledge. Without even looking down, he leaped out toward the catwalk. He landed just a few feet from Benchley, bits of glass tinkling around him.

"You should look before you leap, Bud," Benchley said, "or one of these days you'll find yourself in a mess of trouble."

Battersby moved forward. "Haven't you done enough?" He shoved Benchley aside and then quickly assessed the damage to the printing press. He ripped out the pile of excess newsprint. Then he turned a crank that lifted up the top roller by an inch.

"Why'd you do it, Bud?" Benchley said.

Battersby inserted the paper sheet between the rollers and turned back the crank that lowered the top roller again.

Benchley could hear that Finn and the police officers

were now searching among the debris in the typesetting room.

He spoke to Battersby again. "Far be it from me to presume, but I daresay you owe me an explanation, seeing as you employed a hit man to kill Mrs. Parker, Mr. Faulk—Mr. Dachshund and myself. Not to mention you tried to run us over with a truck full of Bibles. I'd go so far as to say that I'm due—"

Mickey Finn's voice shouted out, "Oh-ho, there you are!" He now stood in the same window where Battersby had just been. He lifted up the tommy gun. Benchley and Battersby both hit the deck. Two officers appeared behind Finn and seized his arms. But the gun still erupted in echoing blasts.

Bullets clanged over Benchley's head, ringing off the printing press. Then the gunfire stopped. Benchley looked up to see Church snatching the machine gun away from Finn.

Battersby, scrambling to stand up, grabbed the lever to restart the printing press. Benchley darted forward and grabbed hold of the lever from the other side and pulled with all his might.

Battersby looked at Benchley as though he were a buzzing insect—an annoyance to be swatted. Battersby raised his shoe—the one that had stomped the cockroach in the Sandman's apartment—and planted it against Benchley's stomach, pressing hard against Benchley's abdomen while he pulled the lever in the opposite direction.

"Ow," Benchley groaned, his fingers slipping but still holding on. "You're taking the 'power of the press' far too literally."

Faulkner's words rolled out of him in a stream of consciousness—without pause, without pretense, and almost without punctuation.

"The flames leaping and dancing and hungry, and he reached and lifted— Don't do it, I said, for the sin punishes not only the one who receives it but the one who commits it. . . ."

They were getting closer to him, she knew. Officer Compson now scaled an alpine mountain of paper rolls. Woollcott followed, slipping and fumbling.

"Mrs. Parker," Compson called, "look out!"

A roll of paper tumbled down toward her like a boulder in an avalanche. She couldn't tell which way it would land. She guessed that it would land directly in front of her rather than bouncing out and landing a few feet behind her. She scurried backward. Luckily, she guessed right. The thing landed with a deep, hollow thump, rolled slowly toward her a few inches, then came to a dead stop.

"Dottie, dear!" Woollcott said aghast. "Are you all right?"

"No need to worry," she said casually, but exhaled deeply. "I've always been good at dodging heavy paperwork."

Woollcott leaned down and extended a hand to draw her up. She grasped it and climbed up to join him and Compson at the top of the pile. "You might want to be more careful about how you throw your weight around, Aleck."

Before he could respond, Compson held up a hand. They understood. Faulkner's voice continued warbling on, but now it was significantly louder than before. They were getting very near.

They descended from the mound and then weaved around a bend, following the sound of his voice.

They came to a narrow cleft and saw a pair of thin legs in gray wool trousers wedged between two rolls of paper. Faulkner's voice warbled from the opening.

"He urged me further and— 'Relinquish me,' I said, 'and relinquish your vanity,' though my words were emitted as a whisper, a ghostly vapor, perhaps only in my thoughts, therefore he would not be persuaded, indeed he insisted he must endure—"

"You can stop now, Billy," she called out, relieved. "I think you found your voice."

The legs kicked and fluttered like the little legs of a happy schoolboy sitting on a porch swing. "Oh, Mrs. Parker, thank goodness! Can I say how grateful I am for all your assistance? And can I say how sorry I am to have put you to such trouble? And can I say—"

"You've said enough. Now, shut up and let us get you out of there."

Benchley continued to struggle against Battersby in a tug-of-war over the lever. Battersby shoved his shoe harder against Benchley's belly, but still Benchley—almost despite himself—refused to let go.

Benchley spoke through gritted teeth. "Just tell me why, Bud. Poor old Mayflower. Was that really necessary?"

Battersby's grip slackened, but only slightly. He didn't let go of the lever.

"That wasn't supposed to happen to Mayflower," Battersby said finally.

"And killing Dottie, Billy and me—that wasn't supposed to happen either?"

"Not at first," he said with a reluctant grin. "But then I realized it would make one heck of a story."

Quickly, Battersby pulled his foot away. Benchley, as if a support had disappeared, flew forward. He would have knocked his chin against the lever, but Battersby yanked it away. The printing press coughed and sputtered, then thundered back to life.

Dorothy, Woollcott, Compson and Faulkner—now freed and relatively unharmed—hurried into the printing-press room. She looked up to see Benchley collapse onto the catwalk. Then she saw Battersby zip up a ladder like a monkey on a vine.

They raced to join O'Rannigan, two police officers and two of Finn's men who had halted at the base of the press.

"Well, don't just stand there," O'Rannigan shouted at them. "Shoot."

Each of them raised and aimed a pistol at the quickly disappearing figure of Battersby.

Dorothy's hand reached out involuntarily and grabbed O'Rannigan's elbow as he fired his gun. His shot sparked off one of the supports that held up the catwalk, missing Battersby's head by inches.

The detective yanked his elbow free and spun around. "What the hell did you do that for?"

For once she couldn't voice an answer, although in her heart she knew why. The thought of O'Rannigan killing that dying horse haunted her. She couldn't stand to see a man, no matter who, shot and killed in front of her eyes.

She glanced over O'Rannigan's shoulder and saw Battersby race across a catwalk that arched over the printing press. Then he was gone.

To her surprise, she saw Benchley chase after him. O'Rannigan turned and followed her gaze.

"Quick," the detective yelled. "Go around to the other side. Don't let him get away." He and the other cops ran off, followed by Finn's men.

She couldn't bear the thought of running all the way to the end of the printing press and then around to the other side. It would be like circumnavigating the globe. Instead, she looked for a stairway to climb up to the catwalk.

Benchley looked down as he crossed over the catwalk. Through the metal grating under his feet, he saw the newsprint flying fast beneath him, the huge rollers spinning, and he had a moment of vertigo. Then he looked ahead and saw Battersby descending to a catwalk that ran alongside the press. Benchley jumped forward and dropped next to him. Battersby stopped and turned.

Benchley reached out to some kind of large knoblike valve. "So help me, I'll turn it."

"Go ahead. Turn it."

Benchley turned the knob. Steam spurted out, scalding his hand, nearly burning his face. He stumbled backward and fell onto the catwalk, knocking his head against something hard and solid.

Battersby stood laughing, as though watching the antics of a hapless clown.

Benchley reached around behind his head. He sat up and found he held a very long-handled monkey wrench—as long as his arm. He clutched it as he stood up.

Battersby held up his hands reflexively.

But Benchley had no intention of swinging the long wrench at him. Instead he held it toward the nearest set of rollers, ready to stick it in.

"So help me, I'll do it," Benchley said. "I'll throw a wrench, quite literally, into the works."

Battersby wasn't laughing anymore. "Put it down. Please just put it down."

"Tell me why. Why did you do it? Why Mayflower? Why us?"

Battersby hesitated, either unsure of what to say or just plain stalling.

Benchley touched the head of the wrench close to the space between the rollers, scraping at the paper.

"Okay, I'll tell you," Battersby pleaded.

Benchley drew the wrench away from the paper but still held it close to the rollers. "Go on."

Battersby's words gushed out. "I found out Mayflower was writing a memoir. I went to him and offered to publish it. But he laughed in my face. He'd publish his memoir elsewhere, he said. So I knew it was going to make the *Knickerbocker* look bad and make me look bad."

"And?" Benchley hoped Battersby would get to the point soon. The damn wrench was getting heavy.

"I knew Knut Sanderson from the war," Battersby continued. "I knew he could be hired for a price. I hired him to see what Mayflower was up to. But Sanderson was only supposed to follow Mayflower, see where he was sneaking off to. Then one day, he followed him into the dining room at the Algonquin, and suddenly they were alone face-to-face."

"So once Mayflower had seen him," Benchley said, "Sanderson knew he couldn't very well continue to follow Mayflower around without being noticed?"

"And Sanderson was always a hothead. Sanderson saw that Mayflower was writing a note."

"To Woollcott."

"Sanderson didn't know what was in the note, but he didn't like it. He probably stood there, giving Mayflower the evil eye. And Mayflower, with that snide attitude of his, must have said something back. Well, you don't talk back to Knut Sanderson."

"So they exchanged nasty words. Then Sanderson grabbed Mayflower's pen and killed him."

Battersby's boyish face suddenly appeared older. "I was as surprised and saddened as anyone. But then later Sanderson found out that your friend Mr. Dachshund had seen him at the scene of the crime. And Sanderson went after not only Dachshund, but you and Mrs. Parker. Sanderson had become a liability to me."

"A liability? He was a one-man plague."

"Exactly. If Sanderson had told someone—the police, Mickey Finn, anyone—that I had hired him, that would be the end of it for me. So I got into his apartment one night while he was sleeping. It was so easy. I turned on the gas stove. I came back in the morning. He was dead."

"You shoved him headfirst into the oven to make it look like suicide."

Battersby's expression now had a peculiar dreamy look. "That was all there was to it. One of the most feared men in the city, and I put an end to him with one little turn of the gas jet. What a thrill that was. You can't imagine."

"A thrill?"

"It opened my eyes. I've always been behind the scenes, trying to prove myself. I finally realized, not only could I simply deliver the news, but I could create the news. I'm sorry to say what fun it was thinking about writing a big news story about the sudden and brutal death of you and Mrs. Parker. I couldn't help myself."

Benchley was tempted to drop the wrench into the printing press, just for the hell of it. But he didn't. Not yet.

"And you had Billy to take care of," Benchley said. "Your one eyewitness link to Sanderson. You were planning to throw him into the furnace?"

Battersby shrugged. "The news must go on."

"Stop right there!" O'Rannigan yelled.

Benchley, startled, let go of the wrench.

The printing press screamed to a halt, its gears squealing. Its motor chugged loudly, but nothing moved. The handle of the wrench stuck out between the immobile rollers.

Battersby yelped like a mother for a child in danger. He shoved Benchley aside and vaulted up the catwalk that arched over the stalled printing press.

Dorothy, moving along the catwalk just moments after the press screeched to a stop, saw Battersby racing toward her. At the middle of the walkway, directly over the wrench stuck into the press, Battersby dropped to his knees and reached down. But the wrench was just out of his reach. She moved toward him, but he didn't notice her. He now fell prone onto the catwalk and leaned the top half of his body over the press.

Benchley approached on the other side of the catwalk.

"Get out of the way," O'Rannigan's voice yelled from below. "Give us a clear shot at him."

Battersby, his arms fully extended, his waist balancing on the edge of the catwalk, teetered forward. From somewhere deep within the press, its motor still churning, came a whistle of building steam. Then Battersby slipped forward and fell the short distance onto the immobile press. He landed safely on top of the metal cylinder that fed the paper into the wide rollers. He was within easy reach of the wrench.

The large rollers squealed. The paper jerked forward an inch.

"Battersby, don't move," Dorothy said. "If you pull that wrench, you'll be sucked in between those rollers."

She hurriedly looked around for a rope or chain—something to lower down to him. She saw the group below like a pack of jackals. Captain Church, Mickey Finn and his men had now joined O'Rannigan and his officers.

"Miss Goosey," Dorothy yelled, "show us your magic. Toss up your glove."

Lucy Goosey understood and reacted without hesitation. Reenacting her famous striptease, she tugged with her teeth at the fingers of her elbow-length silk glove. She slid the glove off her forearm, then lassoed it over her head. With a professional burlesque dancer's accuracy, she snapped it into the air. It streamed in a graceful arc and landed precisely in Dorothy's open hands. All the men watched, slack jawed.

She turned and dangled it to Battersby. "Take it."

Battersby had one hand outstretched toward the wrench. He looked in the direction of Church, O'Rannigan and Finn.

She angled the long glove toward his outstretched hand. "Take it!"

He shook his head. "The news must go on."

His hand gripped the wrench, and he flung it in the direction of the cops and gangsters. The printing press roared back to life. In a blink, Battersby disappeared between the rollers.

There was a sickening crunch, but the press didn't stop or even slow down. The newsprint on the far side of the rollers came out splattered with blood and gore.

Benchley then was beside her. He put his hand over

hers. He smiled gently. Even when everything was going wrong, he never failed to reassure her. She gripped his hand tightly. Thank God for Benchley. He didn't give her much, yet it was as much as she needed.

She didn't know how long they stood there watching the paper flow unceasingly through the machinery. But then Faulkner was standing next to her, and Woollcott next to him. Church and O'Rannigan were behind them.

Benchley spoke in a monotone, but loud enough for all to hear. "Mrs. Parker, what is black and white and red all over?"

She answered on cue, "The *Knickerbocker News*, of course."

Captain Church drew in his breath. "Have you no decency? This is no time for your gallows humor. This is no time for jokes!"

"This is precisely the time for jokes." But Benchley's face held no cheer; his voice was flat. "Mrs. Parker, have you seen who's in today's newspaper?"

"Why, it's Bud Battersby," she answered grimly. "His face is all over the front page. Just like he wanted."

Chapter 44

Two days later, Dorothy walked Faulkner to Pennsylvania Station. He held a one-way ticket for the Crescent, the southbound train to New Orleans, though he would disembark in Mississippi.

They stood on the platform to say good-bye.

"Are you sure you won't reconsider staying a while longer?" she said. "The party's just begun."

He smiled shyly. "There's a saying in Mississippi. You can't drain the swamp if you're up to your ass in alligators—pardon my language. Besides yourself, your friends and a few others I've met, this town seems full of alligators."

"Alligators. Sharks. Wolves. It's like a zoo. That's part of the fun."

He chuckled but wouldn't be persuaded. "Also, as you said, I've found my voice. But I think it speaks with a southern accent. It would be drowned out here." Then he looked to her encouragingly. "But maybe you could come visit sometime?"

"The countryside? I prefer to view the landscape from the inside of a taxi, thank you very much." She shook his hand warmly as the train whistled. "But do come back and visit us. And don't forget to write."

"Write?" He smiled and stepped up onto the train. "Yes, ma'am. Now, that I can do."

*   *   *

Woollcott genteelly spread his cloth napkin on his lap and then greedily dug his fork into his lunch of broiled chicken. He took a bite and waved his fork in the air. "Young Billy would have a bright future if he had stayed in New York. Back in the South, he'll lapse into obscurity. Too bad. I always was impressed by him."

Dorothy looked up from her hard-boiled egg. "You were impressed by him? That's absurd."

"No," Benchley said, "this is absurd. A pineapple, a cow and Pablo Picasso walk into a bar . . ."

It was lunchtime at the Algonquin. Before lunch, they had gathered to attend the funeral of Leland Mayflower, who had finally been laid to rest. Once the story came to light that Bud Battersby had ultimately been responsible for Mayflower's death—and the story was covered in every newspaper for days—Battersby's well-to-do family had offered to pay for the burial and funeral expenses. Lou Neeley had thankfully accepted their offer.

"It was the least they could do," Woollcott muttered, his mouth full of mashed potatoes, "after releasing that black sheep of a son into the world."

Benchley unfolded a two-week-old copy of the *Knickerbocker News*. "What still amazes me is that Bud Battersby as much as told us he was behind it with his own words. Listen to this." Then he read the article they had all read before.

> Consider what a matter-of-fact business it is for an influential editor—flush with the power of his lofty position—to strike out an entire paragraph, or whole pages even. So, too, did this murderer rewrite New York history. It was as easy as this! A simple erasure. A blotting of ink. A word struck through with a line. This was how easy it was for a murderer to strike down the famous yet-frail-figure of Leland Mayflower.

"We thought he was trying to point the finger at us," Benchley said, both amazed and amused. "Here, it turns out, he was explaining his own modus operandi."

"Modus operandi?" Adams took the cigar out of his mouth. "You've spent too much time in the company of policemen and lawyers."

Sherwood leaned forward. "Speaking of policemen and lawyers, did they throw the book at that Mickey Finn?"

"They did, but the book was *Winnie-the-Pooh*," Dorothy said. "And they didn't so much throw it as gently lob it."

Benchley said, "They merely charged him with illegal possession of a firearm. He posted bail and is already back to running whiskey."

Dorothy said, "I'd like to run some whiskey—right down my throat. How about we move this party over to Tony Soma's?"

She spoke to everyone, but she had her eyes on Benchley.

As expected, he stood up and chivalrously offered her his elbow. "I'll drink to that."

Historical Note

The members of the Algonquin Round Table didn't usually let the facts get in the way of a good story. Following their example, this book uses fact to fabricate fiction. But here, allow me to set the record straight of this somewhat crooked tale.

The Round Tablers were all real, though this story takes several liberties with the chronology of their jobs and residences in order to enhance the "anything goes" sentiment of the Roaring Twenties.

For example, Dorothy Parker, Robert Benchley and Robert Sherwood did work together at *Vanity Fair* magazine. And, Dorothy and Benchley did put postmortem photos, clipped from mortician journals, above their desks in order to shock their coworkers. They stopped working at the magazine just months after Prohibition began—yet this story extends their stay at *Vanity Fair* and takes for granted that Prohibition had been in effect for quite some time. (Interestingly, when Dorothy and Benchley first met, she was a infrequent imbiber and he was a staunch teetotaler. But by the end of Prohibition, they were both heavy drinkers.)

Likewise, although Dorothy Parker did in fact live at the Algonquin, she did not live there while working at *Vanity Fair*. Similarly, Alexander Woollcott did have an apartment at the end of East Fifty-second Street, which Dorothy Parker dubbed "Wit's End," but Woollcott did not live there at the time Dorothy Parker lived at the Algonquin.

Although much is known about these famous figures in the public eye, we can only speculate about some aspects of their private lives. Nevertheless, by all accounts, Robert Benchley and Dorothy Parker did *not* have a romantic relationship, though their close friendship is legendary.

Not surprisingly, these people were quite complicated personalities in real life. And, since there were so many unique real-life characters, for most of them I was required to simplify their complexities in order to tell a rousing story. A complex case in point (skipping right past Dorothy Parker) is Heywood Broun. He was indeed a boozy, slovenly sportswriter—but he was also an erudite columnist, critic and champion of civic causes. He founded the American Newspaper Guild, which continues to bestow an annual award in Broun's name to journalists who rail against injustice.

Another complex person was Alexander Woollcott. Although quite a character (and once described as "improbable"), Woollcott was quite real. He was the drama critic for the *New York Times*, but he then wrote for the *New York Herald* and the *New York World* during the Round Table years. In 1939, Woollcott was the model for the insufferable lead character in *The Man Who Came to Dinner*, a hit comedy play by George S. Kaufman and Moss Hart. True to form, Woollcott played the part himself onstage.

Also, every effort was made to portray locations as true to life as possible as my story allowed. The Algonquin Hotel is very real and is still catering to the toast of the town. (The hotel is a designated literary landmark, and a replica of the Round Table sits in the center of the dining room. You can even reserve the table for lunch, if you want.) Dorothy Parker did have a small suite on the second floor of the hotel, but again, this was not at the time that she worked at *Vanity Fair*.

Tony Soma's speakeasy was a favorite hangout for Dorothy and Benchley, although all the action happened in the basement and not on the ground floor, as depicted in this story. It was indeed located on West Forty-ninth Street near Sixth Avenue. In 1930, Tony's and all the other brownstones on this quiet street were torn down to make way for Rockefeller Center. The GE Building (or "30 Rock") stands directly on top of where Tony once served his bootleg liquor.

Interestingly, William Faulkner did indeed visit New York City as an unknown writer in the early 1920s—although there's no reason to believe he met anyone from the Round Table at this time. He did work in the Doubleday bookstore inside Lord & Taylor for a few months, and then went back south. (Elizabeth Prall, the bookstore's manager, married *Winesburg, Ohio* author Sherwood Anderson, who later became Faulkner's mentor.)

By 1930, Faulkner was a literary success. He returned to New York and it was then that he actually met the members of the Round Table, but the group was at its sunset and its members were going their separate ways. Dorothy Parker did express a motherly tenderness for Faulkner, saying, "You just wanted to protect him." This statement formed the basis of the relationship between Dorothy and Faulkner for my story.

Over the years, Faulkner continued to visit the Algonquin Hotel as he rose to fame. In 1949, he was honored with the Nobel Prize for Literature. Before he headed to Stockholm, Faulkner started writing his legendary speech at a room in the Algonquin.

After the Round Table years, the lives of its members were never the same.

Benchley eventually put down his pen and took up acting. He starred in one of the first short films to use sound, and followed that with a string of short comedic films and feature film roles.

Dorothy Parker continued to write. She contributed to the *New Yorker* and *Esquire*, and even earned two Academy Award nominations for screenplays. She took up pet political causes, and numerous pets, and eventually bequeathed her literary estate to Dr. Martin Luther King Jr. After his assassination, her estate passed to the NAACP.

Her collection, *The Portable Dorothy Parker*, has never been out of print. Yet she was largely forgotten at the end of her life. After her death, her ashes sat unclaimed for fifteen years in a filing cabinet drawer in her lawyer's office. (For her tombstone epitaph, she suggested "Excuse My Dust.") Eventually, the NAACP buried her ashes in a memorial garden at its headquarters in Baltimore.

Acknowledgments

I owe considerable thanks and recognition to:

Dorothy Parker, whose genuine wit, insight and humanity far surpass my middling version of her.

Robert Benchley and the rest of the Algonquin Round Table, whose contribution of humor and intellect toward twentieth-century popular culture should not be forgotten.

Marion Meade for her superlative biography of Dorothy Parker, *What Fresh Hell is This?*

Kevin Fitzpatrick, founder of the Dorothy Parker Society, for his essential guidebook, *A Journey into Dorothy Parker's New York*.

James R. Gaines for his encyclopedic handbook of the Round Table, *Wit's End*.

Editor extraordinaire Sandra Harding for her patience, enthusiasm and willingness to take a chance.

Ace agent John Talbot for his hard work and perspicacity.

Mary Logue and Michael Gibbons for their editorial assistance and contributions (and deletions) to the first draft.

Big Bill Murphy and Barbara Beasley Murphy for my first introduction to the Round Table and for their cheerleading and helpful comments.

My sharp-tongued, wisecracking sisters—Cathy, Mary, Barbara and Liz—for showing me what it's like to sit at a dinner table of merry vipers, and my pop, who instigated "pop quizzes" at the dinner table.

My mom for sitting me in her lap as a child and reading countless books to me.

Karin for her optimism, her undying support and for giving me the time to write this book.

About the Author

J. J. Murphy, an award-winning health-care writer in Pennsylvania, has also been a lifelong Dorothy Parker fan. J.J. started writing the Algonquin Round Table Mysteries after the birth of twin daughters, as an escape from toddler television. Please visit J.J. on his Web site at www.roundtablemysteries.com.

"Have you ever wanted to kill yourself?"

Dorothy Parker looked up to see the eager face of Ernie MacGuffin, hovering just inches away. MacGuffin was a third-rate illustrator and a first-rate nuisance.

"Mrs. Parker," he whispered again, only more urgently. "Have you ever wanted to kill yourself?"

"Matter of fact," she sighed, "I'm thinking about it right now."

It was just after lunchtime at the Algonquin Hotel. Dorothy sat at the Round Table in the hotel's dining room. She had been searching in her purse for a cigarette when MacGuffin suddenly appeared. Her usual lunch companions, sometimes called the Vicious Circle, had gotten up from the table. They were saying their see-you-laters and heading back to work for the afternoon. Helplessly, she watched them go.

"Seriously," MacGuffin said, hurriedly taking the seat next to hers, "I want to know."

She looked at him. He was a skinny scarecrow: messy nut-brown hair, cheap necktie, paint-stained fingers, dirty fingernails. She felt both pity and disgust for him.

"Suicide?" She lit her cigarette. "Sure, I've tried it. Who hasn't these days? It's like the Charleston—everyone's doing it."

"I knew it!" He leaned closer. "What happened?"

"What happened?" Her cigarette almost fell from her mouth. "Can't you guess? It didn't stick."

He nodded as if he was about to suggest how she could get it right next time.

"What's this all about?" she asked.

MacGuffin inhaled deeply. He was clearly debating whether he could trust her with something.

MacGuffin was a poor man's Norman Rockwell. He aspired to paint covers for *Collier's*, *Vanity Fair* and *The Saturday Evening Post*, but most of his works were for pulp magazines like *True Crime* or *Old West*. He was not an invited member of the Round Table. Instead, he rode on the coattails of Neysa McMein, a first-rate illustrator and one of the few women, besides Dorothy, who was welcome at the Round Table.

Unlike Dorothy, Ernie MacGuffin took this conversation very seriously. "Your suicide—were you afraid?"

"I was afraid I would wake up." She brushed aside the brunette bangs that shadowed her pretty face. "Again, what's this all about?"

He seemed to come to a decision. "I knew you knew all about it. Now I know I can trust you. Here." He handed her an envelope. "Don't open it until midnight. Promise me."

No one took Ernie seriously. Not his friends, not the art world, not the public. She looked at the plain white envelope and handed it back.

"Nothing doing," she said. "If you mean to commit suicide, don't get me involved. If you go toes up, I don't want that on my head."

He looked disappointed and confused.

She softened. "Don't kill yourself, Ernie. Take it from me. Attempting suicide after lunchtime will simply ruin your whole day."

Ten minutes before midnight, Dorothy and Robert Benchley, her closest friend, were at Tony Soma's, their favorite speakeasy.

Earlier in the evening, Tony had been waltzing around the loud and lively crowd, chatting with all the customers, singing opera and pouring drinks. Now he approached Dorothy and Benchley. His smile had disappeared.

"Mrs. Parker. Mr. Benchley. There's just a little matter I'd like to discuss. It's about the bill."

"Ah, yes," Benchley rocked back on his heels, nearly spilling the drink in his coffee mug. "Our cups and our tab runneth over."

"Tony, you know we're good for it," Dorothy said, gently swatting him on the arm. "We'll pay in full next time."

Tony's deep-set eyes turned darker. "That's what you said last time. It's been weeks since you paid."

He slid his hand inside his vest pocket. Dorothy, less than five feet tall, instinctively edged behind Benchley.

Tony pulled out an envelope. "Your bill."

Benchley glanced at Dorothy. He reluctantly took the envelope and gingerly pried it open.

This prompted Dorothy to remember MacGuffin's envelope. She hadn't given him a single thought since lunchtime. She didn't care much for Ernie, but she hoped he had gotten over whatever itch had been bothering him.

Benchley gasped when he read the bill. Dorothy grabbed her purse and quickly pulled out her horn-rimmed glasses. She scanned down the long column of numbers to the total. . . .

Four hundred and eighty-five dollars! Her big dark brown eyes grew wide. That was more than she earned in a month.

"Have we really drunk all this in a matter of months?" Benchley asked her.

She silently returned his glance. Of course they had. The bill was only a column of prices. It didn't list the many different types of drinks. But she could imagine— double scotches, whiskey sours, gin martinis, gin rickeys, gin and tonics, sidecars, orange blossoms, Tom Collinses,

Rob Roys, old-fashioneds . . . and more Manhattans than they could remember.

Dorothy felt weak. She needed a cigarette—and another drink. She reached into her purse for her pack of Chesterfields, but her hand touched paper. She pulled an envelope from her purse—MacGuffin's envelope.

"What's that, Mrs. Parker?" Benchley asked, his thin mustache twitching. "Another bill?"

"You pay mine first," Tony said, folding his arms over his barrel chest.

"Might be nothing," Dorothy said, holding it in her quavering hand. "Might be something."

MacGuffin must have slipped it into her purse after lunch. He had told her not to open it until midnight. She grabbed Benchley's arm and looked at his wristwatch. Just a few minutes 'til midnight. Something told her to open it right now.

She ripped it open, unfolded the plain white paper and skimmed through the handwritten note.

> *To whom it may concern. At midnight tonight . . . Will meet my fate in the waters beneath the Brooklyn Bridge . . . My last will and testament . . . Once I am dead and gone in this life . . . A new and better life awaits me. Good-bye, cruel world.*

"Oh, crap!" She clutched Benchley's arm. "It *is* a suicide note. That damned Ernie! Come on, we have to go."

She stepped forward, but Tony blocked her way. "Sorry. I cannot let you leave until you pay."

"Tony, what is this?" she said. "A friend of ours—well, a man we know—is about to kill himself. We have to stop him. We have to leave now."

Tony shook his head. "Nobody leaves until the bill is paid up."

Benchley was puzzled. "We don't carry that kind of money around with us. How can we get you any money if you won't let us leave?"

Tony merely kept his arms folded and jutted out his round chin.

"Please, Tony," Dorothy said. "A man might be dying. Right at this moment."

He shrugged, indifferent.

"Oh, Tony, old pal—" Benchley began kindly; his eyes were merry and twinkling.

Dorothy interrupted. She had had enough. "Don't make me make a scene," she said quietly, but Tony heard every word. "Really, is that what you want—a short, hysterical woman shrieking in your speakeasy?"

Underneath it all, she knew, Tony was a softie. His tough facade cracked. His eyes changed from unforgiving to apologetic.

"My friends, I'm so sorry," he sighed, his hands cradling his sagging cheeks. "It's the wife, Mrs. Soma. She's on my back day and night. No more freeloading, she says."

"Freeloading?" Dorothy gasped. "Well, I never." She eyed Mrs. Soma across the room. Mrs. Soma returned Dorothy's glance with an icy glare.

"Look around," Tony said, exasperated but with a touch of pride. "We've paid for a lot of improvements. In case we get raided, we put in trapdoors behind the bar where the bottles can drop out of sight."

Benchley nodded approvingly.

Tony continued, "See all these new potted plants with the big ferns? If the cops bang on the door, you dump your drink in there, and we fill up your cup with tea or coffee. And don't forget all the palms that need to be greased—the patrol cops, the lookouts, the city officials. I can't run the place on goodwill!"

"Of course," Benchley said. He held out a few bills. "Take this for now. We'll pay you the rest as soon as we can."

Tony took them and stepped aside. "Go on. Go help your friend. But please bring in the money soon, okay?"

"Sure," Benchley said, patting him on the shoulder. Dorothy kissed him on the cheek.

They hurried outside and down the steps of the brown-stone. They looked in vain for a taxi. The darkened street of town houses was quiet as usual.

"Stop right there!" Mrs. Soma shouted from the doorway. "You pay your tab or you'll never drink in this club again!"

Tony grabbed her arm to drag her back inside. She shook him off easily and pushed him away.

Dorothy and Benchley paused only a moment. Then they turned and ran.

Mrs. Soma yanked off her apron and threw it back inside. "Tony Junior! Get your backside out here and catch these scroungers! Now!"